THE LAST
REMNANT

BOOK THREE OF THE FOURLINE TRILOGY

ALSO BY PAM BRONDOS

Gateway to Fourline

On the Meldon Plain

THE LAST REMNANT

BOOK THREE OF THE FOURLINE TRILOGY

PAM BRONDOS

SKYSCAPE

SKYSCAPE

Text copyright © 2016 by Pam Brondos

Published by Skyscape, New York

www.apub.com

Amazon, the Amazon logo, and Skyscape are trademarks of Amazon.com, Inc., or its affiliates.

ISBN-13: 9781612184708
ISBN-10: 1612184707

Cover illustration by M. S. Corley
Full cover design by David Drummond
Based on series concept by Chelsea Wirtz

Printed in the United States of America

This book is dedicated to my children.

CHAPTER ONE

The projection microscope hummed next to Nat, filling the empty lab classroom with a buzzing sound. She tossed her sketch of the spherical bacteria on the counter and stared through the eyepiece. Her shoulder muscles tightened.

"I've found the cause, Soris," she whispered to herself when the wriggling organism came into focus. *But I can't figure out how to kill it.* Disheartened, she rubbed her tired eyes and recalled the events leading to her discovery of the bacteria.

Almost a year ago, Estos convinced Nat to travel through the membrane connecting her world and Fourline. During the journey, she and Soris destroyed the tracking device that had prevented Estos from safely returning to Fourline to join the rebel fight against Lord Mudug, but disaster followed their success. The predatory Nala wounded her and bit Soris, turning him into a duozi, a half human, half Nala.

Now, after months of experiments, she knew the tiny bacterium swimming on the slide in front of her was the cause of his transformation. She peered through the eyepiece again and bit her lip, desperate for an answer to the question haunting her: *What kills you?*

The classroom door creaked open. Nat flicked off the microscope and quickly covered her notes.

"If you brought me here for another blood draw, so help me I will make it my mission to give you nightmares for the next two weeks." Annin strode across the lab. Her loose black curls partially concealed the eye patch hiding her Nala eye.

"Try knocking next time, Annin." A pent-up breath escaped Nat's lips and she uncovered her notes.

Annin whistled. "Aren't you a little testy tonight."

Nat held her retort and reminded herself that Annin was in Nat's world by choice to help her find a cure for the duozi. "I've found something." Nat lifted her notes and waved them in the air in front of Annin.

"You found a cure for the duozi?" Annin ripped the papers from Nat's fingers.

"No." Nat dropped her gaze, frustrated by the admission.

"Why am I here then?"

"I finally isolated what causes the transformation from human to duozi." Nat glanced up, expecting to see some excitement from Annin. Instead, Annin's expression soured. She pushed up her sleeve and shoved her blue arm in Nat's face.

"Do you have amnesia, Natalie? Nala venom turns a person into a duozi." She dropped the notes on the counter and shook her head. "Months of poking me with needles, translating that ancient book from Ethet, sneaking into this lab, and skirting the building security guard, and all you've figured out is something we already know? I could be back in Fourline helping Estos and—"

"Just listen to me for a minute," Nat cut in, her aggravation dousing her remaining patience. "Nala venom *isn't* the catalyst. Neither is remnant." She massaged her shoulder, remembering the horrible bond the remnant secretion had created between herself and a Nala after it had cut her and bit Soris.

"I'm listening." Annin tapped her foot but her expression was more interested than irritated.

"I completed the comparison of your blood with mine and Barba's." Nat turned on the microscope and gestured to the eyepiece. "I noted two distinct differences. Your blood has a miniscule amount of polymorphonuclear leukocytes and contains bacteria that aren't in either of ours."

Annin pulled the stool closer, removed her eye patch, and peered through the eyepiece.

"The bacteria are bizarre." Nat felt the now-familiar rush of bewilderment as she continued her explanation. "They've taken over the function of most of your white blood cells."

Annin leaned her elbow against the counter. "So what? I have strange bacteria in my blood. How is that information going to help you or Sister Ethet discover a cure for the duozi?"

"I found no trace of Nala venom or remnant in your blood. The bacterium has to be what caused your transformation." She set her hip against the counter and took a deep breath, still uncertain what she was about to share. "I've tried to kill the bacterium with antibiotics, but it's resistant to everything I've thrown at it, except for one thing."

Annin perked up. "Which is?"

"The meldon concentrate Sister Barba makes you drink every few weeks. I've tested it on your blood dozens of times. There's something in the meldon flower petals that weakens the bacteria. If I can find a way to kill the bacteria with the petals, then—"

"Then no more Nala bacteria in my bloodstream?"

"No more Nala bacteria in your bloodstream, and maybe no more Nala in you." *Or Soris.* Nat glanced out the darkened lab windows and pressed her hands together as she thought about how much time had passed since she'd seen his face. Letting out an aggravated sigh, she focused again on Annin. "I've written all this down for Sister Ethet." She handed the papers to Annin. "Maybe the Healing Sisters can help me. I've got the benefit of all this"—she gestured around the lab—"but I've hit a wall on how to use the flowers to kill the Nala bacteria."

"You want me to go back and grill Ethet?" Annin asked with a twinkle in her eye. "I get to go home?"

"Yes, since Barba's refusing to let me return because of the Nalaide." Nat scowled when she thought of the horrid Nala queen that wanted her hide because she'd freed dozens of duozi children from her den.

"I'll leave first thing in the morning." Annin's smile widened.

"Wipe the grin off your face. It's making me a little sick." Nat felt a pang of jealousy. *I should be the one to consult with the Healing Sisters in Fourline.* Annin pretended to frown, but the smile emerged again. Nat rolled her eyes and walked over to another counter. She retrieved a plastic box from the stainless steel surface. "I do need more of your blood before you go, though," she said. Annin's smile disappeared.

"Ugh, not again. Barba has four vials stored at the costume shop. Isn't that enough?" She held her arm protectively against her chest.

"No." Nat slid open the blood-sample kit. "I'm not going to sit around and do nothing while I wait for word from Ethet." The kit toppled over when she yanked a tube from the case. "Hundreds if not thousands of duozi are at risk of dying at the Nala's and Mudug's hands. I have to keep looking for a cure, and I need your blood. Make a fist," she ordered, and Annin obediently balled up her hand.

She swabbed Annin's inner arm, then deftly inserted the needle into a vein. Blood spurt into the tube. As she watched the tube fill, her mind strayed to the Nala-infested forest Annin would have to travel through to get to the Healing House where Sister Ethet, the other Healing Sisters, and some of the duozi lived.

"I should be going with you," Nat muttered. "Instead, I'm stuck here going to college classes, pretending everything's fine."

"You'd be an idiot if you stepped foot in Fourline right now, Natalie. Don't forget the white Nala that attacked you last spring or the Nalaide—"

"I know, I know, the Nalaide," Nat groused and removed the needle. She taped a cotton ball over the puncture mark. She watched

Annin, trying not to feel resentful. "You know what really gets me, Annin? I'm a Warrior Sister, trained to defend others against the Nala, and instead of fighting, I'm hiding away while Soris and the duozi are at risk." Nat scribbled the date on the tube containing Annin's blood and carefully placed it into a small plastic carrier.

Annin's Nala eye contracted. "Ah, yes, Soris. The real reason you want to return to Fourline," she teased.

"Yes, he is, and I can't do anything to help him." Nat snapped the latch on the carrier and frowned.

"Stop wallowing in self-pity. Soris can take care of himself. Do you think he'd be happy if you put yourself in danger by stepping through the membrane?" Annin slid her eye patch back over her Nala eye. "Focus your repressed Warrior Sister angst and figure out how to kill the bacteria. That's the best way to help Soris and all the duozi right now. I'll take your findings to Ethet and send Oberfisk or Riler with a message as soon as she has something to share with you." Annin gave her friend a reassuring look. "When she learns bacteria, and not venom, cause the transformation from human to duozi, she may have a revelation for a cure," she added.

Nat's frown disappeared at the prospect of a way to heal the duozi. "I hope so. I can't shake the feeling that I've missed something obvious. I'll keep running experiments with the meldon flower while you're gone."

Annin slid off the stool. "Do you have enough flowers to work with? Ethet left a huge store in her laboratory in the costume shop."

"I have a few." Nat glanced at a glass container that held the dried yellow flowers from Fourline. "I've tried tinker's penny from this world since it's the same as the meldon flower, but it did nothing to inhibit the bacteria." The meldon flowers spun against the glass when she lifted the container up to the light. "Something about this flower . . ." Her voice trailed off when she caught Annin eyeing her.

"You'll figure it out, Natalie." Annin gave her a sardonic smile. "Besides, there isn't a rush. It's not like Soris or we other duozi are going anywhere, except maybe to a Nala den or Mudug's mines to work as slaves."

"I hate your sense of humor." Nat dropped the slide and needle into the red biohazard box hanging on the wall and cleared the counter of wrappings.

"Your problem," Annin replied. She glanced at the clock above the door. "Isn't this about the time when our favorite security guard shows up? I wouldn't put it past him to search our bags if he finds us in the biology department's lab again on a Saturday night."

Nat pulled on her coat. "I'd like to see him try. If he so much as touches my bag, I'll break his nose."

Annin gave her a look of mock surprise. "Save the nose breaking for when it counts, Warrior Sister."

CHAPTER TWO

A cold November breeze blew through the trees lining the campus quad when Annin and Nat exited the Science Center. Nat instinctively scanned the tips of the bare branches for Nala. *Stop being paranoid. Nala can't travel into this world,* she reminded herself. She ceased her visual search and turned her attention to Annin. An uncharacteristic smile created dimples in Annin's cheeks. *Of course she's happy. She's finally going back home.* An empty feeling settled in her chest when she thought about Annin leaving her behind.

A cluster of college students stumbled from the entrance of a freshman dorm onto the path in front of Annin and Nat. Their laughter grated on Nat and she paused, pretending to look for something in her backpack to make more space between them. Students, professors, college clubs, classes—anything that interfered with her search for a cure was an irritant and a waste of her time. She spent every spare moment in the lab or training with Barba to hone her skills as a Warrior Sister. She couldn't even remember the last time she'd called home or spoken to her sister Cal, who was in her first year on campus on a dance scholarship. They avoided each other as if by tacit agreement.

A male student stepped unsteadily away from the others and veered toward Annin. "Look! It's a pirate girl!" Anger flamed in Nat as she watched him point at Annin's eye patch and stumble closer. "Did some-one poke your eye out, or did you forget Halloween's over?" His slurred statement brought a round of titters from his friends, and he moved toward Annin, emboldened.

Nat stepped between him and Annin and dropped her bag to the ground. "Let me give you some advice: shut up and walk away."

"I know you." He looked at Nat with hazy eyes. She recoiled at the smell of alcohol on his breath. "You're that runner girl I see each morn-ing on the track. Aren't you Cal's sister?" He whirled around. "Hey, Cal, is this the stuck-up sister you're always complaining about?" Nat scanned the students and spied Cal.

"Yeah, that's my sister," Cal answered curtly and brushed her thick blonde hair away from her face. She gave Nat a split-second glance. A flush crept over her cheeks. "Come on, Ed. Let's get to the party."

Ed shook his head. "Not yet, I want to see what's underneath pirate girl's eye patch." He took a step to the side, and Nat widened her stance, blocking his path to Annin.

"You're not taking my advice, *Ed*." Nat's eyes narrowed as she glared at him.

Ed's smile faded. "You're not taking my advice," he mimicked in a nasal tone. "Get out of my way." He pushed her shoulder. Nat slammed her forearms over his and stepped agilely to the side, sending Ed crash-ing into the pavement. She knelt next to him.

"Are you too inebriated to understand that if you touch me again, I will break your arm?" Nat hissed in his ear. The vine and spear mark-ings on her inner arm rippled as she tensed, preparing to strike him. His bloodshot eyes focused fast enough to see her fist cocked above his face. Confusion and fear clouded his expression. *Pathetic,* Nat thought, and she lowered her fist. She stood, straightened her coat, and kept her eyes locked on Ed. *Why am I stuck here dealing with this garbage?*

Annin picked up Nat's bag and leaned over Ed. "You lucked out," she whispered into his ear. "She could've taken your head off if she wanted to. I've seen it." A sliver of her Nala eye glimmered above her eye patch. To Nat's amusement, Ed scrambled against the sidewalk like a crab running from a bird of prey.

Nat hid her smile and grabbed Annin's arm. "Let's go." She pulled her away from Ed and past his stunned friends. Her eye caught Cal's. "Telling choice of friends, Cal."

Her sister looked at her with a mixture of loathing and embarrassment. "At least mine aren't freaks," Cal spat and gestured to Annin.

Nat paused. Her mind flashed with memories of Benedict hurling insults at Annin and Soris. Anger blossomed inside of her. She retraced her steps and faced her sister. "Don't you ever—"

"Natalie, I don't care what she calls me." Annin grasped Nat's forearm and spun her in the direction of a set of stairs leading to the parking lot.

"You may not, but I do. My sister is an ignorant, self-centered pain," she fumed as she descended the stairs at a clip.

The two of them walked in silence until they reached Andris' rusted orange truck. Nat yanked open the door and shoved the keys into the ignition. Annin slid into the passenger seat and pressed the automatic window button, trying to close the one-inch gap at the top. The electric mechanism for the window groaned and died. Nat drove out of the parking lot and down the hill.

"An observation. You and your sister are about as much alike as Soris and Andris," Annin remarked as she stared into the winter night. A little laugh exploded from Nat. Annin turned toward her. "What?"

"I just had an image of Andris trying to train my sister to fight the Nala. He thought he had it bad with me? Can you imagine? It would almost be worth dragging Cal into Fourline to see that." Nat relaxed her shoulders and the laughter died away. "She'd last ten minutes," she said somberly.

"Five," Annin countered and added, "Maybe that's why you and Soris get along. You both have pigheaded siblings."

Nat laughed again, thankful to Annin for lightening her mood. Her smile faded. She was going to miss Annin's sharp-edged companionship. Annin was her link to Fourline and everything she'd experienced in that strange world. She understood how Nat felt about Soris and how finding a cure for the duozi meant everything to her. Now Annin was leaving her behind.

Nat steered the truck onto Grand Street. The sidewalks were packed with college students. The sounds of a band playing along the riverfront floated through the crack in Annin's window. She watched a young couple dance on the sidewalk in time to the blaring music, and her thoughts strayed to Soris. *What would it be like to dance with him along the river?* she wondered before remembering again that he, unlike Annin, had too much Nala in him to pass into her world. *I have to find a cure.* She tightened her fingers around the steering wheel and looked away from the couple.

Auto repair shops and industrial buildings replaced the restaurants and cafés. As they neared the costume shop, her sharp words to Cal came to mind. Aggravated, Nat let out a long breath and glanced at Annin. "You never told me if you had siblings," she commented.

"None that survived. I am the last of the Afferflys. The Nala saw to that." The glow of the streetlights flashed across her face.

"And here I am complaining about my sister." Nat lowered her head.

"Complaining about her is fine, just don't forget she's family," Annin replied. "I've never forgotten mine, even though I consider everyone I lived with here my family now." Her mouth twisted into a smile. "Two Sisters, a professor, Oberfisk, Andris, Kroner, Riler, and a king. Quite the family."

"Quite the family," Nat agreed and recalled the story Estos had shared with her about Sister Barba leading him and his personal guard through the membrane that connected Fourline to Nat's world.

She drove the truck past Gate's Costumes and parked alongside the connected warehouse. As Annin unbuckled her seat belt and slid the eye patch away from her eye, Nat stared at the entrance to the warehouse. The membrane to Fourline was so close she could almost feel its vibrations beckoning her.

Annin pulled a small book from her bag and set it on the cracked dashboard. Her hand lingered protectively over the cover. "Since I'm leaving, consider this a going-away present. Barba and I finished the transcription key. Now you can read the text."

Nat leaned toward the leather-bound book. Her fingers itched to snatch it from under Annin's hand. Ethet had given the book to her on her last journey into Fourline, when she was trying to understand all the nefarious ways Nala were using their remnant. She and Annin had discovered that its pages contained a series of images and a formula that bolstered her hope that there was a cure for the duozi.

Annin removed her hand. "Oh, and remember Barba has your orb tucked away in there." She gestured in the direction of the warehouse. Nat nodded as she thought longingly of her orb, currently hidden behind a panel in the back bedroom of the costume shop. "Barba said she'd smash it if anything happened to that book. I don't think she was joking. Wisdom Sisters are pretty protective when it comes to books," Annin added with a humorless smile before opening the truck door.

"Do you want me to see you off tomorrow morning?" Nat asked, realizing this was the last time she'd see her friend before she passed through the portal to Fourline hidden at the end of a tunnel behind the warehouse.

"No, spend your time finding a cure, Sister." Annin hopped out of the truck. Nat watched her walk toward the warehouse entrance and punch a series of buttons by the intercom panel. The door clicked open. Annin jerked on the handle. The door held fast. She muttered under her breath, kicked the frame, and pulled again on the handle. The door sprang open.

A protective impulse came over Nat. "Be careful and good luck," she called out.

"Luck has nothing to do with it, Natalie. You should know that by now." She winked her Nala eye and disappeared behind the heavy door.

The stillness of the night settled over Nat. She sat shivering in the cab of the truck, staring at the warehouse door and feeling as if she were suspended between two places, unable to set her feet firmly in either. *I should be going through the membrane with her,* she thought and cranked the ignition before slamming the truck into gear.

CHAPTER THREE

Three weeks later, Nat sat at her desk flicking through the pages of the ancient book for the hundredth time. It fell open to a vivid depiction of the first Sisters' encounter with the Nala. A panel of the illustration portrayed a bitten girl, her arm tinted blue, drinking from a vial of dark-yellow liquid. Nat scanned the final panel. The same girl, now a Warrior Sister, held a dagger to a Nala's throat. The Sister's arm, scrolled with the vine and spear markings, was no longer blue.

Nat closed the book. *My belief in a cure is based on a thousand-year-old illustration.* Even Soris would laugh at how desperately she clung to the image of the wounded girl with a blue arm ingesting the yellow liquid.

Nat stared out her dorm-room window at the sky and clicked off her lamp. The stars struggled to shine through the lights of the campus, but she could make out a few faint flickers of starlight. The pulsing light reminded her of the night when she and Soris lay in a field, looking at the stars blinking above Fourline. An ache settled in her chest. She let out a frustrated groan and ran her hands through her brown hair.

Clicking the light back on, she again opened Ethet's book and found the drawing of the entwined ring of meldon flowers. The bright-yellow flowers with their prostrate stems and ovate leaves bordered a formula for a meldon-petal concentrate that Nat could read thanks to Barba's key. She glared at the formula, recalling how many times she'd recreated the concentrate since Annin left. Each time she tested the concentrate on the bacteria, the results were always the same: it inhibited the Nala bacteria, but never killed them. Her focus strayed from the formula to the glass jar of meldon flowers on her desk.

"Shut the books and the computer and stick those papers where the sun don't shine." Viv, Nat's roommate, slammed the door to the adjoining bathroom. She wore a dark-green dress covered in irregularly cut net material. Her hair was dyed a bright daisy yellow and was arranged in a beehive.

"You look like an electrocuted mermaid," Nat observed and covered the book with a pile of papers.

"Wait till you see what I have for you to wear to my art show," Viv said in a singsong voice. The corners of her bright-red lips curled into a wicked smile.

"I'm not going to make it tonight. Too much to do." She returned to her notes and knew Viv was glaring at her without even looking. *She'll get over it.*

"Oh, you're going, or it's World War Viv. It's the last art show of the semester, dummy."

"I'll catch it later this week."

"No, you won't. You're coming tonight." Viv set her hand on her hip.

The needling irritation Nat felt when anyone interrupted her work settled over her. "I can't. I'm busy."

"I've been working on my pieces all semester." Viv's voice dropped, catching Nat's attention. "You seriously expect me to believe that you can't spare fifteen minutes of your life to show up tonight?"

"Fine! I'll go!" Nat flung her pencil on her table and turned to Viv. "Happy now?"

"No!" Viv yelled back. She grabbed her coat and slammed the door of their room, creating a draft that shifted the papers on Nat's desk.

"Well, neither am I," Nat grumbled to the empty room.

Nat walked down the worn wooden stairs leading to the basement of Brickman Hall. Voices floated up the stairwell from the lower-level art gallery. *I'll stay ten minutes, make up with Viv, and then return to my notes,* she promised herself as she descended the remaining stairs.

Students and a handful of professors from the art department mingled in the brightly lit gallery that extended across the entire basement of the building. A few students nodded in her direction, but most ignored her as she maneuvered her way past the refreshment table. She knew she was an oddball among Viv's friends, but she didn't care. Feeling out of place was her new normal after her adventures in Fourline.

"I wondered if you were coming." Butler, Viv's friend, held a plastic cup out for Nat. He wore a panama hat over his closely cropped black hair.

"I wasn't planning on it, but here I am." Nat shrugged and accepted the drink. "I'm in a rush, Butler. Where's Viv's stuff?" she asked, scanning the crowded gallery interspersed with half walls and sculptures. *I'll be lucky if I make it out of here at all,* she thought as she observed the milling crowd.

"Stuff? Come on, Nat, even geeks like you can show a little culture. Her paintings are at the end, past the performance-art piece. But you can't look at just her creations." He wrapped his brown fingers around hers and pulled her through the crowd. They stopped at a few paintings and a series of ceramic sculptures that reminded Nat of the Chinese terra-cotta warriors. Butler's voice buzzed excitedly in her ear when they stopped at pieces he liked. She nodded appreciatively and kept her mouth shut, hoping to speed up his tour.

"And now prepare to be overwhelmed by my genius." He directed her around one of the suspended half walls. Nat stopped short and gasped. "Amazing, aren't they?" Butler said, taking her expression to mean she was in awe of the series of charcoal drawings. "Remember when I was working on the sketch of her last year?"

Nat stared at the image of Annin and ignored the other portraits. Annin's left hand was near her cheek, pushing away her unruly hair. The portrait had her in profile, so her eye patch wasn't visible. Her lips were parted and her brow curved over her human eye. She looked beautiful and vulnerable.

"She's my secret muse," Butler admitted. "When I sketched her last year, I couldn't get her out of my mind. I watched her whenever I could in class and kept coming back to this expression."

Annin's expression appeared almost longing as she focused on a smeared figure covering the edge of the paper that blended into the black frame. "What's she looking at?" Nat asked, confused by the weakness the portrait exposed. Weakness and vulnerability were anathema to Annin.

"You never noticed the way she looked at him in class?" Butler pointed to the title printed in neat script at the edge of the portrait: *Love's Barrier.*

"Estos?" Images of Estos and Annin coalesced in her mind. She closed her eyes, overcome by a sudden sadness. She knew Estos cared about Annin, but what did it matter how he felt? Because of Mudug's lies, most people in Fourline believed the duozi were as bad as the Nala. What future did royalty like Estos and an outcast like Annin have together unless she found a cure?

"Well, do you think I nailed it?" Butler asked with a hint of nervousness in his voice.

"Yes, Butler. You did." Nat grabbed him and gave him a quick hug, hoping he would take it as congratulations and not see the deep sorrow in her eyes.

"Enough about me," he said sounding satisfied. "There's one more exhibit you need to see before Viv's."

"Butler, I don't have time—"

"It's Erin's performance-art piece about refugee children," he continued, ignoring her protest. "It will rip your heart out."

Butler steered her through the crowd and stopped several paces away from a blank floor-to-ceiling screen. Nat heard a whirring sound. She turned her head and recognized Viv and Butler's friend Erin standing behind a projector.

"Watch," Butler demanded, bringing Nat's attention back to the screen.

The spotlight above them dimmed. Black-and-white images of hollow-eyed children appeared on the screen. A woman, covered from head to toe in a dark-blue bodysuit, stepped in front of the images. A cold tension seeped into Nat, and she gripped her drink. The woman danced in front of the screen, and her erratic movements contorted the children's faces and bodies. A thin layer of perspiration broke out on Nat's brow as she watched the pictures of the children turn blue against the woman's bodysuit.

Nat's stomach lurched. Her mind flashed back to the swarm of emaciated duozi children encircling the amphitheater in the Nala den. She dropped her cup and swayed unsteadily. The cup rolled across the hardwood and stopped at the dancer's feet.

"Nat? You okay?" Butler grabbed her elbow to steady her.

"Sorry," she mumbled, rattled by the memories of the duozi children. "I guess I need a little air." She looked up hesitantly, even though she knew the dancer couldn't be a Nala. She found Cal, face smeared with blue face paint, staring back at her. Butler picked up her cup and led her away from the installation.

"That was Cal?" Nat's voice held a hint of surprise.

"Didn't you know she was working with Erin on her installation?" Butler led her through a press of people clustered around a potato-shaped sculpture.

"I had no idea."

"Close family." He tossed her cup into a bin in the corner of the gallery near a set of stairs. Nat looked longingly at the exit. She wanted nothing more than to leave the gallery immediately, but Butler ushered her toward a triptych hanging on the far wall.

Nat stopped short when she recognized the yellow flowers in the paintings. Disproportionate stems with pointy leaves covered the canvases. The stems bent at odd angles, and the tips of the leaves curled inward almost like fingers. A tiny yellow flower crowned the top of each enormous stem. Nat stepped closer. She felt as if she were looking through a magnifying glass as she studied the crisp, almost photographic detail of the blades of grass, soil, and stems. The petals appeared lost and out of focus compared to their detailed base. She read the card next to the paintings.

"Tinker's penny . . ." Nat's heart beat faster as she stared at the enlarged stem. She stepped back, bumping into Viv. Her roommate gave her a guarded look. Forgetting their earlier altercation, Nat clutched Viv's arm. Wild-eyed excitement flashed across her face. "Viv, these are all tinker's penny flowers."

"You've had that container of flowers on your desk all fall, Nat," Viv said almost guiltily. "They got me thinking about how we naturally focus on only part of an object and often disregard the rest."

"Like focusing on the petals instead of the stem or the leaves." The excitement in Nat's voice grew as she returned to the paintings. She brought her hand to her mouth and stared at the shaded stem. *I've never used the stem in any of my experiments.*

"Right, so you get it?" Viv joined Nat in front of the triptych.

Nat turned to her with a beaming smile. "Viv, you are a genius," she said and gave her a quick kiss on the cheek. "A total genius." She whirled toward the exit and called out over her shoulder, "I have to go, but I'm sorry I yelled at you."

"You just called me a genius. I forgive you," Viv replied as Nat bolted through the crowd and up the stairs.

CHAPTER FOUR

How could I have been so stupid? Nat raced across campus back to her dorm room, mentally kicking herself for focusing all her experiments on the corolla, or petals, of the meldon flower, not the stem or leaves. Barreling through the dorm entrance, she took the stairs two at a time. *It's got to be something in either the stem or the leaves that kills the Nala bacteria.*

Her mind raced as she fumbled with the keys to her door. She hurtled over a pile of shoes and flicked on her desk lamp. Her fingers trembled as she carefully turned the pages of Sister Ethet's book. It fell open to the page of entwined meldon flowers. Her eyes scanned the formula for the meldon concentrate. *It doesn't say petals. It just says meldon.* She scanned the page one more time, then reached for her phone and punched in Cairn Gate's number.

"Professor Gate, yes, I know it's late. I need you to meet me in the lab in the Science Center," she said into her phone. "Yes, now. No, it can't wait until tomorrow morning. I think I've figured it out!" She slowed down and repeated each word. "I'll meet you there. And bring Annin's blood samples," she added. She switched off her phone, placed the book and her jar of meldon flowers from Fourline carefully into her backpack, and burst out of her dorm room.

Nat sprinted across the quad. The glass door to the Science Center flew open under the pressure of her hands, and she dashed into the darkened foyer of the building. Long fluorescent lights illuminated the display cases lining the walls. She nervously danced from foot to foot in front of the cases. "Come on, come on, come on," she said impatiently and glanced at the doors, willing Professor Gate to come through them.

Sister Barba, wrapped in a long black shawl and clutching the plastic bin containing Annin's blood samples, pushed open the door. Cairn followed his wife into the Science Center.

"Natalie, what's going on?" Barba asked.

Nat grabbed the sample case from her Head Sister and raced down the hall to the stairs. "Just come with me," she called out.

Nat turned on the lights to the lab classroom. She removed a distilling apparatus from under the counter and filled a flask three-quarters full with water. She adjusted the flame of the Bunsen burner as it licked the sides of the glass.

Barba and Cairn walked into the lab, both looking perplexed. The pair watched Nat carefully remove a meldon flower from the jar and chop the stem into tiny bits before scraping pieces of it from the blade of her knife into the mouth of another flask. She corked the top and pushed a heavy plastic tube over its sidearm, connecting it to a final glass container. She eyed the three connected flasks nestled in their stands. Water bubbled inside the first, and steam passed through a tube into the next container holding the chopped-up stem.

Barba cleared her throat. "Natalie, would you care to explain—"

"I think I figured out what I've been doing wrong," Nat interrupted. She chewed on her fingernail and watched the steam mix with the stem. Droplets of liquid slowly fell from the angled tube into the last glass container. The droplets had a yellow tint to them, and she sighed with relief. The liquid shown in the book's illustration was yellow, if a shade darker. Using the stem hadn't changed the color. With a gloved hand, she detached the tube from the sidearm and poured the concentrate into a shallow bowl to cool.

"Cairn, turn on that microscope." Nat motioned with her foot to the counter running along the back wall. She took a thin pipette and placed a drop of Annin's blood next to a drop of the cooled concentrate on a glass slide. She secured a coverslip over the slide before clipping it into place under the microscope lens.

When magnified, the spiky, circular Nala bacteria looked like blurred puffer fish next to the red and white blood cells. She increased the magnification. The section of the slide where the meldon concentrate flowed into the blood sample came into view. Nat stared through the lens and her heart sank. She sat back.

"I don't understand." She shook her head. "This should work," she said in frustration and leaned over the lens again. "It's inhibiting the spread of the bacteria." Her fingers fiddled with the magnification. "But nothing more. I don't get it. The stem and leaves should be the answer . . ." Barba slid a comforting hand over Nat's shoulder. "This should work," she said again, then dropped her head into her hands.

"Natalie, it's just a setback." Barba gave Nat's shoulder a gentle pat. "It's good you're going home for holiday break. You need to step away from your experiments for a while. Give your mind space to process what you've discovered and what remains a mystery. You're meant to find the cure. The answer will come."

"I don't need a break." Nat stood up and walked to the counter where the remains of the meldon flower lay scattered over the cutting board. "I'll run the test again. Maybe I skipped something in the formula."

The sympathetic expression on Barba's face disappeared. "Have patience. Progress and answers will come."

"Patience?" Nat dumped the bowl of concentrate into a sink. "Barba, I've been working on a cure for months, and the only thing I've discovered is the bacterium."

"Which was a *significant* discovery, Natalie. It's only a matter of time before you find a cure." Barba's confident statement irked Nat.

"How? I've racked my brains. I have no clue what to try next! I have no one to consult, no one to tell me if my experiments are a waste of time or if . . ." Her voice trailed off and she looked steadily at her Head Sister. "If you let me return to Fourline, I could confer with Head Sister Ethes and Sister Ethet. *Then* I'd make progress." Barba's expression hardened, but Nat persisted. "I have the entire month of January with the fake independent study we set up. I could slip back into Fourline and continue my research at the Healing House."

"No." Lines formed around Barba's mouth. "You're not stepping foot in Fourline as long as the Nalaide's after you."

Nat glowered, wishing she and Annin had never told Barba about the Nalaide and the white Nala with the remnant rings in their chests, or that Mudug and the Chemist knew the Nalaide wanted her.

"I could make it to the Healing House, Barba," Nat argued. "After all these months, why would the Nalaide still be looking for me?"

"Don't underestimate the Nalaide's conviction or her hatred of the Warrior Sisters. You invaded *her* nest, Natalie, and freed the duozi. She won't rest until she sees you dead, or worse." Barba strode toward her, grabbed her arm, and pushed up her sleeve. "A Sister with your markings is a special insult to the Nalaide, and you told me she saw your symbols." Barba's expression darkened. "Your markings represent the beliefs and Predictions of the first Warrior Sisters. Her motivation to find you will be even greater because of them."

Nat shivered and yanked her arm away. "I've been gone for over half a year, Barba. The Nalaide's search for me has to have died down."

"Even if it has, there are likely others looking for you." Barba's green eyes held a look of warning.

"Barba." Cairn stepped next to his wife. "Now may not be the time—"

"No." Barba interrupted her husband. "If she's so convinced it's safe to return, she should know now," she responded, her voice full of authority.

"What? Know what?" Nat asked, glancing back and forth between them.

"The Chemist put a price on your head shortly after you returned to this world, after you aided Emilia." Barba kept her eyes fixed on Nat.

"Why? He can't know I had anything to do with Emilia's escape." Nat braced herself against the counter, suddenly losing a little of her confidence.

"No," Barba replied. "Our spies have heard nothing from Rustbrook about Emilia or her escape. I assume Mudug and the Chemist are still hiding the fact that the queen is even alive, let alone that you, Andris, Soris, and Annin freed her." She gave Nat a shrewd look. "The Chemist must want you so he and Mudug can strike a deal with the Nalaide. His price included the condition that you be brought to him alive. You're not returning to Fourline until we decide it's safe."

The idea of waiting in her world until the committee of Barba and everyone else deemed it safe enough for her to return to Fourline made Nat want to scream. "No one except the Nalaide and the Nala can identify me, Barba," she countered. "How can anyone find me if they don't know what I look like?"

"Your markings would give you away," Barba corrected. Nat rolled her eyes, thinking of the numerous ways she'd hidden her markings and disguised herself while she was in Fourline. "None of us, including Estos, want you to return to Fourline right now. It's not worth the risk."

"It would be if I had a cure for the duozi." Nat gestured to the microscope.

"But you don't, and I am done with this conversation." Barba tossed the end of her black shawl over her shoulder. Nat's cheeks burned from her dismissal.

Cairn cleared his throat and gestured to the door. "I believe we should be going, Natalie."

"I'm not done. If I can't return to Fourline to help the duozi, I'll keep experimenting here." She rinsed a flask and nearly cracked its stem from clutching it too tightly. She glanced up to find Barba staring at her with a pinched look. *She is not pushing me out of this lab.* She grabbed another flask and set up a second test.

"Don't stay too late, and don't rush back from Christmas break," Barba admonished. "Have patience," she added in a slightly less perturbed tone.

Easy for you to say, Nat thought but gave Barba a grudging nod over her shoulder.

"I'm certain my Head Sister is cackling in her grave over this. Wouldn't she delight in seeing me guide such an argumentative Sister," Nat heard Barba mutter to Cairn before they exited the lab.

Nat fumed as she ran through another experiment that yielded the same results. Slumping against the counter next to the microscope, she unclipped the slide, then deposited it in the biohazard box. *This experiment should have worked. I should be on my way to Fourline right now with a cure.* Dispirited, she cleaned the lab and exited the Science Center.

Snow crunched under her sneakers as she made her way back to her dorm. She tucked her chin into the collar of her jacket. *Another failure,* she thought, wondering what Soris would say to her if he were with her. *Maybe he'd think I'm wasting my time, but at least I'd have him to talk to.* She didn't know what was making her crazier: not making any progress on the cure, or missing him and his steady presence.

She stopped in front of her dorm to collect her thoughts. *I feel like I'm running a race but can't reach the finish line.* The lure of returning to Fourline was so tempting. If she could work with Sisters Ethet and Ethes, at least she could rule out what had already been tried. But based on Barba's show of Head Sister authority, she wasn't going anywhere.

"Nat?" Cal stepped out of the shadows near the entrance to Nat's dorm, startling her. Smears of blue makeup still outlined her face and deepened the lines across her brow.

"Cal?" Nat stared at her sister, wondering why she was lingering outside her dorm.

"I've been waiting for you," Cal said in answer to Nat's questioning look. She shoved her hands into her pockets and scrutinized her sister. "Are you going off the deep end again?"

Taken aback, Nat snapped, "What's that supposed to mean?"

Cal took a step forward and frowned. "You know what it means. I thought you'd figured out your issues after you lost it last spring, but after tonight at the gallery, I'm not so sure."

Nat held up her hands. "The problems I had last spring are taken care of, and they never were any of your business." She could never explain to her why she'd had a breakdown when Cal had visited early last spring. The Nala's remnant she'd carried had driven her to the edge until Barba had given her hope and sent her back into Fourline as a fully trained Warrior Sister. Nat contemplated her sister's worried expression and tried to imagine how Cal would respond to her tale of tracking down and beheading the Nala that was linked to her through its remnant. *She'd have me committed.*

"I don't buy it, Nat, not after what happened tonight. Something's bothering you, or was dropping your cup and nearly fainting when you saw me merely a reflection of how much you dislike me?"

"Don't flatter yourself, Cal. Nothing's bothering me. I'm just preoccupied with a research project." Nat took a step closer to the door, wanting an immediate end to the conversation.

Cal grabbed her arm. "Don't flatter myself?" Her cheeks flamed. "How can you be so arrogant and self-absorbed when all I'm trying to do is be your sister and help you?"

All the pent-up anger and frustration from her conversation with Barba surged through Nat. "Listen to me," she said and jammed her finger in Cal's face. "You think I'm self-absorbed? I'd like to see you spend every waking hour in a lab—" She stopped herself and took a deep breath. "What I've been working on this semester and what I will continue to work on over J-term is too complicated to explain."

"Try me." A look of challenge passed over Cal's face.

"You'd never understand." Nat shook her head, but Cal pressed on.

"Look, my J-term's an independent study. I may not comprehend everything you're doing, but I have a brain and plenty of time to listen. I can help."

Nat rubbed her thumb over her right forearm, thinking of the vine and spear markings that were underneath her jacket. Dragging her sister into her dilemma and her life as a Warrior Sister was the last thing she'd ever do. "No, you can't, Cal," she said, suddenly feeling bone weary. "Stop worrying about me. I'll see you when Dad picks us up to drive us home tomorrow."

"Whatever, Nat." Cal released her grip and backed away from her sister. "You know, for being so smart, you're an idiot when it comes to accepting help when you need it."

CHAPTER FIVE

One week later, Nat lugged her black duffel bag through her family's kitchen and deposited it by the back door.

"You're already packed?" Nat's mom removed a steaming casserole from the oven and set it on the stove. She eyed the duffel bag with a disapproving look.

"I told you I was leaving first thing in the morning, Mom. Viv's making a special trip to pick me up before she catches her flight tomorrow night."

"Where's Viv going again for J-term?" her mom asked.

"She's taking an art history course in Italy," Nat replied as she knelt next to her bag and unzipped the padded side pocket. *Ethel's book, my notes* . . . She fingered through the pages of her notebooks, ensuring the crammed binders contained the notations she'd made over the last week. *I'll pick up a sample of Annin's blood and be in the lab on campus before noon,* she promised herself. She'd pored over her notes during the week at home and was anxious to commence another round of tests.

"MC, set the table," Nat's mom called out.

Nat zipped up her bag and heard a door bang shut. A cold draft flooded past her. Nat's dad and Cal walked into the kitchen toward the sink to wash their hands. Cal brushed by Nat without giving her sister so much as a glance.

"Just use paper napkins, MC." Nat's mom sidestepped Nat's little sister and placed the casserole and a bowl of peas on the table before settling into her chair.

"Nat's leaving tomorrow. I want the table to look special." MC folded the last napkin, then sat down and turned to Nat. "I still don't understand why you're leaving so soon."

Nat felt a tugging at her heart. She curled her hand around MC's blonde ponytail and sat down. "The lab work for my J-term class is complicated, MC."

Cal let out a sharp laugh and shook her head. Nat took a bite of food and regarded her sister as an uncomfortable silence settled over the table.

Nat caught her mom glancing at both her and Cal before she said, "Dad told me you're going back early, too, Cal. It wasn't much of a break for either of you."

"Nat's not the only one with a difficult J-term." Cal gave her a stony look, then turned to their mom. "My instructor's leaving campus before January, and I have a huge meeting scheduled with her in two days. Viv told me I could catch a ride when she picked up Nat tomorrow."

"You're coming with us?" Nat asked, surprised. Viv hadn't mentioned that Cal was accompanying them back to campus.

"What?" Cal dropped her fork on her plate and glared at Nat. "Are you mad that Viv's giving me a ride?"

Nat, surprised by the vehemence in Cal's voice, bit back a retort. She took a deep breath and said, "No, of course not."

"Seems like a couple of hours in the car might do you two some good. You've hardly said anything to each other since you got home." Their mom narrowed her eyes.

Nat shifted in her chair, rankled by her expression. "You can't have a conversation with someone who won't speak to you," she replied.

"She doesn't have time to listen to what I have to say. Her life's too *complicated*," Cal shot back. She pushed away her plate of food. "I'm not hungry." She tossed the cloth napkin onto the floor and left the table.

Her dad leaned over his plate and fixed his gaze on Nat. "I don't know what's going on between you two, but figure it out."

"Yeah, I'll get right on it," Nat muttered and shoved a bite of casserole into her mouth. *Right after I solve all my other problems.* She felt a light pressure on her arm. MC slid her hand over Nat's Sister markings and clutched her wrist.

"Will we fight like that when I'm older?" MC's voice trembled slightly.

Nat nearly choked on her bite of food. She coughed and took a sip of water before glancing at both her parents for help. Their expressions left her knowing she had to answer the question on her own. She turned to her sister. MC's blue eyes watered and Nat's heart dropped.

"No, MC, we won't." She placed her hand on MC's shoulder.

"How do you know?"

"Because by the time you're as old as I am now, I'll have had years to learn how to be a better sister."

"You're a great sister. So is Cal." MC wiped her nose.

"I know." She looked intently at her sister. "I know."

Late the following afternoon, Nat entered her almost deserted dorm. Most of the college's students were still on break, and the building was eerily quiet. She surveyed the empty hallway, thankful no one was there. After the morning's ride with Viv and Cal and the disaster she'd just conjured in the lab, she was in no mood to talk to anyone. She inserted her key into her door and tumbled face-first over an enormous black suitcase.

"Viv!" Nat yelled, rising from her knees. "You trying to kill me?"

Viv burst out of their bathroom. "What?"

"Your bag was right in front of the door," Nat snapped, rubbing her elbow.

"Man, you're cranky today." Viv righted the suitcase. "One would think you'd be thanking me instead of yelling at me since I went out of my way to drive you and Cal back to campus. But noooo, you're griping because I left my suitcase near the door."

"Sorry," Nat muttered.

"What?" Viv held her hand to her ear. "I couldn't hear you, was that an apology?"

"I'm sorry, Viv," Nat said in an exaggerated voice.

"You better be." She snatched her furry purple coat off a coat hook. "I've got a marathon flight ahead of me, and you get this palatial spread all to yourself."

"Quit complaining. You're going to Italy for the entire month." Nat dropped her backpack by her desk.

"Yeah," Viv conceded, buttoning the coat. "But you know how I hate planes." She rummaged in her purse. "Passport and plastic. I think I'm ready." She slipped the strap over her arm. "Before I leave, about Cal. You two said approximately one word to each other the entire ride up here. I felt like I was in a silent movie."

"Ugh, Viv," Nat groaned. "Don't start in on my relationship with Cal. Leave with happy thoughts." She forced a smile to her lips.

"Family counselor I'm not, but maybe you could put in a little effort? Your sister's actually pretty funny. If I weren't stuck with you, I'd consider her a decent replacement. Talk to Cal. I'll bring you back a nice present if you do."

"I'll extend an olive branch. When I have time," Nat added.

"So sincere." Viv pulled a crocheted cap over her blue hair. "Hey, promise me you'll do something this month other than peer through a microscope. I don't want to come back and have you any more boring than you already are."

Nat let out a mock laugh. "Funny."

"See you in February." Viv blew her a kiss and rolled her suitcase out the door.

The moment the door closed, Nat settled into her desk chair. Viv's comments lingered in her mind. *If I had my way, I'd be at the Healing House instead of peering through a microscope.* She sighed and unzipped her backpack, checking to make sure the sample of Annin's blood was secure in its carrier. Her phone buzzed inside her pocket. She pulled it out and glanced at a text from Cal.

I've got one of your lab notebooks. You left it on a stack of my books in Viv's car.

I'll come get it now, Nat typed in response, not wanting to risk the chance of her sister losing her research.

No, I'm going out.

Nat swallowed her concern, knowing her notes would be safe enough locked away in Cal's room.

Morning then?
I meet with my professor first thing in the morning to outline my research project. You can get it after my meeting.

Nat frowned and remembered she'd told Cairn she'd be at the shop in the late morning to look through Ethet's lab for an ingredient she wanted to use in her experiments. I'm working tomorrow.

Can you bring it by the costume shop after
your meeting?

I guess. I have to go into town, anyway.

Nat shut off her phone and placed it on her desk. *There, I communicated with my sister,* she thought and pulled her computer from her backpack.

By the time Nat closed her computer and organized her notes, the sky outside her dorm window was ink black. She yawned, arched her aching back, then headed for the bathroom to get ready for bed. *Nothing I'm doing right now is working.* She splashed cold water on her face and yanked a towel from the towel bar. *Barba has to let me go back.* She pushed open the bathroom door and climbed into her bed. She stared at the ceiling and listened to the ticking of the clock. *She has to let me go back,* she thought again, and her eyes fluttered closed.

Nat's dreams faded behind her as she climbed over the rough ledge of her dream space. She stared at the darkened area around her, thankful Estos had taught her to find the place in her subconscious where she was free from her dreams and could imagine and control her surroundings. The moment she'd heard the Nalaide's raspy hiss in her dream, she'd bolted for the ledge of her dream space. Nat was pretty certain the Nalaide was only a memory haunting her sleep, but a Nala had wound its way into her subconscious before when she'd carried its remnant. She had no desire to test whether the Nalaide could track Nat down in her dreams. A hiss echoed on the other side of the ledge, where her dreams played out without her.

"You'll never find me," she whispered, feeling both frustrated and defiant. Her orb appeared above her head, and bars of light shot into the sky along her barrier. She backed away, knowing nothing could cross the barrier unless she let it.

Nat moved deeper into her dream space and imagined a field of meldon flowers. Their delicate yellow faces appeared instantly and angled toward an imagined sun. She settled into the field and picked a stem. *What's your secret?* She spun it between her fingers, perplexed by her failed experiments and attempts to kill the Nala bacteria.

She flopped onto her stomach and stretched out in the imagined sunlight, wishing she could pose her questions to the Healing Sisters. *Why is everyone I want to talk to, need to talk to, in a place I can't go?* Soris' face flooded her thoughts. She dug her fingers between the flowers and pulled a few plants from the rich soil. Delicate roots broke free, and miniscule bits of dirt scattered over the petals of the other flowers. Nat dangled one of the plants in front of her and stared at the dirt falling from the roots onto the ground. She sat upright and knocked her head against her orb floating above her.

The soil!

Nat woke with a start, breathing deep. She banged into a chair as she pulled on jeans. She searched her desk for the container of meldon flowers and held the jar up to the light. A string of fine roots dangled from the base of one stem. Nat could barely make out little bits of soil clinging to the roots. She grabbed her backpack, pocketed the jar, and raced out of the dorm into the early morning light.

Campus was empty as she jogged across the quad. *Don't get your hopes up, Nat,* she told herself as she took the stairs leading to the lab classroom in the Science Center. The dark lab burst with light when she flicked on the light switch. She set up the trio of flasks and sparked the gas line. Flames curled up the side of the first flask. She crumbled the entire meldon flower—stem, leaves, petals, and dirt-encrusted root—into the second flask.

The water boiled, and steam curled through the tubes and sidearms. Dark-yellow droplets formed around the side of the last container. She observed the difference in color from her previous experiments and felt her heart flutter with excitement. *It's the same color as in the illustration in Ethet's book.* She glanced at the ancient volume that lay open near the microscope, prepared a slide, and looked through the lens. The spherical Nala bacteria floated around the blood cells. She sharpened the focus on the microscope, looking for the spot where she'd added a drop of the new meldon concentrate.

There you are. A Nala bacterium came into focus and twisted in on itself, shrinking in size. The bacterium's spikelike hairs flowed off the organism. The same twisting process occurred over and over as she scanned the slide. Her eyes burned from strain. She clicked on the monitor that projected the image from the microscope onto a flat screen hanging from the wall.

All the Nala bacteria were dying.

CHAPTER SIX

Nat slammed her fist against the warehouse door.

"Barba! Cairn!" she yelled and punched in the security code. The door clicked but wouldn't budge when she yanked on the handle. She eyed the wooden frame and kicked the jammed door. "Open up!"

The tinny sound of boots hitting metal stairs echoed on the other side of the entrance. Cairn opened the door, and Nat slid past him like an eel and shot up the stairs.

"Natalie, what on earth?" Cairn hurried after her. The door closed only partway when it hit the doorframe.

Nat ran down the walkway overlooking the interior forest and training grounds. The smell of pine hung heavy in the air. She raced down the steps and through the kitchen and pushed open the heavy doors leading to Ethet's laboratory and the entrance to Fourline. The vibrations emanating from the tunnel cut into the limestone wall and sent a tremor through the soles of Nat's shoes.

Cairn cleared his throat behind her.

"Where's Barba?" she asked as she scanned the empty laboratory.

"Barba left to costume a show in Minneapolis this morning," Cairn answered, breathing heavily.

"What? When?" Nat took a step backward. She glanced at the dark mouth of the tunnel.

"First thing. Now I'm assuming there's a reason you barreled over me to get in here?" Cairn tugged at the bottom of his sweater, pulling it straight.

"I figured out how to kill the Nala bacteria." Nat bounced on the balls of her feet. "It's a compound in the soil that the meldon flowers grow in. It's so obvious now. Come here, I'll show you." She grasped him by the elbow and pulled him toward the counter that ran almost the length of the room. She pulled up two stools and dug Ethet's book from her pack. It fell open to the page with the ornate picture of the small yellow flowers and the formula.

"The book and the formula reference meldon, but the authors didn't mean the flower, they meant the soil where the flower grows. Look." She flipped the page over and pointed to two dots of yellow on an intricate map of Fourline. "Meldon is what the Sisters named the two locations where the flower thrives in Fourline. But they meant the place, the ground, not the flower. I'm guessing after the Rim Accord, the Nala attacks stopped and the knowledge of what really cured a person bitten by them disappeared. Sisters continued to use the flower in their teas and poultices but didn't use the soil."

"Slow down, Natalie." He pushed up his glasses. "Are you telling me the soil itself is a cure?"

"I think a compound in it may be. I had a tiny amount of soil on the roots of a flower. I used it in my experiment this morning, and the concentrate I created killed the Nala bacteria in Annin's blood. It took me a few hours to isolate the compound after I ran my experiment. It is abundant in the soil, but the flower itself contains only a trace. That's why my earlier experiments failed." She held up a vial of dark-yellow liquid and her notes. Her eyes shone with excitement. "I think this may lead to a cure, Cairn. The Healing Sisters live in the middle of a meldon field and may be able to use this discovery to formulate a cure for the duozi. We need to get this to Ethet right away!"

"Yes, of course. Barba will be back tonight, and we'll discuss when and how to send your findings through the membrane." He fiddled with the cuff of his sleeve and fixed his eyes on the vial. He glanced up at Nat and hesitated before he spoke. "I hate to tell you this, but it may be a matter of months before we have a courier."

"Months?" The excitement drained from Nat. "This can't wait that long." She pushed away from the counter, almost toppling the stool. "Mudug's stirred up prejudice against the duozi, so no one questions his use of them as slaves in his mines." Her voice took on a pleading tone. "He's delivering children to the Nala, and those creatures . . ." Her gaze shifted to the tunnel opening leading to the membrane. "If what I found leads to a cure for the duozi, think of how many people we can save from the misery Mudug and the Nala have created."

Cairn frowned. "Natalie, I don't mean to sound indifferent, but a cure can wait, given what's about to unfold in Fourline and the problems with Emilia."

"What's going on?" she asked as she watched his eyes shift from her to the tunnel.

"While you were gone for the holiday, Oberfisk returned with information about the rebellion—and Emilia."

"What's wrong with Emilia?" Nat asked, picking up on the tension in his voice.

"Emilia's memories are returning, but she's experiencing side effects from the Chemist's experiments on her that are putting her and those around her at risk. Estos intends to take her with him and make his way to Rustbrook to reclaim the regency, but the Healing Sisters caring for her are reluctant to let her leave the confines of the House. Barba has extensive knowledge of some of the wilder parts of Fourline. Ethet and Estos sent Ober to her for her advice on the safest route to Rustbrook before Ethet agreed to send Emilia off with her brother. Ober left a few days ago. He did leave a message for you," Cairn added as if it were some sort of consolation.

Nat looked up at the ceiling and clenched her teeth. *A few days ago? If he'd waited, I could have sent these findings with him.* She took a deep breath and brought her attention back to Cairn, knowing she had to convince him to let her pass through the membrane. "If Estos and the rebels are preparing to retake Rustbrook, I need to get my discovery to Ethet *now*." Cairn took a step back when she brushed past him and approached the tunnel. "With a cure, Mudug will have no more negotiating tools with the Nala, no way he can use the Nala or the duozi against the rebels." Nat spun around. "Let me take my findings to the Healing Sisters. I'll make it to the Healing House and back in a few days, Cairn. I'll be in and out, and the Nala will never know."

Cairn shook his head. "The Nala aren't your only problem, Natalie. The Chemist put a price on your head, remember?" He gave her a stern look.

Nat scowled. *Of course he'd throw that at me.* "The Chemist doesn't know what I look like." Cairn's expression didn't change. "Nothing will find me unless I let it. I don't have remnant in me. It's been half a year since the Nalaide had the remotest idea where I was. Cassandra killed the last white Nala that saw me. Bringing my findings to Ethet is worth the minimal risk. I'd be in and out," she repeated, trying to sound calm even though she felt like bolting down the tunnel.

"In and out of the eastern forest?" He lowered his chin and looked over the thick frames of his glasses.

"You're killing me, Cairn." She threw her hands in the air, feeling tension building throughout her body. "How would the Nala find me?" She held up her notebook. "I have a possible way to end Mudug's cozy relationship with the Nala and cure the duozi."

"Fine."

"I can go?" She grasped his arm.

"I didn't say that." Cairn glanced at her hand, and Nat released her hold on his sweater. "I'll call Barba and let her weigh in on this. If she says you can return, then I'll let you go. I trust her judgment, and she is your Head Sister."

"And if she says no?" She crossed her arms defiantly over her chest.

"We wait until Oberfisk or another courier returns. Final decision." He took a deep breath. "Please excuse me. I want to make this call away from the wave of adolescent impatience," he said curtly and left Ethet's lab.

Nat tapped her foot and stared at the tunnel as she waited for him. *In and out, it would only take me a few days. The Nala would never know.*

Cairn returned to the lab, shaking his head. "Her answer is an emphatic no. She feels the risk that the Nalaide would find you is too great."

Nat felt like screaming. "Isn't that my decision to make, Cairn?"

"I'm not going against Barba on this, Natalie." The paternal expression on his face infuriated her. "The decision is made. You're not returning until the matter with the Nalaide is cleared up."

"What if you went?" she suggested, grasping for a solution. *Someone has to take my discovery to the Sisters.*

Cairn's brow furrowed. "Natalie, you know Barba and I have to stay here to ensure the entrance remains secure." His expression softened. "Barba did say she's cutting her work short and will be back within the hour to discuss this with you."

"What a consolation." She looked past Cairn's shoulder toward the dark mouth of the tunnel. The entrance thrummed softly and the vibrations beckoned her. She looked away and thought of everything, everyone, that lay on the other side of the membrane. *I don't care what Barba says. I'm going.*

"We'll get your findings to Ethet." Cairn's voice broke into her thoughts. He glanced at his watch. "I have to go to campus. Do you want a ride, or do you want to wait here until Barba returns?"

Nat's eyes widened, hardly believing her luck. "I'll stay here and work in Ethet's lab until Barba gets back." She dropped her gaze, hoping Cairn hadn't sensed her intentions from her expression. "Maybe there's a soil sample tucked away somewhere here that I can use." She scanned the hundreds of vials and jars lining the back wall as if interested in their contents.

He gave her an appreciative look. "Good. I'd just as soon have you here while I'm gone." He glanced at the tunnel. "I don't suppose you'd mind sending your orb to the end of the tunnel so I don't have to bring down the barricade?"

"Sure," Nat said without hesitation. "I'll go get it." *And my other gear.*

Cairn followed Nat out of the lab, down the hallway, and into the large kitchen. He paused by the dining table and lifted a folded piece of paper off the wooden surface. "Ober's note." He placed it into her open hand.

"Ober in person would be better." She puffed out her cheeks, hoping she appeared defeated, and followed Cairn out of the kitchen. He paused by the heavy metal door leading to the costume shop.

"Trust Barba's judgment on this, Natalie. She has your best interests in mind."

"I know." Nat feigned agreement and gave him a single wave. The door clicked shut behind him. She waited a few heartbeats, then raced up the stairs. The door to the yellow room where her Warrior Sister belongings were stored hit the wall and bounced closed. She clicked a button set into the base of one wall, and her orb shot out of a rectangular opening. "We're going back," Nat said to her orb as she retrieved Ober's note from the floor, where it had fallen. The sphere bobbed by her head, spinning at a rapid pace. She kicked off her hiking boots and read the crude script.

Miss Natalie,

I meant to meet with you in person, but Sister Barba was anxious that I leave. Annin made me promise to tell you that Soris left the Healing House earlier this fall to join Gennes and the attack on the mines. He is living in the western woods of the Keyen Mountains with a band of duozi. Annin thought you should—

Nat stared at the paper. Ober's writing blurred, and a chill of fear for Soris ripped through her. *He attacked Mudug's mines? What was he thinking?* She crumpled the note and grabbed her heavy Sister's tunic. She pulled on her worn leather Sister's boots and yanked her cloak off the hanger. Racing back down the hall, she secured her sword to her belt and adjusted the pack that contained her findings. She grabbed some food from the kitchen and filled her water container. Her orb zoomed toward the warehouse, reading Nat's thoughts.

The improvised armory in the corner of the warehouse was dimly lit by the fiber optics twisting down from the ceiling. She sifted through the remaining weapons and found her small crossbow. A pinging noise echoed through the warehouse, startling Nat. She scanned the indoor forest and metal walkway. *It's nothing,* she told herself and rushed back into Ethet's lab, missing the sound of footsteps clanking down the metal stairs.

Pausing at the mouth of the tunnel, Nat took a deep breath and plunged down the passage toward the membrane with her orb spinning at her side. She thought of Soris as her feet flew over the stone. *If you're not playing it safe, Soris, then neither am I.* She rounded a corner, and the light from her orb shone against the circular, opaque membrane. Nat pushed through the vibrating portal, disappearing just as a voice echoed down the tunnel.

"Nat?"

CHAPTER SEVEN

Nat scanned the forest and hastened from the cliff hiding the membrane. She jogged a few paces in the snow and pocketed her orb. Pausing by the red boulder, she breathed in the cold air and a rush of freedom flowed through her.

I'm back.

She stepped onto the path to the crooked tree and Benedict's cottage, where she intended to spend the night before traveling on to the eastern forest and the Healing House.

"Nat?"

A twig snapped behind her. Nat spun around and froze. The snow-covered boughs of the pine trees framed Cal's pale, startled face. Her sister took a step back and stumbled, landing in the snow.

"What are you doing here?" Nat cried. The elation she'd felt moments before vanished as she stared down at her sister. She extended her hand and helped Cal to her feet.

"I was trying to find you." Cal brushed the snow from her jeans and gaped at the forest around them.

"Why?" Nat barked, overcome by anger as the disastrous consequences of Cal's presence in Fourline crashed over her like an icy wave.

"You told me to meet you at the shop with your notebook. Remember?" She held up the binder containing some of Nat's experiment notes. "The front of the shop was closed, but the back door of the warehouse was open." Cal's gaze traveled up and down Nat's heavy cloak.

Nat groaned. Cairn must not have secured the door after her, and he hadn't set up the security measures because Nat had told him not to.

"I saw you," Cal continued. "You were in the corner of the warehouse and then disappeared down that tunnel . . ." Her voice trailed off as she gaped again at the forest. "Where are we and what was that weird door I passed through?"

Nat shook her head in frustration and clenched her fists. Cal shifted from foot to foot, shivering in the cold and waiting for an answer.

Nat unhooked her cloak and passed it to Cal. "Put this on. It will keep you warm," she said, feeling anything but generous.

As Cal accepted the cloak and draped it over her shoulders, Nat silently weighed her options. *Barba will return soon. If I take Cal back now, I have to come up with some convincing lie to keep her from blabbing about the tunnel and Barba may catch me. Why did she have to follow me?* Nat kicked a stump near her feet. She looked up and caught Cal's startled expression. A cold realization settled over her and dampened her fury. *She's coming with me, and Annin will have to erase her memories,* Nat decided.

"Nat, did you hear me? Where are we?"

Thinking quickly, Nat answered, "We're in a forest on the other side of the cliff behind the shop. You've never been here?" she asked and tried to look curious even though she felt like attacking something. She took Cal's elbow, steered her away from the boulder, and set a brisk pace. Cal fell in step next to her.

"No, but what about that tunnel and the weird door?" Cal asked. Suspicion permeated every word.

"It's just a tunnel that cuts through the cliff and an unusual reflection of light," Nat lied, keeping her face averted so her sister couldn't read her expression. She quickened her steps, wanting to increase the distance between Cal and the membrane. "I've used the tunnel a bunch of times to check on a house Cairn and Barba have a little ways past the woods. Cairn asked me to look in on it again today. Run with me. I want to get there as soon as I can. I'll take you back after I'm done." She gave Cal what she hoped was a reassuring look and skipped over a log.

"I don't know." Cal hesitated and slowed her pace.

"Finding your way back on your own might be tricky, and I'm in a rush. I promise I'll take you back." Nat dug her hand into her pocket and readied her orb in case she had to knock her out if she refused to come.

Cal glanced over her shoulder at the cliff. The tall pines hid most of its craggy surface. "Okay," she reluctantly agreed. Her long legs matched Nat's stride. "But I hope this doesn't take too long. And why are you dressed up like Robin Hood?" She gestured to Nat's tunic and tall boots.

"It's just a costume from the shop I like to wear sometimes."

"Weird," Cal muttered.

Nat ignored the comment and ran onto the path with Cal following her. She glanced up at the tips of the trees, hoping both of them would make it to Benedict's before anything else went wrong.

Nat slowed to a jog when Benedict's cottage came into view.

"Rest here a second." She gestured to a wooden fence Benedict used as an enclosure for his mule. "I have to check that old shed before I open up the cottage."

"Fine with me." Cal breathed heavily and leaned red-faced against a wooden post. "I hope Barba and Cairn have a car somewhere around this dump, because I am not running back to the shop. You nearly killed me at that pace."

Nat bristled at her sister's whining. "I thought dancers were supposed to be in good shape," she shot back as she jogged through the snow toward the cottage.

"I am in good shape, but that was a minimarathon you made me run!"

Nat ignored Cal's reply. *I can't believe she followed me.* She ducked around the other side of the cottage so Cal wouldn't see her and pulled out her orb. She wiped a circle of grime off a window and peered inside. It was completely dark. *I'll get her settled, then tell her just enough to keep her in line. Annin can erase it all later, anyway.* She glanced at the bedraggled thatch roofline and then at her orb. The sphere shot up the pitch of the roof and disappeared down the chimney. A rattling sound erupted from the interior of the cottage. Nat pressed her forehead against the window again and shielded her eyes. Her orb, streaked with soot, spun through the room, filling it with beams of light. The cottage was empty.

She hurried to the wooden front door and listened. The sound of her orb rolling against wood met her ears. She closed her eyes and tried to remember what the interior latch looked like. The orb rolled up the door and spun under the latch. Nat gripped the knob and twisted. The door sprang open.

Nat examined the dusty interior. The air smelled stale. Cobwebs clung to the sconces set into the wall and hung from the iron chandelier suspended from a wooden beam crossing the ceiling. The orb bobbed over surfaces and dipped into corners. A frightened mouse froze in the light, then scurried under the legs of the cabinet. Nat scowled when she looked at the cabinet, remembering the images Annin had shared of her captivity in the Hermit's cottage.

Nat pocketed her orb and leaned out of the entrance to beckon to Cal. She dropped her bag on the wooden table across from the narrow bed, then set about making a fire.

"What is this place?" Cal asked as she ducked under the doorframe. "Some kind of off-the-grid shack? There's not even a sink and I'm dying of thirst."

"Shut the door and have a seat," Nat ordered. Cal's whining set her on edge. "I'll get you something to drink after I get this fire going." The spark from the tinderbox set the cobwebs clinging to the logs ablaze. She sat back on her heels and watched the tiny flames creep along the underside of the wood until they curled around the dried bark and roared to life.

Benedict had been far from her mind, but now, sitting in front of his hearth, a dozen unsettling thoughts popped into her head as she wondered what had happened to him. The last time she'd seen the Hermit was right before she, Soris, and Andris had rescued Emilia from the Chemist's quarters at the castle in Rustbrook. *He hates the duozi more than anyone I know,* Nat thought, recalling his cruel words to Annin and Soris. If her findings really could cure the duozi, then his paranoia and absurd accusations about all the other duozi would be put to rest. *If he's alive.* She poked the logs with a heavy hooked rod. Cal coughed behind her, bringing her attention back to the immediate problem of her sister. Cal stood with her arms crossed tightly over her chest, looking around the cottage. Her shadow flickered against the wall. *Time for a little truth.*

Nat gestured to the worn chair in front of the hearth. "Sit down, Cal. I have something I need to tell you."

Cal cupped the chipped bowl in her shaking hands as Nat finished explaining where they were. Nat watched her from the hearth, added a few more meldon flowers to the teakettle, then set the heavy kettle on a hook near the flames. She lifted a mug balanced on the edge of the hearth and sat down.

"This is some kind of trick you're playing on me, right?" Cal narrowed her eyes.

"No." Nat looked steadily at her sister.

"I don't believe you." Her full lips were set into a thin line.

"I swear on MC's life, everything I just told you is the truth."

Cal stiffened and drained of color. "I don't understand how—"

"Don't try," Nat cut in. She took a sip of her tea and stared at her sister. They sat in silence. The wind howled outside the small cottage.

Cal wrapped a moth-eaten blanket tightly around her shoulders. "None of this is real. I must be dreaming."

"I wish it were a dream, because your being here is a big problem." Nat stretched her legs in front of her, trying to ease some of the built-up tension in her body.

"Then why did you bring me? Take me back. You said you would."

"I will." Nat poked the fire and angry sparks flew above the burning logs. "But I can't right now. I have to find some people I know before I take you back."

"I'll find my own way, then." A flare of defiance flickered in Cal's eyes.

"No, you won't." Nat leaned toward her sister, feeling both aggravated and protective. She studied her sister's face, wondering what else to tell her to keep her in line, and thought of the Nala. *A little more truth right now won't hurt, since Annin will change her memories.* "You're staying with me because the forests around here are infested with a creature that will either kill you or infect you with nasty bacteria. I'm trained to protect people from the creatures, but you have to—"

"Are you serious?" Cal cut in and stared at her sister as if she were a deranged stranger.

"Yes. Completely. You're going to stay by my side, we'll find my friends, and then I'll make sure you get home." Nat waited for some smart remark or argument, but her sister just stared at the rush mat on the floor. "Get some sleep, Cal. We have a long day ahead of us tomorrow." She pointed to the tiny bed.

Cal stood up slowly as if she might topple to the floor. Her shoulders hunched, she shuffled toward the bed. Nat felt a tinge of guilt, remembering how confused she'd been when she first entered Fourline.

"Cal." Her sister turned around. "I'll get you back home, I promise. But you have to promise me something. Whatever I ask you to do while we're here, you need to do it. No arguments, no questions—just do it."

"Whatever," Cal mumbled. She looked pale in the shadows by the bed. "I'm going to wake up tomorrow morning knowing all this was a dream, anyway." She lay down with her back to the fire, her long legs dangling off the side of Benedict's bed.

Nat sat in front of the fire and stared at the flames while she sipped her now-cold tea, wishing it really were a dream.

CHAPTER EIGHT

The next morning, Cal stiffly followed Nat from the Hermit's cottage into the woods, muttering about long dreams and sleepwalking. Cal's comments ceased the deeper they traveled into the woods, and hours flew by without so much as a peep from her. Now, as Nat scanned a riverbank, looking for a good place to ford, Cal stared at her with an anxious look in her eyes as if the truth of what Nat had told her had finally started to sink in.

"Take me home," Cal said quietly.

Nat touched the thin ice near the bank of the river, then regarded her sister to try to gauge Cal's mental state. *She knows she's in over her head and needs me if she wants to find her way back home,* she thought, feeling more coldhearted than she liked. *But she's holding it together. She won't bolt.*

"Can't, at least not yet," she responded and averted her eyes. She glanced downstream and recognized the cliff where she'd jumped into the river to escape a Nala. *A jump like that today would kill us.* "This is as good a place as any to cross," she said to Cal as she pointed to an uprooted tree that spanned part of the river, its bare branches sticking up like gnarled fingers.

"Are you crazy? I'm not crossing there. The tree's not even close to the other bank." She stamped her feet on the riverbank and blew into her hands. Little puffs of breath curled around her fists.

"The water won't kill you," Nat said, struggling to stay patient with her sister.

"You're refusing to take me home. I'm freezing because you burned my clothes and shoes and made me wear these rags." She lifted her arms. The sleeves of the coat Nat had fashioned out of one of Benedict's blankets flapped in the breeze. "And now you want me to jump into a river?"

"It's the best option. I've been down this river before, I know. Would you just trust me? Please," Nat added, desperate to avoid another argument. She scanned the towering line of trees above Cal's head. The tips swayed in the breeze.

"Trust you?" Cal let out a sharp laugh that echoed down the river valley. Nat winced at the sound. It would be a miracle if the Nala didn't know they were in the forest by now.

"Cal, I'm going to explain this one more time," she said through clenched teeth. "There are creatures in these woods who will happily kill both of us. We're in danger and need to move quickly through this forest. Challenging everything I say is not helping." A creaky groan that sounded like a tree bending in the breeze caught Nat's attention.

"Yeah, the creepy monsters." Cal rubbed her chilled hands together and met Nat's eyes. "How do I know you're not lying about that just to get me to do what you want? You lied about this place and tricked me to get me to come with you . . . What's wrong?" Cal stopped talking as Nat's complexion paled.

"Get on the tree in the river now," Nat whispered to her sister. She unsheathed her sword. *"Now,"* she repeated. Cal glanced nervously at Nat's sword and stepped onto the slippery wood of the uprooted tree. Nat turned and searched the branches of the tall pines bordering the river.

"What is *that*?" Cal cried. A Nala, blue as glacial water, dropped from a naked aspen. The creature landed with all four limbs on the riverbank, and its emotionless eyes settled on Nat. A hiss shot from the creature's mouth like a leak in a steam pipe.

"Keep moving, Cal," Nat said through barely parted lips. The muscles in the Nala's long limbs twitched. She pointed her sword in the crouched creature's direction and took a tiny step forward, wanting all its focus on her and not Cal.

Cal took a swift step across the tree. The damp wood creaked. The Nala's concave eyes swiveled from Nat to Cal. It opened its mouth and bit at the air. Nat felt like the creature was sizing them up, but its facial features were devoid of the crazed anger she'd seen in the remnant-infused white Nala. She released her orb, and it flashed toward the creature's head.

As the Nala swatted at the bright sphere, Nat backed onto the trunk and glanced over her shoulder, searching for Cal. Her sister leapt from the mangled end of the tree onto the opposite bank. Her long legs easily covered the distance, and her foot barely touched the ice. Cal turned and Nat caught a glimpse of her face. It was the color of the gray ice clinging to the surface of the riverbank.

"Sisssssster." The creature drew out the word in an unpleasant exhalation of breath as it whapped her orb to the side and crawled onto the fallen tree to scramble after her. It sprang off its back legs. Nat's orb slammed against its side, and the Nala landed in the icy water.

"Where'd it go?" Cal yelled. She held a forked branch in her hand and sidestepped along the bank.

"It's underwater," Nat called out and crouched low on the tree as she scanned the river. Dark-blue water surged from underneath the fallen trunk. "I know you're there," she whispered and held her sword tip above the bubbling surface.

"Maybe it swam away." Cal's voice trembled.

"No, it's waiting." Nat tightened her grip on her sword and sent her orb closer to Cal.

"For what?"

"For—"

A crashing sound exploded behind Cal. "Duck!" Nat screamed and sprinted down the fallen trunk. A second Nala launched itself from an aspen tree near Cal. Cal spun around and smacked the Nala in the face with the long branch.

"Keep it away from you!" Nat yelled. Her orb flew across the bank and pelted the Nala in its compressed abdomen. The creature slumped to the ground, then scuttled across the pebbled bank. The sphere slammed against the top of the Nala's head, and it wobbled to the side.

Nat steadied herself on the end of the fallen trunk, then jumped toward the shore. She slid across the ice and skipped onto the pebbles. The Nala shook its head, righted itself, and looked up. Its faceted eyes contracted when it saw Nat's sword descending down upon it. Nat thrust the sword between its bony shoulder blades. The creature's mouth formed a dark *o* as it wailed. The Nala's body jerked, then slumped onto the pebbles. Nat pulled her sword from its back and cut off the creature's head.

"Behind you!" Cal yelled and grasped her branch. She lunged at the Nala erupting from the river behind Nat. The point of the branch punctured the creature's belly, and it lurched forward. Nat pivoted around Cal and struck the back of the Nala with her sword.

"Is it dead?" Cal's voice squeaked as it rose in pitch.

Nat freed the blade and brought her sword down a second time. The Nala's head rolled to the side of its body. "It is now." She curled her hand around the Nala's head and tossed it into the middle of the river.

She picked up the other creature's bulb-shaped head. It sailed into the air and landed in the water like an oversized skipping stone.

"The bodies need to go into the river, too," Nat ordered, still holding her sword and refusing to think how close her sister had just come to being bitten. She grasped the slick blue skin of one of the creature's arms. An image of Soris' blue skin flashed in her mind as she stumbled on the icy pebbles. Cal took a few uneven steps closer to the body, then grabbed a leg. The sisters heaved the creature into the river. It clipped the edge of the ice, then floated away. They tossed the second body into the water, and it disappeared in a torrent of bubbles. Nat scanned the opposite bank, but saw no Nala. Her orb skimmed the water and wove around the trees, then returned to her hand. Cal followed the sphere's movements, transfixed by fear, and hardly noticed Nat running her hands over her sister's arms and sides to ensure there were no bites.

"Did it touch you anywhere?" Nat asked, not hiding the concern in her voice.

"N-no." Cal's voice shook. She kept her eyes locked on Nat's orb as it hovered protectively above both of them. "Everything you've told m-me's been the truth." A look of dread clouded her face. Her body trembled so much Nat could see her coat shaking.

Nat sheathed her sword and wrapped her arms around her sister. "Yes, it is, Cal." The harsh realization that Cal could've been bitten or killed made her stomach roil.

"Will you take me home now, please?" Cal's hands trembled and her eyes were filled with fear.

Nat closed her hand around Cal's and shook her head, feeling wretched for dragging her here. But she knew now there was no choice. They had to make it to the Healing House, and quickly. "Too danger-ous. Any Nala that heard the fighting will be on this bank and after us soon." *Including the white Nala.*

"So what do we do?" Cal looked at her sister in desperation.

"We're headed in the direction of a place those creatures won't go near," Nat said, thinking of the Meldon Plain around the Healing House. "But Cal, you have to run with me now, faster than you've ever run. Can you do that for me?" she begged as she dragged her sister closer to the forest.

"I don't know." Cal's grip on Nat's hand grew painful. "What if those things catch us?"

"I'll keep you safe, I promise," she said, hoping her words would calm her sister. "Stay by my side and I promise to keep you safe."

"Okay," Cal said in a shaky voice and held tight to her sister's hand as they plunged into the forest.

CHAPTER NINE

Rain streamed from the branches of the soaring pines. Thunder boomed above the trees. Nat felt the crackle of electricity in the air. She glanced over her shoulder. Cal ran wordlessly behind her. Her mouth was pinched with worry and concentration. The blanket cloak covering her was drenched from the rain and hung off her shoulders.

"Stay with me, Cal." Nat slowed her pace and swallowed the feeling of panic building inside her. Cal caught up, her blonde hair stuck in wet strands against her cheeks. "We're getting close," Nat said in a lame attempt to sound certain. *Please let me be heading in the right direction.* The cloudy sky and her vague memory of this part of the forest filled her with doubt. *Have we run too far south?*

Another cannonade of thunder broke from the sky. Nat slowed their pace, glanced uncertainly to her right, then set off in a direction she hoped led to the west. The rain let up enough that she was able to hear her footfalls on the forest floor. She dug her water container from her bag and took a quick sip before passing it back to Cal like a relay race baton. Cal took the container and stopped running. Her chest heaving, she leaned her arm against a tree before taking a sip.

"Can't stop," Nat said, retracing her steps to Cal.

Cal's head shot up and she stared at the nearby trees. "Did you hear that?" Her eyes widened.

"What?" A nervous shiver ripped through Nat.

Cal stepped away from the tree and turned around. "I swear I just heard it," she said with a tremor in her voice.

"What?" Nat demanded.

Cal's eyes met Nat's. "It sounds like someone saying 'sister.'"

Nat grasped Cal's hand. The moment their fingers touched, Nat heard a distant drawn-out hiss. An enormous branch cracked and flipped end over end until it crashed onto the forest floor far behind them. Nat jerked Cal into motion, and they sprinted away from the noise.

The forest transformed into a murky green blur. They raced over the damp organic sludge coating the ground. The sound of breaking branches followed them. From the corner of her eye, Nat spotted a Nala landing near the exposed roots of a tree not far behind them. She clung to Cal's hand and veered to the left toward a dense cluster of trees. A Nala sailed across the treetops above them and landed in front of Nat. Its face was inches from hers, and its jaws expanded until its black mouth seemed to extend to its chest. Cal screamed. Nat punched the creature's flat nose, and its head jerked back. The Nala's reaction gave Nat enough time to unsheathe a dagger.

The creature lashed out at Nat, grasping her shoulder with its pointed hand and drawing her close. Nat shoved her dagger deep into its abdomen. A mossy smell like river mud filled the air around them as the Nala spit out its last breath and doubled over her blade. Nat cut off the creature's head and it rolled over Cal's feet. She leapt from the pool of blood and let out a muffled cry. Nat put her finger to her lips. She motioned for Cal to follow. They ran from the now-decapitated body into a clearing. A distant flash of yellow caught Nat's attention.

She shrugged off her pack and tossed it to Cal. Her sister caught the pack and held it in her hands.

"See the field?" Nat whispered and handed her dagger to Cal.

Her sister took the weapon and glanced nervously through the trees. "Yes," she replied and turned back around.

"Run to it. You'll be safe once you hit the flowers. But don't stop running until you find a building. It looks like a fortress. Annin should be there." She pushed Cal in the direction of the field. "Don't come back into the forest."

"You're not—?" Cal froze and her eyes grew as big as saucers. Three Nala hit the ground in front of Nat. Their slick blue bodies glistened with rainwater.

"Go, Cal!" Nat whipped around and faced the Nala as they scuttled closer. She sent her orb directly above the Nala's heads and raised her sword. "You're beyond the boundary of the Rim Accord. Leave this area!" she yelled at them. Her orb blazed with light. The creatures brought their forearms to their eyes as a shield against the glare. "Are you deaf?" she yelled and stepped closer to them. "Leave now."

One of the Nala lowered its arms. "We take no orders from Sisters." The creature's lips curled away from its sharp teeth as it spoke.

Nat could still hear Cal's footfalls behind her. A Nala glanced past her shoulder and shifted its weight to the side as if it were about to spring away. *No, you don't.* She pushed up the sleeve on her right arm, exposing her markings. The Nala's eyes contracted and an angry hiss filled the air.

"The Sister the Nalaide seeks," one of the creatures hissed.

Her orb shot toward the Nala and zipped through the space between their limbs. Nat ran straight for the creatures, cutting into their blue skin as she passed between two of them, then took off running in the opposite direction from Cal. Looking over her shoulder, she saw the creatures jumping between trees, chasing her. Cal was nowhere to be seen.

Nat slumped against the base of a tree, exhausted. Her chest heaved. Hours had passed since she'd fought the remaining Nala, but running through the woods had worn her out. She forced herself to slow her breathing and pulled her hand from the rip in her sleeve. Her fingers came away smeared with blood. She examined the deep stab in her arm. Blood seeped out of the puncture wound and glistened in the pale moonlight. She leaned her head against the trunk and let her hand drop to her side.

Don't fall asleep. She forced her eyes open and listened to the distant crash of waves. A salty-smelling breeze wove through the thin line of trees. The chase had taken her to the coast. She thought about running again, but quickly gave up on the idea. The forest would be crawling with Nala, and she had no idea how close she was to the Nala den set into the cliff along the coast. Staying in one place, at least for the moment, was her best chance of avoiding another run-in with the creatures. *Maybe they won't think to look for me here. Who'd be dumb enough to hide out next to a known Nala den?*

She winced and dug out the small kit she kept in her cloak pocket. Besides her sword and orb, the kit was the only thing she had with her. All her supplies, water, and food were in the pack she'd given Cal. *How could I have been so stupid to take her with me?* The uncertainty over whether Cal had made it to the lower Meldon Plain and the Healing House plagued her.

She unwrapped the kit, removed a yellow vial, and drank the contents. The bitter taste of the meldon juice made her gag. *When Soris finds out what I've done, he'll be furious,* she thought, feeling like a hypocrite as she recalled how upset she'd been when she'd learned he'd invaded Mudug's mines. She wondered who had the bigger death wish. *But he didn't put someone else's life in danger like I did.*

She pushed the thoughts of Cal and Soris away and focused on cleaning and binding her wound with the store of supplies from her kit. The puncture in her arm from the Nala's pointed hand still bled. *At least I don't have to worry about its remnant.* She recalled its startled expression when her blade had cut into its throat.

The lower branches of the trees in front of her swayed in the breeze. She struggled to her feet and stumbled forward, looking for a good place to hide. Clouds floated above her, and a sliver of moon provided a cold light. She spotted a trio of trees ringed by a winterberry bush. She burrowed under the bush and listened as the wind and waves lashed the cliffs. Her eyes fluttered for a moment, and she drifted into a nightmare.

CHAPTER TEN

Nat crawled through the mist clouding her dream and peered over a ledge. Fear clutched her heart when she recognized the open cavern of the Nala den where she had found and rescued dozens of duozi children months before. Now, instead of children, blue Nala filled the cavern and circled a silvery pool of water in the middle of the amphitheater.

A white limb slithered across the surface of the pool. The Nala procession halted, and each creature dropped to its four limbs and bowed. The crown of the Nalaide's head breached the surface of the water. A shiver ran through Nat when the Nala queen's black eyes peered over the rim. She pulled herself out of the water, revealing her long white torso and limbs. She stood and towered over the prostrate creatures.

A Nala lifted its head and approached the queen. Its feet slapped against the smooth stone floor inlaid with a spiral of blue stone, then it paused in front of the Nalaide. The queen blinked her concave eyes and, in a sudden movement, pressed her mouth against the Nala's chest. The Nala arched its back, and its blue skin turned white. The Nalaide unlatched her mouth from the creature, and it stumbled away in a dizzy motion. The circular opening on its chest fused shut and a white ring of the queen's remnant pulsed beneath its skin.

Heart pounding, Nat edged away from the rim. Her hand brushed a loose rock, and it tumbled down and crashed against the amphitheater floor. A piercing cry echoed through the cavern, and hundreds of disc-shaped eyes turned in her direction. Nat jumped to her feet, spun around, and bolted for a narrow cut in the cavern that led to an empty tomb with steps carved into a wall. She raced up the stairs and vaulted the ledge of her dream space. Sucking in a breath, she yelled, "Lights!" Brilliant beams shot up along the protective barrier.

"Nat!" The sound of Soris' voice broke through the hissing of the Nala that were lashing out at the barrier between the safety of her dream space and the horrors in her dream landscape.

"Soris?" She lifted her head and squinted against the light of the beams. A figure floated above the creatures. She took a quick step toward the ledge, and her eyes met his. "Come in!" she yelled, frantic to have him by her side.

The lights dipped, and Soris leapt over the top of the beams before they shot back into the endless sky. He wrapped his strong arms tightly around her before she could say anything. She felt the pounding of his heart as he clutched her close to his chest. His touch sent a surge of strength through her, and the light barrier brightened with a white heat that sent the remaining Nala scurrying away from her ledge.

Soris pressed her face between his hands. His broad cheeks were flushed, and his eyes were filled with worry. "Are you hurt? Did the Nala catch you?"

She shook her head, momentarily losing her voice as relief in having him in front of her choked away her fear.

"Then where are you?" Nat didn't need to see his expression to know he was holding back his frustration and concern. She could hear it in the tremor of his voice.

"I'm near the edge of the eastern forest by the coast." Her voice wavered. "I think I fell asleep close to the Nala den, but I'm not sure. I—" A razor-sharp pain coursed up Nat's forearm and she gasped. Soris faded in front of her, and a black fog swallowed him whole.

Nat opened her eyes. A shadowy figure bent over her and trailed the tip of a sharp stick against her exposed Sister markings. Nat jerked her arm back and scrambled to her feet. Her sword cut through the branches tangled around her as she lunged toward the figure.

"Put down your weapon," a female voice ordered. A ray of morning sunlight cut through the mist and flooded the forest floor. The figure stepped into the light and lowered her hood. A woman with a shock of short brown hair and brown eyes framed by long lashes held up her hand, gesturing for Nat to lower her sword. Nat caught sight of a marking of a bird between the woman's gloved hand and her tight sleeve. "I'm a Sister." Her voice was calm, and her pale lips were set in a firm line that reminded Nat of Barba.

Nat's shoulders drooped and she lowered the sword. "Am I glad to see you."

"From the looks of you, I'm surprised you're alive to see anyone." The Sister scanned Nat from head to toe and arched her brow. She stepped next to Nat and ushered her away from the bushes with a gentle guiding hand. "Come, fresh air will do you good."

They walked along the thinning tree line. A cold breeze hit Nat's skin, slowly shaking her free from the hold of her nightmare and the shock of seeing another Sister in the eastern forest. She glanced at her, wondering how she'd ended up this far up the coast, too.

"I took the liberty of checking your markings before I woke you," the Sister said before Nat could ask any questions. "Your markings are quite intriguing. I've never seen them on a Warrior Sister, at least not one that was living. What House holds your oath?" The woman tilted her head in Nat's direction.

"I'm from the fringe." Nat pressed her arm protectively against her stomach, suddenly remembering the bounty the Chemist had put out on her.

"The fringe." The woman nodded and led Nat out of the tree line.

"How about you? Your markings are Emissary. Where was your House?" Nat asked, wanting to know more about the Sister before she divulged additional information.

"My House no longer exists," the woman replied evasively. She settled on a flat rock overlooking the waves that rolled against the cliffs.

Nat breathed in the sharp smell of the sea. She looked up the coast. Dark pinnacles cut through the water in the distance. A tingle of fear shot through her when she recognized them. *We're near the Nala den.*

"Sister, I don't know what you're doing here, but this isn't the safest place to stop." Nat gestured to the ring of rocky pinnacles. "The Nala have a den nearby." She scanned the coastline and then the forest behind them, feeling uneasy out in the open.

"I'm well aware of the Nala den." She uncorked a water flask. "Drink. You sound parched." She pushed the flask into Nat's cramped hand. Overcome by thirst, Nat set her sword on the ground so she could grasp the flask with both hands and not send the water pouring down her chin. She took a long drink, quenching her dry throat. The Sister's dark eyes followed her every move.

Nat handed the flask back. The Sister accepted it and capped it without taking a drink herself. Nat glanced again at the pinnacles in the sea and shook her head. "We need to move."

"In a moment," the Sister responded. She dug in her small satchel and pulled out an oily brown wrapper. "I've heard fringe Warrior Sisters were returning from the north, but I never imagined one would wander alone this far into Nala territory." Her eyes held Nat's as she unwrapped a square of cheese.

"I had an encounter with the Nala yesterday." Nat touched her forehead, feeling a sudden wave of dizziness. "The fight led me here."

"Did it now," the Sister remarked with casual ease as if Nat were discussing a minor mishap. She broke a clump of cheese from the square and offered it to Nat. "Eat," she demanded.

"No. The Nala will spot us out here. We should return to the forest and head south." Nat bent to retrieve her sword, but it blurred in front of her eyes and she stumbled to the side.

The Sister reached for the hilt. "I'll carry your sword for you. You look a little pale." She tucked the long blade in her belt. Nat tried to reach for it, but the Sister moved to the side and Nat's hand missed her by inches. Nat blinked quickly as the woman spun around behind her. A pulsing rush filled her head. She turned and felt as if she were moving in slow motion. Her eyes fell on the woman's water flask. *Something was in the water.* "Give me my sword." Her mouth felt fuzzy when she spoke.

"Steady now, Sister," the woman said and slipped her hand inside Nat's cloak. In a blink, she grabbed Nat's orb and slammed it into a small cage she produced from the folds of her garments. The orb beat feebly against the curved bars. Nat heard a small snap and a wire securing the cage's latch fell to the ground, but her orb drifted to the bottom of the cage, unable to free itself.

Nat's head drooped and her vision clouded as she watched the woman examine the broken latch and Nat's now-inert orb. "No matter, she'll be dead soon enough," the woman muttered to herself. She clutched the cage in one hand and dug her other fist into Nat's wound. "Don't pass out on me yet, Sister."

Nat screamed in pain. The Sister pulled her close and dragged her toward a cluster of boulders that hung precariously over the edge of the coastline. Nat pushed feebly against the woman, but she merely tightened her grip and shoved Nat onto a bowl-shaped rock. She loomed over her, her breath hot on Nat's cheek. "You have the markings of the

Sister who was foolish enough to free duozi filth from the Nalaide's den. What are you doing here?"

Nat shook her head, refusing to answer.

The woman slapped her cheek. "Answer me!"

"You're not a Sister." Nat's retort was nothing more than a cracked whisper.

The woman straightened and glared at Nat. "Oh, but I am, fringer, and the last one you'll ever see." She shoved Nat against the rock, then turned her head to scan the trees. Nat heard a snapping sound like breaking branches. The tips of the trees shook, and three Nala emerged from the forest. Nat sucked in a breath. Her chest tightened as a single Nala scurried closer. She waited for it to attack both of them, but it bowed its head slightly toward the Sister, then noticed Nat.

"What is this, Emissary Malorin?" the creature hissed as it pointed at Nat. "We were to discuss the number of children your Lord Mudug must deliver if we are to provide him with more adult duozi. Your courier said you would come alone, not with another."

Malorin? Nat turned the name over in her mind until she remembered Mudug's saying it in the Chemist's garden.

Malorin walked over to Nat and nudged her with her boot. Nat slumped over the rock with a glazed look in her eyes. "The terms of our duozi trade must wait for another time, as I have something more important to discuss." Her expression turned shrewd when she faced the Nala. "The Nalaide agreed to aid Lord Mudug in finding and destroying the rebels' outpost if we delivered something to her, did she not?"

The Nala's eye contracted. "She did."

"Then she must deliver on her promise, because I've found the Sister the Nalaide's seeking."

The creature crawled toward Nat and ran its hand over her cheek. The slick, cold skin felt like steel pressing against her flesh. She struggled to move, but her body barely flinched at its touch. The creature's form grew blurry as it leaned over her and wrapped its arm around her wrist, shoving away the folds of fabric. A drop of venom fell from its mouth onto her Sister markings.

The creature arched its long back and addressed Malorin. "She will be pleased. Very pleased." Malorin bowed her head, handed the Nala Nat's caged orb, and stepped away from her. The Nala bit at the air, and the other Nala drew closer. "Tell your Lord that the Nalaide will satisfy her promise soon. We will discuss the duozi some other time."

Malorin set her cold, unfeeling gaze on Nat as the Nala bound her wrists with a green cord. "How ironic given those markings of yours," she said wistfully.

"Malorin," Nat whispered as the Nala lifted her into the air. But no one, not even Malorin, heard her as her vision faded to darkness.

CHAPTER ELEVEN

A moldy smell crept into Nat's nose. She groaned and a wave of nausea rolled over her.

"Sister wakes."

Nat stiffened at the sound of the hissing voice and opened her eyes. A blurry Nala perched on the edge of a rock near her feet. She flinched and tried to kick the creature, but a wet, fibrous net clung to her body.

The Nala's lips curved into a macabre smile. A stream of venom trickled from the corner of its mouth. "Struggle if you like. It will do you no good. You are bound as Mudug's emissary advised."

Malorin, Nat thought, and the image of the treacherous Sister burned in her mind.

The creature hopped off the stone where Nat lay and crossed the dimly lit cave. Nat's heart raced and she struggled against the bonds, but the net held her firmly in place.

"Where am I?" Her breath caught in her throat when the creature spun on its pointed feet. It opened its black mouth, exposing sharp fangs.

"Have you forgotten so quickly your invasion? Your desecration of this sacred place?" the Nala hissed. Its arm muscles rippled as it removed a silver basin from an alcove chiseled into the wall. It met her eyes with a hate-filled glare. "We have not. We have not forgotten what you took from us."

The creature brought the basin to her lips and poured salty water into her mouth. The water spilled over her neck and face. She thrashed her head back and forth, coughing and sputtering for breath, but the Nala pressed its forearm against her nose. "To purify for our queen," it muttered and poured more water into Nat's mouth. She choked on the foul water, and her lungs burned with want of air. The last drop trickled onto her cheek, and the creature released her. She gasped, pulling lungful after lungful of air into her mouth.

"You would be so easy to kill, Sister." The Nala placed its sharp hand next to her neck, and the muscles in its shallow cheeks twitched. Nat's skin crawled and she spat at the creature. It narrowed its eyes until they were nothing more than silvery slits. "If She were not most anxious to see you . . ." The creature lowered its hand and scuttled toward Nat's feet. "Yes, She is most anxious to see you, Sister," it said and rolled the net off Nat. "She has great plans for one so undeserving of life."

The fabric made a squelching sound when the Nala tugged it off her chest. The creature wrapped its hand around her arm and yanked her onto the floor. Nat looked around, frantically searching for something she could use to attack it, and spotted a faint glow from beneath her balled-up Sister's cloak jammed into a corner of the cave.

My orb.

The Nala dug its sharp hand under her arm, lifted Nat to her feet, and thrust her toward the cave entrance. Nat stumbled forward, keeping the image of her orb in her mind. A faint rattle echoed behind them as they emerged from the cave onto a narrow footpath overlooking the subterranean amphitheater. Nat glanced over the edge of the path and paled. Like in her nightmare, ring after ring of Nala swayed on their blue limbs in the amphitheater. She scanned the darkened crevices of the cavern around the creatures. *No duozi slave children.* She felt somewhat relieved in spite of the presence of so many Nala. *All I have to worry about is myself.*

Nat purposely slowed her steps and called again for her orb, but the Nala thrust its daggerlike hand into her back, forcing her to quicken her pace. She stumbled down the path to the amphitheater. The horde of Nala scuttled to the side to create a narrow way to the center of the cavern, revealing the Nalaide pacing in front of the pool ringed with rocks. The pale creature's arched back resembled the curve of a wave. She lifted her smooth head, and her dark disc-shaped eyes met Nat's.

Fear locked Nat in place. Four Nala wrapped their hands around her wrists and ankles, hoisted her into the air, and carried her closer to the white creature. She twisted and writhed, trying to free herself, but the Nala held tight. The Nalaide, standing high above the other creatures, watched the procession with intense interest. She hissed and the Nala released Nat, sending her crashing onto the stone floor in front of the Nalaide. A stream of gray venom dripped onto the floor by her hand.

"Stand before the queen, as your own do." The hissing command was followed by daggerlike hands jerking Nat upright. "Do you know what I am?" The creature crossed her angular arms over her abdomen. Nat took a breath and lifted her shaking head. The Nalaide was twice the size of any other Nala she'd seen.

"Yes," she said, clenching her jaw to keep her teeth from chattering.

"Sister, you with those vile markings, have taken our vessels, our duozi." The Nalaide jumped onto a rough stone ringing the pool. Her pointed feet made a sharp tapping sound against the stone as she stepped around the ring in a furious burst of movement.

"The duozi were never yours." Nat's voice trembled.

The Nalaide hopped off the ring and set the tip of her hand on Nat's shoulder. "What did you say?" She snaked her hand around Nat's neck, constricting her throat and lifting her into the air. Nat kicked at the empty space beneath her feet, and the cavern grew dim as the muscles in the Nalaide's hand constricted. She suddenly let go, and Nat fell to the ground, wheezing. Through the pain, she scrambled to think of something to hold the Nalaide at bay.

"The Nala agreed never to harm the Sisters." Her voice sounded pathetic and weak, but she pressed on. "You are in violation of the Rim Accord."

"Accord?" The creature brought her face close to Nat's. "Ancient restrictions confining us to the rim where the forest meets the sea are no more, just as the Sisters are no more." A glob of venom fell onto Nat's cheek.

"You're w-wrong." Nat clung to the image of her orb in her mind while facing the Nalaide's fangs. "Sisters survived. Mudug didn't kill all of us. He left enough of us alive to fight you."

"He killed Sisters as I asked," the Nalaide hissed, but Nat sensed doubt as she watched her eyes narrow. "Just as I asked." She circled around Nat, scraping her hand over Nat's back. "But you"—she grasped Nat's arm and pinched her markings—"your existence surprised me. Your kind died out long ago. None like you should be alive."

The curious look on the Nalaide's face disappeared, and a cold rage swirled in her eyes. She ripped Nat's sleeve in one swift movement and dug her hand into the crook of Nat's elbow. A scream burst out of Nat's mouth as the Nalaide cut through her vine and spear markings, splitting Nat's skin with her pointed hand. Pain seared through her and blood poured from her forearm. The Nalaide thrust Nat aside and addressed the throng of Nala.

"She has taken our life links, our duozi," the Nalaide cried. A chorus of hissing reverberated around Nat. She clutched her arm to her chest and shook violently. Shutting out the image of the black and silver eyes leering at her, she imagined a glowing ball of light sailing through the air.

"As punishment, I will make this Sister a duozi. She will be a vessel for my remnant," the Nalaide proclaimed to the horde. The hissing grew louder, echoing through the cavern. "She will carry my remnant and die one day so that I may regenerate!" She opened her fanged mouth and flipped Nat onto her back with a swift flick of her hand, preparing to bite and infuse Nat with her remnant.

Nat's orb, bulging through the broken cage door, skimmed the cliff wall then burst free and swept past the heads of the frenzied Nala. The cage clattered against the ground, and the freed orb cracked against the Nalaide's skull, sending her crashing upon the rock rim surrounding the pool of water. The sphere swung around the Nalaide's head and slammed into her cheek. Her head jerked to the side, and her gaping mouth snapped shut.

Nat pushed herself to her feet and stumbled backward, away from the Nalaide. The orb hit the phalanx of Nala surrounding her with lightning speed. She ran toward the curve in the rock wall of the amphitheater where a path led to the cavern exit. Spikelike hands lashed out, reaching for her arms and legs, but her orb ricocheted off the pursuing Nala's limbs, keeping them from grasping her as she ran. She slid over the smooth stone and skipped sideways onto the footpath.

An arrow flew past her ear.

"Run, Sister!" Cassandra, the mad Warrior Sister, cried from a cleft above the path. Nat thought she was hallucinating, but Cassandra let another arrow fly, and it struck the heart of a Nala lunging toward Nat. "Run, you fool!" she cried again. She jumped from the cleft and hit the path behind Nat. A Nala landed in front of Cassandra. Her red dreadlocks whipped it in the face as she slammed the spiked tip of her bow into its heart and severed its head with a sword clenched in her other hand. She whirled around and pounded after Nat as a mass of Nala filled the path behind them.

They burst onto the rocky ledge above the heaving sea. Cassandra held her sword high in the air and screamed, "Jump!" before pushing Nat off the cliff.

Wind rushed past Nat. She fell free, and her orb plunged with her toward the sea. The foaming white crest of the waves was the last thing she saw before her body crashed into the icy water and sunk beneath the surface.

CHAPTER TWELVE

Water slapped against the side of the weathered rowboat. Nat groaned and rolled onto her back. A tilting motion sent her rolling in the opposite direction.

"She must have a death wish." Nat recognized Cassandra's voice, followed by the sound of wood grinding against metal.

"Not any more than you, Cassandra." Nat tried to place the second voice, but her ears felt like they were filled with cotton balls.

"I don't have a death wish, Rory. I merely live a life of calculated violence." Nat heard a harsh burst of laughter from Rory. "Laugh away, Rory. My ethos is child's play to the Sister's here. Traipsing into the Nalaide's den with a bounty on her head." A low whistle followed her words.

"I didn't traipse anywhere," Nat retorted as she opened her eyes to find Cassandra leaning over her. Water dripped from her red hair onto Nat's face. Her tunic clung to her thin, wiry body.

"Nice to see you alive, Sister Natalie." Rory sat on a cross seat of a small rowboat, pulling oars through the water. Her cheeks were bright pink from exertion and the cold air.

"How'd I get in a boat?" Nat sat up and looked around, confused. A tingling sensation ran up and down her right arm, and she glanced at the blood-soaked bandage wrapped around it.

"Cassandra tossed you off the cliff," Rory answered. Nat massaged her forehead as the memory of hurtling off the cliff outside the Nala den came back to her. Sharp daggers of pain dug into the base of her neck. "Apparently your situation was pressing enough that throwing you into a free fall was preferable to scaling down the cliff to meet me as planned." Rory shot Cassandra a disparaging look.

"Jumping from a cliff was better than a face-off with a hundred Nala," Cassandra replied and wrung her hair out over the side of the boat. "My calculated violence doesn't include suicide missions."

Rory snorted. "Both of you could've broken your necks from that fall."

"Better odds with the fall." Cassandra shrugged and leaned her arm over the side of the boat. The flaming scar running from her temple down her left cheek puckered when she frowned at Nat. "I'm disappointed, Sister. You let the Nala catch you." She tsk-tsked. "I had greater expectations of you."

"I didn't let the Nala catch me," Nat snapped. The ache in her head was incessant, but not painful enough to blot out her anger with Malorin for tricking her. She closed her eyes to stop the boat from spinning in front of her. *I let her take my sword, I let her drug me, I let her lead me to the Nala.* Nat's eyes snapped open. "Cal!" A flood of concern for her sister washed away her anger. "How did *you* find me?" she asked, hoping Cal had encountered the Sisters.

"Through Soris and a slightly deranged young woman," Rory replied.

"You found Cal?" Nat's heart slowed its pace.

"We found a woman named Calpurnia, if that's who you mean. Now tell us how you landed in the Nala's clutches," Cassandra ordered and sucked on the gap in her teeth.

Relieved by the news of her sister, Nat acquiesced. "A Nala pack came after me close to the Meldon Plain. I had Cal with me and diverted the Nala's attention so she could escape." Cassandra grunted in approval. "I let the Nala chase me far into the woods before I took them down. The next thing I knew I was on the edge of the forest near the coast. I fell asleep and an Emissary Sister woke me." She glanced at Rory with a scowl. "Her name is Malorin. Ring any bells?"

Rory pulled up on her oars. "Malorin? Did I hear you right?" Rory asked. Cassandra let out a feral snarl at the mention of Malorin's name.

"Malorin," Nat repeated. "Short brown hair, dark eyes. Best I can tell, she drugged me, dumped me with the Nala, and took off with my sword." Cassandra made a low clucking noise and shook her head. Nat tried to ignore her, but the ease with which Malorin had tricked her left her embarrassed and angry. "You both know her?"

"Yes." Hard lines formed around Rory's mouth. She lifted the oars and resumed rowing. "She was the Emissary Sister assigned to the Representatives' Building in Rustbrook. Mudug was the chair of the representatives. She and Queen Emilia locked horns over certain subjects."

"Let me guess, the duozi?" Nat asked, remembering how Malorin had described the halflings.

"Yes, and she's a snake." Rory gripped the oars tightly. "Emilia ordered an inquiry into Malorin's involvement in the disappearance of several Emissary Sisters who had openly challenged Malorin's opinions about the duozi. Mudug wrested control of Rustbrook and commenced his destruction of the Houses before she was formally charged. We never knew what happened to her."

Nat suddenly remembered the cache of dead orbs she'd discovered in the ruins of the Emissary House months before. Her anger flamed as she wondered if Malorin had killed the makers of those orbs. "She's alive and working for Mudug. I think she's his emissary to the Nala. Before I passed out, I heard her talking to the Nala about a deal Mudug had with the Nalaide." She gritted her teeth, unable to get Malorin's face out of her mind. Her arm throbbed, and she clutched her side of the boat to stay steady. *I let Malorin turn me over to that monster who cut me.*

"Do you know the terms of the agreement between Mudug and the Nalaide?" Rory prodded, oblivious to the horrible pain and realization gripping Nat.

"Yes." The answer came out in a forced whisper. "The Nalaide promised to find and attack Gennes' rebel outpost in exchange for me." She shuddered, recalling the creature's gaping jaw near her chest. "Malorin turned me over, and the Nala . . ." Nat's voice trailed off, her eyes fixed on her bandaged arm.

Rory leaned over Nat, casting a shadow across her. "I didn't see any bite marks on you when I hauled you into the boat, Sister. You're not at risk of becoming a duozi."

"I know. I escaped before the Nalaide bit me, but she sliced my arm," Nat replied, feeling the weight of her words. "She cut me with her hand." She averted her eyes from Rory. "I'm carrying her remnant, even if it is a small amount."

"Did you behead her?" Rory asked, her voice urgent.

"I wasn't in a position to take the Nalaide down, Rory." Nat gave the Sister a deprecating look. *But now I'll have to.*

Cassandra let out another low whistle and Rory swallowed. Nat looked up at the pale winter sky. She'd lived through the nightmare of carrying a Nala's remnant before. She knew all too well that the only way to destroy the remnant and the connection it created between a Nala and a carrier was to sever the neural pathway between the Nala's brain and the gland that produced remnant. Even if only a small amount had been transferred from the Nalaide to Nat through the cut, there would still be a connection between them.

"You were fortunate at least that Calpurnia made it to the Healing House and Soris told us where to find you," Rory said, breaking the silence that had settled over the boat.

"Where is Soris?" Nat asked, wanting to think about something else. She remembered how upset he'd sounded in her dream space. What would he think after he learned about her wound?

"He's in the west with a band of duozi that the rebels freed from Mudug's mines," Rory replied as she pulled the oars. Before she could say more, Nat heard a distant cry and gingerly turned her head. A vessel with square sails cut through the water. Rory shifted her grasp on the oars and turned the rowboat parallel with the oncoming vessel. She dug into the water with the paddles. The rowboat clipped the bow of the vessel. A head popped over the side, and a rope ladder tumbled toward them.

"Up you go, Sister." Cassandra lifted Nat to her feet.

Nat eyed the thick end of the rope ladder, wondering how she was going to scale the vessel with only one hand. "I don't know if I can, Cassandra." Exhausted, she grasped the rope with her good hand to keep from falling into the water.

"You can. You faced the Nalaide, Sister, and lived." Cassandra clasped Nat's shoulder. "You lived, Sister," she repeated. Nat listened to the woman she'd once believed irretrievably beyond the edge of sanity and felt a rush of gratitude.

"I lived because you risked your life to save me. Thank you."

"I'm under oath to protect other Sisters, just as you are. Now climb up the ladder," she demanded.

Cassandra's words spurred Nat. She turned to the rope ladder and pulled herself up the first rung, not wanting to disappoint her. Her wound throbbed and her muscles screamed with pain, but she climbed rung after rung until she reached the top. She muttered a low curse under her breath when she saw Andris standing a few feet from the gunwale. A deckhand grasped her wounded arm in an effort to pull her aboard, but backed away when she yelled a string of unintelligible words.

"Demeanor hasn't improved." Andris gripped her under her arms and lifted her onto the deck. His blond beard, gathered in two spiked points, brushed across her cheek. She stumbled, drained from the climb and aching from her injuries. Andris eyed the tattered bandage wrapped around her arm. Nat caught a look of concern on his face and blinked, certain she'd misread his expression.

"Welcome back, Sister." He steadied her with his hand and eased her down to the sun-bleached boards of the deck. "You're timing is, as usual, impeccable." He turned and cupped his hand to his mouth. "Get Annin down here!" he yelled. Nat squinted against the winter sun and saw a man disappear from an upper deck down a set of stairs.

Cassandra hauled herself over the side and landed with her feet firmly on the wooden planks. Rory was right behind her. She tossed a satchel and weapons onto the deck before climbing over.

"She picked up some intelligence you'll be interested in, Andris." Rory unhooked the satchel and retrieved a circular object. "And this I fished out of the water for you, Sister." Rory pressed Nat's orb into her hand. Her fingers curled around the warm sphere, and she closed her eyes, silently thanking both the orb and the Sisters for saving her life.

CHAPTER THIRTEEN

Stripped and shivering under a light blanket, Nat sat on a narrow berth in a tiny cabin on the ship. Annin stood at the opposite end of the cabin, mixing green and yellow liquids in an empty vial.

"Barba let you pass through the membrane?" she asked while stirring the contents of the vial.

"No." Nat shifted her eyes away from Annin's.

"Safe to assume Barba didn't give the go-ahead for Cal, either?" Annin thrust the glass tube under Nat's nose. "Drink up."

"You've seen Cal?" She downed the liquid, tasting the bitter undertone of the meldon extract.

"Yes. She found the Healing House, and lucky for you she did." Annin pulled up a squat stool next to the berth and peeled the edge of the filthy bandage away from Nat's arm. "After calming Cal down, Ethet figured out what had happened to you. Do you remember our little friend Neas, one of the duozi children you saved from the Nala's den?"

"I'd never forget him," Nat responded, thinking of the little boy she'd first met in Yarsburg and later saved from the Nala.

"You owe him a word of thanks. I'd already left the House with Riler when Cal showed up, apparently hysterical and screaming for someone to help you. Ethet knew Soris could find you, so she had

Neas contact Soris in his dream space. Soris latched on to your dreams fast enough to figure out where you were, then connected back with Neas, who told the Sisters. Cassandra and Rory were leaving the Healing House with the remainder of our party and split off to track you down."

Nat's head spun as she listened to Annin's description of the search.

"You look confused," Annin remarked as she tucked the blanket tighter around Nat and looked intently at her friend.

"I am, explain it—"

"Doesn't matter how we found you, Natalie, just be thankful we did." Annin shifted and placed Nat's arm on her lap. A dull pressure weighed against her arm as Annin probed the broken skin and muttered foul words under her breath. Sweat broke out on Nat's brow. "Why'd you come back, Natalie?" A look of disappointment crossed Annin's face. "I told you I'd return or send a messenger. Now you've got this to contend with." She shook her head and examined Nat's arm.

"I think I found the cure for the duozi, Annin. That's why I came back. I would have been in and out, except Cal . . ." She stared at the floor, knowing her excuses would sound pathetic after what had happened.

"Whatever you found wasn't worth risking both your life and your sister's." Annin pushed her gently onto her back. The movement sent a raking pain down Nat's spine. She struggled to sit up again, chafed by Annin's harsh statement.

"Annin, I need to get to the Healing House. What I found . . . I don't know if Ethet will understand the notes I had in the pack I gave Cal." She glanced at her arm, knowing she needed to return to the Healing House and, for other reasons, the eastern forest.

"Not happening, Natalie. We're already behind schedule because of you, and I don't see Estos turning this boat around."

"Estos is here?" she asked, surprised.

"Estos and Andris, Sisters Rory and Cassandra, and Emilia, plus a few others." Annin returned to the opposite side of the cabin and grabbed a roll of gauze.

"Emilia's well enough to travel?" Nat asked, thinking about her conversation with Cairn before she'd left for Fourline.

Annin shrugged. "We'll find out. She's why we're seabound. We're meeting Soris and the duozi rebels near the Keyen Mountains before the rebels move on to Rustbrook. The sea route is safer for Emilia than inland. With the number of times she's tried to escape from the Healing House, Estos and Sister Ethet decided this was the best way." She dabbed Nat's forearm with the damp cloth. "Andris has pretty much glued himself to her side. Not that he kept her from scaling the Healing House walls," she said with a little contempt in her voice. "That man does not understand women at all."

"Why was she trying to escape?" Nat's teeth chattered.

"She has these episodes. I'm sure you'll see one." Annin frowned as she wiped Nat's arm a final time.

"But both Estos and Emilia together? What if something happens?" Nat knew the time for Estos to claim the regency was drawing near.

"If this ship goes down, the rebellion is sunk." A humorless smile passed Annin's lips. She set aside the bloodied gauze she'd used to clean Nat's arm and covered it with a clean cloth. "Are you ready to see this?" she asked, keeping her eyes steady on Nat.

"No, but show me anyway." Nat steeled herself as Annin lifted the white cloth. Swollen gray skin surrounded a deep gouge running the entire length of her forearm. The puffed-up flesh distorted her vine and spear markings.

"With a cut like this"—Annin gestured to the wound—"the Nalaide didn't have to bite you to infuse you with remnant, Natalie. You know that."

"Yeah, I know." She let out a deep breath.

The hatch door burst open and boots clomped down the stairs. Cold air rolled into the small cabin.

"Where is she?" Cal dipped her head beneath the low ceiling. Her blonde hair was pulled back tightly.

"What are you doing here, Cal?" Nat bolted upright at the sight of her sister.

"Settle down," Annin ordered and shoved her onto the berth.

"I thought she was safe at the Healing House. How could you bring her?" Nat struggled back up only to have Annin glare at her and push her back down again.

"It's not Annin's fault. I made Andris take me when I heard they were looking for you." Cal jumped down the remaining stairs. "What happened to you, Nat?" She cringed when she saw her wound.

Annin caught the pleading look in Nat's eyes. *Cal can't know what happened to me, or what I'll have to do to purge the remnant,* Nat thought. Annin gave her a slight nod and looked at Cal.

"She cut her arm on some rocks." Annin's lie slipped easily off her tongue. "Tuck that around her, except her arm." She motioned to an extra blanket draped loosely over Nat's feet. Cal obediently tucked it under Nat's legs and left arm. Annin brought a cloth close to Nat's face. It smelled cloyingly sweet.

"Hold up. What's that?" Nat protested, lifting her uninjured arm to block Annin.

"I have to remove the skin near the cut and cleanse the wound to prevent infection. Would you prefer to be awake when I do that?" She held the cloth a few inches above Nat. Nat lowered her arm. "About time you listened to somebody," Annin griped and pressed the white cloth to her nose.

CHAPTER FOURTEEN

Nat opened her eyes. A soft light filtered in through the square window set above the berth. Cal, resting her head on her crossed arms, snored next to Nat. Her back lifted slightly with each breath she took. Nat touched a strand of Cal's blonde hair. Her hand trembled slightly. *I almost lost both of us to the Nala.* The harsh realization brought on a wave of nausea. Nat swallowed. *How am I going to get both of us out of the mess I made?*

Cal stirred. "Morning," she said and stretched her arms above her head. Her fingers brushed the cabin ceiling. "How did you sleep?"

"Fine," Nat replied, realizing she hadn't dreamed. She propped herself up on her good arm and winced slightly. A fat bandage encased her right forearm, which throbbed with a heavy, painful pulse.

"Annin said to make you drink this when you woke up." Cal held a cup to Nat's lips, and she drank the bitter meldon extract, grimacing at the taste. She looked over the edge of the cup and caught the intense expression on Cal's face.

She's worried about me.

"How about you, Cal?" Nat asked quickly, before she choked on her own guilt. "How are you handling all this?" She gestured to the air around them.

"I have my own personal freak-out every few minutes. Other than that, I think I'm holding it together pretty well, considering . . ." Her voice trailed off.

"Considering you ended up someplace that shouldn't exist with creatures that shouldn't exist when all you meant to do was bring me one of my notebooks?"

"Yeah, that about sums it up." Cal pressed her hands together and shook her head. "I don't know a fraction of what's going on here. But I've seen and heard enough to know how much you mean to these people and that you've done things they didn't think were possible. Sister Ethet literally freaked when she read the papers in your bag. And that crabby old lady who runs the Healing House, what's her name?"

"Sister Ethes," Nat answered. A smile crossed her lips as she thought about how Ethes, the Head Sister of the Healing House, would respond to Cal's description.

"Yeah, she had the whole place in an uproar, ordering people out into the field to bring in cartloads of dirt and flowers, yelling about a cure for the du . . . do—"

"Duozi," Nat corrected and let out a little laugh, imagining the scene.

"Yeah, the duozi. It was nuts. Sounds like you discovered something big that will help them."

"I hope so, Cal. But I don't know for sure." The cabin suddenly felt claustrophobic, and Nat suppressed an urge to jump from the bed. *What good am I doing lying here?*

The hatch above them flung open and water-stained boots appeared on the stairs. Annin bent over in the stairwell, and her black curls tumbled over her shoulder. She held a bundle of clothes in one arm and gave Nat an irritated look.

"You're still in bed?" She jumped the last two steps. "Move out of the way," she said to Cal, who shifted just enough for Annin to slide in front of her. Annin lifted Nat's chin and looked into her eyes. She examined the wrapping on her forearm, then pressed her fingers to Nat's uninjured wrist. "Stand up," she ordered. Nat pulled the blanket aside and swung her legs off the narrow bed. The wooden planks felt cold underneath her feet, but her legs felt strong and steady.

"Go make yourself useful upstairs," Annin said to Cal, motioning toward the door. "You've been here all night. Get something to eat."

"I'll stay here." Cal put her hands to her hips.

"No, you won't. Does not listening run in your family? Go away. Get some fresh air." Annin pushed Cal toward the stairs.

Cal cast a sour look over her shoulder at Annin. "You okay if I leave?" she asked Nat.

"I'm fine, Cal," Nat said with a small smile, hoping to reassure her sister.

Cal nodded, then glanced at Annin. "I liked you better with the eye patch." She narrowed her eyes, then turned and exited the cabin.

"She's no more likable here than in your world, is she?" Annin asked as soon as the hatch closed behind Cal.

Nat remained mute, knowing she was the last person who should insult her sister after what she'd put her through.

"Any dreams last night?" Annin asked after Nat failed to respond.

"No, nothing." Nat's smile vanished. She shuddered to remember the nightmares she'd had the last time a Nala's remnant was in her. She didn't want to think about what her dreams would be like when the Nalaide attempted to invade her subconscious.

"Good. I'll keep giving you the same draft each night. If the Nalaide can't find you in your dreams, she may think you're dead." She pressed a thin white undergarment into Nat's hands.

"You can't drug me every night of my life, Annin. She'll figure out I survived the fall from the cliff." Nat raised her bandaged arm and grimaced. "You and I both know what this means. As long as she's alive, I'll carry her remnant. I'll have to face the Nalaide sooner or later and behead her." She focused on the garment instead of looking at Annin.

"Later would be better, and stop being so dramatic. We have an idea how to help you."

"Who is 'we'?"

"Me, Estos, and Soris."

"Soris knows what happened?" Nat clutched the clothing to her chest.

Annin rolled her eyes. "You look like a lovesick puppy, Natalie. Yes, he knows what's going on. I dream-spoke with him last night." She gave Nat a long look. "When you see him, expect him to be *mildly* upset that you risked your safety."

"And when will I see him?" Nat swallowed, feeling a flutter of nerves at the thought of seeing Soris again. *I'll be amazed if he's just mildly upset.*

"After we pass through the swamps. He's to meet up with us and take us to a band of duozi rebels." Annin gestured to the clothes. "Get dressed. Estos wants you upstairs so we can have yet another committee meeting." She made a disgusted face and cleaned up the supplies she'd used to bandage Nat's arm the night before.

Nat slid her good arm through the armhole of the undergarment and shimmied the fabric over her body. "What is this made of?"

"The belly hair of a bastle. It hardens on impact. Estos insisted you wear it in case you do something stupid *again*, like returning to Fourline when you should have stayed home." Annin handed Nat a pair of thick woolen socks, followed by her leggings and tunic.

"I told you my reasons." Nat pulled the tunic over her head and tightened her belt. "You of all people should understand." She beckoned her orb. The sphere rose from the corner of the berth and hovered next to her head.

"Reasons mean nothing if you're dead, Natalie." Annin focused on Nat's belt. "Did you lose your sword?"

"No, I didn't." Anger swept through her. "A Sister named Malorin took it, and I intend to get it back." Her fingers trailed over the empty belt loop. *Malorin, when I catch up to you . . .*

"You sound slightly perturbed, Sister," Annin remarked as she climbed the stairs toward the hatch. "But if I were you, I'd direct my energy to solving more pressing problems." She gestured to Nat's wounded arm. "Now finish dressing and meet us above deck."

CHAPTER FIFTEEN

The sea was a shade of grayish blue that reminded Nat of Estos' and Emilia's eyes. She took a deep breath, enjoying the fresh air after the confines of the cabin. Cold wind lifted her hair and twisted it around her face. *Not where I expected to be,* she thought as she observed the white peaks of water beyond the bow of the ship.

"Sister!" Rory beckoned to Nat from the wind-whipped deck. Nat retreated from the bow and followed Rory as she climbed a set of stairs and slipped inside a narrow passageway out of the wind. "This way, Sister." Rory slid open a wooden door. Nat moved to follow her, but Andris blocked her. Nat stepped back, startled by his sudden appearance.

"Bit jumpy, Sister? Maybe you should have stayed home. I know a few people, including my brother, who share that sentiment." Andris gripped the rounded frame, barring the entrance.

"Soris will get over it." She scowled at Andris, angry with him for inserting his opinion where it didn't belong. "Are you going to move or just stand there like a brainless block of wood?"

He ignored her insult and gave her a look of false concern. "You were supposed to stay in your phlegmatic world, remember?"

"And you were supposed to keep Soris at the Healing House." She leaned close until she was just a few inches away from him and jabbed her finger at his chest. "You didn't keep your promise."

"Soris can make his own decisions," Andris replied with little show of emotion.

"Well, surprise, so can I." Nat pressed her shoulder into his arm blocking the doorway. "Don't expect me to believe any of your promises again. Now move out of my way."

"Listen, Sister—"

"Let her in, Andris," Estos said from inside the crowded room. There was a bustle of movement as chairs scraped against the wood floor. Andris barred her entrance a moment longer, then stepped to the side. Nat shot him a cold look and brushed past him.

A draft whistled through the room and rustled papers strewn across a rectangular table occupying the center of the cabin. Estos leaned over the table with his fists planted on its surface. Annin stood against the dark-wood wall next to him.

"Where's Emilia?" Andris glanced around the room.

"What, you lost her again?" Annin teased.

"She's downstairs with Cassandra and Calpurnia," Rory answered. Hearing her sister's name roll off Rory's tongue left Nat feeling disjointed. Rory shifted closer to Annin, allowing space for both Nat and Andris to join them at the table.

"Good to see you, Natalie." Estos smiled at Nat and gestured for her to step closer to where he stood. *At last, a friendly greeting.* His pale eyes widened when he saw her bandage. Unnerved by his worried expression, Nat tucked her wounded arm close to her side. Estos cleared his throat and smoothed his hand over a map. "You're just in time. We're working on a different route to the dam at the base of the Keyen Mountains," he explained.

"I thought an attack on the dam was in the works months ago?" She examined the light trail sketched on the map near the western coast of Fourline.

"We postponed our plans while Emilia convalesced at the Healing House," Estos replied. He stood up straight and leaned against the wall. Next to Annin, he looked like a giant. "Gennes and Soris used the time to hit Mudug's mines in the north." Nat tensed, but Estos didn't notice. "They gained control of mines located here." He touched a mark on the map northwest of the rebel camp in the canyon. "And here." His finger landed on a spot far west of Rustbrook.

"Why did Gennes go after a mine that far west? That's a ways away from any supply route." Nat studied the section of the map showing the western edge of the Keyen Mountains.

"He didn't. Soris did," Andris cut in. "He discovered Mudug was working the duozi slaves to death in the western mine and led the attack himself." A look of challenge flashed over his face. A bitter feeling rose in Nat, and she wondered if Andris had ever intended to keep Soris at the Healing House.

"It *is* far from supply routes, but it's been a boon for us." Estos sounded grateful. "The duozi that Soris freed had a rebel movement in place with an excellent leader. She's been aiding Soris with insurgent attacks on Mudug's posts throughout the mountain range."

Nat stared at the map. *Insurgent attacks?* The weight of Andris' admonition that Soris could make his own decisions, even dangerous ones, settled over her.

"Natalie, are you all right? You look pale." Estos' look of concern reappeared, and he turned to Annin. "Should she even be out of bed?"

"Her physical state's not her problem," Annin said, focusing her keen eyes on Nat. "Is it, Natalie?"

"I'm fine." Nat brushed off Annin's dig. "Tell me the rest."

"Soris and the duozi have Mudug's guards stretched thin, and Gennes has control of the northern supply routes. The final step is to take over the dam in the mountains and then invade Rustbrook." He rolled his shoulders and rubbed his neck. "Emilia and I will reclaim the regency once we've taken the capital. I know our return will strike a blow to Mudug given the lies he's spread about Emilia's murder and my disappearance. We'll use that to our advantage and finish him."

"We anticipate Mudug will hole up in the bluffs surrounding Ballew if we don't catch him. It's a secure spot, but it has disadvantages for him." Rory pointed to a dot on the map. The edge of the eastern forest abutted the city.

"It's close to the Nala." Nat glanced up and caught the wicked look in Rory's eyes.

"It is indeed, Sister. We know Mudug's relationship with the Nala is tenuous. Pressing it to the brink should work in our favor," Rory added.

"You arrived at a complicated but opportune time, Natalie," Estos said and crossed his arms. "You are aware the Chemist put a bounty on your head?"

"Yes," she responded, feeling uncomfortable as all eyes shifted to her.

"From what I understand, the one thing the Nalaide wanted from Mudug, besides duozi children, was you. Rory tells me Sister Malorin turned you over to the Nalaide."

"Do you know Malorin?" Nat asked, feeling roiling anger at the mention of her name.

"Not well," Estos acknowledged. "But Emilia does." A worried look crossed his face, then faded away. "I anticipate the Nalaide will demand Mudug offer you up once more even though you escaped from her. Knowing he delivered you once, the Nalaide may refuse to do anything Mudug asks, including attacking our rebels, until he delivers you again."

"He won't get the chance." Nat fingered her orb.

"No, but with your remnant tie to the Nalaide, we now have a way to manipulate her into believing Mudug has you and is refusing to turn you over." He gestured to her arm. "If we push Mudug south to Ballew, he'll be trapped between us and some very peeved Nala."

The draft in the room prickled Nat's skin. "How do you propose to make the Nalaide believe Mudug has me?"

"I'll implant you with a fake memory of Mudug capturing you," Annin answered. "Then you'll show the memory to the Nalaide when she comes after you in your dream space."

"Are you serious?" Nat backed away from the table. "You want me to willingly let that creature into my dream space so she can see a counterfeit memory? Are you crazy?"

Annin's expression sharpened. "If she wants you as much as we think she does, she'll be after Mudug in a heartbeat if she believes he's holding you."

Nat turned to Estos. "You really think this will help?"

He nodded. "I do. And the lives we'll save if we can get them to battle each other . . ." His voice trailed off, and Nat noticed how burdened he looked. "There are risks to you, though, Natalie."

"I know. I've carried remnant and let a Nala into my dream space before," she replied, remembering the awful experience.

"Allowing the Nalaide into your head will be much worse," Annin said with a frown. "She's more powerful, and she'll want to take up residence in your mind once you let her access your memories."

"And if she doesn't leave?" A wave of apprehension washed over Nat.

"That's the risk. But I have a possible solution," Annin added.

"A *possible* solution?" Nat blanched. "You have a *possible* solution to get her out of my head after I let her in and reveal my inner thoughts to her?"

"My solution should—"

A cry interrupted Annin. The door to the cabin opened and a frantic-looking steward burst through. "She's trying to jump overboard!"

Andris chased after the steward, and Estos hurtled over the table. Wind blasted against Nat when she followed everyone to the deck. Grasping a worn handrail, she watched figures tussling on the lower deck and recognized Cassandra dragging Emilia away from the gunwale.

"You can't stop me from finding him!" cried Emilia. Estos and Andris pinned her flailing arms to keep her thrashing body in place.

"Do you want to die before you get to him?" Cassandra yelled at her. But Emilia took no notice and continued to wail and curse. She stomped on Andris' foot, elbowed Estos, and slipped out of Cassandra's hold. Cassandra gripped Emilia's shoulder as she ran for the side of the ship and slammed her to the deck. Stunned, Emilia rolled onto her back, her black hair covering her cheeks and mouth.

"We've got to lock her up. She's going to kill herself with one of these stunts," Rory said sharply. She leaned down and brushed the hair from Emilia's face.

"No," Estos said as he massaged his side. "That only makes it worse. Andris, Annin, help me, please." He and Andris lifted Emilia to her feet. Her rage seemed to have faded, and she looked around in confusion. Nat could hear Andris' soothing voice as he carried her across the deck, away from the others, with Estos and Annin trailing behind.

"Want to fill me in on what's going on?" Nat asked Rory as she joined Rory, Cal, and Cassandra.

"Emilia's memory is coming back just fine, but she has these occasional fixations," Rory answered. "She's remembering what the Chemist did to her and wants him dead—now."

"So she's jumping off boats trying to get to him?" Nat asked in disbelief.

"I saw her scale the Healing House walls," Cal spoke up and shivered in the wind.

"Boats, wagons, the Healing House walls. When the memory comes back, she loses all compunction and rational thought. She just wants to kill him. Doesn't matter what's in her way." Cassandra grimaced and rubbed a spot on her arm where Emilia had ripped into the sleeve of her tunic.

Rory's cloak billowed behind her in the wind. "You are part of her guard now, too, Sister," she addressed Nat. "Help us keep her under control, because unless someone is there with her ready to hold her down when the memory floods back, she may end up killing herself trying to get to the Chemist."

"Maybe that's what the Chemist wanted all along," Cassandra added, leaving the others with the unpleasant thought as she strode away.

CHAPTER SIXTEEN

Nat scraped the wooden bucket against the floor of the punt and dumped the sludgy swamp water over the side. The water swirled around the boat. Nat sighed as she thought of her growing list of concerns. *The Nalaide, my sister, Soris, and now Emilia . . .*

"A little more bailing and a little less daydreaming, Sister Natalie," Cassandra chided. Nat glanced over her shoulder. Cassandra shot her an impertinent look and lifted a pole hand over hand from the murky water. She set the tip of the pole back in the water, and the punt continued its gentle glide forward.

"I wish I were daydreaming," Nat replied and filled the bucket again.

Angry voices in the distance echoed through the mist, and Emilia twisted around on the bench in front of Nat, listening. Only her pale lips were visible from beneath the hood of her cloak. When they'd embarked from the boat in the early morning hours in the thin-shelled punts, Nat had wondered why Cassandra, and not Estos or even Andris, had accompanied Emilia in their boat. Now as she listened to the men's voices cutting through the mist from the other punt, the match made perfect sense.

"They are arguing about me again." Emilia lowered her hood, and her startling eyes looked out over the swamp.

"Is it a wonder?" Cassandra asked as she lifted the pole again. "A brother arguing with his sister's suitor?"

"I suppose not," Emilia responded.

A suitor? Does she mean Andris? Nat peered through the mist and shook off the thought.

"Sister Natalie, hand Emilia that bucket," Cassandra ordered. "There's more water in this sieve than around it."

Nat passed the water-swollen pail to Emilia, who accepted it with an irritated expression. "Keeping me busy, Cassandra?" she asked as she bailed water onto the roots of the bleached tree towering above them.

"No, just keeping us afloat, Emilia, keeping us afloat."

"But with you and Rory around, I have no need to bail. You'd fish me out of this lovely water if we sank or if I fell in, wouldn't you?"

"How about I toss you in, Emilia, and we'll find out," Cassandra snapped.

"Sister Cassandra," Rory admonished from the front of the boat. "Control your tongue, Emilia's merely baiting you, as usual."

"I'll happily use her as bait," Cassandra growled, and Nat chuckled.

A curve of a smile played over Emilia's full lips, and she winked at Nat. Her gaze traveled to Nat's side. "I notice you're carrying a borrowed sword, Sister. Did you lose yours?"

"No." Nat self-consciously touched the hilt of her new sword and felt the familiar anger against Malorin rekindle. "Someone took it."

"Who took your sword, Sister?" Emilia's pale eyes fixed on her. She held the bucket over the cloudy water. Nat hesitated, uncertain if mentioning the treasonous Warrior Sister's name would set Emilia off.

"A malcontent," Rory responded from the front of the boat before Nat could say anything.

"Do you have plans on how to find your sword and get it back?" Emilia bailed another bucketful of water.

"Not yet," Nat said, thinking of the plans everyone else already had lined out for her. "But I'll figure out a way."

"You should. I remember your sword." She looked out over the desolate swamp. "It was special. If someone took something that special from me, I'd be certain to—"

A birdcall pierced the air, interrupting Emilia. Rory dug her pole into the muck, and the punt shifted direction. It banked gently, then righted itself. Nat glanced at the surface of the swamp. The murky water clouded even more as the boat scraped the shallow bottom.

"I see them ahead." Emilia pointed to the faint form of another boat tilted to the side on a solid patch of land. Andris came into view. He lifted an armful of supplies and dropped them near the base of a white tree whose limbs disappeared into the shroud of mist hanging above him. Cassandra and Rory steered their craft until its tip bumped the edge of the bank.

Estos grasped Emilia's hand before the punt came to a stop. "We have to make the Western Wisdom House before nightfall," he said to his sister. "Are you well enough to make the journey, or should Andris and I fashion a seat and carry you?"

"Don't be ridiculous, Estos," she said. "I can walk on my own. I am *not* an invalid."

"Of course you aren't." He bowed his head slightly and helped her farther up the bank.

Nat watched the interaction with interest, then stepped out of the boat just as Cal jumped out of hers.

Cal rolled her eyes. "Bet your ride was quieter than mine," she muttered under her breath.

"That bad, huh?" Nat responded.

"Worse than riding in a car with you and MC." Cal scrunched up her nose. "Those two bickered nonstop about what's best for Emilia."

She nodded toward Andris and Estos. "I mean, I know she's a bit loopy—"

"Grab a bag and weapons," Andris barked before Cal could finish. "Rory in the lead and Cassandra on rear defense." His eyes settled on Nat and Cal, and he frowned. "Annin, walk with the neophyte and the Sister."

"Neophyte?" Cal scowled at Andris and hefted a bulky bag onto her back.

"Let's move. Stay alert." Andris strode toward Emilia, and he and Estos flanked her. Nat noted how Andris' hand lingered a little too long in Emilia's as he helped her over the exposed roots of a tree.

"It's a wonder those two let her take a breath on her own," Annin observed as she dropped back with Cal and Nat. The three women followed Rory, who was creating a path by slashing thick stalks of reeds with her sword.

"I don't blame them," Cal piped up. "Emilia's fast like a snake. I saw her scale a stone wall. She moved like she had a flame under her—"

"Cal." Nat gave her sister a sharp look.

"Well, she did." Cal shrugged and inspected the hacked-up black reeds scattered on the ground. "This place just gets weirder and weirder." With a few steps of her long legs, she was ahead of Nat and Annin.

"You sure you have the same parents?" Annin asked in a low voice.

"Cut her some slack," Nat said and kicked a cluster of reeds. "I think she's handling this place remarkably well considering."

"Considering she shouldn't be here in the first place. Barba will string you up when she sees you."

"The Nalaide has first dibs, Barba may not get a chance." Nat held up her bandaged arm and Annin shut up. Nat scanned the land shrouded in mist as they walked in silence. They passed a few naked trees in the flat field. She felt as if the world had turned monochromatic.

Even her brown cloak—an extra Sister's cloak borrowed from Rory, since she'd had to leave hers behind in the Nala den—looked dull against the gray landscape.

"Hard to believe there's a Wisdom House out here," Nat remarked as she recalled Annin's telling her they were going to meet up with Soris there. She scanned the half-submerged terrain.

"The House is farther inland, but I don't think the Sisters there cared much about the landscape so long as the rest of Fourline kept its distance. They were the scholars who liked to be left alone." Annin rolled her eyes. Nat raised an eyebrow and gave her a questioning look. "Wisdom Sisters who eschewed distractions lived there. Colorful bunch," she added.

"You've been there?"

"Only once, when I accompanied Sister Barba. I don't know if Mudug even bothered sending his soldiers to destroy it. The place is so bizarre and out of the way. The House may be intact, which will help."

"With what?" Nat narrowed her eyes.

"With what you and Soris need to accomplish tonight. You'll be seeing him quite soon," Annin said and jogged ahead to join Cal, leaving Nat dead in her tracks.

The band traveled at a steady pace, and the swamp disappeared behind them. Long, dry grass replaced the reeds. Nat tripped over the uneven ground. A sharp blade of grass sliced her finger when she fell forward. *This place is wretched,* she thought as she sucked on the cut and rose to her feet. In front of her, Cal jumped from spot to spot near a tall white tree, her balance never faltering. *She makes walking through here look easy.*

She took a tentative step forward and examined the white tree trunks that grew in thick clusters as far as the eye could see. Brown bands encircled the trunks, giving them a striped appearance and providing the only color to the landscape. Nat bent to inspect a colored ring on one of the trees. The band glistened. She was about to touch the ring with the tip of her finger when a hand clamped over hers.

"I wouldn't if I were you." Rory's breath warmed Nat's ear. She released her grip, and Nat let her hand fall to her side.

"Why not, is it poisonous?" she asked as she peered at the band. Small globules popped and oozed over the bark.

"No." Rory shook her head, a mischievous glint sparkling in her eyes. "But if you brush your bare skin against a band, you'll be flat on your face in a few moments, dreaming of your mother—or in your case the Nalaide."

Nat stood up straight and eyed the Sister, wishing she hadn't mentioned the creature.

"The sap from these trees is the main ingredient of a resin you used on Emilia when you rescued her from the Chemist's quarters," Rory added.

"This is what was in Benedict's resin?" Nat asked, remembering swiping Emilia with the sticky substance to knock her out when she'd tried to flee.

"It is indeed," Rory replied and ushered Nat away. "The Healing Sisters used it on the queen a few times to control her outbursts, but Estos demanded they stop when he found out what they were doing."

"Why?" Nat asked. She spotted Emilia and Estos walking together up a gently sloping hill. Andris trailed behind them, scanning the dry grass.

"She'd been under the Chemist's control for years, Sister. Drugging her now to keep her docile is just another form of restraint."

"Even if she's trying to jump off a ship?" Nat wondered at Sister Rory's attitude.

"No, of course not." An annoyed expression crossed her face. "But how will she learn to direct her rage if she's knocked out every time she has a fit?"

"It seems like Estos is walking a fine line between letting her learn how to live unrestrained and risking her killing herself during an irrational moment."

"He's her brother. He knows her mind better than most. I'll defer to his judgment. Certainly you understand. I didn't see you sending your sister back to the Healing House when we disembarked from the ship this morning." Rory gestured in Cal's direction. Cal and Cassandra loped up the hill, racing each other to the top.

Nat let out a sharp laugh. "My sister's presence has nothing to do with how well I know her mind, Rory. Cal didn't give me any choice this morning. She threatened to walk into the eastern forest when I told her she should go back with the ship and the rebel guard to the Healing House. She's like a tick, once she makes up her mind, she won't budge. I knew better than to argue with her, and at least I can keep an eye on her if she's with me."

"Sounds to me like you know her better than you think," Rory said. She gave Nat a shrewd look.

"Maybe," Nat replied as she watched Cal outpace Cassandra. *That's an unlikely friendship,* she thought as she observed her sister egging on Cassandra.

The grass swished under the hem of the women's cloaks as they walked. Rory turned suddenly and scanned the hilltop. "We're missing Annin," she said. She cupped her hands to her mouth. "Annin!" she called out. Annin appeared from behind one of the banded trees. "We haven't got all day. Wisdom House by dark." Rory's voice rang out in warning across the gray field.

Annin waved her arm in their direction. She secured her satchel and jogged past a cluster of trees, but stopped suddenly in the grass and turned.

"Annin!" Rory yelled. "Stop dawdling."

Annin glanced up, and Nat could tell something was wrong. Annin's eyes were wide and she sprinted toward them. Out of the corner of her eye, Nat saw the grass behind Annin undulate as if something were shaking its roots.

"Buler bugs!" Annin called out and leapt over the decaying remains of a fallen tree.

Rory reached for her sword and ran for the edge of the tall grass. Nat followed in her steps, unsheathing her own sword.

"Get out of the grass!" Annin yelled. She dashed from the vegetation to the base of the hill. Two crablike pincers bigger than Nat's hands cut through the dry blades. A sausage-shaped body that looked like an engorged millipede emerged from behind the claws. It glided toward Annin on thousands of tiny legs. A long ribbonlike tail with a sharp tip lashed out at her. Rory dodged around Annin and swung her sword like a pendulum, cutting the creature's claws from its body. A reeking smell like swamp gas filled the air.

"Annin, move out of the way," Rory ordered, her voice tense as she clutched her sword.

"No," Annin said sharply. "I can feel a pack approaching. There are too many for you to kill on your own. They'll overrun you in seconds, and you know what their tails can do. I'll try to control them and push them away."

The grass moved like a wave not far from where they stood. Nat drew her sword and stepped next to Rory. Annin clenched her fists, concentrating. Her grim expression reminded Nat of the time she had used her ability as a duozi to control an enormous tunnel eater spider that had crawled onto Nat's shoulder. Nat had never seen anything as disgusting as a buler bug before, and she tightened her grip on her sword, wondering if Annin could control a pack of the creatures.

Annin fixed her eyes upon the grass as it waved closer and closer. Her Nala eye contracted as sets of claws scythed through the vegetation.

The ribbonlike tails brushed the grass, and the blades shriveled into a fine white powder that floated to the ground. The thudding sound of fast-approaching footsteps made Nat look quickly over her shoulder and away from the onslaught of bugs. Her jaw dropped when she saw Soris rushing past her. He skidded to a halt next to Annin. A buler tail lashed out, missing his shin by an inch.

"How many?" he asked Annin as he focused on another set of claws hacking through the grass.

"Ten, maybe more." Sweat poured from Annin's forehead. "And they are not responding well to my commands," she said through clenched teeth. An oversized insect rushed Annin and grasped the edge of her cloak in one of its pincers. Annin struggled to unhook the garment while Soris focused on the bug. It flitted from side to side as if uncertain which way to move. Annin loosened the clasp, and the cloak fell to the ground just as another bug surged ahead. Nat stepped forward and cut one of the bugs in half.

Soris grabbed her arm and yanked her back. "Natalie, go!" he yelled. "Get to the base of the Wisdom House!"

More bugs undulated from the grass, and Soris whipped his head around to focus on them. Nat could see the strain in both their faces as they fought to control the insects' minds and push them back. *They can't handle this many bugs. We've got to help them.*

"You take the right, I'll take the left," she whispered to Rory. Rory nodded and crept silently behind Annin. Seven bugs now darted in and out of the grass. Nat held her sword low as she approached Soris' side.

"Now!" Rory yelled and swung her sword, splitting two of the creatures in half. Nat thrust her sword under one of the bugs. It clamped onto the tip of the blade as she impaled another lunging toward Soris. Nat flung the bug into the air and sliced off its claws. Her blade whistled as it then cut its body in half. The bisected bug's claws clacked together involuntarily as its halves landed on the ground. Soris and Annin, expressions focused, pushed the remaining bugs away with their minds until the creatures retreated. Nat scanned the scene. Pieces of dead bugs lay strewn over Annin's cloak. A horrid smell filled the air.

"Thank you." Annin sat back on her heels and let out a deep breath. "Brazen little beasts are almost as hard to control as gunnels."

Soris leaned over, slowing his rapid breaths. His blond hair was damp with sweat and flecked with green buler-bug blood. He turned his head and looked at Nat. "You should have gone when I told you to." He straightened, grabbed her hand, and pulled her up the hill away from the grass.

"Soris, let go!" Nat yelled.

"No," he said over his shoulder. "When I yell for you to go, I mean it."

Nat felt a flush of anger rise in her cheeks. She'd imagined a quiet, intimate reunion, not some juvenile fight over obedience. "I just saved you back there! What did you want me to do, just abandon you and Annin?"

"What I want is for you to stop throwing yourself into the middle of trouble and getting hurt." He spun around and pulled her to him. Lifting her chin with his fused fingers, he brushed her hair from her eyes. His touch felt like a craving to her, but she stopped herself from reaching for his hand when she saw the disappointment in his eyes. "Why?" His face creased with pent-up concern. "Why did you come back here and put yourself at so much risk?" His gaze traveled to the bandage around her arm, and he shook his head.

His pained look cut into her heart and she blurted, "I came back because I discovered something that may cure the duozi."

His expression changed to confusion. "You what?"

"I discovered something that may cure the duozi," she repeated, controlling the emotion in her voice. "Returning was worth the risk if Ethet and Ethes can use my findings to create a cure."

"Nothing, not even a possible cure, is worth that." He gestured to her arm. Nat stumbled back, feeling as if a barrier had suddenly come between them. Stung by his comments, she stormed up the next hill.

Soris followed, matching her strides. "Natalie—"

"You may not think it's worth it, but I do," she interrupted him. "After what we saw in the Nala den last spring. You of all people should understand."

"No, I don't understand. You have the Nalaide's remnant in your body!" he yelled.

Annin and Rory sprinted ahead of them both. "Would you two stop arguing?" Annin yelled, grabbing their attention. Her cloak billowed behind her as she ran. "We have more buler bugs on our tail, and the Wisdom House is over the next hill. We need to warn the others, now move!"

CHAPTER SEVENTEEN

A clacking sound echoed behind them.

"Run to the Wisdom House, now!" Rory ordered. Soris grasped Nat's hand again without hesitation, and they took off through the forest.

Voices penetrated the early evening, and Nat spotted the rest of their traveling companions near an enormous tree. Andris knelt at the tree's base, his hand curled around a stake and a mallet. Emilia stood a few paces away, staring into the twisted limbs high above their heads. Nat let out a little breath of relief. Emilia looked confused but calm. *The last thing we need right now is Emilia taking off, especially with buler bugs in the woods.* Nat followed Emilia's line of sight and gaped when she glimpsed the shadows of beehive-shaped structures nestled in the crooks of the high, sturdy branches.

"Buler bugs are headed this way, Andris, why isn't the access door open?" Rory called out.

"Someone's up there and they won't let us in!" he yelled back, his voice seething with anger as he gestured to a tube connected to the tree. Cassandra, face inches from the tube, appeared to be speaking into its mouth. Cal stood apart from the others. Still holding Soris' hand,

Nat ran over to her sister. Annin followed, glancing nervously over her shoulder.

"What's going on?" Nat asked, taking in Cal's worried expression.

"Cassandra and Andris tried to pry open an access door with those stakes, but it's sealed." Cal pointed to the dark outline of a door cut into the tree above the second band of sap. Stubby metal pegs led from the base of the tree to the door, creating a precarious set of stairs. "When they tried to open the door, we heard this weird squawking noise, almost like a siren. Completely freaked me out." She shook her hands in front of her chest. "When they couldn't open the door, Estos tossed a rope ladder to that limb up there. I guess there's a rush to get us off the forest floor." Her forehead creased when she looked into the darkening forest.

"Yeah, there's a rush," Nat answered and was about to tell her sister to get on the rope ladder when Cal asked, "Who are you?" She stared straight at Soris, and Nat realized she was still holding his hand.

"This is Natalie's boyfriend, Soris." A smirk passed over Annin's face, then faded away quickly. "Soris, when you're done introducing yourself, help me with the buler bugs. I sense two more approaching," she said and sprinted back into the woods.

"Boyfriend?" Cal gave Soris an appraising look, then leaned closer to Nat. "I didn't know you had a boyfriend. He's cute but kind of blue," she whispered. Nat cringed.

Soris regarded Cal. "And who are you?" The lines around his Nala eye deepened.

"I'm Nat's sister," Cal said, holding her head high.

"Another Warrior Sister?" Soris glanced at Cal's arm, searching for markings.

"No, I'm her *real* sister."

Nat gave Cal a little smile, surprised at how proud she sounded.

Soris looked at Nat, aghast. "What is she doing here?"

"Long story," Nat replied.

"Not really." Cal shook her head. Her eyes focused on Soris' tapered hand. She parted her lips to speak, but Annin's voice interrupted Cal before she could say anything more.

"Soris, a little assistance down here! Just two bugs, but I'd like a little backup!" Annin yelled.

Nat felt Soris' hand slip from hers. "I'll call out if we need help. Get that door open." He gestured to the access door. She pushed aside the mix of emotions in her and nodded, knowing he and Annin could manage two bugs.

"Sister Natalie, over here," Rory beckoned as Soris ran toward Annin.

"Get over to that rope." Nat gently pushed Cal in the direction of the rope ladder. She heard a faint voice coming from the tube when she joined Rory and Cassandra.

"Only Sisters are entitled to access this House. We do not offer accommodations to gutter-spewing frauds claiming to be Sisters." A woman's voice flowed out of the tube.

The skin around Cassandra's puckered scar twitched. "Come down and say that to my face!" she yelled.

"Control is an attribute of all Sisters. Again, your lack fuels my certainty. You are not a Sister." The voice sounded contemptuous and tinny.

Cassandra's face contorted in rage. "Listen, you mildewed piece of rot. Under your oath, I demand you open this access door now!" She drew her sword, and for a moment Nat was afraid she was going to attack the tree.

Rory stepped closer to the tube. She quieted Cassandra by touching her shoulder.

"Claims I'm not a Sister and not entitled to access the House." Cassandra glared wild-eyed toward the canopy.

"Are they seriously not going to let us up?" Nat looked over her shoulder, then at the high limbs of the tree. "There are buler bugs down here!"

Rory tapped the metal tube. "This is Sister Rory from the Central Warrior House."

"There is no more Central Warrior House," came the reply.

"You are quite correct," Rory said patiently. "But that was my House nonetheless. We had no idea this House was still occupied, or we would have requested hospitality immediately before attempting to enter your access door. As a Sister, I formally request hospitality afforded all Sisters. Please open the hatch so we may enter."

"As you conceded, you have no House. You claim the right of hospitality but offer no explanation as to how you survived Mudug's treachery while so many other Sisters died. Suspicious? I believe so," the voice prattled on, not giving Rory a chance to respond. Even from a foot away, Nat could feel Cassandra tensing with rage. The voice continued, "Suspicion founded on fact precludes me from providing you any benefit you claim."

"Sister," Rory replied with an edge to her voice. "We are not only Sisters down here. We have under our protection individuals who you are under oath to protect."

"And who might that be?" The voice sounded amused.

"The regents of Fourline." Rory placed her hand to her forehead and looked up at the hives. Estos grasped Emilia's hand and took a few steps away from the trunk so whoever was high above could see them.

A high-pitched chuckle floated from the tube. It turned into a full-throated laugh that reverberated in the air around them. "Those two? The regents of Fourline? Such entertainment I haven't had in years," the voice said.

Nat looked back into the woods with a worried expression as she heard a clicking sound drift through the air. She watched Soris and Annin join hands, preparing to hold back the bugs. *We don't have time for this. We need to get off this forest floor.* She approached the tube. "Sister, will you open the door if we send our orbs to you as proof that we are Sisters?"

A moment passed, and then the voice piped out from the opening, "And you are?"

"Natalie."

"Do you claim to be a Sister like the other two, or are you a regent of Fourline?" the bemused voice asked.

"I'm a Sister, and if you let me up, I'll be happy to introduce myself," she said through clenched teeth.

"Who was your Head Sister?"

"Sister Barba Gate."

"Well, well," the voice responded. "The little sprat has her own House. This is an orb I need to see. Send them up, all of them!"

Nat dug her orb out of her cloak pocket. It bobbled above her hand. *Find that voice and get us in. I want to see the face of the person who calls Barba a little sprat,* she thought as she focused on her orb. Cassandra's and Rory's orbs joined hers. They ascended the tree and disappeared over the curved roofline of one of the central hives.

"I'm not waiting for a reply," Andris said tersely. "Climb the rope ladder, Emilia." He helped her up the first rung. "Calpurnia, you're next."

Nat heard Annin cry out in warning as the clicking sound of the buler bugs grew even louder. She stepped closer to Cal. "Get on that ladder," she ordered.

"We're in a bit of a rush down here!" Rory shouted into the tube.

"The three claiming to be Sisters may come up, the others must remain below while we test your orbs."

"What?" Rory lost all patience and slammed her fist against the trunk. "We sent you our orbs in good faith. We have five others with us who will not be left to fend off the buler bugs."

"Is there somewhere isolated you can keep the others while you test us?" Nat asked, trying to find a middle ground.

A hushed conversation floated down the tube. Cal slipped from a rung on the rope ladder. Emilia thrust her hand down and grasped Cal's arm as she clung to the rope with one hand.

"All of you in the lift," the woman's voice rang out of the tube. The access door clicked open.

Andris stared at the door in disbelief. "Calpurnia, Emilia, back down," he ordered. He grasped Cal around the waist when she was a few feet from the last rung and spun her toward the steps. "Could've mentioned that idea a few minutes ago, Natalie," he carped as she helped Cal balance on the first step. Andris and Estos guided Emilia off the twisting ladder and ushered her to the stairs.

"How was I supposed to know what they'd agree to?" Nat shot back, then ran toward Soris and Annin as soon as Cal disappeared into the opening.

A buler bug scuttled around a tree and sent its lashing tail toward Nat's leg. She felt something lift her off the ground just before it struck. Soris pressed her body tightly against his and sidestepped the bug. "Hold on to me," he said without looking at her. He stared at the creature and threw his dagger. The blade sliced into its body and the insect trembled, then flopped to the ground.

"The door's open," she said, suddenly not caring that he'd acted like an annoying oaf before. Soris set her on the ground and retrieved his dagger. Nat heard more clacking. Another bug darted toward Annin.

"Go. I'll be right behind you," Annin called out while keeping her concentration focused on the remaining bug. Nat and Soris turned and sprinted for the door. Rory poked her head out of the opening and grasped Nat's hand as she clambered up the steps with Soris on her heels. He dove through after her and skidded to a halt on the dusty floor.

Nat leaned out. A buler bug raced over the ground and latched on to the edge of Annin's cloak with one claw as she swept up the stairs. Nat lifted her sword and sliced the bug in half as Annin jumped into the room. Rory, poised behind the door, slammed it shut, plunging Nat and everyone else into darkness.

CHAPTER EIGHTEEN

The wood floor beneath their feet jolted upward, sending them all onto their backsides. Nat felt a hand wrap around hers and saw the faint outline of Cal's frightened face. The floor vibrated, then shot up so quickly, wind pushed against her cheeks. They flew through the darkness, hurtling upward until the room stopped suddenly, sending all of them and their supplies hovering a few inches into the air before crashing back down to the floor. A door swung open and a bright arc of light spilled in. Nat blinked and brought her hand to her brow to shield her eyes from the pulsing light and heat.

"A wall of orbs," Emilia said in awe and tried to stand, but Andris' arm was wrapped around her waist. "I'm steady enough now, Andris. You can let go of me." Nat caught a flush of embarrassment color Andris' face as he dropped his arm. Emilia approached the lights, beckoned by their luminescence. The orbs began to shake violently.

"Emilia, don't touch them!" Rory cried out. She bolted in front of the queen, barring her from moving closer. "An orb wall has enough energy to blast all of us through this tree," she warned and looked over her shoulder at Nat. "Can you find yours?"

Nat examined the wall and picked hers out immediately. "Third one two rows up from the bottom," she answered, then holding her sword at her side, she joined Rory in front of Emilia.

"Cassandra?" Rory turned to the other Sister.

"Dead center," Cassandra said with certainty. She pushed her dreadlocks away from her face and nudged Rory, pointing out her orb.

"Can you break through it?" Estos asked. He wiped the back of his hand across his brow. The room was growing uncomfortably warm from the heat of the spheres.

"I'll retrieve mine, maybe that will release the wall." Rory unhooked her cloak. The dark-gray material slid off her shoulders onto the ground. Sweat rolled down her temple. She lifted her arm in the direction of her orb and closed her eyes. A ball bulged from the upper corner of the wall, then retracted into its original position. "My orb won't come to me. It's bound in place," Rory gasped as she stared at her empty palm. "Cassandra, try to retrieve yours."

Cassandra stared at the bright center. Another orb pulsed out and then returned to its original spot.

Nat scanned the wall, thinking quickly. "The Sisters are testing the three of us to see if our connection to our orbs is genuine. Maybe they think we're orb thieves," she said as sweat dropped from her brow into her eyes.

"Orb thieves?" Cassandra cried. "Enough with this!" She pulled her sword free and lunged toward the light.

"No!" Rory and Nat yelled at the same time as they pulled back her writhing body.

"Use your mind, Cassandra!" Nat yelled. "Look at the position of the orbs." She drew an imaginary line connecting the location of their spheres in the now-blindingly bright wall. "The wall should break if the three of us together pull our orbs out at the same time." Sweat dripped down her back, and she felt as if her exposed skin were burning. The three women faced the wall and beckoned their spheres. They protruded from the wall but remained stuck.

"Try again," Rory panted. "And call up the memories you used to imbue your orbs."

The women closed their eyes against the heat. Nat took a quick breath as memories flooded over her.

Cal crawled into her bed, shaking like a leaf. A late summer thunderstorm rattled the window of their childhood room. Nat wrapped her arms around her little sister.

"Make it go away, Nat." Cal's voice trembled. Her blue eyes were wide with fright. An electrifying light flashed through her window.

"Under the blanket." Nat flipped the quilt up, and the two girls ducked their heads under it before the next flash of lightning. "Close your eyes, Cal," she said as they burrowed beneath the quilt. "Imagine it's not lightning, imagine we're at the fair with Dad, and the noise of the thunder is just the sound of the roller coaster." The thunder rattled their window again, followed by a sharp cracking sound. "Do you hear the roller-coaster cars clanking up to the top, Cal?" she said, trying to sound excited as the thunder shook the sky above the house. Cal nodded with her eyes screwed shut. "We're at the top now. Get ready," Nat said. "Here we go!" she cried just as the next lightning strike lit up the room.

Nat's eyes fluttered open. She could smell the river coursing behind her and looked down at Soris cradled in her lap. Blood wept from the Nala bite on his shoulder. "Soris, wake up, please," she pleaded as fear swept through her.

"Natalie." A gentle hand shook her shoulder. She opened her eyes. Soris crouched next to her, supporting her with his arms. "You did it," he said as he helped her stand.

Did what? She looked around, confused. The strange elevator was now empty except for Soris and bits of buler bug. She glanced in front of her. The wall of orbs was gone.

"Where's my orb?" Panic washed over her as she searched the curved wooden walls for the sphere.

"Here." Soris held the glowing ball in his hand. The light sparkled in his Nala eye. The sphere floated into the air and hovered between them. "When your orb broke free, the other orbs spun away down the hall. Rory and Cassandra ran after theirs. I sent everyone else on. Are you steady enough to walk to the hallway? I'd like to get out of this room before it drops on us."

Nat walked across the wobbly floor with Soris' arm still wrapped around her waist. They stepped into a long curved hallway with a rounded ceiling. Cool air rushed over her. Her face stung where the orb wall had burned it.

"Natalie." He reached for her hand. "I said some things I regret earlier on the hill." He averted his eyes a moment, and Nat leaned closer to him, drawn in by the emotion shown in his expression. "I *do* understand why you came back." His eyes met hers and she felt lighter, as if a heavy weight had been lifted from her shoulders. "But do you understand why I was, why I still am, disturbed that you returned?"

"Yes," she admitted. "I understand, because I feel the same way about you." He gave her a puzzled look. She continued, "You're upset because I put myself in danger by returning here, but I'm upset at what *you* risked by leaving the Healing House to attack Mudug's mines. And then there's the part about you and the other duozi hitting his mountain outposts. That one got me a little riled up, too."

"Annin's been busy filling you in, hasn't she?" Soris did not look amused.

"It wasn't just Annin. I found out from your brother and Estos what you've been up to since I left."

They stared at each other in silence.

"I'd like to say we're even, but I believe you topped me." He carefully lifted her bandaged arm.

"Yeah." Nat sighed and stepped closer. "I did." She gazed at him and felt the tension of love mixed with burned-out anger. "You and I don't have the best track record when it comes to reconnecting, do we?"

Soris shook his head and smiled. "No, we don't. I haven't seen you in months and here we are, upset because neither of us did what the other wanted."

"From the moment I left you last spring, all I wanted was to see you again." Nat's eyes misted over, and she struggled to hold back her tears. "The only thing that kept me sane was trying to find a cure."

Soris glanced at the floor. "Maybe that's why I left the Healing House, Natalie. To stay sane, too."

She let out a breath as his words sunk in. *We've both done what we needed to do to carry on.* "Can we try again? Pretend that the last couple of hours never happened?" Still exhausted from the effort of retrieving her orb, she leaned against the curved wall and studied him.

"No," he answered, and she noticed the warm look in his human eye. "I have a better idea." He drew closer, and Nat shuddered at the sensation of the cold wall behind her and his body against hers. Her lips found his and she ran her hands through his hair, wondering why they'd ever argued in the first place.

"You have no idea how much I missed you, Natalie," he whispered and buried his face in her hair. The tension in her muscles evaporated. She tucked her head into the crook of his neck and breathed in his warmth before kissing his salty skin.

"Excuse me."

Nat and Soris broke apart at the sound of a woman's voice. A Sister with short pepper-colored hair and piercing blue eyes stood in front of them. She arched a single brow, assessing them. Nat straightened her shoulders and adjusted her sweat-dampened cloak.

"Welcome to the Wisdom House." The woman bowed her head slightly. "I am Head Sister Judith Wash. If you are done with your amorous acts, please follow me," she said with a tinge of condescension. Judith pivoted, and her wide green cloak embroidered with a single thick vine swirled behind her.

CHAPTER NINETEEN

"Estos personally asked that I fetch you." Judith spoke with an impatient authority as she strode in front of them. She glanced over her shoulder, and looked down her angular nose at Nat and Soris. "Please quicken your pace. Your dawdling is wasting precious time I could use to speak with the regents. Both Emilia's and Estos' presence here are nothing short of miraculous."

Nat stared at the back of Judith's cloak as she and Soris trailed after her down the curved hallway. The Head Sister's unabashed rudeness flamed the ember of anger within her. "You wasted plenty of time mocking us when we requested access to this House."

"We, as a rule, ignore anyone at the base of our House and rarely welcome visitors as we have you." Judith held her head high.

"A burning wall of orbs was a welcome?" Nat caught up with Judith and grasped her elbow. "My skin feels like it's ready to peel off my face."

Judith paused and gave Nat an icy look. Nat released her grasp but openly glowered as the Head Sister examined her skin. Judith gave her a satisfied look.

"The wall worked well. We take all necessary precautions, and the orb wall was the best way for us to ensure you were who you were claiming to be. We *did* respond to your request and allowed you to ascend to the House," she said, as if she had rolled out a red carpet for the travelers. "Most people that attempt to enter our House are left to their own devices. The buler bugs generally take care of them." Judith turned and continued to stride down the hall.

"You've left people on the forest floor to die?" Nat asked, stunned by the woman's callous disregard for the lives of others.

"No. I leave fools who travel this close to the swamps alone," Judith corrected. "Their fate is in their own hands, Sister, not mine. Most people believe this House is deserted. I have no interest in correcting that assumption."

"I'm surprised you let us up at all," Soris broke in.

Judith gave him a sidelong glance and pursed her lips. "If you or the other duozi had been alone, you'd still be on the forest floor," she said in a perfectly reasonable voice.

"Wait a minute. Why wouldn't you let a duozi come in?" Nat's orb spun swiftly above her head.

"Control your orb, Sister." Judith's eyes looked as if they contained ice.

"Answer my question," Nat responded, not trying to hide the threat in her voice. She expected Wisdom Sisters to be free of any prejudice.

"Anyone, including duozi, is a potential threat to the existence of this House. We are vigilant in protecting it and its contents. Can any other House, any other Head Sister, claim the same?" The pale skin around Judith's eyes wrinkled as she waited for a response from Nat.

"That is a grand statement, Sister," Soris spoke up. "What have you really done other than hide? Do you seriously think this House would survive an attack like the ones Mudug unleashed on the other Houses?" Judith bristled at his suggestion. "Mudug probably thinks the Sisters of this House deserted or died out. He has no interest in this part of Fourline, and I know for a fact that the Nala haven't ventured this far west—yet. I doubt you've faced a real threat."

"Do you? Maybe you'll change your mind after your brief visit here." An unpleasant smile crossed Judith's lips. She brought her attention back to Nat. "I've spoken briefly with the other Sisters that arrived with the regents. You must be the one who was mentored by Barba?" Judith cocked her brow.

"Sister Barba," Nat corrected, disliking her disdainful expression. "Yes, she is my Head Sister."

"How unfortunate for you."

"What's that supposed to mean?" Nat scowled and followed Judith with Soris on her heels.

"Barba led a misguided life in this House." She flicked her hand in a dismissive gesture, ending the subject, then opened a heavy wooden door carved with the vine patterns of the Wisdom House. The three of them entered a dark passage. The smell of spices filled the air. Nat squinted against the light at the end of the passage and tripped on a ripple in the floor. When she looked up, her jaw dropped. *I'm in the middle of a beehive.*

Linked hexagons created a domed ceiling above her. A hexagon-shaped table occupied the space beneath the dome. Rory, Cassandra, and Estos stood near the doorway, speaking to three Wisdom Sisters. Nat passed by them, keeping her eyes fixed on the extraordinary ceiling. Not looking where she was going, she bumped into a chair.

"Watch it, Sister," Andris growled. He righted the high-backed chair and turned his attention to Emilia, who wandered around the edge of the room, touching and examining the colorful tapestries that hung from dull metal rods.

Judith cleared her throat and the conversations ceased. "Please, have a seat. A simple meal will be served soon, but there is much to discuss." She paused next to Emilia. "Your Grace." She gestured to the chairs, but Emilia didn't move. Her eyes held a faraway look.

"Excuse me, Sister. She's had a difficult afternoon, as you know." Andris bowed his head respectfully, but his voice had a sharp undertone to it. He ushered Emilia away from the Head Sister and guided her into a wooden seat. She slouched against the back of the chair. Andris immediately took the seat next to her and locked his hand around hers as if holding her in place. Estos caught sight of his sister and walked quickly around the table. He sat in the empty space next to her and placed his hand over hers just as Andris had. Judith took a seat next to Estos and immediately engaged him in conversation. Soris pulled out a chair for Nat next to Cal.

"Thanks," Nat said and slid into the seat while keeping her eyes on Emilia. The queen stared at the highly polished surface of the wooden table. Andris whispered into her ear, and she let out an odd laugh. Andris, eyes animated, chattered away, and Emilia laughed again.

Nat leaned closer to Soris. "What is your brother doing?" she whispered as she observed the strange scene.

"Trying to distract her," he replied.

Before Nat could ask what he meant, Judith stood and tapped her spoon against a glass.

"Welcome to our Wisdom House." She lifted the glass in the air. A half-dozen Wisdom Sisters entered the dining room and settled into the chairs around the table. "We rarely have such esteemed guests." She bowed to Estos and Emilia. "Please accept our hospitality." Judith took a sip of the clear liquid and sat down. Estos, his hand still clasped around Emilia's, leaned toward Judith and resumed their conversation. *For someone who wanted to leave us to the buler bugs less than an hour ago, she sure is laying it on thick,* Nat thought.

Cal took a wheezing breath and set down her glass. "That is not water." She dabbed at her eyes with a napkin. "Seriously, Nat, try this stuff. It is wicked." Her sister gestured to Nat's glass and took another sip from her own.

"Then maybe you shouldn't drink it," Nat replied and frowned. She was in no mood for Cal's antics. The hexagons loomed over her, and she shuddered, imagining the entire structure collapsing. The wound in her arm pulsed, and Cal chatted annoyingly in her ear. Ignoring her sister, she scanned the faces, walls, and tapestries. Aside from the presence of Soris, her friends, and her sister, everything felt foreign. An anxious feeling gripped her when she thought about how far away she was from the Healing House. Nothing had gone as she'd planned. Remembering her disastrous encounter with the Nalaide, Nat shook her head and realized maybe Soris had been right about her coming here not being worth the risk. *I'm carrying the Nalaide's remnant because I was impatient, and I have no idea if the Healing Sisters can even use my discovery to find a cure.*

She glanced at Soris as he engaged in conversation with a Sister sitting next to him. Finding his fingers under the table, she clasped his hand, wanting his touch to steady her whirling emotions.

He broke off his conversation with the Sister. "What's wrong?" he whispered in her ear and squeezed her hand.

"Other than the obvious—"

"I'm Sister Hanni Roven." The woman sitting next to Cal introduced herself to Cal and Nat.

"Calpurnia Barns," Cal responded and took another sip from her half-empty glass.

"Are you an apprentice?" Hanni inquired as she passed a plate laden with a crusty brown bread to Cal. Nat scrambled to think of how to explain what Cal was to the Sister.

"Calpurnia is an apprentice of Head Sister Ethet, aren't you?" Soris interceded, reaching over Nat's arm for the plate of bread.

"Yes, indeed. Apprentice to Sister Ethut," Cal replied, mangling Ethet's name. A rosy flush spread across her cheeks. Nat let out an exasperated breath as Cal took another gulp of the clear liquid. Nat sniffed the contents of the glass in front of her. Her eyes watered. *What is this stuff?*

She leaned close to her sister. "Stop drinking, Cal. You're getting sauced," she warned.

Cal rolled her eyes. "Don't boss me around," she said, swaying in her chair. "After what you've put me through, I deserve a drink or two, or three." She held up three fingers, but a confused look crossed her face and she lowered her hand as if forgetting what she wanted to say.

Nat pushed her chair away, intending to escort Cal away from the others before she made a scene.

"And you?" Hanni leaned across the table and extended her hand to Nat just as she was about to stand. Another Sister placed a wooden plate with a crustacean-looking entrée in front of her.

"Sister Natalie," she answered, reluctantly scooting her chair closer to the table. She reached across Cal and shook Hanni's hand. The tip of a spear marking right at the edge of Nat's wrist peeked out from beneath the bandage.

"From what House?" Hanni inquired. She peered at Nat's wrist in the dim light.

"I'm from the fringe," Nat replied.

"How fascinating. I've never met a Sister from the fringe. Who is your Head?" Hanni asked.

Nat's orb hovered over her. She wondered why Hanni still held on to her hand. "Sister Barba, Barba Gate."

"I must have misheard you." Hanni let go. "Did you say Barba?"

"*Sister* Barba Gate. Do you know her?" She wondered if Hanni could shed some light on Judith's obvious dislike of the Wisdom Sister who had trained her.

"I did know Barba—very well in fact." Hanni glanced in Judith's direction and cleared her throat.

"What's this?" Cal asked, her voice slurring slightly. She pushed at the pink meat puffed over the exoskeleton with her fork. She wore the same expression when she complained about their mother's cooking.

"Buler bug," Sister Hanni answered as she peeled the exoskeleton from the pink flesh. Nat dropped her fork and it clattered loudly against her plate. "We raise them here for food. They are easy to manage if you remove their tails at birth. Excellent protein." Hanni cut a bite, dipped it in a honey-colored sauce, and popped it into her mouth. "I believe this is the bug that came up with you." She chewed. "Yes, much gamier than the ones raised here."

Nat eyed her plate, pushed the piece of buler bug to the side, and nibbled on a radish-looking vegetable. A bitter taste filled her mouth and she reached for her glass. The drink burned her throat and she spit it back. Tears poured from her eyes.

"Bit strong for you?" Hanni asked. Dimples appeared on her ample cheeks.

"Y-yes. What is it?" Nat wheezed.

"Bone-leaf liquor. We brew it ourselves," Hanni said with a tinge of pride. "The alcohol counteracts any poison that remains in the buler bug's body. The second sip will go down smoother than the first," she assured them.

"The whole glass is even better," Cal interjected. Her cheeks were fully flushed and the tip of her nose was pink. Her glass was empty. She stood, brushed across Nat, and tugged on Soris' sleeve. "So are you really her boyfriend?" Her voice rang above the quiet conversations occurring around the table.

"Cal, sit down and be quiet." Nat pried her fingers from his sleeve.

Cal waved her off and focused her glazed eyes on Soris. "Because if you are, there are a few things you should know." Everyone turned in her direction as her voice grew even louder. "She's bossy, she never listens to anyone, she always tries to fix everything like a Ms. Do-Gooder—"

"Knock it off." Nat glared at her sister.

"No!" Cal's voice echoed around the room. Sister Hanni's eyes widened and the entire table grew silent. "You dragged me here! I'll do whatever I want!"

The fragile thread holding Nat's anger in place snapped. "Right! Just like you always do." She pushed Cal back into her chair. "You say I don't listen to anyone? When was the last time you did something I asked you to do without whining, complaining, or challenging me?"

"Are you serious?" Cal stood up again and knocked the chair over.

"Yes, I'm serious! Anytime I ever ask you to do anything at home, you shrug me off like I'm some massive pain. And here, the one place you'd think you'd do what I ask you to do, you ignore me as well. I told you to go back with the ship to the Healing House where you'd be safe, but did you do it? No! Now I've got you to deal with along with everything else."

"You dragged me to this crazy place!" Cal screamed. "And you're blaming me for wanting to stay with you? It's the same here as it is at home. You're always trying to shut me out! Why don't you let me in just a little?" Cal lowered her voice. "Trust me a bit?" She sucked in a huge breath.

Nat paled. Cal's words felt like a physical punch. "I do trust you."

"No, you don't." Cal shook her head. "You trust MC more than me, and she's in elementary school!" Her blue eyes were bloodshot and full of a pained fury. "It's 'cause I'm not good enough, smart enough, for you, am I? That's it, isn't it? Even here." She spun around. "You trust these people more than me, and I'm your sister! Your *real* sister!"

Cassandra, who had crept behind Cal without her noticing, clamped her hand over Cal's mouth, muffling her cries. Cal kicked her legs ineffectually against her. The Sister merely shook her head and lifted Cal's long figure off the ground.

"I believe the young apprentice has had a little too much to drink," Cassandra said as if commenting on a change in the weather. Cal stopped kicking and her skin turned a shade of green. Cassandra let her hand drop from Cal's mouth. "Let's get some air and take a walk, Calpurnia, and I'll tell you a story about the first time I met your sister . . ." Her voice trailed off as she led Cal from the dining room.

Nat moved to follow them, but Soris grasped her hand. "Let her go," he said, holding her in place.

An uncomfortable silence settled over the room. Shame over losing her temper with Cal ran through Nat like a flame burning through paper. She squared her shoulders and addressed the remaining diners. "I apologize for the outburst."

"I'm certain Sister Barba would be quite proud of your decorum, Sister." Judith's voice rang through the room. Nat averted her eyes, unable to meet her cold glare. "Perhaps you, too, should get a little air." She shifted in her chair. "Hanni, escort the Sister and her friends to the resting room in the Library. Estos advised me they have a matter to attend to this evening." She gestured to Annin and Soris, who stood close to Nat. "And I want no further outbursts interrupting my conversation with the regents."

"Certainly, Head Sister." Hanni bustled from her chair and gestured to a passageway.

Nat lowered her head and darted toward the passageway without looking at anyone. Free of the confines of the room, she pressed her forehead against the wooden wall. She dug her fingernails into the wood as Cal's words and accusations replayed in her mind. Her emotions brewed inside her like a spring storm.

"Take a deep breath, Natalie." Soris slipped his hand over her shoulder.

"I can't believe that just happened. I can't believe I said those things, that she . . ." Nat banged her head against the wall.

"Your family relations are not improving," Annin remarked sarcastically as she stepped next to Nat, but she placed a comforting hand on her back. The three of them stood in the hallway together as Nat cleared her mind. She finally turned around and faced her friends.

Soris tightened his hold on her. "Andris and I have had worse rows than that, Natalie. He threw me in a water trough once, and I gave him that little scar under his left eye by whipping him with the end of a willow branch for breaking a bow I'd spent three months making." Nat sniffed, feeling slightly heartened. "Just remember that what you do after the quarrel to make amends is what really matters."

Nat heard a quiet coughing behind her. "This is a bit awkward." Sister Hanni shifted her weight and gave them a pensive look. "Shall I take you to the Library now?"

CHAPTER TWENTY

An earthy smell pervaded the curved hallway as Nat walked next to Hanni. Soris and Annin spoke in low voices behind them. Nat overheard Annin whisper "Nalaide," and she shivered. *I don't know if I can handle the Nalaide in my dream space tonight,* Nat thought, feeling as if her emotions were stretched to their limit after the fight with Cal.

She trailed her fingers over the veined honey-colored walls and felt a sharp sting. "Ouch," she muttered and sucked on her finger where a sliver of wood had pricked her skin. She examined the walls. Notches and grooves marked the curvature. She suddenly remembered Barba's description of this House. *Wood and mud, not some marble monstrosity.* "I had no idea Barba's House was so . . . different."

"Different?" Hanni stiffened at the description.

"I don't mean it as an insult, but you have to admit, compared to the other Wisdom Houses, this one *is* different."

"True," Hanni conceded. "But for a Wisdom House, content is more important than structure. This House contains the single largest collection of ancient scripts." Her eyes gleamed with pride. "Many predate the original Sisters and the First House. Our Library possesses volumes on every conceivable area of study. The texts your Head Sister used as source material exist in no other library in Fourline. And I should know, because I spent two years assisting her by searching the ancient scrolls in the other Houses." She stopped in front of an arched doorway carved with thick vines and lifted her chin. The tight collar of her tunic pinched her neck.

Her interest piqued, Nat asked, "You worked with Barba?"

"Yes," Hanni said in a brusque manner. She adjusted her short cloak around her shoulders and addressed Soris and Annin, who had gathered behind Nat near the door. "It gets brisk this time of evening. Hold on to the ropes and don't stray far behind," she warned and pushed open the door. Wind sent Hanni's cape flapping into Nat's face. "Please, shut the door once through," Hanni instructed. "No light must be seen from below."

Hanni disappeared into the gloom of the night. The three passed under the doorway and Soris closed the door behind them, extinguishing the dim light of the hallway. Nat took a step forward. Her foot slipped on something. Her eyes adjusted to the darkness. A bridge made of thick slats of wood, bound in place by bristly rope, stretched from the end of a tree branch to the shadowy shapes of three enormous domed structures nestled in the neighboring tree. Nat realized she was standing on a rope bridge leading to one of the beehive structures she'd seen from below.

"Don't look down," Soris said and touched her elbow.

"Too late." Nat gaped at the forest floor far beneath them and clutched the rope handrail. Feeling a wave of dizziness, she moved cautiously across the bridge. A strong breeze whipped against her, and the bridge swayed. When she reached a wide veranda-like ledge that projected from the neighboring tree, she hastened away from the bridge and caught her breath.

Annin passed her and approached a door set into the domed structure. "Your orb, Natalie," she requested. "I can't find the handle."

Nat pulled the sphere from her cloak. It pulsated with light and revealed an arched door carved with a vine pattern. Even the blackened metal handle was in the shape of a leaf. Annin wrapped her hand around the handle's edges and tried to turn it, but the door held fast. *Where's Hanni?* Nat wondered, not relishing the idea of crossing over the bridge again. The door swung open. Nat's orb flew behind Sister Hanni, casting light into the darkened room.

"Put your orb out at once!" Hanni demanded. Nat's orb dimmed and spun above their heads. Hanni gripped Annin's cloak and pulled her into the room with surprising strength. Nat and Soris stumbled over the threshold behind her. "We never use lights outside at night," Hanni scolded while shutting the door.

"Why? Are you afraid the buler bugs will see you?" Annin wisecracked as she sidestepped a stack of books.

"More travelers come through this area than you would expect. And Mudug has an outpost a day's travel from here," Hanni replied, giving Annin an irritated look. "We've remained undisturbed for years by making this House appear unoccupied and inaccessible. What will a passersby think if they see a glowing light hovering up in the trees?"

"That giant fireflies are on the prowl?" Soris suggested.

Nat smacked him on the arm to quiet him. Hanni scowled.

"I didn't mean to cause a problem," Nat said, trying to mollify the Sister.

"Next time, use your mind, Sister, not your instinct." Hanni tapped her forehead. "The lure of the sap in the surrounding trees brings a mixed breed of the reckless and criminal this way," she explained as she led them through the narrow room packed floor to ceiling with books. The faint light from Nat's orb cast rectangular shadows across the floor. "The sap is immensely valuable. Once or twice a year, we disguise one of our own and send her with a barrel of sap to a small trading post east of here. Our one barrel brings more in trade and needed provisions than you could possibly imagine. The sap is valuable enough that others are willing to risk venturing into these woods and the lands bordering the swamps. We've only avoided detection through great care. There is too much at risk here."

"Understood, Sister," Nat said, thinking of the ruined Houses.

Hanni seemed pleased by her apologetic tone. "Excuse this area." She gestured to the books. "We are constantly moving and transitioning collections and books to be copied and stored in other locations. I'll lead you to a resting room the Sisters use. But please understand you will need to remain within the Library until I retrieve you in the morning. Head Sister Judith is quite strict about movement after dark."

"That suits our purposes, Sister," Annin said. Nat scrutinized her, wondering exactly what she had planned for the evening.

Hanni approached a set of double doors almost as high as the ceiling of the narrow room. "Then welcome to the Library." She beamed as she pushed open the doors. Nat came to a halt.

"Would you look at that," Soris said as he stepped next to Annin and Nat. Warm, subtle light from an unseen source filled the enormous domed room. Ladders connected seven tiered floors lined with shelves of books. Nat breathed in, smelling the pleasant but musty smell of thousands of written works.

"Come this way to the next sublibrary," Hanni beckoned. Her tunic swayed over her wide hips as she walked in front of them.

"There's another library in here?" Nat asked in a small voice. She looked around in awe.

"Three in total," Hanni clarified and strode across the wood floor. An inlaid vine of dark wood wound down a center aisle that extended to another structure. "You could spend a lifetime within these walls and barely scratch the surface of the works contained here," she said with pride. "Most, like your Head Sister"—her eyes caught Nat's attention—"limit themselves to one area of study."

"What was Barba's?" Nat asked as she gaped at the books, trying to remember.

"I couldn't help but notice the spear tip of your marking." Hanni gestured to Nat's bandaged arm. "Surely given your markings . . ." Her voice trailed off and she gave Nat a curious look. "Barba never discussed her study of First House Predictions with you?"

"No, not in depth." Nat rubbed her bandaged arm and slowed her steps. *Predictions, Barba said during training that she'd studied Predictions.*

"Well, I'm surprised she didn't make the time, given what I can only guess covers the rest of your arm. The spear marking I can see on your wrist is linked to the Prediction foretelling the return of the First House and the annihilation of the Nala by a single Sister. The Predictions were specific in identifying a Sister with your very markings as the one who would end the creatures."

The hair on the back of Nat's neck stood on end.

"Sister Hanni, what do you mean by Prediction? Do you mean a prophecy?" Annin asked.

"No, no, no." Hanni's voice echoed through the Library. "Nothing as nonsensical as that. The first Sisters, especially the Wisdom Sisters, were very adept at observation. They made several predictions based on their observations of animal and plant life, weather patterns, that type of thing. However, their predictions concerning the Nala veered away from the scientific. That's the reason it was never a formal area of study in this House until Barba took it on. Several Sisters, including Judith, considered it a complete waste of time."

"What did the Sisters predict?" Nat asked, not sure she wanted to hear the answer.

"They observed the Nala's progression and behavior as the creatures transitioned from sea to land. They predicted that based on the creatures' manner, they would infiltrate farther and farther into Fourline. When the Emissary Sisters negotiated the Rim Accord, a few Sisters argued against the premise of granting the Nala any territory, based on these Predictions."

"What did the Predictions say about the single Sister ending the Nala?" Annin asked the question Nat was dreading.

Hanni paused at a round door set into the passage between two sections of the Library. "That was the sticky part for Barba, because there is little written about the social structure of the Nala. The Prediction was based on only a few observations of the Nalaide," she said. "It stated that if a single Sister killed the Nalaide, the colony life of the Nala would disintegrate and they would be like a head without a body."

Nat dropped her gaze to her bandaged arm.

"The Nalaide has always been an elusive creature. She hasn't been seen for hundreds of years. She is either dead or was merely the creation of an overly imaginative Sister. And yet the Nala thrive, don't they? So much for the Prediction."

"Oh, the Nalaide's alive all right," Nat said in a low voice.

Hanni gave her a skeptical look. "Well, even if the Nalaide is alive and a single Sister could eliminate her and the Nala, what about the duozi? Pardon me for saying, but there's a bit of the Nala living on in each of you," she said to Annin and Soris. "I recall our Head Sister grilling Barba on that very question before Barba left, but she was never able to provide an adequate answer to that wrinkle in the Prediction. How could she?"

"You can destroy the Nala in the duozi by curing them," Nat said, unable to help herself.

"Blessed me. A cure? What a ridiculous notion." Hanni stopped laughing when she saw the challenge in Nat's eyes.

"Maybe it's not as ridiculous as you think." Nat scanned the rows of books around her, feeling both emboldened and frustrated that Barba had never shared any of this with her. "You said you helped her. Could you find the books she studied?" *Maybe one of them holds more answers.*

"I could, but it would take me weeks to track down her source materials. As I mentioned, we constantly shift and move the materials to ensure they are well cared for. Do you intend to stay here that long?"

"No, we're moving on in the morning," Soris said. It sounded like an order rather than an answer. He set his arm protectively over Nat's shoulders, and she could feel his muscles tense.

"Well, perhaps on another visit I may assist you." Hanni opened the door. "Here we are. The resting room. Quietest place in the House. Feel free to use your orb in here, Sister. The space is sealed. I will come to get you in the morning," she reminded them. Nat, Annin, and Soris stepped through the entrance, and Hanni shut the door behind her.

"Well, well." Annin cocked her head to the side. "Nothing like a Wisdom House Sister to spread a little enlightenment. I always wondered why Barba gave you First House markings."

CHAPTER
TWENTY-ONE

"Do you really think Sister Barba believes Nat can take on the Nalaide and the Nala on her own?" Soris ran his hand through his hair and paced around the room. He looked more upset than Nat had ever seen him.

"Why else would she have given Nat those markings?" Annin answered. "I always thought they were a precautionary measure in case Natalie encountered the Nala. You know, to scare them off. But after hearing what Hanni had to say, I'm not so sure." They both looked intently at Nat as if she had the answer.

"I have no idea what Barba was thinking." Nat raised her hands in a frustrated gesture. "But after I finished my training, she told me the markings were a symbol of her faith in me and my ability to do what needs to be done. She couldn't seriously have thought I'd be able to eliminate the Nalaide and the entire species?" She felt stunned.

"Well, Natalie." Annin hesitated. "You *are* heading down that road. You carry the Nalaide's remnant. You have to kill her to be free."

"I know." Nat stared at the ground.

"But it doesn't have to be Natalie that kills the Nalaide," Soris broke in. "Someone, anyone, could behead the creature and sever the remnant tie." He gave Nat a reassuring look, but the lines in his forehead deepened.

"Let's talk about the Predictions and killing the Nalaide later." Annin dropped her satchel on one of the tables. "Right now, we have work to do." She removed a vial of clear liquid from her bag and set it down before fixing her gaze on Nat. "Tonight, I want to ensure we have safety measures in place before I go to the trouble of disrupting your memories tomorrow evening." A shiver rippled down Nat's spine at the thought. "You also need to understand the consequences of allowing the Nalaide to traipse through your dream space."

"I know what I'm getting into, I've had a Nala in my dream space before." Nat's retort came out sharper than she meant. The frustration over discovering Barba had yet again withheld information from her—along with the thought of eventually having to face off against the Nalaide—set her on edge.

Annin shot Nat an impatient look. "I explained before that your prior experience will be vastly different than what's coming your way, Natalie. This time you must relinquish the control you have of your dream space and let the Nalaide see your thoughts so she believes Mudug has you." Nat opened her mouth to tell her she understood, but Annin hushed her. "Before you tell me you understand *again*, listen to what Soris and I have learned from working with other duozl."

"Fine." Nat acquiesced and pulled out a chair, preparing herself for a lecture.

"You remember the duozi children we freed last year, how there were ones who remained immobile while the others fled?" Annin leaned her hip against the table.

"Of course I do. How could I forget?" Nat replied, thinking of those children's glazed expressions.

"A few of them tried to flee from the House back into the woods, and some became totally withdrawn," Annin said. Nat scrunched up her face in surprise. "I managed to get access to their dream spaces and discovered the cause. The duozi children were infused with remnant from Nala that were still alive, still awake." Annin leaned closer to Nat, her eyes wide. "And the Nala were inhabiting their dream spaces, day and night. The creatures were compelling them to return to the den."

"What?" The idea of the Nala infesting the minds of the duozi children made Nat's stomach churn.

Annin's expression turned grim. "It gets worse, Natalie. Ethet investigated our theory about the Nala using the children to regenerate. We were right. One duozi child we rescued from the den witnessed the process. I won't go into the details of his description, but the end result was a child willingly transferring the remnant back to the Nala to resurrect the creature. The process ends the remnant carrier's—the child's—life." Anger poured from Annin as she spoke. "Remember how Soris responded in the Nala's den?"

"Yes." Nat's shoulders tensed in response to the memory of Soris cleansing the Nala's wounds. She would never forget that. She glanced at him. His arms were crossed tightly over his chest, and he averted his eyes from both of them.

"The remnant creates a compulsion in a duozi to serve the Nala. It's our belief that the Nala's ability to occupy a duozi's dream space and thoughts allows them to direct all a duozi's actions when it's time for a Nala to regenerate."

Nat instinctively touched the bandage on her arm and remembered the Nalaide's hissing words. *She said she wanted to make me her vessel.*

"The Nala's occupation of a dream space occurs in adult duozi as well." Soris dropped his arms and paced in front of her. "Luriel, one of the duozi rebels, and I fought a Nala who inhabited the dream space of one man for years. I can't even begin to describe the horror of what I saw." He swallowed and a visible shudder shook his body. "After Luriel and I ejected the creature from his mind, the man woke up. When he saw Luriel, she had to assure him he was alive. He said he thought he must be dead, because he finally had peace and quiet in his own mind."

Nat tried to imagine the toll of having a Nala in her mind for years.

"You'll meet Luriel tomorrow," Soris continued, distracting her from the unpleasant thought. "After we leave here, we're joining with the band of duozi rebels I left behind before I came here to meet you."

"What Soris said about fighting the Nala is the key, Natalie. Even when a Nala is allowed to take over someone's dream space, the creature can still be ejected. After Estos and I learned you had the Nalaide's remnant, we discussed the idea of using your connection to her to trick her into turning on Mudug. But we never would've followed the thread of the idea if we didn't believe Soris could help you expel her once she'd seen your altered memory."

"It's the only reason I agreed to the plan," Soris added.

Nat shifted in her seat, perturbed by the idea that she was left out of the initial conversations. "Any other uplifting news you have to share with me?"

"The memory manipulation Annin plans will be tough. It has to be in order for you and the Nalaide to believe it." Soris paused, letting the thought settle in.

"I can handle that," she responded, sounding more confident than she felt.

"I should hope so." Annin brushed her dark curls away from her brow and eyed Nat. "The manipulation will be a walk in a sunny field compared to facing the Nalaide. The second you give her so much as a handhold in your mind, she will dig in like a bastle flea," she warned.

"If you're trying to freak me out, it's working."

"Good. You should be afraid. It may keep you from doing something stupid—*again*." Annin gestured to Nat's bandaged arm.

Soris knelt in front of her chair and took her hand. "Are you still willing to do this?"

Nat settled her head against the back of the chair and tightened her hold on his hand. She thought of the duozi children and the nightmares both Mudug and the Nala had subjected them to.

"You won't be alone, Natalie. I'll be there with you, helping you fight her." Soris sounded certain, which quelled a bit of Nat's unease.

"Yes, I'm up for it."

"Then to the details." Annin walked around the other side of the table to one of the beds that lined the wall of the room. She pulled back a wool blanket and motioned for Nat. "Before I even try to manipulate your memory and you allow the Nalaide in, we have to be certain that Soris can access your dreams at will and stay in your dream space. If he can't pass across your barrier without an invitation, there's no point in attempting any of this." A hint of skepticism flickered behind her human eye. "I want to see if the link is really strong enough."

"What link?" Nat asked, looking back and forth between them. She felt as if she'd arrived late to the conversation.

"The link between you and Soris," Annin replied. Nat gave her a confused look. Annin shook her head. "Soris, tell me you told her about the link after you started accessing her dreams?" She set her hands on her hips and shot an irritated glare his way.

"I told her a few things, but never explained the full meaning to her." Soris glanced to the side at Nat. "The time wasn't right."

"She needs to know. Do you want *me* to explain it?" Annin threatened.

"What am I missing here?" Nat asked.

"Annin, give us a little space," Soris requested. Annin didn't budge. "Please," he added through clenched teeth.

"Fine, but don't take all night. We have too much to do to get mired down by your failure to communicate." Annin walked to the door, glanced over her shoulder, shook her head again, and exited into the Library.

Nat's orb hovered in the space between them, pulsing with a soft light. Soris took a deep breath and stood up. He looked into her eyes. "Do you remember how I explained that as a duozi, when you're close to someone, you can easily access that person's dreams and find their dream space?"

"Yes," she answered and sensed that Soris' nervousness matched her own.

"Sometimes, if the bond between two people is strong enough, no invitation is necessary to cross the barrier protecting the other person's dream space." He paced back and forth in front of the tables before continuing. "A duozi with a strong bond to someone who isn't a duozi can guide the person to their own dream space as well. The ability becomes reciprocal."

"Like Estos and Annin." Nat watched him intently, wondering where the conversation was heading.

He nodded. "If the level of trust is great, it's even possible to access a person's thoughts while in their dream space, but not in a coercive way like the Nala."

Nat's orb vibrated above her head as the implication of his words sunk in. She grasped the sphere, pulling it close, and watched Soris' expression carefully as he continued his explanation.

"For what Annin and Estos have planned with the Nalaide to work, I'll need uninvited access to your dream space and your thoughts in case the Nalaide takes control and you can't eject her on your own. The bond we have has enabled me to see your dreams, but for me to have unimpeded access to your dream space and thoughts, you have to have profound trust in me." He tilted his head, and his gaze flickered nervously to her orb before settling again on her eyes.

"And you're not sure if I do?" Nat asked. *Does he really not know?*

A doubtful expression crossed his face. "I know you care for me. Your feelings have made it easy for me to find your dreams even without trying. That's the link Annin was describing. But I don't feel certain your feelings aren't grounded in something more than compassion because I'm a duozi. There is a difference between wanting to protect someone and . . . deeply trusting someone. What I've seen, what I've been through, since you've left has only solidified that in my mind."

The brutal honesty of his words twisted her up inside. Nat swallowed, remembering all the times she'd told him she wanted him safe and was staying in Fourline to make sure of that. *I can't blame him for being confused.* The light of her orb intensified, and she tucked it into the folds of her cloak, knowing she needed to express her emotions herself.

"After what we've been through, you are the only person I would trust that much," she said. Soris still looked doubtful. She took a deep breath. "My feelings for you extend beyond wanting you out of harm's way." She swallowed. A sense of vulnerability overwhelmed her and she looked away from him. *Is this what he meant by trusting someone?* "I admit that after you were bitten, I wanted to protect you to cure you, but finding a cure means I'd get what I want."

"Which is?" He drew nearer.

"To keep both our worlds from getting in the way of building something with you," she replied, feeling completely exposed.

His gaze traveled across her face. She felt her throat tighten and stared at a single curl wrapped around his ear.

"Well," he said suddenly and brushed his hand down her arm. Heat washed over her. "I always knew your judgment was a bit off." He leaned closer, and a mischievous smile appeared when he looked into her eyes. "But given that I feel the same about you, I'll do my best to overlook that fault if you stop trying to get yourself killed. Agreed?" he asked, his breath tickling her skin.

"Agreed," Nat whispered. The space between them dissolved as Soris' lips brushed hers.

When Annin returned, she gave each of them a coy smile. "Both of you are easier to read than any of those books out there. Let's get started.

Nat, take the bed at the far end, and Soris, sit here," she ordered, pulling a chair out from one of the tables.

"We don't need to touch?" Nat asked, thinking of the physical tie the three of them had made before when she'd let a Nala into her dream space.

"I need to test how strong the link between you two is in the event you and Soris are separated. I'll put you in a dream state, and Soris will attempt to find you and your dream space. He'll have to cross over your barrier tonight without you inviting him in." Annin spoke as if giving a lecture. "And I'll warn you, Natalie, the Nalaide will be out there looking for you. This will be the first night she will be able to find you since I've kept you in a dreamless state the past few nights, so be prepared. The wound in your arm may hurt now, but the pain will explode once the Nalaide realizes you're alive. Keep her out of your dream space tonight."

"I know." Nat sighed, not needing a reminder. Soris set his elbows on the table and watched Nat settle uneasily in the bed.

Annin turned her attention to Soris. "Tonight's as much about tempting the Nalaide and letting her know Natalie's alive as it is about ensuring you can cross over without an invitation. Don't try to thwart the creature's attempt to seek her out, but for all you hold dear, do not let the Nalaide access her dream space yet."

"We've been over this," Soris said gruffly.

"No harm in reminding you, is there?" Annin didn't wait for a response. "You ready?" she asked Nat as she held out the vial.

"Yeah," Nat replied. She took a shaky breath. Annin passed her the vial and she downed the contents. Annin's expression grew serious as she leaned over Nat, adjusting the pillow behind her head. "Trust him," she whispered. "You don't stand a chance against the Nalaide unless he can access your dream space and help you fight her."

Nat opened her mouth to respond, but drifted to sleep before the words passed her lips.

Nat dug her feet into the white sand of a craggy cove's beach. Water lapped over her toes. She slowly spun around, sensing someone was watching her. A fog descended, and the rolling mist stopped at the edge of the ocean. Nat stepped into the water to escape the growing sense of claustrophobia caused by the blinding fog.

The warm sea caressed her ankles and pulled her away from the shallow sands and a jagged reef. A smooth white form cut through the water in front of her just as the outgoing waves slammed against her back, submerging her. Nat felt suddenly cold. The warm water flowing through her fingers turned into an icy current pulling at her arms and legs. Kicking frantically, she swam toward the surface. A sharp object brushed her leg, and a flash of white appeared beneath her. Nat broke through, and the waves thrust her against the reef. She pulled herself over the rocks and flopped on the ground, shivering violently.

When she opened her eyes, a dim blue light filled the space around her and she realized she was in the Nala's den. The sound of splashing water brought her scrambling to her feet. The Nalaide emerged from the pool and towered over Nat. Water poured off her head and cascaded down her long limbs. Her emotionless stare dug into Nat. Tremors shuddered through Nat's body as she struggled to breathe, to move. Blackness snuffed the light from Nat's thoughts, and a suffocating feeling swallowed her.

Just as the blue light around her dimmed into nothingness, an arm encircled her waist and jerked her away from the approaching Nalaide. Nat felt herself flung into the air, and she gasped for what felt like her first breath when she hit the hard floor of her dream space. Her eyes flickered open. Soris bent over her, frantic with worry.

"Send up your lights—now!" he yelled.

"Lights up." Nat struggled to find the breath for the words. The lights slowly rose from the barrier between her dream space and her dream landscape. The Nalaide curled her white hand around the beams on the opposite side, and a sizzling steam rose from the creature's flesh as Nat intensified the lights in her mind. The Nalaide let out a hissing shriek and let go. Nat took another shuddering breath and collapsed into Soris' arms. The throbbing sensation in her arm grew in intensity.

"It's okay, Natalie, it's okay." Soris held her shaking body. "She's on the other side and can't get in. It's your dream space. Use it to block her. Use it to block the pain." As he caressed her hair, the pain slowly receded and she stopped trembling.

The Nalaide peered through the bars. A hungry look seeped from every inch of the creature's face. Nat shuddered. She imagined a wall of orbs and hundreds of spheres appeared, completely blocking the Nalaide's view of her dream space. A sibilant sound reverberated from behind them. The orbs hummed, drowning out the hissing.

"Well done," Soris said and lifted Nat to her feet.

"You made it over," she whispered, suddenly realizing she hadn't invited him in. He smiled his wide, familiar smile.

"I did." Soris linked his arm in hers. "I guess you do trust me."

"Annin will be so proud," she said and attempted to smile, but her smile faded when she saw the intense look he gave her.

"Come, let's walk away from the barrier."

A yellow meadow of meldon flowers appeared in front of them, instantly chasing away the darkness. A sense of calm settled over Nat as they moved deeper into the field and away from the orb wall and the edge of her dream space. Soris gestured to a spot in the field and took a seat. Nat settled next to him.

"It's time to let me see a thought, a memory. Something you feel uncomfortable sharing with me." He gave her an odd look. "Show me the memory, then push me out. The process will give you a sense of what you'll need to do with the Nalaide."

"Something I'm uncomfortable sharing . . ." The memory came quickly and she blushed.

"That looks about right." Soris laughed when he saw the flush creep up her cheeks. "I may actually enjoy this. Let me see it, then push me out," he repeated.

"How?" she asked.

"It's your dream space, Nat, you can do whatever you want. You just have to muster the strength." He gestured to the air around them.

"Okay." Nat settled her mind on the memory and glanced at Soris. *Trust him,* she reminded herself. She felt him pushing into her thoughts and created a tunnel leading to the memory.

"Do you know what I dream about each night, Annin?" Lightning *flashed on the hill above the house, and the lights flickered in the kitchen. "I dream about all those duozi children dead in that Nala cavern. And I dream about Soris—but not some flowery-field reunion. I dream he's dead, too, crumpled at the base of a rock bed, in some Nala nest or in Mudug's mines with me standing over him, helpless to do anything."*

She turned. Annin's eye patch hung around her neck. The lights flickered again, then went out. The humming of the refrigerator ceased, and the kitchen was utterly silent as the two women stared at each other.

"I wondered," Annin said quietly.

"Wondered what?" Nat tossed the hand towel onto the counter.

"You do love him."

"Yes," Nat said haltingly, admitting it to herself for the first time. "I do."

Nat yanked the memory away from Soris. She stared at the flowers, unwilling to meet his eyes. "Other than my family, I've never said that about anyone before." She felt the flush return to her face. "Was that good enough?" she asked, finally meeting his eyes.

He touched her cheek. "Yes, Natalie, that was good enough."

CHAPTER
TWENTY-TWO

The next morning, Nat followed Annin as she alighted from the access door to the Wisdom House onto the forest floor. She shielded her eyes against the bleak morning sun and rubbed her right arm. It burned, reminding her that the Nalaide now knew she was very much alive.

"Move on, Sister," Andris said gruffly. He held Emilia tightly against him and gestured for Nat to step out of the opening. Nat caught his apprehensive expression as he turned his attention to helping the queen. She dropped her satchel onto the exposed gnarled roots of the tree and balanced on the stairs before descending. Soris followed.

"What's the plan?" she asked him, feeling a tinge self-conscious after her revelation, but he hadn't run away screaming. She smiled at how he'd reacted to her memory.

"Luriel and the other rebels are waiting about a half day's walk from here," Soris replied, helping Nat adjust her pack over her shoulders. "They'll have transportation for us that we'll use to get to the dam in the mountains."

"Horses?" she asked while eyeing the gray sky. Heavy clouds were rolling in from the west, and she felt a distinct chill in the air.

"No, Natalie, they're duozi, remember? Not particularly keen on horses," he chided as he strapped his crossbow to his pack and gave her a knowing smile. He glanced toward his brother. "I'll see you in a bit."

He jogged over to Andris, who was in deep discussion with Estos and Rory. Soris' expression grew animated as he gestured to a faint path through the trees. *He looks hopeful,* Nat realized. His grim mien, so common the last time she was in Fourline, was gone. She smiled and wondered how much of his demeanor was due to their conversation and experience the night before.

She heard someone groaning next to her and turned around. Cal leaned against a tree and held her head in her hands. Nat watched her, uncertain what to say after the fight in the dining room. Then she remembered Soris' words.

"How's your head?" she asked. Cal dropped her hands, and her bloodshot eyes met Nat's.

"Do you really care?" Cal responded. A tangled mat of hair hung around her pale face.

Nat paused with a retort on the tip of her tongue, but held her comment. She was the one responsible for Cal's presence in Fourline. She'd made a promise to her sister to get her home. Fighting the rest of the way would do neither of them any good.

"Go ask Annin if she has anything to help with your headache. We have a long day ahead of us," Nat suggested.

"You're not going to lecture me?" Cal's focus sharpened and she looked surprised.

"No, I'm not, Cal. I think you're past needing any lecture from me. Especially after what you said to me last night." She sighed and helped Cal lift her pack.

"I didn't mean—"

"Yeah, you did." Nat cut her off. "And I had it coming."

Cal looked slightly stunned. "I guess I did, too," she replied and walked unevenly toward Annin.

"Sister Natalie," Andris barked, disturbing the quiet, cold morning. Nat's gut wrenched at the angry undertone in his voice. She straightened her shoulders and walked briskly to where he stood next to Estos and Soris. *What could Andris possibly be mad about?* she wondered as she watched him tug at his beard, a sure sign he was agitated.

"I will handle this matter." Estos held his hand in front of Andris as Nat approached. Soris stood next to the young king. His grim look had returned.

"Natalie," Estos said. "Soris tells us he had unimpeded entry into your dream space last night." His expression was encouraging.

"Yes, he did," Nat replied, feeling a little embarrassed. Estos had to know what that meant. She gave Andris a quick sidelong glance, wondering if he knew as well. Andris again tugged at his beard and glared at her.

"Good. We have less than two days' journey to the dam. Annin will manipulate your memories tonight." Estos looked at her for some sign of approval.

"Or I could just find one of Mudug's guards and save Annin all the hassle." Nat put on a fake smile. Estos' pale eyes widened in surprise. "I'm kidding, Estos."

"You have a strange sense of humor, Sister." Andris gave her a withering look. "Maybe you'll find the trouble your sister caused last night funny as well." His voice dripped with sarcasm.

"My sister and I had a fight, that was it. I apologized already." Nat shifted uncomfortably.

"It wasn't that, Natalie." Estos set his hand on Andris' arm before he spoke again. "Cassandra was guarding Emilia last night and left her post when your sister stumbled out of her room and threw up in the hallway." He paused. "Emilia had been distraught at the end of dinner. Something set her off, and she snuck out when Cassandra was occupied tending to Calpurnia. She cut one of the rope bridges and was scaling down the tree when Rory found her."

"What?" Nat's head snapped back as if slapped. She twisted around and searched for Emilia. The queen paced near the base of the now-sealed entrance. Rory and Cassandra flanked her.

"Fortunately no harm came to her, but she was very close to falling. I can't have an incident like that happen again. For all the progress we made at the Healing House with restoring her memories, Emilia's fits seem to be getting worse. It takes Andris, myself, and all the other Sisters to calm her at times." The scar running from Estos' ear down his neck stretched when he turned his head toward his sister.

"Your sister nearly got the queen killed because you were ignoring your responsibility to watch over her," Andris burst in. "Calpurnia is your sole responsibility, not some burden for the rest of us to manage."

"Natalie was not ignoring her sister last night," Soris interrupted and stepped between them. "She was preparing herself to endure something horrible to help all of us, brother."

"Stop." Nat put her hands up. *There's already been enough fighting.* "She's my sister, and I'll make sure she understands the situation. You don't need to worry about her. What happened last night won't happen again."

Andris tugged once more at his beard. His gaze moved from Soris to Nat. A glimmer of disapproval flickered behind his eyes. "Make certain it doesn't," he growled. "Estos"—he turned toward the regent—"we need to move out before this storm hits."

"Agreed," Estos said, and Andris immediately began barking orders.

"Cassandra on rear guard, Rory in center with Emilia. Sister Natalie, with Calpurnia. The rest up front with Estos and me. Soris in the lead," he said pointedly before turning and striding away into the woods with Estos. Annin flashed by, running to catch up with them.

"Next time you're in my head, I'll show you a memory of my true feelings toward your brother." Nat squeezed Soris' hand, then let go.

"I don't need to be in your head, Natalie. It's written all over you." He gave her a humorless smile before reluctantly dropping her hand and catching up with his brother.

They walked through the woods in silence. After an hour, snow began to fall and drifted down from the high branches before settling onto the forest floor. Cal walked quietly next to Nat, occasionally letting out a low groan.

"You two mend your fences?" Emilia's voice startled Nat. "I haven't witnessed a fight like that in some time," she remarked as she joined them. Rory walked next to her, her sharp eyes watching Emilia's every movement.

"The fight was my fault," Cal replied and blushed. "I'm sorry I got drunk and lost control." Nat felt a tug at her heart when she saw the remorse on Cal's face. "It won't happen again, I promise."

"From my perspective, both of you lost control, but only one of you was inebriated." Emilia leveled a look at Nat. Now it was Nat's turn to blush.

"You're right," Nat responded, even though she disliked being called on the carpet by Emilia.

"My advice to both of you is find a way to communicate those pent-up emotions of yours before they blow again. A sibling is a precious thing." Emilia's gaze traveled to Estos. "I thought my brother was dead at one point." Her expression clouded over. "To have him back in my life is a blessing. Some are not as fortunate. When my husband was killed, Andris and Soris lost their brother."

"You were married?" Cal asked.

Nat glanced back at Rory, wondering if the line of conversation was safe. Rory gave her a wary look.

"You sound surprised." Emilia fixed her pale eyes on Cal. Rory adjusted her steps so she was directly behind the queen.

"No, no, you're beautiful and a queen," Cal backtracked. "Of course you'd be married. I just didn't know. There's a lot I don't know." Her normally perfect posture slumped.

"Thank you for the compliment, but neither my looks nor title predisposed me to marriage. I never intended to marry, but circumstances required that I marry one man to avoid marrying another." Emilia shivered under her heavy black cloak.

"Did you like the person you married?" Cal asked, and Nat wondered why she was so interested.

"Yes, I did," Emilia acknowledged. "I grew to like him quite a bit. He was so very different than his brothers." Nat followed her line of sight to Andris and Soris, who were walking with Annin and Estos up a winding, worn foothill edging the base of a snowcapped mountain. "Not a bit like Andris, not to say that Andris doesn't have his charms." Emilia's lips formed a crooked smile.

"You like Andris?" Nat couldn't help herself.

"I'm not quite sure why, but I do. Although I often wonder if anything makes him happy." Nat kept her uncharitable smile hidden as she imagined Andris' response if he heard her. "Now Soris, the one you're so enamored with"—Emilia made the comment in such a casual way that it took Nat completely off guard—"he's much more like my husband was. It's a shame he's a duozi. Your relationship will be plagued with difficulty, and you'll be forced to live on the edge of society." She gave Nat a pitying look.

"That makes no difference to me," Nat said, irked by Emilia's expression. "I've been living on the fringe for a long time. I'm from there, remember?" The truth of her own words struck her. *I haven't fit in anywhere since I first stepped foot into Fourline. I really am from the fringe, even when I'm home.*

"My words were not meant as an insult to you or the duozi, Sister. I spent years advocating for duozi rights before—" The queen turned as white as the snow beneath their feet and gripped the side of her cloak. "Before the Chemist—"

"Take rear guard, Sister," Rory cut in. Nat obediently dropped back and watched in dismay as the queen's body shook violently. Rory beckoned to Cassandra, who sprinted to Emilia's side.

"Stay with me, Cal." Nat reached for her sister as Rory and Cassandra sandwiched the queen between them and walked up the gently sloping hill.

Cal shook her head. "She is messed up. One minute you're in a normal conversation, and the next thing you know, she's off in a different world. Estos seems pretty normal. Do you have any idea what happened to her?"

"Yeah, I do. A man called the Chemist happened to her," Nat replied.

CHAPTER
TWENTY-THREE

Andris hailed the travelers to a halt in a low valley at the base of the Keyen Mountains. Nat helped Cal remove her pack, then brushed snowflakes from her eyelashes as she scanned the party for Soris. *Where is he?* A stinging sensation shot through her arm, and she dropped Cal's pack on the snow-covered ground.

"Nat?" Cal wiped snow from her shoulders and studied her sister. "Is something wrong?"

"I'm fine." She covered her grimace with a cough, not wanting to worry Cal. Annin strode by them through the snow, looking grim. *Maybe she has something that can take the edge off the pain.* Nat backed away from Cal to follow Annin, then paused, remembering Andris' order.

"Cal, you okay on your own for a few minutes? I need to speak to Annin."

"I think I can behave myself while you're talking to her, if that's what you're worried about." Cal gave Nat a deadpan look, and Nat felt a pang of guilt.

"I didn't mean . . . You've been . . ." Nat bumbled. "I shouldn't have even asked you. It was a dumb question given how well you've managed." A rush of remorse for all the harsh words she'd said to Cal came over her. "You've been nothing short of amazing, and I owe you."

"Oh yes, you do." Cal chortled and pulled on an extra pair of gloves. "You're doing every last one of my chores for the rest of my life when we get back home."

When we get back home . . . The image of the Nalaide's black eyes flashed in Nat's mind as she faced her sister. *I have to make things right with her in case something happens to me.* "I am sorry about last night, about everything I said to you."

"I'm sorry, too." Cal averted her eyes and took in the snow-covered mountains on the horizon. "I guess the good news is unless we completely stop talking to each other, things between us can't get much worse." She gave Nat a rueful smile and patted her arm. Nat hid her wince.

"You are a ray of positive thought," Nat replied, keeping her voice light. Her eyes watered from the pain coursing through her arm. "I'll be back."

"I'll be here."

Nat jogged through the snow toward a flat rock where Annin was unpacking her apothecary kit. A flash of movement in the trees above Annin caught her eye. Nat quickened her pace and joined her friend.

"Did you see that?" she asked.

"See what?" Annin removed three vials and didn't look up.

"I thought I saw something move on the bluff above the trees."

Annin grumbled, lifted her head, and scanned the granite slabs at the base of the mountain. "Duozi, several if my senses are right, are coming this way."

Nat's gaze lingered on the rock and trees, and for a moment she wished she had her friend's ability to detect the Nala and duozi. The sting in her arm intensified, and she brought her attention back to Annin.

"My arm feels like it's about to explode."

"Not surprising now that the Nalaide knows you're alive. Expect it to get worse." Her voice held little sympathy.

"Do you have anything to numb the pain?" Desperation colored her voice.

"That pain? No, I don't."

Nat groaned. "Nothing?"

"Stop being so whiny. Later, I'll dilute some of the resin I took from the ghost trees back in the swamp to numb your arm without knocking you out, but right now, I don't have time."

Nat started to complain but saw the tense, harried look on Annin's face as she poured liquid from one vial into another. "What's wrong?" she asked, momentarily forgetting her own problems.

"See that woman over there?" Annin thrust her hand in Emilia's direction. The queen slouched under the trees, shivering in her cloak as Andris tried to cajole her into eating some food. "She's about this close to snapping again." Annin held her thumb a hair's breadth away from her index finger. "I have to figure out a way to calm her without sedating her—*again*." Snowflakes floated onto her eyelashes as she gestured to Estos. "See that man over there? He thinks I can perform miracles and expects me to whip up elixirs for his crazy sister at the drop of a hat."

"He's only asking because he knows you can, Annin," Nat said.

"I'd like him to do more than simply ask me to solve his problems." An edge of bitterness crept into her voice.

Nat glanced over Annin's shoulder. Estos set his hand protectively on Emilia's back as he conferred with Cassandra. "He's stressed out, Annin. Put yourself in his shoes: Mudug, the rebels, the regency, his sister, Fourline. All of it is sitting on him. He has a lot to lose."

"I know." Annin gave her an irritated look. "But he's not alone in carrying the weight. This isn't just his fight." She held a vial in the air and tapped the side. "We all have a lot to lose."

Nat removed her orb and it spun next to the vial, giving Annin extra light. She examined Annin's duozi features, silently agreeing with her friend. If the rebellion failed, if her discovery didn't lead to a cure, so many people she cared for and loved would continue to suffer. The depressing thought settled heavily over her.

Annin capped the vial. She wordlessly cleared her medicines and supplies from the rock and walked through the snow toward Emilia, leaving Nat alone. She clutched her arm close to her side when another harsh thought struck her. *Regardless of what happens with the rebellion or the cure, I still have to kill the Nalaide.* She sighed and followed in Annin's tracks, so lost in her thoughts that she failed to notice a half-dozen figures emerge from the rocks and trees above the travelers until she heard Cassandra's cry of warning. Nat unsheathed her sword and sprinted toward the trees.

"Hold up, Sisters!" Rory cried from atop a snow-covered rock. A fur-clad woman stepped next to her and removed her cap, revealing a full head of white-blonde hair. Even in the weak light of the colorless winter sky, Nat could see the blue tint of her face. "Soris' recruits have arrived!" Rory called out as she and the duozi woman climbed down the rocks toward the travelers.

"Let's hope they make good on their promise to get us to the dam," Nat heard Andris say to Estos with a hint of distrust as he helped Emilia to her feet. He brushed snow from her cloak. Heavy lidded, Emilia gazed past Nat toward the end of the valley. Annin took a few steps away from the queen and tucked an empty vial into her bag.

"The duozi have plenty to lose if Mudug stays in power, Andris. They will keep their word, and you have to trust your brother's judgment in bringing them in to aid us," Estos replied.

"I do trust my brother's judgment." Nat felt Andris' eyes settle on her and he scowled. "With some exceptions," he added. He shouldered his bag and turned away from Nat.

Anger replaced her depression and she glared at him. "What might those exceptions be, Andris?"

"Nothing worth noting," Andris shot back.

"Am I interrupting something?" A clear voice broke through the tension. The white-haired duozi woman stepped from the trees with Rory, and they halted in front of Estos. Her eyes were silver discs and her skin was blue like the color of the sky. Nat caught Cal gaping at her and yanked on her sleeve.

"No, you have not." Estos gave Nat a curious look, then focused on the woman. "Thank you for coming. You must be Soris' friend."

"Luriel Evers, my lord," she introduced herself and glanced around at the travelers. Her eyes lingered on each person. Nat frowned, disliking the cold, unfeeling way she looked at her companions. It was as though she were assessing each person's worth. "Soris asked me to gather you. He's traveled on to check that the transport we arranged for you is suitable. We are to accompany you to ensure your safety."

More duozi rebels emerged from the trees behind her. Some had regular eyes while a few had partially transformed faces that looked far more Nala than human. Nat wondered what the Nala bacteria had done to the rest of their bodies wrapped under their heavy winter clothes.

"What form of transport's waiting? Don't tell me my brother has a line of pushcarts up there." Andris gestured to the upper slope of granite.

"Nothing as useless as that, Andris," Luriel said, cocking her head to the side as she said his name. The fur lining her cape moved in the light wind that was now sending snow in every direction. Andris paused and gave Luriel a suspicious look. "Soris said you'd be the hardest to please, but I think you'll be satisfied." Her Nala eyes danced with humor, and one corner of her mouth turned up, making a lopsided smirk.

"We'll see," he snorted.

"Are you ready to leave?" Luriel asked.

"Of course we are," Andris snapped, then turned to his companions. "The cliffs are slick. We'll travel in groups. Estos with Calpurnia, Rory and Cassandra with Emilia, Annin, you'll come with me, Sister Natalie is on rear guard," he barked and ignored her surprised expression. *Why is he pairing Estos with Cal after lecturing me that Cal's my responsibility?* she wondered.

The duozi rebels dispersed and joined the pairs while Annin remained in the trees talking to Luriel. Estos and Cal hiked up the slanted rocks. Cal cast a glance over her shoulder. Nat waved to her, and her sister waved back before ducking under some tree limbs and passing out of sight with Estos.

"What a touching send off," Andris sniffed.

"Why'd you send her with Estos?" Nat asked. Between the pain in her arm and his attitude, she felt as if she were teetering on the brink of losing herself again to her anger. "This morning you lectured me about keeping my thumb on her."

"I need a rear guard, and my choices are limited. Head Sister Judith told me Mudug has a remote outpost east of here. More of a ramshackle post for miscreants and louts from the Head Sister's description, but an outpost nonetheless. After we're all past the crest and out of sight, I want you to wipe this location clean of any sign we were here. Wait a good interval under cover to ensure we weren't followed, then join us. The last thing I need is Mudug's guard crawling up my—"

"I got it." Nat held up her hands.

"So refreshing not having to explain things to you twice." He turned to go, then paused. "I'll have a rebel wait for you on that covered outcropping on the ridge." He motioned toward a distant spot, half hidden among the snow-covered trees. "Pay attention even after you leave the valley. We don't have the luxury of time to deal with any unwanted encounters now."

"Of course I'll pay attention," Nat replied. Her orb pulsed by her head, and she felt the familiar stab of pain in her arm. Andris watched her as if waiting for her to complain. "What are you waiting for?" she asked, swallowing her anger.

"Nothing," he said, his voice colder than the air around them. He beckoned to Annin, then walked away, leaving Luriel and Nat behind.

"You're the peculiar Sister Soris talks about." Nat turned to find Luriel watching her. Up close, Nat could see the shadow of a human eye behind one of her Nala eyes.

"I guess I am a little peculiar," Nat said, trying to warm up to the rebel.

"I'd say. Any Warrior Sister who forgets to behead a Nala when she kills it is at the very least peculiar. Be quick up the slope after you clean up down here. Soris mentioned you were slow as well." Luriel bounded up the granite as if it were nothing more than a gentle slope. Nat gaped after her, stunned. She stood beneath the trees for a moment, collecting her thoughts. *Why would Soris tell her those things?* A prickle of hurt cut into her as she watched the rebel disappear. Grasping the end of a fallen branch sticking out from beneath a drift, she attacked the band's tracks with vigor. Snow flew above her swift strokes. The movement warmed her cold body but didn't take away her bitterness.

After wiping away the tracks, Nat walked briskly toward a cluster of trees, figuring it was a good spot to watch the valley before climbing up the granite slabs. She slapped her hands together and brought her orb closer to her face, hoping to steal a little of its warmth. She rolled her shoulders, trying to relax the tightness in her muscles, and wondered why she felt so peeved by Luriel's comments. Of course Soris would share his past with the duozi from the mines, the duozi he'd been living with for months. A little puff of breath clouded the air in front of her face. "You've got other things to worry about than what Soris told his companions," she muttered to herself, thinking about her inevitable encounter with the Nalaide. She pocketed her orb and watched the lines from the branch strokes disappear under a layer of snow.

"And who do we have here?" The low voice startled Nat. She spun in place, but one of the tree branches clung to her cloak, pinning her temporarily to the tree. Two figures emerged like apparitions from the thick snow behind her. Thick hands thrust her face into the tree trunk, scraping her cheek against the rough bark and pine needles. A hand clamped over her mouth before she could cry out. She bit down on the woolen-gloved finger. The person holding her face let out a string of muffled curses.

"Do that again and you'll lose an eye," the low voice threatened. The steely point of a dagger dug into her cheek. Nat's heart hammered when she saw the gloved hand and a wool cuff an unmistakable shade of blue pressed against her cheekbone. *Mudug's guards.*

The dagger angled away from her face, and a cloth hood was pulled tightly over her head. She brought her foot down on the shin of the man behind her and jabbed her elbow into his abdomen before reaching for her sword. She heard the breath whoosh out of his lungs, and his hands fell away from her. The ground was slick beneath her feet as she stumbled to the side and tried to yank the hood off her head.

"Get her down!" another voice barked.

Nat heard a whirring sound. A hard, flat object smashed into the back of her head, and her chin slammed into her chest. The blow tore off the sack covering her and sent her onto the soft snow. The last thing she saw before her world went black was a single scuffed-up boot racing toward her.

Cold.

A jolt sent Nat's shivering body floating into the air, then crashing against a hard, flat surface. She opened her swollen eyes and tried to focus. Pain shot through her head and she groaned. When she swallowed, she tasted blood. She gingerly ran her tongue over her teeth. Two bottom teeth wiggled, and her mouth filled with more blood. She lay still, trying to gather her wits as her head pounded with pain.

Slats of splintered wood and a deer carcass next to her legs came into focus. She felt another jolt and braced herself before her body hit the wood beneath her. Snow tumbled off her shoulder onto her cheek from the impact. She licked the snow into her swollen mouth before lifting her head even higher.

A small man bundled in furs sat atop a winter-coated horse in front of her. Nat's vision improved, and she realized she was in the bed of a wooden sled. A smooth white blanket of snow spread over a flat expanse of land to her right. She turned her head only to be rewarded with another sharp stab of pain. She swallowed the bile in her mouth and forced herself to look around. The Keyen Mountains were distant streaks of blue and white in the still-cloudy sky. Nat rested her head on her arm, wondering how long she'd been passed out and how far away from the others Mudug's guards had taken her. An intense pain brought her attention to her bound hands. Someone had torn part of her protective bandage away, and the bristly rope fiber binding her wrists and lower arms stung her still-open wound. Nat gagged when she examined the exposed skin. The once-vibrant tendrils of her vine and spear were barely visible against the grotesquely discolored skin.

She took a deep breath and focused again on her surroundings. A series of structures far in front of the rider caught her attention. She squinted, trying to get a better view. "Whoa," the rider said, quietly bringing the horse and sled to a slow stop a ways away from the tall spiked fence surrounding a cluster of low buildings. Snow crunched around the sled. Nat turned her head carefully, searching for the source of the noise. A burly man with a dark beard appeared next to the sled and threw a blanket over her.

"She's awake, but I've covered her," the man said. Nat recognized his voice as that of one of her attackers.

Nat listened through the layers of fabric to the rider's voice. "Good, that blow of yours could've killed her. No good to us if she's dead, is she, Fergus? I'm surprised it only knocked her out half a day." He spoke in a nervous pitch.

Nat remained still, her heart thudding as she pondered his words. She knew now she'd been traveling less than a day. Had any of her companions or the duozi rebels seen her abduction? And what about Cal? Nat forgot her own predicament for a moment when she thought of her sister. *Annin and Soris will keep her safe,* Nat assured herself.

"I didn't hit her that hard," Fergus objected.

That's what you think. Nat's tongue again found her loose teeth.

"Larkem should be back from hunting soon," Fergus continued. "He'll help us take her on to Rustbrook. Let's slip her in through the side gate."

Rustbrook? Nat tensed.

"You're sure she's the one the Chemist is looking for? If we're deserting the post, we better be certain. Commander will have our heads." Nat's heart sank as she remembered the bounty the Chemist had put out on her.

"The commander is likely flat on his face from the ghost-tree sap and won't even notice we're gone," Fergus said. "If we slip a few coins to the cook and the gate guard, they'll keep him in the dark until we arrive in Rustbrook. Nothing he can do to us then. And yes, I am certain she's the one the Chemist wants. Her markings match the description in the Chemist's bounty notice exactly. I still can't believe our luck finding her on our hunt."

She took a deep breath and pressed her inner arms to her sides, searching for any weapons the guards may have missed. *My orb,* she thought and pushed against the fabric of her cloak. She felt nothing but the folds of cold material. Nat closed her eyes, seeking her orb. A sound like striking rocks rattled above her.

"Finally remembered your orb, did you?" Fergus' voice floated above her. "Don't waste your energy, Sister, it's locked up. That old cage is working like a charm."

"You've got the wrong person. I don't know who the Chemist is looking for, but it's not me," Nat said, suddenly not caring about keeping her thoughts to herself.

"Ho-ho, that's a long one, Sister. No other Sister has markings like those, at least not anymore. Nope, you are the one he wants. Did you slice yourself up in hopes that no one would recognize you?" Fergus asked. Nat bit her lip and silently cursed Barba for giving her the symbols. "Move on, Hamil," he ordered after Nat failed to respond to his accusation. The sled lurched forward, gliding over the snow. Nat struggled with her bonds again, but stopped moving when the sled slowed and she heard an exchange of voices.

"I'll lock her up and find Larkem while you get the bigger sleigh and handle the gate guard," Fergus' low voice rumbled. She heard a squeak of assent from Hamil and pulled the blanket clear of her eyes just in time to see the arch of a gate above her. The sled moved forward once more. The sound of clucking chickens and a plaintive mooing muffled the sound of the sled as it slid to a stop. She struggled into a sitting position to get a look at her surroundings. A chicken coop in front of a bleak row of wind-warped barracks lay off to her right. A chicken hopped onto the side of the sled and peered down at her.

Fergus dismounted from his horse and stormed over to the sled. "Scat." He thwacked the chicken off with his arm. "Couldn't stay covered, could you?" he growled at Nat. He picked her up as if she were a feather and shoved her into an enclosed pen next to the chicken coop. "Welcome to your Sister accommodations." Fergus gave her a mock bow, then tossed the cage holding her orb into the enclosed pen and locked the door.

CHAPTER
TWENTY-FOUR

Nat scanned the enclosure for a way to escape. Thick wooden posts buried deep in the ground made up the walls of the pen. A matted layer of straw bulged between slats of wood supporting the low roof. She jumped up and struck one of the slats with her bound hands. Dirty hay showered her.

She cleared the hay from her eyes and noticed her orb glowing inside a cage similar to the one Malorin had used. She flipped the cage with her boot and frowned when she spied the locked door. *Hold on,* Nat thought and struck the heel of her boot against the latch. The cage ricocheted off the walls of the rank enclosure. A cacophony of clucking erupted, and the door to the pen creaked open.

A guard with a ginger beard stood in the doorway. He narrowed his green eyes and snatched the cage from the ground. "Waste of time, Sister. This cage is orb-proof."

"Nothing's orb-proof, Larkem," Nat said, guessing that this was the guard Fergus had mentioned. She eyed the heavy fabric of his riding coat, took a quick step, and kicked him in the groin. He doubled over, dropping the cage. Nat skipped forward, slammed her knee into his chin, and brought her elbows down onto his back. Larkem fell to his knees, groaning. She grasped the cage, bolted for the door, and ran straight into Fergus and Hamil.

"Bind her legs, Fergus," Larkem said, wheezing. Nat brought her knee up sharply again, striking Fergus' chest as he descended on her. He grunted but closed his hands around her upper arms and pushed her roughly to the ground. He and Hamil looped a thick belt around her ankles, binding her legs together.

Larkem straightened. Clutching his hands protectively over his groin, he shot a murderous look at Nat. "I will enjoy delivering you to the Chemist, Sister."

"Commander's passed out, Larkem." Hamil's face twitched, and he backed closer to the door as Nat writhed against the bonds. "We've bribed the gate guard and the cook. Now's as good a time to leave as any."

"Help Fergus throw her into the big sled, and don't forget the orb. The Chemist will want that as well," Larkem spat and walked unevenly out of the enclosure. Fergus and Hamil lifted her into the air. Her head hit the low doorframe as the men carried her wriggling body.

They released her, and she tumbled onto the back of the raised bed of a sleigh. Pain blinded her when she landed against her wounded arm. Gasping for breath, she barely noticed Larkem settle onto a low bench in front of her. Fergus and Hamil mounted the riding seat and whipped two draft horses into motion. Larkem tossed blankets over her and smashed the heel of his boot into her lower back.

"Stay still if you know what's good for you," he threatened. He kicked her in the side, and the sled pitched forward. She clutched her stomach, groaning under the stench of the manure-encrusted blankets.

Hours passed in a freezing blur. She nodded off only to snap awake again when the sleigh bounced over a bridge or struck a rock. Her feet grew numb from the constriction of the belt. She raised her ankles and struck her feet against the sleigh bed a few times to get the blood flowing again. After the third bang, Larkem ripped off the blankets and clamped his hand on her legs.

"What's your plan, Sister?" A frozen globule of snot clung to his mustache. "Think you can kick a hole in the sleigh?" he sneered.

"I can barely feel my feet. Loosen the belt or I'll keep kicking."

The smirk faded from his face. He hit her cheek with a gloved hand, sending her head crashing against the sleigh floor. "You demand nothing, Sister." He pulled her hair back, and his green eyes seethed with a burning hate. "Consider yourself blessed the Chemist wants you in one piece, or I'd have thrown your body to the gunnels that prowl the land near the outpost." He released her hair. She pushed herself up with her good arm, feeling a mixture of fear and rage as Larkem settled back into his seat.

Fergus glanced nervously over his thick shoulder. "Easy, Larkem, she's no good to us damaged," he advised.

"You should listen to him." Nat touched the tender spot on her head. Larkem slowly turned his head her way. The ire in his expression made her cringe. *He's mad about something other than my kicking him in the groin.* "Do you know why the Chemist wants me?" she asked quickly, hoping to quell his rage.

Her query caught him off guard, and he relaxed his fists. "Haven't a clue." He pulled his glove back into place.

"He's going to deliver me to the Nalaide." She grimaced as she struggled to sit upright. *That will throw them off.*

Instead, Larkem's mouth curved up into a smile. "Ha!" His red hair brushed his shoulders as he laughed. "Did you hear that? The Sister thinks the Chemist's offering a fortune for her hide just so he can deliver her to the mythical Nalaide." He set his elbows on his knees and contemplated Nat. "Do you take us for fools, Sister? Not only is the Nalaide a piece of Sisterly fiction, but the Chemist has no cause to aid the Nala." His pale brow crinkled. "The Nala are our enemies. You Sisters let them wrest control of the eastern forest, and they've run rampant ever since."

He gave her a suspicious look, and she remembered the lies Mudug had spread to justify his destruction of the Houses. "I lost my brother to the Nala years ago," he continued. She couldn't tell if the pink shade of his skin was from the cold or his rage. "Your House failed to protect the route he was traveling. If the Sisters had done their duty and lived by their oaths, he'd still be alive."

That's why he's so mad at me. She sat quietly in the bitter cold, wondering how to use Larkem's emotions to her advantage. A thought occurred to her. *Annin was going to implant a memory of me being held captive by Mudug, and here I am, with a trio of his guards.* She looked straight at Larkem.

"Mudug killed or exiled the Sisters," she said in a steely voice. "Whatever happened to your brother is at Mudug's feet, not the Sisters'." He twisted his lips into a frown. Nat continued, "And the Nalaide is very real. Real enough to threaten Mudug and the Chemist into agreeing to turn me over."

"You're not even a good liar, Sister," Larkem said, shaking his head. "If the bounty he put on you months ago is any indication, he's not sending you anywhere, let alone turning you over to those vile creatures."

"Really? Then why did one of the Chemist's collaborators hand me over to them last week?" She kept her voice low and watched Larkem's expression. She noticed a slight twitch in his left eye.

"What was that you said?" Fergus asked as he turned from his position on the driver's bench to listen. Hamil kept his slight figure facing forward.

"The Chemist's collaborator turned me over to the Nala as a reward from Mudug and the Chemist."

"A reward?" Larkem stared at her in disbelief. "For what, terrorizing the southern coast?"

"For the Nala's assistance in creating more adult duozi to work Mudug's mines." Nat paused and prepared her verbal bomb. "Are you certain your brother's dead? It's possible that he's toiling away underground as a duozi slave for Mudug." Larkem stiffened. She sat a little straighter and took a breath before launching her final attack. "You do know Mudug's been sending children to the Nala for years in exchange for adult duozi, don't you?" She punctuated every word. A stormy look crossed Larkem's face, and Nat braced herself for another blow.

Fergus burst out in a deep laugh. "That's a tale, Sister." His smile disappeared. "But it has more holes than a sieve. If what you say is true, you wouldn't be here having this pleasant conversation with us."

"Why not?" Nat asked, wanting to push the men further to get the memory she needed to trick the Nalaide.

"Because you'd be dead." Fergus' dark eyes held little warmth. "The Nala would have killed you."

"I'm not lying, Fergus." She met his forceful stare with her own. "If the Chemist or Mudug want me, it's to turn me over to appease the Nala."

"Enough of your lies!" Larkem's blow to the side of her head was swift and painful. A buzzing sound nearly drowned out the rest of his words as he spit in her face. "Neither Mudug nor the Chemist cares what the Nala want. You'll die in the Rustbrook dungeons or on the gallows wishing for a quick death, not in some infested Nala hole!" He kicked her in the stomach. She gasped and brought her knees protectively to her chest. Another blow rained down on her back. She cried out in pain, but clung to Larkem's words. *Neither Mudug nor the Chemist cares what the Nala want. You'll die in the Rustbrook dungeons or on the gallows wishing for a quick death, not in some infested Nala hole.* Blow after blow struck her head and back until a yell erupted and the sleigh slid to a stop.

"Stop it!" Fergus bellowed and lumbered from the bench toward Larkem. Nat opened her eyes, and the blurry image of Fergus clasping his sausagelike fingers around Larkem's wrists wavered in and out in front of her. "You kill her, harm her, we have nothing, understand?

Nothing!" Larkem's chest heaved and he glared at Fergus. "We've been stuck in that hell of an outpost for years." Fergus yanked Larkem closer to him. "She is our ticket out. She's our ticket to what we want!"

"She's a liar!" Larkem growled as he struggled against him. Hamil crept nervously from the bench and stood by Fergus' side.

"I don't care if she calls my mam a horse's butt, she's worth a fortune. We've a mile to the Elem River. How are we to convince a boatman to transport a dead body to Rustbrook? How are you going to explain to the Chemist what you did to his prize? If we're lucky, we'll get nothing if we show up with her damaged. More likely, he'll throw *us* in the dungeons." Fergus finished yelling at Larkem, and a visible shudder trembled through Hamil.

"Then keep her quiet." Larkem wiped his mouth and glared at Nat. She collapsed against the floorboards of the sleigh, sensing the danger of another beating had passed. *Thank you, Fergus.*

"She's not saying anything now. Sit up here with me." Fergus gestured to the riding bench. "Hamil can watch her. When we get to the harbor, we'll lock her in the hull of the boat. And I'll shut her in the back of the wagon after we disembark. You won't have to look at her until we reach Rustbrook." Fergus loosened his hold and Larkem shook him off. He shot a deadly look at Nat but clambered onto the riding bench. Hamil slid next to Nat. He averted his eyes and refused to look at her.

She listened to the swishing of the sleigh blades and the occasional snort of the draft horses. Her head felt heavy and the residual sting from Larkem's blows kept her in place, afraid to move for fear of sending a shock of pain through her limbs. She curled her neck to her chest and settled her breathing. *It was worth it,* she told herself, wincing at the pain in her back and arm. *I have the memory I need to trick the Nalaide.*

CHAPTER
TWENTY-FIVE

Only a thin layer of snow blanketed the road when the sleigh arrived at the small harbor town on the Elem River. The sled scraped against the exposed rock and dirt as Fergus brought the horses to a halt. Larkem jumped from the rider's bench and strode toward the lonely boats bobbing in the river, leaving Fergus and Hamil alone with Nat. She groaned as she peered over the sleigh bed. Two globe lights illuminated the ice-covered dock. Larkem disappeared beyond their glowing circles into the mist.

"Don't give us any problems now, Sister," Fergus warned. Little icicles clung to his black beard as he held a moth-eaten blanket in front of her. "I'll untie your legs, but if you bolt, that wound in your arm will look like a scrape when I'm done with you." He hefted a ten-inch serrated dagger in front of her face. Nat let out a nervous laugh and Fergus' expression soured. "Don't tempt me," he growled. "I know how to run a Sister through as well as Mudug's special guard." Nat could see his look of wounded pride. *Chip on his shoulder,* she thought as she inched away from the tip of his dagger.

"I wasn't laughing at you," she explained. "I laughed at your describing the wound on my arm as a scrape . . ." She paused, seeing the confusion in his face even in the dim light. "I won't run," she added, knowing she wasn't lying. Her feet were completely numb, and her muscles were beyond stiff and sore.

Fergus cautiously unbuckled the strap and pulled Nat to a standing position. Slowly, a painful stinging sensation crept into her feet. She grimaced and shuffled forward. Fergus tossed the blanket over her head and around her shoulders, shrouding her. True to his word, Nat felt the tip of his dagger against her back. She walked with clumsy steps and found herself on the iced-over wood planks of the dock. Fergus led her up a narrow set of stairs onto a boat.

"Put her in the hull," Larkem's voice rang out above them.

"In you go, Sister." Fergus removed the blanket and gestured to a square opening in the middle of the deck. Nat peered into the darkness and noticed something small scuttle across a stair. "Don't mind the rats. They're good company," he said and pushed the dagger point deeper into the folds of her clothing.

Nat sucked in a breath when the tip nicked her skin. "I thought you didn't want me damaged," she muttered, tensing to elbow his side if he pricked her again.

"Just get in there," Fergus grumbled. Nat stepped over a wooden lip and carefully descended into the darkness. When her head was barely even with the opening, Fergus threw the blanket in after her and slammed the hatch closed. Nat ducked just in time to avoid having her head smashed. A metal clanking sound, like a lock clicking into place, clacked above her. Footsteps and distant voices followed, then nothing more.

She extended her arms in the pitch blackness, wishing she had her orb. Her fingertips brushed one wall, and she shuffled around the perimeter of the cramped space, checking for openings other than the sealed hatch above her head. Finding nothing, she braced herself against the side of the hull and slid to the floor. She thought of Soris and her sister, and a single tear trickled down her cheek. The rats scampered away from her as she considered her predicament.

The boat rocked slightly, and Nat felt it drift away from the dock. The sound of water slapping against the side of the boat calmed her. She sniffed, wiped her nose, and wrapped the old blanket over her chest to keep out the bone-chilling cold. She pulled the tattered edges of the bandage hanging from her arm together and pressed her forearm to her abdomen, not wanting to draw the rats any closer. *Barba was crazy to believe I could end the Nala. But if I can convince the Nalaide that Mudug has me, then maybe I can do some good before they turn me over to the Chemist.*

She settled her bruised body as comfortably as she could against the wall, hoping the memory of Larkem's beating would anger the Nalaide enough that she'd attack Mudug just as Estos and Annin had intended. She closed her eyes, knowing for the moment she still had the freedom of her dreams and dream space, until she let in the Nalaide. The boat rocked side to side, lulling her quickly to sleep.

The dream came almost at once. Nat found herself in theater class, staring at the stage glowing under bright spotlights. Long strips of silken blue fabric billowed away from the wall, as if a breeze were pushing the cloth. She sat alone in the front row, watching the fabric undulate like a wave.

A spotlight creaked, and a piercing beam of white light landed on Nat. The brightness blinded her and the beam burned into her skin. She launched out of the chair, away from the light and the searing heat. The beam swirled, and the Nalaide emerged from it. The creature opened her pale lips and hissed, filling the theater with a sound like oil sizzling in a hot pan.

Nat bolted toward an aisle, but the audience chairs expanded in size, blocking her way. The tail end of one of the strips of blue fabric snapped in front of her. She grasped the edge of the material, braced her legs against the wall, and climbed up hand over hand. The Nalaide leapt toward the trailing fabric, but Nat yanked it up before the queen's pale, spiked hands could grasp it. Her dark eyes burned with a black fury. Nat tightened her grip on the slippery fabric and continued to climb. The cloth disappeared at the edge of her dream space, and she slapped her hand on the barrier.

"Natalie!" Soris' voice rose from the depths. He stood in the middle of the stage with his arms lifted toward her. The Nalaide twisted her elongated neck and fixed her inky eyes on him.

"Catch!" Nat yelled. She tossed the end of the fabric toward the center of the stage. Soris leapt into the air and grasped the hem. He shimmied up the cloth, gathering the folds behind him. Nat pulled herself over her dream space barrier when Soris reached her, and the two of them fell onto the floor.

"Lights!" Nat yelled, and the protective beams blazed to life.

Soris grasped her arms before she even had a chance to stand. "I've been looking for you for hours! Where are you?"

"I'm in a boat on the Elem River." Her chest rose with a shaky breath. "Two guards stationed at the outpost found me while they were hunting." Out of the corner of her eye, she caught the movement of a white limb jabbing one of the protective beams. The Nalaide glared at her through the lights, and pain flamed in her arm.

"Soris, help me . . . help me get away from here," she gasped. Soris wrapped one arm around her waist and lifted her into his arms. He raced away, pressing her protectively to his chest. The pain in her arm ebbed the farther he ran. *This is my dream space, my dream space*, she thought, trying to control the pain.

"I'm okay. You can put me down," she said after her thoughts cleared.

"You look anything but okay, Natalie," he said, but set her gently on her feet. "Now tell me everything."

"The guards saw my markings. They know about the Chemist's bounty on my head and want the money. They're bringing me to him.

They said something about switching to a wagon before we get to Rustbrook." The words tumbled from her mouth.

Soris rubbed his chin. "Sunton, they must plan on switching to a wagon at Sunton. It's the only town with a harbor before Ballew and a day's ride to Rustbrook. I'll find you." He took a step away.

"No, Soris." Nat grasped his hand. "I can take care of myself, and you can't reach me before we arrive in Rustbrook, anyway. I need you to watch out for Cal, and I have to continue with what we planned."

"What do you mean?" He shook his head in confusion.

"The Nalaide. I can convince the Nalaide that Mudug has me and won't turn me over to her. The guards that captured me said enough that I think I can use those memories to trick her. It's still the best chance Estos has of pitting them against each other before he takes Rustbrook."

"Natalie, Annin had a complex memory alteration planned for you. I don't know if a few words from an outpost guard will make the Nalaide believe anything other than you're lying to her." Soris gave her a wary look.

"I have to try, and I have to try now. I may not have another chance if I can't escape from the guards."

She saw Soris' expression waver. He let go of her hand. Tiny buds poked through the ground around them and burst open, revealing the yellow petals of the meldon flower. He regarded the flowers, then met her steady look. "Only you would imagine flowers at a moment like this," he said, letting out an exasperated breath. "All right. We'll do it, but not the way Annin wanted. Create a protective barrier like you did when you let in the Nala that bit me."

"The flowers will protect us." Nat gestured to the yellow field.

Soris scanned the delicate petals near his boots. "Flowers? Not an impenetrable wall of orbs, a pack of wild gunnels, or an impassable river?" he suggested, looking desperate.

"Trust me." Nat knelt to the ground and dug her fingers into the soil, thinking how the fields of meldon flowers always repelled the Nala.

Soris took another deep breath and puffed out his cheeks. "I trust you," he said, but gave the ground another wary look. "Flowers," he muttered as he glanced at the wisp of white light streaming past Nat's barrier lights. He rubbed his palms against his thighs. "The moment you let her in, show her the memories from your captivity, nothing more. As soon as she's seen those, force her out and run back to the flowers. I'll help you. We can't risk giving her time to worm any deeper into your thoughts," he warned. He knelt next to her, and the yellow glow from the flowers enveloped his face. "As soon as she's out of your dream space and I know you're safe, I'll leave and tell Estos and the others what's happened."

Nat dug her fingers deeper into the soil and focused on Soris' green eye, trying to pull every ounce of courage she could from his presence.

"Mudug has two outposts between the dam and Rustbrook. Depending on the fight, it may be two, three days before we take Rustbrook. Can you make it that long?"

"Yes," she said, trying to keep her voice confident. "You said it's a day's travel from Sunton to Rustbrook?"

"At least a day."

"Good. Then at the most I'll be in Rustbrook two days before you arrive. I can manage the Chemist for a couple of days. It will give me a chance to cause some mischief." She lowered her gaze, afraid he would see the fear in her eyes.

"Mischief?" Soris gave her a startled look. "Forget mischief, Natalie. Just do whatever you can to stay alive in Rustbrook." He ran his fingers through her hair and kissed her with such need that Nat felt lost in the moment, forgetting where they were. The hissing of the Nalaide broke them apart. Nat took a deep breath and reached for his hand.

"Are you ready?" he asked.

"I'm ready." She took another deep breath as if it were her last. "Time to let her in."

CHAPTER
TWENTY-SIX

The light barrier disappeared. Nat braced herself, leaning against Soris. He wrapped his arms around her waist and pressed her back protectively against his chest.

The Nalaide ceased thrashing against the ledge and settled her chilly glare on Nat. Her skin emitted its own light as she hovered on the other side of the barrier. The pale, opaque color reminded Nat of a clouded orb. Her own orb popped into the air above her head, startling Soris. Nat glanced up, and warmth washed over her face.

"They can't cage you from my mind," she whispered to the sphere. She lifted her trembling, wounded arm above her head and grasped the ball. The Nalaide's eyes narrowed, and a ripping pain seized Nat's forearm. The ball fell from her fingers and landed on the bed of flowers. She inhaled sharply and cleared her mind. The orb inched off the ground.

"No, leave it there." Soris' voice was so low Nat could barely make out his words as he whispered in her ear. "Make her believe she has control over you, just as if you were a duozi." He tightened his grasp on her waist. The sphere fell back onto the flowers, and Nat lowered her head as if submitting.

"Come in," Nat said, barely above a whisper. The Nalaide's mouth curved into a hideous smile. The creature stabbed the barrier with her hands and vaulted over the ledge, landing without a sound. Nat's arm throbbed with each piercing step the Nalaide took closer to her. Nat clung to Soris, pretending to cringe as the creature approached. The Nalaide frowned, dark eyes forming needlelike slits.

"Send him away." The Nalaide's teeth ground together as she stared at Soris. Nat's back arched as another bolt of searing pain exploded in her forearm. She screamed and collapsed against him.

"I'm letting you go so she stops hurting you," Soris whispered in her ear as he bent over her. "Let her into your memories quickly. I'll be back to help. I promise. Remember where you are." He pressed his lips to her hair. Nat gave an imperceptible nod and he released her. She imagined a path of meldon flowers under his feet as he moved to the ledge and disappeared over the barrier. A satisfied looked crossed the Nalaide's face.

Nat kept her eyes trained on the flowers. Her breathing quickened as she waited anxiously for the Nalaide to do or say something. More pain shot through her arm and her legs buckled. She landed with her face in the flowers. *This is my dream space,* Nat reminded herself, but along with the pain in her arm, she was beginning to feel the Nalaide's pull on her.

The Nalaide let out a barking hiss. Nat's head involuntarily jerked up as if invisible hands were forcing her movement. "Where are you, Sister?"

Nat averted her eyes and focused on the flowers, drawing strength from their simple beauty as she listened to the Nalaide rant.

"You must pay for an eternity of Sisters' wrongs *and* your thievery." The creature drew back her lips and bared her sharp teeth. "You will be my vessel and I will regenerate through you."

"You l-lost your chance." Nat's lips trembled as she spoke. "Mudug's guard found me. He and the Chemist won't turn me over. You'll never see me again." She forced herself to meet the Nalaide's glare.

"No." A drop of dark venom trickled from the side of her mouth. Nat felt a pressure in her mind, like a probe being inserted in her head. "No, they will bring you to me. We have an *agreement*. Tell me where you are, and I will find you."

Show her the memory. Soris' voice was a whisper in her head.

Nat rose unsteadily to her feet and stepped out of the protective ring of flowers. The Nalaide loomed over her like an eagle over its prey and grasped Nat's head between her slick hands. Nat's muscles spasmed. She forced herself to think of Larkem and his sneer as her head rolled back under the force of the Nalaide's grip.

The Nalaide squeezed her head. Nat opened her mind to the creature, leading her into the memory of Larkem beating her. Her back flinched under his blows. The white circle on his blue uniform flashed with each strike. "Mudug has me," she whispered, her voice raspy. She saw nothing but her memories now. The hatch above the hull slammed over her head, sinking her into darkness. Rats scurried across her feet. She collapsed in the cold darkness of the memory, shivering, sobbing. "I'll die in the Rustbrook dungeons." She repeated Larkem's words.

She felt the Nalaide searching through her thoughts and brought the image of the meldon flower to the front of her mind, hoping it would repel the creature from her dream space as it did in real life. The Nalaide's hands snapped away from Nat's head as if it were on fire. Nat fell at the Nala queen's feet and crawled toward the bed of flowers, but the Nalaide lunged for her, arms outstretched. Just as the creature touched her ankle, a loud thwacking sound filled the air.

"Expel her, Natalie!" Soris yelled. The Nalaide brought her hand to the side of her head as he struck her again. He lowered his arms and skirted the space behind the creature. Nat rose on shaky legs. The Nalaide rounded on Soris, knocking him away with a single blow.

This is my dream space, Nat repeated over and over in her mind. Meldon flowers sprang up around her and Soris, enveloping them in a yellow light. The Nalaide scuttled back, away from the flowers. Her lips quivered and her glare seared into Nat. A sensation like a thousand shards of glass cut into her arm, and she fell to her knees.

"I will have you, Sister." The Nalaide seethed. Her body expanded in size. Nat cradled her arm, blinded by the pain. Her concentration ebbed. The flowers at the edge of the tiny field withered and crumbled. The creature inched closer, scraping her feet over the dead flowers.

"This is your dream space, Natalie!" Soris yelled and leapt onto the Nalaide's back. A simple shake of her immense body sent him sailing through the air. His face and knees hit the barrier at the same time, and he landed with his back toward Nat. The Nalaide pivoted, and in three long steps was bent over Soris. She scooped him into the air, preparing to toss him over the barrier.

"No," Nat breathed, barely able to lift her head. A blur of light shot over her, and her orb crashed into the Nalaide's skull, then spun around and slammed into the creature's mouth. Soris tumbled to the ground as the Nalaide struggled to free the sphere from her maw. Nat heard a grinding sound as her teeth crunched against the orb, then she spat it out. The Nalaide's pale chest rose and fell, reminding Nat of the horrid remnant rings she'd found in the Nala that had attacked her months before. The creature pivoted and a dark anger flamed in her spiderlike eyes. She launched off her hind limbs in Nat's direction.

Pushing herself into a kneeling position, Nat hunched over the flowers. She stuck her fingers into the remaining patch of dirt rooting them. The soil separated into tiny particles that floated into the air, whipped into a long funnel point, and spun toward the creature. The whirlwind of soil surrounded the Nalaide. Her body disappeared inside the funnel as it twisted over the ledge. Silence settled over her dream space.

"Lights," Nat whispered. The light beams rose and hummed to life along the protective barrier. Her orb wobbled in the air toward her.

"We did it." Nat rose unsteadily. "If that doesn't get her mad enough to come after Mudug to get me, I don't know—" She stopped midsentence and searched the base of the barrier, where she'd last seen Soris. "I don't know what will." She finished the thought, knowing she was alone again.

CHAPTER
TWENTY-SEVEN

The memory of the Nalaide searching her thoughts lingered in Nat's mind long into the next day. As the wheels of the wagon brought her and her captors closer to Rustbrook, a sliver of doubt pricked at her thoughts. She wondered if the Nalaide would seek out Mudug in search of her based on the flimsy memory Nat had revealed to the queen. After hours of worrying, she pushed the doubt aside and listened to Hamil's whiny voice as he grabbed a blanket from inside the wagon and joined Fergus on the rider's bench.

"When I get my money from turning the Sister over, I'm building the snuggest cottage and won't set foot from it until spring." Hamil sniffed and wiped his nose. "I'm sick of being cold all the time."

"Quit your grousing, Hamil. It's giving me a headache." Larkem pushed his guard's hat from his eyes and stretched on the bench across from Nat. She frowned, wishing he'd slept longer.

Hamil shrugged and tucked the blanket around his legs. "How about you, Fergus? What will you do with your share?"

Fergus scratched his head and snapped the reins of the wagon. "I'll pay off my sister's and her husband's debts so they can leave the Rewall.

Been there for more than four years now." He snapped the reins again. A deep frown settled over his features.

Nat scooted over a pile of hides, closer to the driver's bench. "Are you certain they're still in the Rewall?" she asked, seizing the opportunity to sow seeds of fear and doubt in Fergus. She'd survived a night with the Nalaide in her head. Now she had to find a way to avoid the Chemist until the rebels seized Rustbrook.

"And where else would they be, Sister? Traded to the Nala?" Larkem's voice was ripe with sarcasm. Nat shifted on the hard wooden seat, away from Larkem, flexing her hands bound together at her wrists.

"The Chemist rounds up Rewall residents and experiments on them." She met Larkem's glare. Fergus' back tensed, and she heard him grumble from the front of the wagon. Larkem balled his fingers into fists. No one had tried to hit her since they'd pulled her from the boat hull early in the morning, but Larkem's tense expression made her nervous. Nat let out a deep, raspy cough, and his fingers relaxed. *I must look pretty bad,* she thought, figuring he was restraining himself out of fear of what the Chemist would say if he delivered a mashed-up mess of a Sister.

Hamil turned from the rider's seat and peered through the opening in the canvas wagon cover. "How do you know what the Chemist's been up to?"

Nat glanced from Fergus to Hamil. "It's common knowledge," she lied.

"Not to us it isn't." Hamil shot Fergus a sympathetic look.

"How long have you been stationed at that backwoods outpost?" she asked, trying to sit a little straighter. The pain in her forearm was beginning to ebb, but it still felt as if the Nalaide were ripping into her arm.

"What has that got to do with anything?" Larkem removed a small knife from his belt and stripped a thin piece of leather from a torn bridle.

"If you're heading into Rustbrook, don't you think you ought to know what's happening in the city?" The men said nothing. "Suit yourself," Nat said dismissively. "You can figure it out on your own." She leaned her head against the canvas shell of the wagon and closed her eyes.

"Hamil was sent to the outpost five years ago. Larkem and me, four." Fergus snapped the reins again. "Now tell us what you know of the Rewall."

"Shut up, Fergus." Larkem split the bridle and tossed the leather to the side.

"What difference does it make if she knows how long we've been in that no-man's-land? If she has information that can help me get my sister out of the Rewall, I'm willing to listen. So tell us, Sister, what's going on in the city?"

"First tell me why you were stationed at the post," Nat asked, thinking the information about the men could prove valuable. From what little she'd seen, the outpost's location struck her as a last resort.

"Hamil went off on a lark when his company was near Daub Town." Fergus' eyes crinkled and his cheeks turned into little apple-shaped knobs when he grinned.

Hamil turned toward Nat. "I didn't do anything wrong. We were near my hometown, and I was only gone for a few hours to see my beloved." His eyebrows knit together. "And I got an indefinite post."

"I'm sure your beloved is waiting indefinitely for you." Fergus chuckled.

"What about you?" Hamil smacked Fergus' burly arm with the back of his hand. "Refusing orders to deliver a family to the Rewall."

"I'd do it again." Nat could see the firm set of his profile. "Sending an entire family to the Rewall because the son had thieved an old mule to get his mam to a quack healer? I knew the family myself. They'd just fallen on hard times, that's all. Didn't deserve to live in the Rewall." He snapped the reins with an agitated flip of his wrist.

Not a fan of the Rewall, Nat thought. Her eyes met Larkem's.

"Don't ask, Sister," he warned.

"Come on, Larkem, we're all sharing. Not like she'll be spilling our secrets where she's going," Hamil goaded.

"Makes no difference why I was stationed out there," Larkem growled.

"No, I guess not." Nat shrugged in feigned agreement. "But you've been separated from the rest of Fourline too long to see the damage Mudug's inflicted on the people."

"You have special insight into Mudug's doings?" Larkem leaned forward, settling his elbows on his knees as he regarded Nat.

"Finding out what the Chemist and Mudug are up to isn't difficult when you travel across Fourline," she said, trying to keep her response vague. She didn't want to feed Larkem information he'd turn around and tell the Chemist if she couldn't escape before they reached the castle. *The Chemist must know I slipped out of the Nalaide's grasp, but he can't know I had any involvement with Emilia . . .* A chilling thought gripped her and she sucked in a quick breath.

Benedict.

Nat blanched. If a castle guard had caught the Chemist's twin brother after he'd fled during their attempt to rescue Emilia, the Hermit could have told the Chemist and Mudug everything. A well of panic formed in her chest. Why hadn't she thought of Benedict before?

"You don't look certain of yourself now, Sister." Larkem flipped his knife in the air, catching the handle. "Maybe all Mudug and the Chemist want is to rid Fourline of troublemakers like you so the country can find peace again."

"He won't bring peace," Nat said in a distracted tone as she thought of the Hermit's wrinkled face. "Only the regents and the Sisters can do that."

"The regents?" Larkem's brow crinkled, and his knife clattered onto the floor of the wagon bed. The tip landed precariously close to Nat's bound ankle. "They're dead, Sister. And you say we're out of touch."

Nat settled against the cold canvas, refusing to respond to Larkem. Her eyelids drooped from exhaustion and her new worries over what lay ahead if Benedict had been caught. She glanced at her captors and her orb swinging in its cage from a bowed beam. If she could free her orb and locate a Sister passage in the castle, there was a chance to escape before the guards turned her over to the Chemist. Her mind whirled with possible escape routes, remembering the passages near the Chemist's quarters.

Larkem's gaze followed Nat's to the orb cage. He gave her a cold smile and tucked his hand into a faded pocket of his coat. *What has he got hidden in there?* Nat wondered as she watched the outline of his fingers press against the fabric as if clutching something.

"Get us something to eat, Larkem. I'm starving up here," Fergus called out.

Larkem grumbled and removed a greasy wrapper from a leather bag. He cut a few slices of cold meat off a fat drumstick and passed them to Fergus on the tip of the knife. Fergus looked over his shoulder and tossed a slice in Nat's direction. A hunk of meat landed in her lap.

"Eat up, Sister," Fergus said. Nat pretended to struggle to pick up the meat with her bound hands. The slice fell to the floor.

Larkem gave her an irritated look. "I haven't seen many Sisters recently, but you are by far the most pathetic." He bent over to retrieve the food and Nat lunged forward. She shoved her fingers into his pocket and grabbed a small key. She tucked it under the rope binding her wrists and rammed her shoulder into Larkem. He snatched at her leg, sending her falling forward into the thick canvas wagon cover. The material cushioned the fall, and she slumped onto the wagon bed.

"Try a stunt like that again—" Larkem held his fist inches from her face.

"Larkem, Rustbrook's ahead," Fergus said from the rider's bench. "Leave her be."

Larkem lowered his fist, looking as if he'd lost a prize. He wrenched her off the wagon bed and shoved her back onto the bench. Nat pressed her arms tightly to her stomach, hoping the key had stayed in place. She glanced through the open canvas flap, past Fergus' and Hamil's heads. A wide wooden bridge spanned a river directly in front of them. Beyond the river, she spotted the geometric castle crowning the hill overlooking Rustbrook.

Larkem straightened his coat and glared at her. "End of the line, Sister."

CHAPTER
TWENTY-EIGHT

The wagon ground to a halt. From beneath the hides Larkem had heaped over her, Nat heard footsteps and the creak of the stairs. Muffled voices rose from the other side of the canvas cover. Nat peeked out and glanced toward the front. Fergus and Larkem were nowhere in sight, but Hamil sat hunched over on one side of the rider's bench. Nat could see only the curve of his back. She scanned the empty wagon bed.

Fool, she thought as she glimpsed the knife Larkem had used to slice the meat. Its greasy handle stuck out from between the two leather bags situated near the rider's bench. Nat slipped off the bench. Staying low, she crept toward the bags and snatched the knife before Hamil could notice her movements. The handle almost slipped out of her hands, but she caught it before it clattered against the wagon bed. Once back on the bench, she picked at the rope binding her wrists with the knife's sharp point. It hit the key tucked under the rope, and she slid the key into her tunic before attacking the rope again.

"Delivering a report from the Western Outpost to the captain of the guard." Larkem spoke in a loud voice, and Nat heard him clearly through the canvas cover.

"The Western Outpost? What are you reporting? Which way the wind's blowing?" A contemptuous laugh filled the air. Nat dared to peek through a rip in the cover and watched Larkem blush.

"Got a sense of humor, do you?" Fergus' deep voice chortled. He slapped his hand on Larkem's shoulder in a restraining gesture. "No, we have a report on some possible rebel activities. Our commanding officer sent us," he added. Nat heard Hamil let out a little nervous squeak, then cover it with a cough.

"If your commanding officer sent you, where are the orders?"

"Here." Larkem thrust a folded paper into the guard's hand.

Fergus shifted nervously as the guard scanned the forged paper. "Seen much rebel activity around here?" he asked.

"No, all the action is everywhere but here," the guard replied. "Which is a good thing, because between you and me, the city's feeling a bit tense these days. Leave whatever report you have here. I'll see it's delivered to the captain."

Nat continued to listen as she cut at the rope with awkward movements. Sweat trickled down her face. She glanced up. Hamil's back was still to her.

"No," Larkem responded quickly. "We have to deliver the report in person. Commander made us memorize it. The information's too sensitive. He didn't want to risk its falling into the wrong hands if we were caught by rebels."

The gate guard snorted. "I'd like to see the captain when he hears that one."

The rumbling sound of hoofbeats surrounded the wagon. The canvas cover vibrated, and the draft horses strained against the wagon brake, twisting their heads to the side.

"Merchant convoy. Twenty-six wagons coming," a voice called out from behind the wagon.

"And all needing to be searched," the gate guard grumbled. "Go on through."

He passed the papers back to Larkem and disappeared from view. Nat lay quickly on her side, pulling a hide back in place just as Larkem ducked under the canvas flap. She shoved the knife down the front of her tunic. He silently adjusted the hide to conceal her entirely.

"I want this reward, but I will kill you if necessary, Sister," Larkem whispered in warning.

You're not getting the chance. She pressed the hidden metal blade against her chest. The wagon rolled through the gate and into Rustbrook.

"Where now?" Fergus asked in a hushed tone. "We can't take her to the captain. He'll want to turn her in himself."

"I know," Larkem replied. "We'll take her to the Chemist ourselves. I saw a map of the castle in the commander's office and have a good enough idea where to go. Bring the wagon up to the kitchen. We'll bluff our way in. No kitchen maid will question a soldier."

Hamil snapped the reins and shouted for someone to move. Nat closed her eyes, trying to visualize where they were in the city as the wagon rolled through the streets. She fumbled in her tunic and slowly retrieved the knife. Angling the tip down, she picked at the rope again. The wagon increased its speed, and she nicked the skin above her wounded forearm. Biting her lip to keep from crying out in pain, she continued to drag the blade across the rope. She flexed her hands. The tension of the rope loosened. Nat tucked the knife back into her tunic next to the key.

After a long series of turns and Hamil cursing, Larkem spoke up. "Next right, Fergus."

Nat dared a peek from underneath the hide. She caught a flash of brick beyond the guards' heads. The pungent smell of garbage wafted into the wagon just as its wheels crunched over gravel.

"Stop here. Cover the orb, Hamil." Fergus reached for one of the leather bags and handed him a cloth that smelled of soured milk. Hamil covered the cage, hiding Nat's orb from sight.

Larkem ripped the hide off Nat. "Spare cloak." He snapped his fingers. Fergus pulled a long black cloak from the bag. "Hold her,"

Larkem demanded as he stooped to unbuckle the strap around her legs. Fergus set his large hand on Nat's shoulder and gave her a look of warning. "Straight through those back doors and into the kitchen. Let me do the talking if anyone stops us," Larkem ordered. Fergus and Hamil grunted in agreement, but Nat caught Hamil shooting Fergus a nervous look. "I meant what I said, Sister." Larkem flashed his dagger in front of her face. Nat pressed her wrists close to her chest. He grasped her and shoved her head back. "Do you understand?"

"Yes," she said through her swollen lips. Her thoughts of escape blazed under his glare.

Larkem pulled her up by the shoulders and threw the oversized cloak over her. Hamil clutched the orb cage under his arm and clambered down from the wagon. Larkem followed, pulling Nat after him.

She tested the ropes binding her wrists as they climbed the icy steps leading to the scullery. *I need to make it to a Sister passage and then to Wesdrono Street,* she thought, planning out her escape. The run-down bookstore where her friends Matilda and Mervin lived would offer a safe refuge until Estos and the rebels arrived in Rustbrook.

The rope loosened a little more.

Fergus opened the scullery door, and a blast of warmth settled on Nat's skin as they walked into the kitchen. Three open hearths crackled with fire. Near one hearth, a girl turned a spit and ladled a liquid over the crisping flesh of a pig. The drippings sizzled and filled the kitchen with an unpleasant burning smell that overpowered the aroma of baking bread. A plump woman, holding a long-handled circular paddle laden with steaming loaves of bread, looked their way. Nat recognized her immediately as the cook she and Soris had slipped past on the day they'd tricked the Chemist. She ducked her head, letting the folds of the hood hide her face.

"What's this then?" the cook asked, sliding the bread onto the wooden table that ran half the length of the kitchen.

"Guard business," Larkem said briskly and elbowed Nat toward the stairs. Her foot caught on the cloak, and she stumbled onto the stained stone floor. The cloak billowed away, revealing her bound wrists and bandaged arm.

"When did the captain say my kitchen was a route for prisoners? I'll have words with him if he intends to let you guards tread through here." She waved her paddle in Larkem's direction.

"Better for you if you don't ask questions," Larkem replied and took a menacing step toward her. She lowered her paddle, and her cheeks grew red as she huffed out a breath.

Fergus lifted Nat to her feet, pinched the front of her cloak together, and pulled her to the set of stairs that led to a balcony overlooking the kitchen. He urged her up the stairs with a rough hand.

"Then use the guard entrance instead of mucking up my kitchen with your filthy boots. It's not right traipsing through here like it's your private barracks," the cook grumbled. She held firmly to her paddle and didn't back away from Larkem. The girl stood from her stool and joined her. Larkem gave them both a contemptuous look and followed Hamil up the stairs after Fergus and Nat. Hamil glanced nervously over the balcony ledge and tripped on the top stair. The cage fell from his hand and crashed onto the balcony floor. He scrambled after it, wrapping the old cloth around it and hiding the orb from sight. Nat watched the girl's eyes widen before Hamil could cover the cage.

Fergus thrust open the door at the top of the stairs, and Nat found herself shoved into the familiar hallway.

"Get yourself together, Hamil," Larkem growled. Crimsoned faced, Hamil shut the door behind him. Larkem repositioned himself behind Nat.

"You do know how much trouble you're going to get into when the cook rats you out to the captain?" Nat knew nothing of the captain but figured the threat might rattle the guards and hamper their focus. Fergus frowned, and Hamil wiped his sweaty brow.

"Won't mean anything after we turn you over to the Chemist," Larkem said, but he glanced anxiously down the hallway. With Larkem looking the other way, Nat focused on Hamil. The cage hung by its brass ring from his fingertip. She inched closer to him, but Larkem grabbed her arm and pushed her down the hallway.

They walked quickly and passed a guard who gave them a curious look. Fergus, Larkem, and Hamil strode by with stony expressions.

"Keep moving, Sister," Larkem whispered.

They escorted her deeper into the castle, through corridors she'd never seen and down a steep set of stairs, until they reached a long hallway. At the end of the hall hung a faded, dusty tapestry Nat recognized immediately. Hope welled in her. She glanced to the right and spotted the door where she and Andris had exited the Chemist's garden before slipping behind the tapestry into a Sister passage.

"This is it." Larkem paused by the door. He faced Hamil and Fergus. "I'll talk to the guards and make sure the Chemist is in his quarters. I don't want to bring her into view until I know he's there." He placed his hand on the door's black metal knob.

"What are we supposed to do if someone comes this way?" Hamil asked. Sweat continued to trickle down his brow, and he looked almost green in the dim light of the hallway.

"Make something up," Larkem said through clenched teeth. "But don't let her escape. We didn't come all this way to lose her now." He opened the door with a creak and cringed at the sound, then slipped through. Fergus peered out, watching him. Hamil stood next to him with the fingers of one hand pressed against the doorframe. Neither paid any attention to Nat.

She furiously twisted her wrists back and forth under the cloak, hardly believing their inattention after Larkem's admonition to watch her. The rope broke and landed near her boots. She slipped one hand down the front of her tunic and retrieved the knife before edging closer to Fergus. She whipped her cloak open and kicked Fergus in the groin from behind. His eyes crossed and he doubled over as his head knocked against the door, slamming it shut on Hamil's fingers. The cage slipped off his other hand and crashed to the floor. Nat grabbed it and took off running down the hall toward the tapestry.

Footsteps sounded behind her. Hamil bowled into her legs, knocking her to the ground before she could lift the dusty tapestry away from the wall. The knife fell from her hand, and her orb clattered against the bars of the cage as it rolled away from her fingers. She reached for it, but a black boot kicked it out of her grasp and stepped on her arm, grinding into her wound. Her screams echoed down the corridor. She felt a heavy weight on her back, and she hit the stone floor face-first under the forceful thrust of someone's hand. A long green robe brushed against her cheek, and the boot lifted off her arm. The hem of the robe swished in front of her, exposing an irregular large heel on one of the boots visible only to Nat.

"Your Chemistness." She heard Fergus' anxious voice above her.

"Is this who I think it is?" The drawl of the Chemist's voice made Nat cringe.

"Yes." Expectation rang in Larkem's voice. Nat tried to lift her head, but Fergus held her fast. "It's the Sister you're looking for."

"Surprising you made it this far with her, given she almost slipped from your fingers just now," the Chemist responded with a nasal tone. "Lift her up so I may look at her."

Fergus jerked Nat into a sitting position. She took in the heavy embroidery of the green robe and the golden leaf-shaped clasp, then met the Chemist's eyes with her own.

"You've done well," he said a few inches from her face.

Nat's eyes widened when she recognized the slight kink in his nose. "Benedict," she mouthed, barely moving her lips.

He brushed his finger over his lips, warning her to stay silent. "Welcome, Sister. I've been waiting quite a while for someone to bring you to me."

CHAPTER
TWENTY-NINE

"You are certain no one else knows she's in the castle?" Benedict asked as he walked with a slight limp through the Chemist's gardens. Nat kept glancing at his long robes and his full head of hair, wondering where the Chemist was and how Benedict had managed to pull off disguising himself like his twin brother. Had he fooled everyone with long robes and modified boots to hide his atrophied leg?

Larkem shook his head. "Not a soul," he responded as he easily matched Benedict's stride.

"Except that devil in the kitchen," Hamil remarked. He clapped his hand over his mouth when Fergus elbowed him in the side.

Benedict drew to a halt under a trellis covered in dried-out vines. "The devil in the kitchen?" He gave Hamil a withering look.

"We brought her through the kitchen. Thought it the most discreet way to bring her into the castle," Larkem rushed to explain. The tips of his ginger beard bobbed up and down as he spoke. "Just the cook and her maid saw us. No one else," he added, shrinking back a step as Benedict continued to glare.

Nat scanned the gardens and the front of the Chemist's quarters, looking for more guards. The courtyard was empty. She gave Benedict a fleeting glance, but his attention was on Hamil. He held out his hand. Hamil's eyes filled with fear.

"The cage." Benedict gestured for it. "Give me the orb cage and the key."

Hamil handed the cage to Benedict. Larkem fumbled in his pocket. "Had the key somewhere in here." He flushed as he emptied his pockets. Nat hid her smile. "It must have fallen out in the hallway during the struggle."

"Don't tell me you've lost the key?" Anger seeped from Benedict's voice. He turned his back on the guards and walked to the end of the long building that made up the Chemist's quarters. Looking uncertain and worried, Larkem, Hamil, and Fergus followed him, pushing Nat ahead of them. A wooden screen Nat had never seen before shielded the porch, hiding the three entrances to the quarters from direct view. Benedict opened the last door and closed it in Larkem's face.

"What do you think he's about?" Fergus asked Larkem under his breath. "Does he mean to leave us here with the Sister and not give us a reward because you lost a key?"

Larkem held up his hand, silencing him. "Just shut up and wait," he said, his voice a tense whisper.

"You had to lose the key, didn't you," Fergus said, unwilling to hold his tongue. His fingers tightened around Nat's arm.

The door opened and Benedict emerged. He curled his upper lip into a sneer, reminding Nat of all the times he'd given Annin and Soris hateful looks. He pressed a heavy bag into Larkem's hands.

"Your reward, with a deduction for the lost key. Leave this castle and Rustbrook immediately. If I learn you dallied in the city longer than it takes to saddle your horses, I'll have your hides." Benedict grasped Nat's arm. Hamil gulped audibly.

Fergus let go of her as if she were on fire. "Do you want us to bind her again, your Chemistness?" he offered. "She's a slippery one."

"And where would she run?" Benedict glowered at him. "I have Mudug's personal guards at my command. They know every nook in this castle. She'd be found and strung up in minutes."

"Not if she's knocked you out first," Hamil added. His mouth snapped shut as Benedict took a menacing step forward.

"Do I look like an imbecile?" he bellowed. "Get out of my sight!" He jerked lightly on Nat's arm and she pretended to fall forward. He shoved her inside the room before hastily closing the door.

"Hush," Benedict said, silencing the questions already forming on her lips. He walked with a more pronounced limp to a glass disc set between two crammed bookcases, adjusted a knob around the disc, and looked through the glass. Nat, still feeling the weight of stress and dread she'd been carrying since the guards captured her, collapsed onto an overstuffed chair in the center of the room and looked around.

The chamber was richly furnished with a single four-poster bed covered with heavily embroidered bed curtains, ornate bookshelves, and two octagonal side tables inlaid with mother-of-pearl. A merry fire danced in a small hearth in a far corner of the room. A kettle steamed above the fire, letting off a piping hiss.

"They're gone." Benedict let out a breath, stepped away from the peephole, and limped to the hearth. He wrapped his hand in a heavy flannel pot holder and removed the kettle from a metal rung. "My apologies for stepping on your arm, Sister." He poured hot water from the kettle into a teacup. "The Chemist is not known as a person with a delicate manner. I had to play the part."

"It was a stellar performance, Benedict." She laughed in spite of the pain, too relieved to care about her throbbing arm.

"I'll fix you up." He handed her a cup of steaming tea. "If you don't mind my saying, you look like a bastle trod on you, Sister. Had a rough go of it with those guards?" he commented, giving Nat a crooked smile.

"You have no idea, Benedict."

"I hid in the passages for weeks," Benedict said, answering Nat's question about where and how he'd evaded capture after he'd fled from Emilia's rescue party. He capped a jar of ointment he'd used on a cut on her forehead, then scooted to the side to examine her arm. "Let me see your forearm, Sister." Nat tensed as Benedict peeled the putrid bandages away from the wound.

"Weeks?" Nat stared at the Hermit as she settled more comfortably into the overstuffed chair. After the beatings and the wagon ride, the soft chair felt like a cloud beneath her.

"You doubt I could hide in this castle that long without someone finding me?" Benedict responded from his perch atop a pouf next to Nat's chair.

"No." Nat shook her head, thinking of all the times Annin had called Benedict a rat. "Andris and the others said you'd find your own way out. I'm just surprised you stayed after the rest of us escaped with Emilia."

"I considered it." He gently touched the side of her forearm and Nat winced. "But when I discovered you, Andris, and those half-breeds had successfully made off with her, I knew the Chemist would be on edge." Nat frowned at his description of Annin and Soris. "I couldn't pass up the opportunity to torment my brother." His eyes gleamed. Nat flinched as he spread more ointment over the wound, and wondered what he meant.

"Mudug never found out Emilia was gone," Benedict said in response to her questioning look. "He and the Chemist went directly to the Sisters' accommodations when they noticed the guards were missing after you'd escaped. The frenzy in finding the dead guards and then the dead Nala prevented the Chemist from even noticing Emilia had disappeared until the next day, and by then Mudug was so enraged with him that my brother dared not tell him about her." He wrapped a new bandage around Nat's arm. "I hid and watched as he grew increasingly paranoid over Mudug's discovering Emilia's absence." The deep lines etched in his forehead wrinkled. "She is safe? Tell me she's safe."

"Yes, she's safe," Nat replied, remembering that Benedict had been one of the queen's tutors and advisers when she was younger, and that he, too, had taken an oath to protect her.

Benedict exhaled and set his elbows on his knees. "Thank the Rim," he muttered. Dark circles colored the wrinkled skin under his eyes, but he looked relieved.

"Thanks to Soris and Annin," Nat added, unable to help herself. "Emilia never would've made it out of the castle without them," she said pointedly, recalling how Benedict had fled after accusing Soris of trying to kill Andris. Soris' arrow had grazed Andris' hip while he was subduing one of the Chemist's guards during the rescue mission. Nat's memory of Benedict's hateful words toward Annin and Soris still lingered in her mind. Benedict frowned at the mention of the duozis' names.

"If the Chemist never told anyone Emilia was missing, what happened after we left?" Nat asked. "Mervin said guards were searching for us near the river."

"The Chemist spun a story that since the Nala were looking for you, you must have been the one who ransacked the Sisters' accommodations and killed his guards."

"Me?" Nat squeaked.

"He had the description of your markings from the Nalaide's messenger and put a price on your head. I think he meant to use you as a scapegoat or some leverage with Mudug and the Nala."

"Where is the Chemist now?" she asked and glanced around the lavish room.

Benedict gave her a pained smile. "With our blessed parents, may they rest in peace."

A tight knot of nerves inside her disappeared at the news. "How did he die?"

Benedict stood slowly and ambled back toward the hearth. "My brother kept an impressive array of poisons in his laboratory, including rhododendron honey." He gestured to a glass jar on a shelf next to the hearth. Crystallized globules clung to the side of the jar.

"Never heard of it."

"Causes mild paralysis and a few other nasty symptoms. My brother always did like tea and honey," he said almost wistfully.

"You poisoned your brother?" Her voice rang out in the room. She'd been mad at Cal before, but what level of madness would she have to reach before she'd even consider the idea of poisoning her own sister?

"He tortured our queen." Benedict gave her a fierce look. "I've read his journals. The evil he raged on Emilia and others was unforgivable. Justice called for his immediate death, and under my oath, I was more than happy to deliver."

Nat carefully set her cup on the floor. The idea of Benedict handing out justice made her uneasy.

He leaned against the hearth and continued his story. "Sneaking into his quarters was simple enough. I waited until he left, then appeared dressed in this ridiculous wig and a long robe to hide my limp and doctored his supply of honey." He brushed his hand over the wig. "His guards were none the wiser, especially since they were newly assigned to him. After a few weeks of consuming the honey in his tea, my brother was barely able to hobble out to his garden. I added a touch of water hemlock to his own elixir and watched him die." He drew in a long breath through his nose. "I took his place and no one was the wiser. I blamed my gait on the lingering effects of the illness and the crook in my nose on a fall I faked."

"What about his body?" Nat asked, once again glancing around the room. "Surely someone noticed a dead body or at least the smell?"

"Ha! Around these quarters? Hardly." Benedict gave her an unabashed look. "I'm not an idiot, Sister. I did dispose of the body eventually. The residents of the Rewall were quite helpful in that regard."

"What did you make them do?" Her stomach lurched at the memory of the dead Rewall resident on the Chemist's exam table.

"Since I assumed the Chemist's identity, I've been busy, Sister, but wary. I couldn't go handing out daisies to everyone and proclaiming Emilia's and Estos' imminent return now, could I? I had to placate Mudug, get him to leave me alone."

"What do Rewall residents have anything to do with that?"

"They've had everything to do with it." He gave her a shrewd look. "I've kept up the Chemist's practice of kidnapping people from the Rewall. But when the guards bring them here, I enlist their services. They've aided me in both tricking Mudug and forming a rebel movement in the Rewall. I demonstrated my breakthrough riven antidote against the Nala venom on three of them with Mudug watching from behind a screen. He's received an infusion each week and believes he's completely protected against the Nala."

"But he's not," Nat said, thinking of the meldon compound.

"No, he's not." Benedict smiled. His crooked teeth gleamed in the light of the fire. "Not in the least. It's all a fake. But he thinks he is." He chuckled.

"What about your test subjects?" Nat asked, warming a little to the Hermit's tactics.

"They returned to the Rewall. There's an entire movement there just waiting for word that it's time to strike against the usurper's regime. Each of them also carted off certain larger specimens in need of disposal and deposited them in the refuse pit in the Rewall." Benedict gave her a knowing look.

"Meaning the Chemist." The notion of Benedict cutting up his brother's body and sending it off in pieces sent waves of nausea through Nat.

"Yes," Benedict replied. "Now that the Chemist is gone, I have Mudug in my sights. Tell me, Sister: Are Emilia, Estos, and the rebels to take Rustbrook soon? The city feels on edge, ready to lash out against Mudug after years of his abuse."

Nat picked up her cup and sipped from it, thankful she tasted nothing sweet like honey, and considered what to tell him. "They will be here in a few days," she responded.

Benedict slapped his hands together, and his expression turned from dour to excited. "Blessed news," he said gleefully. "Emilia will restore balance to Fourline, bring the Houses back, divest the Nala of control . . ."

Emilia will be lucky if she can tie her bootlaces without flipping out, Nat thought as she listened to Benedict prattle on about the queen's future accomplishments.

"Defeating the Nala and restoring balance will take more than one person," Nat interrupted. Sister Hanni's surprising revelation about the Predictions that one Sister would bring down the Nala came to mind. "No single person can do that," she said more to herself than Benedict.

"Yes, Estos of course will be at her side. But he is still not much older than a boy, and his proclivity toward the duozi will do nothing to heal this country." *Here we go,* Nat thought, steeling herself as Benedict launched into a tirade. "The duozi will fester in our society if not rooted out and sent away. Estos' mistaken belief that half-breeds can live among us will inhibit Fourline from returning to its former glory. It is Emilia who must lead the people back into the balance and the light."

His old invective grated against Nat. How many times had she thought of Benedict's hateful words when she'd been searching for a cure?

"Benedict, the duozi have suffered more than anyone under Mudug's control. Integration and acceptance are what they deserve, not a perpetuation of prejudice."

Benedict pinched his thin lips together and Nat let out a long breath, knowing her words fell on deaf ears.

"All will play out as it should." Benedict brushed off her comment and poured more steaming water into his cup. "Now, a more pressing question is what to do with you. I'd all but forgotten the Chemist put a reward on your head before he met his deserved fate. It was a stroke of luck that guard happened upon me in my garden without anyone else around, or we would not be having this conversation." He settled back on the pouf and rubbed his chin. "I don't believe Mudug would turn you over to the Nalaide again, since she failed to aid him as promised after Malorin delivered you to her door." His wiry eyebrows rose as he sipped his tea.

"Mudug knows Malorin found me and turned me over?" Nat scowled at the mention of the Sister's name.

"Oh yes, she brought your sword to him." He gave her a deprecating look. "Mudug almost refused to believe her. A Warrior Sister willingly relinquishing her sword?"

"I didn't know who Malorin was," Nat said, glaring at the Hermit. "But I promise you, if I meet her again, she'll lose more than her sword. I have a score to settle."

"Ho-ho, the fringer's grown a spine." His eyes narrowed. "Don't underestimate Malorin. She's killed more than her share of Sisters. Developed that little contraption holding your orb as well." He gestured to the cage. "The Chemist mentioned Malorin frequently in his journals," he continued. "She had a part in creating the tracking orbs that you destroyed and pulling the memories from Emilia." He stared past Nat at the far corner of the room. She followed his gaze. A narrow door was set into the wall. Nat's eyes widened as she realized the Chemist had access to Emilia's old cell from this room. "According to the journals, Malorin was merciless to Emilia the first several years the Chemist held her."

"That must be why Emilia doesn't seem overly fond of the Emissary emblem," Nat said, remembering the queen's violent response to the bird symbols after they'd rescued her.

"I'm not surprised. Malorin has a fascination with the queen and pesters me to see her, even more so than Mudug. I am relieved to hear your news that the rebels will arrive soon. I wasn't sure how much longer I could keep up the ruse that Emilia was still the Chemist's captive." He frowned. "Malorin is due back here soon. Mudug sent her south to see if she could pacify the Nala. Something's riled them up, and they are attacking Mudug's posts near Rim Town. We'd best figure out where to hide you in the event she shows up before the rebels arrive."

"I can handle Malorin." Nat bristled and glanced down at her bandaged arm.

"Like you handled her before? No, Sister. I think not. Now is not the time for confrontation. Wait until the rebels hold the city. I believe the residents will turn in their favor quickly, but we mustn't take a chance until that time." Benedict scratched his wig.

"What about hiding at Matilda and Mervin's?" Nat suggested. "I'd be out of the castle."

"A possibility, but how to get you there? I've had no contact with either of them. I doubt they or Gennes' rebels know I've taken the Chemist's place." A thoughtful look crossed his face. "I do have a little snitch in the kitchen who's been running messages for me after I freed her brother from the Rewall. I could get some clothes and baskets from her. If you can find your way through the Sister tunnels out of the castle, you'd look just like a scullery maid going to market. Yes, that might work. I certainly can't keep you here, too many unwelcome visitors," he grumbled. "I'll see to it now." He stood and limped toward the door. He adjusted his wig in front of a cloudy square mirror, pulled his long robe from a hook, and draped it over his shoulders.

A sharp rap on the door startled Benedict and sent him tripping backward over his trailing robe. Nat leapt from her chair, catching him before he crashed to the floor.

"Chemist! Open up." A familiar female voice spoke in a harsh, loud voice.

Benedict, cradled in Nat's arms, turned his head, and a look of fear settled over his features. "Malorin," he mouthed.

CHAPTER THIRTY

The sharp rap repeated, sounding like an angry woodpecker drilling into the door. Nat lifted Benedict to his feet. He pivoted the moment he was standing upright and herded her to the corner of the room.

"Stay in here," he whispered as he set his hand on the knob of the narrow entrance leading to Emilia's old cell. It opened with a creak.

"No." Rage simmered in Nat as she thought of Malorin on the other side of the Chemist's door. "I want to—"

"Do not show your face," Benedict interrupted and pushed her into the cell. "I'll get rid of Malorin." He waved her in with a frantic motion of his arm. The door swung shut, but Nat stuck her foot against it before it completely closed. She peered through the crack and listened to Benedict's footsteps.

"Took you long enough, Chemist." Nat's anger flamed at the sound of Malorin's voice.

Benedict let out a wheezing cough. "I was in with the queen," he lied through gasping breaths.

"Odd, you look as if you were on your way out." Malorin's voice held a hint of suspicion. Nat moved into the shadows of the cell, her heart pounding as she looked around for something to use as a weapon.

"That was my intent. I was merely administering another sedative before leaving," Benedict said tersely.

"Good, Mudug wants both of us in his chambers immediately. He's preparing to lead his guard south to the outpost in the bluff above Ballew." Malorin strode into Nat's line of view. Her black robe whipped against the edge of a chair.

"Why? I've been told all rebel activity has been north and west of here," Benedict drawled, falling back into the Chemist's pattern of speech.

"The Nala are reneging on all our agreements," Malorin fumed. "They've attacked almost all our outposts in the south. Soldiers on the merchant road I just traveled advised me of attacks not far from Ballew. I spoke with a soldier I sent to deliver more children to placate the Nala. He was bitten, Chemist, bitten by the creatures!" She leaned over the chair. "He informed me the Nala claim we are holding something the Nalaide wants. I assume it's that Warrior Sister." Malorin's expression hardened.

It's working, Nat thought, not in the least sorry for the soldier. *The Nalaide's attacking Mudug's men.*

"Your negotiating techniques with the Nala failed, Malorin?" Benedict asked in a deprecating tone.

"None of this is my doing. Those creatures let that Sister escape. I don't understand why they think we have her." A moment of silence followed. "Where did you get that?" Malorin's voice was as sharp as a sliver of ice.

"What?" Nat followed Malorin's finger as she pointed at the cage containing her orb that lay in a corner of the room.

My orb!

"Oh, the cage." Benedict scowled, feigning irritation. "A soldier delivered it, claiming it was the Warrior Sister's and demanding the bounty I offered." He sneered.

Nat felt a surge of hatred as she watched Malorin lift the cage and shake it violently. "Looks as if it's dead." Her gaze swept from the cage to Benedict. "Did the guard say what became of the Sister?"

"He said he killed her, but I'm sure he's lying. Probably picked that orb up while scavenging the Houses."

"No." Malorin examined the orb through the bars. "I recognize this orb. It's hers. It's the Sister's." She turned the cage over and the orb rolled against the bars. Nat clenched her fists at her side. "This gives me an idea." She tapped the cage. "The Nalaide must be desperate to have the Sister if she's sending her scourge to attack southern outposts. She knows Mudug will retaliate. If we offer this as proof that the Sister is dead, the Nalaide may temporarily come back into our fold. We still need the Nala to aid us against a rebel attack."

She shook the cage again and rage clouded Nat's mind. She thrust the door open and lunged for Malorin's legs. The startled Sister dropped the cage. Nat plowed into her shins, sending Malorin toppling to the side and crashing into one of the Chemist's ornate tables. Teacups clattered onto her head and chest, spilling their lukewarm liquid. Nat crawled quickly over the Sister, wrapped her arm tightly behind Malorin's neck, and pinned her to the ground.

"Surprised to see me?" she said an inch from Malorin's wet face.

"What are you doing?" Benedict clutched his hands to the side of his head and his wig went askew. Malorin gave him a desperate look. Nat shifted onto her side, ground her weight into Malorin's chest, and locked her arms, squeezing the Sister's neck tightly with her wounded arm.

"It's called payback. Get me a rope and a piece of cloth," Nat barked at Benedict while keeping her eyes locked on Malorin. Her arm burned, but she ignored the pain and squeezed harder as the traitor struggled beneath her. The Hermit cursed and ripped open a drawer in an ornate bureau. Garments fell to the ground as he rummaged in its depths and retrieved a thin coil of rope braided tightly around wire. He tossed it to Nat.

"Chemist, stop her," Malorin said, gasping for breath.

"This was not well thought out, Sister," Benedict said, ignoring Malorin. He brought over the cloth. "She'll be missed."

"You traitor!" Malorin said, wheezing, when Benedict offered her no aid. She thrashed under Nat, but Nat tightened her grip.

"Shut up!" Nat yelled. "So help me if I had my sword right now! Do you have any idea what you did to me by turning me over to the Nala? What you did to Emilia?" Anger poured from her. "You're the traitor, a traitor to every one of those children bitten by the Nala, every one of the Sisters you betrayed by working with Mudug. A traitor to your own queen, your own people."

Malorin turned from red to white. "All for the greater good!" she said, twisting her head away from Nat.

"Greater good? Mudug's used the Nala to create a slave population for him. That's your greater good?" Malorin's eyes bulged. "Estos and Emilia are returning, Malorin. You're done, do you hear me? Done!"

"Never." Malorin gasped for breath as Nat squeezed even harder. "Emilia's half-dead, and Estos is nothing more than a ghost."

"Shove the cloth in her mouth. I'm sick of listening to her," Nat ordered Benedict. He ripped the fabric and balled up a strip. Malorin clamped her lips shut, but Benedict plugged her nose. The moment her lips parted for a breath, he jammed the wad of fabric into her mouth and wrapped the rope quickly around her head to hold it in place. He sliced the end with a stubby blade produced from the folds of his robe. Nat released her grip, grasped Malorin's shoulder, and flipped her onto her stomach. Malorin's orb rolled out from underneath her robe.

"Cover her orb!" Nat yelled. Benedict landed on the sphere, slamming it into the ground. His eyes crossed as the breath rushed out of his lungs from the impact.

"You're wrong about Emilia and Estos, Sister." Nat quickly jerked her adversary's hands together and bound them in place, wrapping the cord tightly around her wrists. Malorin shook her head furiously and screamed out muffled curses. Nat yanked her to her feet, removed her cloak, and patted her down. A short sword and dagger clattered to the floor.

"Would you hurry?" Benedict was flushing red from the strain of holding Malorin's orb to the ground. Nat shoved her headfirst into the cell. She grabbed an empty shackle secured by a chain to the wall and locked Malorin's leg into place.

Nat's own orb was rattling in the cage when she burst back into the room. She retrieved the key and opened the tiny lock. The cage door sprang open and her orb flew free. Nat carried the cage over to Benedict. His body jerked a few inches in different directions as Malorin's orb strained to lift him off the ground.

"Careful now," Nat cautioned. She positioned the cage near Benedict and held the cage door open. Malorin's orb shot out from beneath him into the cage, and she slammed the door, almost losing a finger. The orb ricocheted off the bars.

"Well, Sister," Benedict panted. He leaned heavily against the back of a chair. "That was by far the stupidest thing you could have done. Mudug's expecting both of us. What am I supposed to do?" he whined.

"Do you think I was going to let her walk out of here with my orb?" Nat's sphere settled in her hand. "And maybe try 'thank you' instead of insulting me. At least Malorin's not in a position to cause any more problems."

Benedict glared at her. "That doesn't help me with Mudug, Sister."

Nat waved her hand in the air. "You'll think of something. Tell Mudug that Malorin received a message on your way to see him. She wouldn't tell you what it said and just took off without another word."

"Oh, he'll believe that," Benedict grumbled and adjusted his cloak.

Nat straightened his wig. "While you're at it, see if you can get my sword back from him."

"And how am I to do that?" he asked, the color in his cheeks rising.

"Charm him," Nat said and shoved him out the door.

When Benedict returned two hours later, he bustled through the door with a large basket. He tossed Nat's sword onto his bed.

"We both have luck on our side, Sister. I fed Mudug some gibberish about using your sword to track you. Complete bollocks, but he bought it. He's willing to grasp at anything right now. His chambers were in chaos—soldiers streaming in and out, him yelling orders. He hardly acknowledged my presence. The Nala are attacking the southern towns, and he has half his men spread across the north right now trying to retake the mines the rebels took weeks ago. His remaining battalion is on the move to secure the outpost in the bluff above Ballew. Mudug's preparing to join them tonight. He thinks the Nala may converge on Rustbrook and is scampering away to safer ground."

Nat listened, amazed by the turn of events.

"I heard of another disaster in the making just as I was leaving that sent Mudug completely over the edge. It seems there's a bit of a problem with the dam at the base of the Keyen Mountains that controls the flow of the Rust River. The floodgates are apparently malfunctioning. Rustbrook will be desperately low on water in a few days. He was scrambling to find any men to send into the mountains to correct the problem before leaving. The capital will be almost completely empty of soldiers by morning."

A wide smile broke over Nat's face.

"I see that the news isn't a surprise to you." Benedict thrust the basket into her arms. "Put those on. I need you out of these quarters, Sister. Mudug's sending a courier for extra vials of my fake antidote to the Nala's venom. I'll have enough on my hands keeping Malorin quiet without you underfoot to foul up something."

Nat ignored the Hermit's nasty glare and strapped her sword to her belt. The feeling of the sheath against her leg brought another smile to her face. Her orb glowed above her head as she rummaged through the basket and draped a tattered shawl over her head and shoulders.

"If you take the Sister passage under the tapestry and stay to the left, it leads to the carriage house. I'll make sure the way is clear." Benedict limped to the door, not hiding his anxiety.

"You certain you don't want any help with Malorin before I go?" Nat asked, feeling guilty for putting the Hermit at risk.

"No." Benedict shook his head with vigor. "I will handle her. My brother left a plentiful store of sedatives." He cracked the door and motioned for Nat to follow. She slipped out after him, and they walked in the darkness through the garden. Benedict motioned for her to remain behind a trellis and hobbled through the door leading to the hallway where Hamil had tackled her. His hand appeared from behind the door, waving in her direction. Nat sidled up next to him and peered down the empty hallway.

"Avoid capture, Sister," Benedict warned. "We are too close to victory now."

"You, too," Nat replied, feeling an odd affection for the Hermit. "You, too," she whispered once more, then padded down the hall and slipped behind the tapestry.

CHAPTER
THIRTY-ONE

The dark lanes of Rustbrook were eerily quiet. Nat dashed past a frozen fountain occupying the heart of the empty square. Her basket caught on a broken fence post as she ran down an adjacent alley. Cursing under her breath, she tucked the basket behind a handcart. It had already caused her enough headaches in the Sister passage. After fumbling into a room of sleeping servants from a tunnel she'd thought led to the castle's carriage house, Nat had knocked over a spindly-legged table. It had come within an inch of landing on a sleeping housemaid before Nat had caught it.

She glanced down the empty alley at the sheen covering the broken cobblestones. The fine, cold rain had turned to sleet, coating the uneven alley with a slick glaze. She instinctively curled her hand around the hilt of her sword. The touch of the metal made her think of Malorin and her overwhelming desire to see the Sister suffer, to make her experience the pain and misery she'd caused. If she'd had her sword when she'd attacked Malorin, would she have meted out her own angry revenge like Benedict had on his brother?

I think I understand Emilia's fixated rage on the Chemist, Nat realized as she considered how overcome with anger she'd been in that moment.

The similarities between her outbursts and the queen's episodes were too close for comfort. She paused behind the bare branches of a tree jutting into the alley, realizing anger and impatience had directed so many of her recent actions both in her world and this one. She shook her head and thought of the price she had paid for her impatience and rage: the wound on her arm and the fractured relationship with her sister. Barba had said over and over that her mind was her greatest asset, but Nat felt like her growing instinct for retribution was overtaking her rational thought. *You need to keep it under control. You've got too many challenges ahead to let anger rule you.*

A faint orange light spilled out onto a lane at the end of the alley. Figures moved behind the grimy window of a tavern. The signs of life brought Nat's attention back to the pressing need to find Matilda and Mervin's bookshop. She let out a relieved breath as she read the words "Wesdrono Street" on a weathered sign affixed to the upper corner of the tavern's exterior. She peered down the street before inching into the lane. The tavern door burst open, and Nat retreated into the shadows before anyone could see her. A cold rage flowed through her when she saw Fergus, Larkem, and Hamil step out of the doorway. They wore heavy cloaks hiding their guard's uniforms. The door slammed shut behind them, silencing the chorus of voices inside.

In the damp cold of the night, Hamil stamped his feet and addressed the others. "We should leave now, like the Chemist said. Were you listening to any of the talk in there?" He jerked his thumb toward the tavern entrance. "Either the rebels or the Nala will be at Rustbrook's gates soon, and those weren't just grumblings I heard. If the rebels show up, it sounds like the city will hoist Mudug's arse before the rebels even lay a hand on him."

"Tide's definitely turning against Mudug," Fergus agreed. "But I'm not leaving Rustbrook until I get my sister and her family out of the Rewall slum."

The men crossed the street, coming close to Nat's hiding spot. She quietly unsheathed her sword, feeling the familiar surge of anger when her gaze landed on Larkem.

"It's no time to be wearing a blue uniform in this city for certain." Larkem tossed a bag of coins into the air. "If we stick around, chances are we'll be found out and pressed back into service to fight the creatures, the rebels, or the city's people." He placed his hand on Fergus' arm. "I understand your need to stay here, but I'm leaving tonight. Take care and get as far away as you can once you've bought your sister back." He slapped the large man on the shoulder.

"And what about me?" Hamil whined.

"Bribe yourself onto a boat heading to Daub Town and find your beloved. You have more than enough money." Larkem shrugged. "Best of luck, fellows, in avoiding the Nala, the guard, and the rebels." He let out a little chuckle and disappeared down the gloomy street.

"You can stay with me if you like," Fergus offered.

Hamil shook his head. "No, he's right. Daub Town will be a sure sight safer than Rustbrook if what we heard in the tavern is true. Come with me," he urged.

It was Fergus' turn to shake his head. "I can't leave my sister."

Hamil squared his shoulders and extended his hand to Fergus. "Then luck be with you and your sister." He bobbed his head and took off down Wesdrono Street in the direction of the docks.

Fergus stared uncertainly after the little man. Nat felt a stirring of sympathy as she watched her former captor's massive shoulders slump. He was risking his life by staying in Rustbrook to save his sister. Cal's face flashed in her mind, and she knew she'd make the same decision. After a moment, Fergus stroked his black beard, turned, and walked right in front of Nat. She flicked her sword up so the tip pressed into the folds of skin hanging from his neck.

"Hello, Fergus," she whispered as she motioned for him to move farther into the alley, away from the light and noise of the tavern.

"Sis-sister. The Chemist—"

"Shame he didn't take you up on your offer to bind me up. I turned out to be a little too slippery, even for the Chemist," Nat lied, hoping she looked menacing even though she had no intention of hurting the man.

He drained of color and held his hands in the air. "Don't kill me, too."

Nat put her finger to her lips, hushing him. "I won't, unless you do something stupid. Take that handcart at the end of the alley and fill it with garbage. You'll get past Mudug's guards stationed at the gates of the Rewall without a fight if they think you're delivering refuse to the Rewall pit." She pulled her sword back a few inches.

Fergus' nervous gaze moved from the sharp blade to Nat's eyes.

"I have a sister, too," Nat said. "I'd do anything to get her out if she were in the Rewall." She paused, hoping her words would make him receptive to her request. "And in exchange for letting you go, I need a favor." Fergus' brow wrinkled. "When you reach the Rewall, tell as many of the residents as you can to ready themselves for a fight to take out the guards. Do as I ask and I'll make sure the rebels know to spare you, because they are coming, Fergus. Mudug's reign is nearing its end," she whispered. His eyes grew wide. Nat lifted the sword again. "But if you say a word to any other guard, I'll see to it that the rebels hunt you down. And trust me, they're not the forgiving type," she threatened and lowered her blade. "Now go."

Fergus stumbled down the alley. Nat watched him run, grab the handcart, and roll it past the fountain. She sheathed her sword and quickly crossed the street, hoping she hadn't pressed her luck by trusting the man. *He'll do what I asked,* she assured herself, and her trust felt like a little ray of light cutting through all the anger and fear inside her.

She jogged down the lane, looking for the familiar gate and trees obscuring Matilda and Mervin's backyard. She slipped through the gate and padded over the stone path leading to the back entrance of the bookshop. The tension in her body ebbed when she opened the shop's back door.

A soft light burned from the circular stairs concealed behind the counter. Nat heard muffled voices, then quick footsteps. Mervin's head appeared. The light highlighted his long, angular jaw, but his eyes were in shadow.

"You always seem to arrive a little late, Sister," Mervin said as if expecting to see her.

"Who is it, Mervin?" Matilda's voice rose from the base of the stairs.

"Someone Soris will be happy to see." Mervin smiled, and Nat's heart leapt as she heard Soris anxiously calling her name. She raced down the stairs, brushing past Mervin's tall frame, and crashed past Matilda. She flung herself into Soris' arms, burying her head in his chest. His fingers eased the tight muscles in her back, releasing the remaining tension in her body.

"You're wounded." Soris tilted up her chin and examined the cut on her forehead. His fingers brushed over her swollen lips.

"Just some scrapes," she lied, not wanting him to worry. She pressed her head to his chest and clutched the back of his tunic. "I don't think I can let you go," she whispered as she felt his breath on her hair.

"You will have to at some point, Sister," a female voice said.

Nat's eyes popped open. Luriel stood next to Soris, her white-blonde hair and contrasting blue skin shining under the room's lights.

"Natalie." Soris slid his arm around her waist and stepped to the side. "You've met Luriel Evers, leader of the duozi rebels we helped free from Mudug's mines."

Nat smiled at her. Luriel leaned against the stair rail and crossed her arms. "Yes, we've met, but didn't have much of a chance to speak, especially since the good Sister managed to get herself kidnapped."

Nat's smile disappeared.

CHAPTER
THIRTY-TWO

After brushing off Soris' repeated concern over her battered appearance, Nat listened, slightly shocked, to his story of how easily Estos and the others had taken the dam and northern outposts. Matilda pressed a plate of food into her hands. Nat grabbed a slice of bread stacked with a thick cut of meat. Her stomach grumbled as she took a huge bite. Soris watched her with an amused smile as she attacked the food.

"I don't understand how you were able to move so quickly," she said after swallowing her mouthful.

"We used gunnels as transport," Soris answered with a wicked smile.

"You rode gunnels?" Nat thought of the wild bearlike creatures who'd attacked the Nala last spring. "I didn't think Nala or duozi could control gunnels like other predators." Seeing Luriel's concave Nala eyes fixed upon Soris, Nat inched possessively closer to him.

"You can't if you *try* to control them. It's more a matter of persuasion with a gunnel," Luriel responded, taking a sip from her teacup.

"How do you persuade a gunnel?"

"You'd be amazed at what a creature will do if you convince it you can kill it." Luriel balanced the delicate cup on her knee.

Nat's appetite vanished and she set her plate on a bench.

"Luriel had an entire pack waiting to take us to the dam." Soris slid his arm behind Nat's shoulder and she relaxed. "We made it there in half the time we expected. The gunnels jumped the rock crevices and climbed up the slopes like they were nothing more than anthills." He waved his free hand in the air.

"I'm sure Andris loved that. I can't imagine he was too happy to see Emilia on a gunnel." Nat caught Matilda's reproving expression. At least someone else in the room saw the folly in using gunnels as transport.

"Emilia had no problem once she saw they were safe to ride," Soris assured her. "She and Calpurnia rode side by side."

"You put my sister on a gunnel? What were you thinking?"

"We couldn't very well leave her behind," Soris replied. "Cassandra and I looked after her. No harm came to her, Natalie. She's safe outside the city now." He tightened his hold around her shoulders, and she let go of some of her concern.

"I knew you'd take care of her." She glanced at the floor. "It's just that I've already put her at so much risk."

"Calpurnia was quite willing to ride the animals. I sensed no hesitation on her part." Luriel glanced back and forth between them.

"She doesn't know any better," Nat said, struggling to find the words to explain the protectiveness she felt toward her sister.

Soris removed his arm from her shoulder and joined Luriel. "The good news is you should see her soon. Since we were able to travel so quickly, the attack on Rustbrook has been moved up. Estos and the others will rendezvous with Gennes north of the city in the next hour. They will attack at first light."

"What? At first light?"

"Yes." Soris gave her a puzzled look. "Why are you upset?"

Frustrated, Nat shook her head and thought of the Hermit. *He'll be stuck in the castle during the attack.* "I could have used that information a few hours ago." She stood, and a little gasp escaped her lips from the pain of the bruises covering her body.

Soris moved to her side to help her stand. "Natalie, what's wrong?"

"I'm fine. Just a little stiff." Nat waved him off, not wanting to share that her muscles ached from Larkem's multiple beatings.

"Then sit down and rest."

She ignored the concerned look in his eyes. "No, I need to return to the castle to warn Benedict. He doesn't know the rebels are coming so soon. If he gets caught up in a fight at the castle, someone may mistake him for the Chemist."

"Benedict's alive?" A sour expression crossed Soris' face at the mention of the Hermit's name.

"Yes, he's alive." She took a deep breath and launched into her story about all that had transpired after Larkem and the others had delivered her to Benedict.

"You told Benedict the rebels were coming?" Soris pressed his fist into his open palm. "He deserted us, Natalie. Don't you remember? No one's heard anything from him since we rescued Emilia. How do you know he's not under Mudug's control?"

"He's been pretending to be the Chemist this entire time, fooling Mudug with a placebo antidote to the Nala venom, lying about Emilia still being captive, and establishing a rebel movement in the Rewall." Soris continued to regard her with a look of disbelief. "I know you don't like him, Soris, and you know he's no favorite of mine, but he's done everything he can to undercut Mudug and protect the Rewall residents. And he saved me."

Unswayed, Soris pressed on. "Benedict's interest in protecting the Rewall residents won't extend to the duozi. What did he say when you told him the duozi had joined the rebellion?"

"I didn't tell him," she admitted, feeling guilty. "He wanted to know anything I could share about Emilia. I didn't have time to reveal much else." She knew the excuse sounded pathetic.

"What do you think this Benedict will do when my duozi rebels show up in the city with Estos and Gennes' men?" Luriel broke in. Her question irritated Nat.

"He'll keep his oath to Emilia and do whatever he can to secure the regency for both her and Estos," Mervin interrupted in a low voice.

"Benedict's prejudice toward the duozi may not matter much longer, anyway," Nat added, thinking of her possible cure.

"Why not?" Luriel asked. "If he's close to Emilia, anything he says could influence her."

"It may not matter, because I think I found—" Nat stopped mid-sentence. Soris' eyes were bulging. He mouthed "no." "B-because Estos won't tolerate any prejudice toward the duozi," she said, wondering why he didn't want her to mention her discovery. Luriel snorted.

"You seem to lack faith in Estos," Matilda said to Luriel, breaking the silence she had kept while listening to Nat. Her dark eyes searched the rebel's angry expression.

"Faith? I was kidnapped from Rim Town at seventeen by Mudug's guards, taken to the Nala to be transformed into a duozi, and sent to work in Mudug's mines. I lost faith a long time ago, Matilda. Now revenge is all that matters to me. If Estos offers me a way to even my score with Mudug and the Nala, then I'll follow him willingly. But Estos' promises of future tolerance are meaningless to me. He may have taken a liking to a duozi, but what does that mean for the rest of us?"

"Building up Fourline again will require more than settling scores," Nat said. Her skin prickled at Luriel's description of Estos and Annin's bond.

"I want Mudug and the Nala dead. I couldn't care less about Fourline. I'll leave the rebuilding to your kind, Sister, since the Houses did nothing to keep Fourline from crumbling in the first place."

Luriel's words were like the sting of a wasp. "You're dead wrong," Nat quickly retorted. She thought of Cassandra, Rory, Barba, Ethet,

Ethes, and all the other Sisters who had sacrificed so much to save Fourline.

An amused expression played over Luriel's face. "Am I? What have any of the Sisters, including you, done to really help us?"

"Luriel, that's enough. Natalie's sacrificed more than you can know to help us, to help all the duozi." Soris placed his hand on Nat's shoulder, and she tensed, not wanting anyone to touch her.

Luriel ignored Soris' rebuke and let out a sharp, humorless laugh. "Yes, I am sure the Warrior Sister's guilt about letting a Nala bite you has left her with a heavy burden. I'm not surprised she shows an attachment to you and other duozi. Shame is a hotbed of strong emotions."

"That was out of line, Luriel." Soris glowered.

Nat's hands had started to shake. She struggled to keep her anger under control. Breaking eye contact with Luriel, she pushed the discomfiting question of why Soris had told Luriel about her failure to protect him aside and let the anger flow out of her. *What good will it do to fight with her?* Benedict, and more specifically what to do about him, was the critical problem she needed to solve now.

"Benedict told me Mudug's on his way out of the city, heading for the outpost in the bluffs above Ballew." Feeling tight with emotion, Nat cleared her throat and continued, "Matilda, are you still a light bearer?" Matilda nodded. "Can you confirm tonight whether Mudug's left Rustbrook?" Nat would go regardless, but the return trip to the castle to get Benedict would be much safer without Mudug and his guards, and waiting a short time to see what Matilda could learn might serve her well.

Matilda's normally sharp expression softened. "Yes. I know where to inquire. I'll leave immediately."

Nat turned to Soris. "You should try to contact Annin and the other duozi with Estos." She spoke quickly, glossing over the tension that lingered from the earlier conversation. "If you dream-speak with Annin, she can inform Estos about Mudug's movements before the attack. Gennes and Estos may want to send the Sisters and a band of rebels after Mudug if he really has left Rustbrook." She paused. "She can tell him about Benedict, too." Soris rolled his eyes, and Nat felt a wave of aggravation.

"Use Annin's old room upstairs," Matilda offered. "It's quiet if you'd prefer to attempt to reach her dream space without us around."

"I'm certain Soris and I can manage even with distractions, but if a quiet place is available away from discussions of ill-conceived alliances, and an overemotional Sister, I'll take it." Luriel cast a scornful look Nat's way, then climbed the stairs after Matilda.

Nat stared at a box of dusty books, smothering her desire to chase after the rebel and punch her in the mouth. Soris shifted closer to her and placed a hand on her back.

"Sister." Mervin's gaze settled on Nat. "Why don't you rest here? You look as if you could use some quiet yourself. I'll have Matilda wake you when she returns with any word of Mudug's movements."

"I don't need any rest, Mervin," Nat said, hiding a yawn under her hand. The last thing she wanted to deal with was fending off the Nalaide if she followed her into her dreams again. She'd avoid sleep as long as she could.

Mervin's bangs flopped into his eyes when he nodded. He climbed the stairs, leaving Nat and Soris alone.

"Nat—"

"I can't believe you'd tell someone like that . . . Why did you tell her about what happened to you at the river?" The old guilt she carried from not protecting Soris from the Nala resurfaced.

"That's what's upsetting you?" Soris gave her an incredulous look.

"One of the many things."

"I did it because all the duozi we rescued from the mines shared their stories with me. I didn't intend for anyone to take it as a condemnation of you."

"Well, Luriel certainly did," she replied, feeling a tinge of betrayal.

"Natalie, don't take her demeanor personally. She's understandably callous and jaded because of her past. She and the other duozi have lived so long without any hope."

"Then why didn't you want me to say anything about my discovery? There's hope in a possible cure, and fighting for hope is a sure sight better than fighting for revenge," she said, unable to keep the hurt out of her voice.

He held up his hands. "Until we know for certain the Sisters can use your discovery to actually cure the duozi, I don't think we should tell them. It would be cruel to dangle the possibility of a cure in front of someone who's suffered so much only to have it not work the way you believe it will."

Nat searched his face and read the doubt in his expression. "You don't believe my discovery will lead to a cure, do you?"

Soris averted his eyes. "It's . . . it's too much to hope for, Natalie. I think you understand?" He looked up and she read the reluctance in his eyes.

"I trusted you enough to show you my heart. Why won't you trust me and believe in me enough to hope for the impossible?"

"I've trusted you since the moment I met you, Natalie." He gripped the stairwell. "But life's taught me to have little belief in the impossible." He walked up the stairs, leaving her alone.

CHAPTER
THIRTY-THREE

Too much to hope for? Nat slouched against the bench, waiting for Matilda's return. Her orb spun above her head, then stilled its movement. *A cure is all I've been hoping for.* She closed her eyes and lowered her head into her hands. Cal, Benedict, the Nalaide, the battle for Rustbrook, and now Soris' doubts . . . Her list of concerns seemed to double every time she turned around.

"What a mess," she whispered, feeling the heavy weight of her emotions pressing down on her.

"Indeed."

Nat's head snapped up.

Luriel descended the bottom step and walked into the room. "Has Matilda returned?" she asked. Her indifferent expression nettled Nat like a needle pricking her skin.

"No." Nat stood and distanced herself from her. "She may be gone awhile yet." *So why don't you go away?* Luriel was the last person she wanted to be near.

"See that she finds me when she returns. Soris is searching for Annin's dream space, but it's pointless for me to reach out to my people

until we know if there's any truth to what you said about Mudug."
Luriel shifted her gaze away from Nat, and her Nala eyes contracted.

"Benedict had no reason to lie to me." Nat held her arms tightly at
her sides. *Don't let her goad you.*

"So you think."

Nat felt a little tickle behind her ear and brushed at her hair. A
coin-sized spider scurried across her hand as she swept it off. It fell to
the floor and ran in Luriel's direction, then ceased its scurrying and
froze in place between them. When Nat looked up, Luriel wore an
unpleasant smile.

You did that. Nat's orb floated next to her, spinning quickly. She
imagined her orb slamming into Luriel's mouth as it had the Nalaide's,
but pushed the image out of her mind when the orb jerked toward the
duozi.

"Not afraid of spiders, are you?" Luriel asked, gesturing to the
arachnid.

Nat took a step forward. The spider crunched under her boot.
"No."

"How fortunate." Luriel dropped her gaze to Nat's boot. "Since
there are so many in the cracks and crevices of this building." Her eyes
glimmered in the light of Nat's orb.

"Are you threatening me?" Nat narrowed her eyes, wondering at
her motivation.

"No, merely a friendly warning." She observed Nat's orb pulsing erratically and retreated up a few stairs. She paused. "I'm curious,
Sister," she said without looking at her. "You seem capable of wiggling
out of each mess you make. Why, then, is Soris so concerned about your
safety? It certainly weighs on him, like an obligation he can't shake." Not
waiting for an answer, Luriel climbed the remaining stairs.

Every muscle in Nat's body tensed as she listened to Luriel's footfalls
fade. *Obligation? Is that what he really thinks of me?* She stared at the
stacks and boxes of books that occupied the corners of the room. They

reminded her of the Wisdom House Library and sharing her memory with Soris. She leaned her head against the wall, feeling shaky, and thought of his parting words to her. *Who do you trust, Soris or Luriel?* she asked herself. Knowing the answer, she sighed and brought her orb into her palm. The heat from the sphere radiated into her wounded arm, providing warmth and solace.

A scraping sound pulled her from her thoughts. Nat walked toward the stairs and peered up the stairwell, hoping Luriel wasn't making a return appearance.

"It's me, Sister." Matilda's cloaked figure materialized at the top of the stairs.

"Any news?" Nat asked as she ascended, feeling her bruises with each step she took.

Matilda lowered the hood of her light-bearer cloak. "Mudug's gone from Rustbrook. He left a few hours ago for Ballew with a battalion and sent a company north to fix the dam. Only one small company remains here."

Mudug is heading right to the Nala. A sense of relief fluttered in Nat, calming her earlier agitation.

Matilda unhooked her cloak and continued in an excited voice, "I connected with two of Gennes' men scouting in the city. Estos and Gennes should reach the outskirts within the hour. The scouts expect Gennes to divert men to follow Mudug once Rustbrook is taken."

Nat ruminated over this last bit of information. If the Nalaide was following Mudug's movements, she might personally come after him at Ballew. *I may have a chance to attack and behead her outside her lair if I go with the rebels,* Nat realized. *But I need to get Benedict to safety first.*

"Any idea how the battle for the city will play out?" she asked, knowing she could reach the castle beforehand, but the Hermit's leg would hinder a quick escape, especially if the castle and city were in chaos.

A wide smile broke across Matilda's face. "The city will turn quickly. I witnessed two skirmishes between guards and residents on my return. The people are ready to stand up and fight to end Mudug's reign of corruption and violence." Her eyes gleamed in the light of Nat's orb.

"Good." A pent-up breath escaped Nat's lips. "I'll sneak back into the castle and get Benedict now before the rebels arrive so he's not caught up in the battle." She reached for her orb and fastened her cloak. "I'll send him here."

Matilda placed her hand on Nat's. "It would be wise to wait for Soris or Luriel to accompany you, Sister."

Nat frowned at the idea of either of them going with her. The Hermit had treated Soris and all other duozi with nothing less than outright suspicion and disdain. She wouldn't ask Soris to help her, and Luriel was completely out of the question. "With only one company in the castle, I shouldn't have a problem." Nat glanced at Matilda's hand resting over hers. "I can handle this one on my own."

Matilda pressed her thin lips together. "Likely you can, but should you? Soris will be plenty worried when he learns you've gone. You should wait until he's done dream-speaking with Annin," she said but released Nat's hand.

Nat suddenly remembered Andris' harsh explanation months ago of why he'd purposely left her behind and traveled to Rustbrook with Soris to rescue Emilia. "I don't want emotions to muddle this," she replied to Matilda, parroting a version of Andris' rebuke. "And I owe Benedict. If the real Chemist had been in his quarters when the soldiers delivered me, I'd be dead or in the hands of Mudug's guards on the road to the Nalaide right now. So no, I'm not interested in waiting," she said as politely as she could. "None of us are going to get through the next few days by putting our own needs over others'." She opened the door to the backyard.

"Your decision, Sister." Matilda stepped to the side and Nat slid out. "Good luck," she whispered.

"Thank you, Matilda."

In a haze of fatigue, Nat rushed through the empty lanes. Faint morning light broke over the horizon, and a flash of movement caught her eye. She ducked into the narrow foyer of a shop entrance just as two guards ran down the street in front of her. She peeked cautiously around the corner. The soldiers' blue coats flapped against their legs as they rounded an intersection leading to a nearby square.

A cry erupted. Nat stepped onto the street and sprinted in the direction the guards had taken. The unmistakable clang of swords clashing made her pick up her pace. A dozen rebel soldiers and a handful of citizens surrounded the two guards. The rebels cut the guards down and raced up an adjacent lane, followed by the citizens.

Nat chased after the band, fearful she'd be too late to get Benedict out now that the fight for Rustbrook was beginning. The cobblestones beneath her feet turned to gravel, and she ran like mad onto the wide arcing drive near the castle's carriage house. She slid to a halt as guards spilled from the side entrance of the castle and clashed with a throng of residents and rebels.

After one quick glance at the chaos surrounding the castle doors, Nat took off around the corner of the carriage house, scrambling to think of another way in. *I have to get Benedict out—now.* A rancid smell assaulted her as she ran. She followed her nose to the lane by the scullery and crept silently toward the single soldier guarding the entrance. Nat released her orb, and it walloped him on the side of the head. She hurtled over his slumped figure and through the open door, and burst into the darkened kitchen.

The sound of footsteps reverberated from the floor above the kitchen. She dashed up the stairs to the balcony and kicked open the door. It struck a guard fleeing from two rebels. He tottered on his feet and fell unconscious onto the thick carpet.

Skirting the rebels, Nat took off toward the opposite end of the hall. Her orb blazed a path in front of her. She skidded around corners and flew past surprised servants. Time blurred as her feet fell on the same steps where Larkem, Fergus, and Hamil had dragged her the day before. She jumped the last few steps of the stairwell. Dread seized Nat as the door to the courtyard came into view, hanging wide open and letting in the gray morning light. Yelling assaulted her ears.

Throwing caution to the wind, she bolted into the garden, crushing row after row of herbs under her feet. Andris appeared in front of the Chemist's quarters. He dodged the blow of a spiked morning star brandished by a guard, then blocked the sword of another inches before it struck his leg. Nat let out a guttural cry as she sped toward him with her sword raised and her orb flashing in front of her.

One of the guards spun around, momentarily stunned as Nat's orb flew toward him. The sphere crushed his nose, and blood gushed over his face.

"For once your timing is good!" Andris shouted as Nat raced to join him. He lunged forward with his sword, stabbing a guard through the abdomen.

"Is this what it takes for you to be happy to see me?" she yelled back and blocked a blow with her sword. She skipped to the side as the guard with the morning star flung the weapon in the direction of her face. Andris brought his sword down, slicing through the guard's uniform and cleaving into his bicep. A high-pitched scream and the sound of splintering wood erupted from the Chemist's quarters.

"Emilia's in the Chemist's chambers!" Andris lunged after the wounded soldier retreating toward the quarters. "Protect her!"

Nat backed away from the skirmish and ran into the Chemist's private chambers, where she'd last seen Benedict. Broken furniture and books were strewn across the floor. Benedict, curled up protectively near the hearth, clutched his hands to his chest. His eyes were wide with fear as he cringed away from Emilia. The queen's body shook violently as her serrated blade cut into his cheek.

"You! You thought you could break me, Chemist!" she screamed.

"Emilia, it's me," Benedict pleaded. He fumbled to pull the wig from his head.

"Emilia, don't!" cried Nat, but Emilia paid no heed and brought the sharp edge of the dagger across Benedict's throat.

"*No!*" screamed Nat. She charged at Emilia, knocking her to the side. The dagger hit the wood floor and spun around until the tip pierced the wall.

"Get off her, Natalie!" Andris yelled as he ran into the room. He yanked Nat violently away.

"Let go of me!" Nat wrenched herself free of Andris' grip and scrambled to the Hermit. He made a horrible gurgling sound as his eyes met hers. "Stay with me, Benedict." She fumbled with the edge of his cloak, pressing it against his throat. The Hermit's eyes glazed over, a wheeze escaped his lips, and his hands dropped lifeless to his lap. The life faded from his face.

Nat released the pressure on his neck and slumped to the side.

"Benedict?" Andris took a hesitant step toward the Hermit. Confusion clouded his features.

Nat's throat was so tight she could hardly breathe, but she leaned over and pulled his wig away, revealing the Hermit's short chestnut hair. Emilia crawled from the corner where Nat had pushed her.

"Hermit?" the queen said uncertainly as the rage faded from her eyes only to be replaced by a look of horror. Andris pulled Emilia to her feet and away from the Hermit's body. "What have I done?"

Nat brought her hand over Benedict's eyes, closing them forever. Her chest tightened as dozens of memories flashed in her mind. The Hermit's expression the first time she met him, when he opened the front door of his cottage with a grumbling welcome. Riding behind him on a donkey through the ruins of Ethet's Healing House, comparing herbs. His gleeful look when he and Gennes shared their plan for how Soris and Nat would break into the Chemist's quarters. His somber tone as he told her about his duozi sister and how he believed she'd lured their mother from the family. The poisonous expression he wore when he cursed Soris near the stable of the Emissary House. How he tricked the Rustbrook guards into believing he was the Chemist the day Andris, Soris, Annin, and Nat snuck into the castle to rescue Emilia. His joyful expression just the night before as he spoke of Emilia reclaiming the regency. Nat averted her eyes and clutched her knees to her chest, too overwhelmed to do anything more.

"Andris!" voices yelled from the courtyard.

"In here," Andris replied, still staring in disbelief at Benedict and holding Emilia close to his chest.

Estos and Sister Rory ran into the room with jubilant expressions. "We've taken the castle," Estos cried, but his smile faded when he saw his sister crying in Andris' arms. He rushed to her side. "What happened?"

"I didn't know . . . I thought . . ." Emilia hid her face in Andris' coat and sobbed.

"She killed Benedict," Nat whispered.

"What?" Estos stepped past his sister, then froze when he saw Nat huddled near Benedict's body.

Rory knelt next to the corpse. "Emilia killed the Hermit?" she asked Nat, looking completely confused.

"She thought he was the Chemist," Andris answered, running his hand over Emilia's long black hair as she wept openly in his arms. "It's my fault. I brought her here intending to kill him for her. I thought it would help ease her mind to know he was gone, but the guards attacked as soon as we entered the courtyard and Emilia ran straight for the quarters. She didn't know it was Benedict," he said in an anguished voice.

Gennes passed through the doorway. "Blessed Rim," he muttered as he took in Benedict's slumped form and the sobbing queen.

"Where is the Chemist?" Estos asked as he stared at the Hermit.

Nat stood on shaky legs and leveled a look at the king. "He's dead. Benedict killed his brother months ago," she replied in a flat voice. She laced her fingers together and pressed her hands atop her head.

The thought of the minutes—seconds—she'd wasted in Matilda and Mervin's basement made her sick. *I should have come straight here as soon as I found out about the early attack.*

Andris pressed Emilia closer to his chest and led her out of the room. Her sobs faded as they disappeared from view. Nat pulled a blanket off the Chemist's bed and draped it over the Hermit's small body. Rory helped her and adjusted the cloth over his withered leg.

A heavy banging from the corner of the room interrupted the silence. "Malorin," Nat growled, anger replacing her grief. She took a step toward the cell door with her hand on her sword hilt, then caught herself as she thought of the result of Emilia's unrestrained violence. *You're too angry, Nat,* a voice inside her whispered. *Harming her won't help or change anything.* She backed away, feeling a sudden need to flee from everything.

"Malorin's in there?" Rory reached for her sword.

"She's locked up in Emilia's old cell." Nat released the tight grip she had on her hilt and turned, intending to escape the room. *Let Rory deal with Malorin.* She brushed past Estos without looking at him but paused next to Gennes. Both he and Estos needed to know what the Hermit had accomplished. "Benedict established a rebel group in the Rewall, Gennes. I sent someone there last night to tell them to prepare to fight." Her voice was gravelly and barely more than a whisper. "They may be of some help to you in taking and holding the rest of Rustbrook."

The tips of Gennes' parted beard twitched. He stepped out the door and issued a string of orders to a rebel soldier before returning. "Thank you, Sister. That information may save lives today." He bowed his head.

Nat's body shook at the thought of the lives already lost. She lowered her gaze to the floor, wanting nothing more than an end to the fighting. A pain shot up her arm, reminding her of the Nalaide. *If I kill the Nalaide, her death could mean an end to so much of this conflict.*

"Gennes, find me before you leave for Ballew. I want to come to the front with you," she told him. If the Nalaide truly believed that Mudug had her as his prisoner, Nat would break off from the rebels at the front, sneak as close to Mudug as she could manage, and wait for the creature to come after both of them.

"That's a promise, Sister," Gennes replied before joining Rory by the door to Malorin's cell.

"Natalie." Estos reached for her arm. She held herself stiffly in place. "Are you all right?"

"No, Estos, I'm not," Nat admitted and stepped out of the room before he asked more questions. She dragged her sword tip on the ground behind her as she wandered past rebels knocking down doors and searching the Chemist's quarters. She quickened her steps and entered the castle. A cold gray stairwell stood to her right. She climbed the uneven stairs away from the misery behind her.

CHAPTER
THIRTY-FOUR

"What an odd place to hide out." Annin's voice echoed in the empty hourglass-shaped hearing chamber. Nat looked up from where she sat on the granite platform supporting the regent's empty throne and Mudug's richly carved chair. Annin's black cape lifted above her shoulders as she strode through the hearing chamber's doors. "I've been looking for you everywhere."

"I wasn't hiding." Nat stared numbly at her friend. "Benedict's dead."

"I know, Estos told me. Sounded pretty awful." A genuine look of sympathy crossed Annin's face. She sat down next to Nat on the polished stone platform. "He was a rat, but even after all these years he kept his oath to protect and uphold Emilia's regency. His death was . . . unfortunate," she said as she watched the banners above the empty throne tremble from a cold draft coursing through the room.

Nat pressed her fingers against the hard granite. "He was a horrible person to be around, Annin, even if you weren't a duozi," she conceded, feeling guilty for speaking ill of him but unwilling to gloss over the truth. "But he didn't deserve to die, especially at Emilia's hands."

"They'll give him a proper burial," Annin said briskly.

Nat looked away and focused on a column near her. Annin's dislike of Benedict ran deep, like the vine carved in the column. She refrained from saying anything else about the Hermit. Annin would never understand the loss she was feeling. Nat wasn't sure she understood it herself.

"Malorin's dead as well," Annin said. Nat's eyes bulged. "By Cassandra's hands."

"Thank her for me," Nat said, then realized how cold her words sounded.

"No reason to thank her, she was just doing her duty as a Warrior Sister. Malorin attacked Rory while they were transporting her to the castle dungeon." Annin shrugged. "She probably figured she had nothing to lose after she found out the Chemist was already dead. Cassandra cut her down while she fought with Rory." She rose and trailed her fingers over the back of the regent's throne. "Now just Mudug's left."

"And the Nalaide," Nat added, thinking of her plan to take off on her own after she reached Ballew and the front with Gennes.

"Would you revel a little in our victory before bringing me down? Rustbrook has already rallied behind Estos, and he'll soon sit on this throne. Think of all the changes that will follow." She perched on the edge of the throne and looked intently at Nat. "The Houses will be rebuilt. Estos will reinstate the representative system Fourline had before Mudug took over, *and* he intends to create positions for the duozi so they have a voice and representation in the government. Won't that be a strange new world?"

"Strange, no. Deserved and hard won, yes." Nat wondered how long it would take the population to accept the duozi. When Mudug's deceits were revealed and misconceptions about the ties between them and Nala dispelled, would people be more accepting? Her heart hoped so, but she wondered. Her thoughts strayed to the reason she'd returned to Fourline. "Annin, you believe I discovered something that may lead to a cure, don't you?" she asked, thinking of what Soris had said the night before.

"Yes." Annin stood and resumed her position next to Nat.

"Then why do you still talk as if there will be duozi?"

Annin pursed her lips. "Despite being around you and your experiments, I admit the concept of a cure has been difficult to fathom. Duozi have been around forever. Personally, I don't know if I would change, Natalie, even if I could," she confessed. "It's what I've been for so long. I'm not sure who I'd be. The idea of changing frightens me in some ways." She shook her head, and her curls bounced around her shoulders. "The possibility of being fully human again, of having a choice, where before there was none, fills me with both fear and a sense of freedom I've never felt. Does any of that make sense?"

"Yes," Nat replied. *A choice.* She'd never considered a cure in that light. She hugged her knees and regarded her friend. Annin's life journey was her own, and Nat would support her in whatever decision she made. "It makes perfect sense. You are an amazing person, Annin. Estos is lucky to have fallen in love with you."

"What?" Annin sat up straight.

"You know very well what I mean." Nat gave her friend a tired smile. She brushed a streak of dirt off her tattered cloak and stood. Annin gaped at her, speechless. "Why were you looking for me, anyway?" she asked, changing the subject to a more neutral topic. She held out her hand and pulled Annin to her feet.

"The inner circle is meeting in the Representatives' Building to plan the move south to take out Mudug. Your presence is requested." Annin found her voice and matched Nat's pace.

Mudug. I'll be leaving soon with Gennes for the front and need to make sure Cal's taken care of. She glanced at Annin as they strode through the empty halls in silence, worried about how to frame her request without letting her friend know of her plan.

"Annin," Nat finally said, "I know this goes without saying, but if something were to happen to me, make sure Cal gets home."

Annin continued walking. "*Nothing* will happen to you, Natalie, unless *you* let it," she replied without so much as a glance in Nat's direction. "Gennes, Estos, and Soris will all see to your safety."

Nat decided not to press the matter. *Annin and Soris will take care of her,* she assured herself. "I assume Estos and Gennes are calling the shots on attacking Mudug?" she asked as they headed down a wide hallway lined with floor-to-ceiling windows. Two rebel guards dressed in layers of fur and wool stood near a set of doors at the base of the stairs.

"Yes, but Sisters Rory and Pauler are the voice of all the Sisters who've returned from the fringe. Matilda's there, and so are Soris and Luriel."

Nat slowed her pace and frowned.

"Too many duozi for your liking?" Annin said sarcastically, catching her unhappy expression.

Nat's frown deepened. "It's not the numbers, it's the personalities," she said.

"I don't like Luriel, either, but she is the leader of the duozi rebels. And Soris seems to trust her." Annin gave Nat a long look.

"What's the plan for attacking Mudug?" Nat asked, not wanting to dwell on Luriel or any of the doubts she'd stirred up in her mind.

Annin cocked her head to the side but didn't challenge Nat's change of subject. "Since your little ruse with the Nalaide appears to have worked even without my memory-altering skills, they're discussing how best to use that to their advantage." Nat's arm tingled with pain at the mention of the Nalaide. "There have been multiple schemes, but Estos wants your input before they make the final decision."

"Why does my input matter?" Nat asked, feeling bone weary as she walked.

"It always does, Natalie," Annin said. "You should know that by now."

The Representatives' Building had an unimpressive square facade made of the same pale stone as the castle and reminded Nat of a child's play block. When Annin pushed through the carved doors past more guards, Nat's impression changed immediately. The doors opened into a long antechamber with a wooden floor that shone in the sunlight from the windows set along the long entrance wall. The rich hue of dozens of different types of wood formed the shape of the House emblems. Awed by the beauty, Nat bent to touch a vine inlay.

"Mudug had a carpet placed over this." Annin gestured to two rolled-up rugs nestled at both ends of the hall. "But some things aren't meant to be covered up." She gave Nat a smile and ushered her to a set of doors directly across from the entrance.

Nat followed her into a square room with a massive circular table ringed with chairs. Luriel and another duozi were speaking with Sister Pauler and Andris near a window. Estos, Rory, Soris, and Gennes stood in a tight cluster at the far end of the table, talking to Matilda. Soris glanced Nat's way and waved at her, but she averted her eyes. Her exhaustion and grief over Benedict's death had left her feeling numb. She knew she needed to speak with him, but all she wanted to do right now was collapse into a heap on the floor. The sound of pounding footsteps diverted her attention. She stumbled back as Cal, pale faced and watery eyed, flung her arms around her.

"Don't do that to me again, okay? Don't disappear like that. I had no idea where you went or what happened to you. Annin and Soris said you were fine, but I knew they were lying," Cal whispered in Nat's ear.

"I'm okay, Cal." She stepped away and took in Cal's wan face. "How about you?"

"I've been better." Cal wiped her eyes with the back of her hand, and Nat's eyes watered as well. "I don't even know how to describe what's happened the last two days, but I'm in one piece. Cassandra and Soris made sure I was okay."

"Couldn't have been in better hands, but why did they bring you here? Soris told me they were keeping you away from the city," Nat asked, shooting a look in Soris' direction.

"Cassandra is with Emilia, and Estos seemed to think you might want me here." Cal shrugged.

"Would everyone please sit." Estos' voice rang out and he gestured to the chairs. He watched the others claim seats, then his pale eyes settled on Nat. She took Cal's hand in hers, walked around the table, and pulled out a chair next to Sister Pauler. "Before we begin," he continued solemnly, making eye contact with each person sitting at the table, "what are the reports of the wounded?"

"Minimal casualties, Your Grace," Gennes said. "The handful of Healing Sisters that accompanied Sister Pauler are seeing to them. Rustbrook itself fell with little effort. The citizens were more than anxious to join our cause."

A look of relief passed over Estos. Nat couldn't help but think of Benedict. She lowered her head.

"What's wrong?" Cal whispered.

"Someone I knew died today," Nat replied in a hushed voice. She clutched her orb under the table and listened to Estos ask about the status of the rebels and intelligence reports gathered by scouts who had followed Mudug and his guards' movements north and south of the city. Her ears perked up when Gennes, looking uncomfortable in the tight confines of his chair, stood and cleared his throat.

"My canyon band and the fringe Sisters are in place between Rustbrook and Ballew. They are poised to pursue Mudug." Estos gave Gennes an appreciative look. "Our rebels in the city are preparing now to head south with you toward Ballew," Gennes added.

Sister Pauler leaned over the table. "Another band of Sisters is set to join Gennes' rebels within the day. They've taken the outposts near Daub Town and along the central trade route."

"All good news, but we leave Rustbrook exposed to the guard Mudug sent north once we pull out for Ballew." Estos pondered the quandary. "We need all rebels and Sisters in the attack against Mudug and the Nala, but I can't leave the city vulnerable."

"Luriel and the duozi rebels can guard the city," Soris suggested. A sliver of light coming from a gap between the curtains cut across his face.

"No," Annin shook her head in disagreement. "If we leave the city occupied by duozi troops, we may lose Rustbrook."

"Are you intimating my rebels aren't capable of holding Rustbrook?" Luriel glowered at Annin from her seat next to Soris.

"No." Annin gave Luriel a disagreeable look. "We were able to easily take the city because people believe Emilia and Estos have returned. Nothing's changed in their attitude toward the duozi. If you flood the streets with duozi patrols, the hold will vanish like that." She snapped her fingers.

"I'd like to see a Rustbrook citizen try to take on my rebels," Luriel snarled.

"Brilliant idea, start another battle in the city right after we've taken it." Annin leaned past Soris and glared at Luriel. "I'm not backing anything that will weaken Rustbrook's support for Estos. Now isn't the time to thrust a duozi occupation on the residents."

"You may be willing to be cast aside and suppressed for the sake of the regency, Annin, but I'm not." Luriel stood abruptly, knocking over her chair.

Nat listened to the argument with growing irritation. *Would Luriel be this antagonistic if she knew of the possibility of a cure?* she wondered.

"This regency is the duozi's chance to claim a foothold in Fourline. You knock it down now, there will be no future for any of us!" Annin yelled back, crushing a piece of paper under her hand.

"The solution to the problem is simple!" cried Nat, breaking up the fight. She saw Soris sit up abruptly in his chair at the sound of her voice.

She turned to Gennes and Estos. "Send the duozi rebels north and have them create a perimeter. They know the terrain. They can protect the capital from any outlying guard that tries to retake Rustbrook from the north."

"That still leaves the city itself exposed if any of Mudug's guard remains here," Andris said.

Nat took a deep breath. "Just once, be a ray of sunshine in my life, Andris," she muttered under her breath. Pauler cast her a sidelong glance and curled her lips into a little smile. "No, it won't, Andris," she countered loudly. She rose from her chair and walked over to the window. She whipped a drape to the side and gestured toward the city. "Estos and Emilia should publicly reinstate themselves as coregents." She fixed her eyes on the king. "Leave a small contingent here and use the Rewall rebel network and those citizens that helped you take Rustbrook to guard the city. They have plenty to lose if Mudug returns. Matilda and Mervin will know more people in the city who can be trusted to help." She glanced at Matilda, who bobbed her head in agreement. "With the duozi rebels guarding the northern access to the capital, the Rewall rebels and citizens should be more than enough to keep the city under control."

"You forget the queen's condition, Natalie." Andris leaned across the map toward her. "She can't be expected to make a public appearance, not after what she's been through."

"I'm forgetting nothing, Andris," Nat snapped. "She doesn't have to make a speech and shake everyone's hand. The Rustbrook residents put up a fight because they were told the regents are returning, so a simple appearance at the castle entrance with Estos would be enough for now. I think she can manage that. She had plenty of strength this morning," Nat said and instantly regretted her words.

Andris stormed over to her and shook his finger in her face. "She didn't know he was the Hermit!"

"You're right." Nat glimpsed his concerned expression but refused to back down. "She didn't. But she has a chance to do something good now, Andris." Her weariness and emotions took hold of her, and her voice wavered. "Give her a chance to be a part of bringing Fourline out of the darkness Mudug created. She can be strong for Fourline. It's in her. I know you care for her, but she'll wither just like she did when she was imprisoned if you keep treating her as if she's incapable of making her own decisions."

A hush fell over the room. Andris paled and Nat averted her eyes, knowing she'd pushed him too far. She steeled herself, waiting for his wrath.

"Well said, Natalie." Rory broke the silence. The tension Nat felt rolling off Andris seemed to lessen at the sound of the Sister's voice. "A public reinstatement needs to occur, anyway. It may be just the thing to keep all of Rustbrook in our camp until we root out Mudug." She gave Nat an encouraging nod.

Nat walked back to her chair and settled next to Cal, thankful for the presence of all the Sisters. "I agree with Sister Natalie," Rory continued. "There is a sufficient rebel contingent among the Rewall indentured servants and the citizens to keep control *if* the citizens know Estos and Emilia have returned. I also agree that Luriel's guard are well trained and can fend off anything from the north."

Luriel pressed her fists against the table. "I have more than enough people to protect the city from the north, but I'm not sending all of them to act as a buffer for Rustbrook while you go after Mudug and the Nala. They are the real prizes."

"Leave the duozi with remnant to protect the north," Soris spoke up. "They'll be no good the closer we get to the Nala, anyway." His comment reminded Nat of the hold remnant created, and a shudder rippled through her body.

"And the rest of us?" Luriel narrowed her Nala eyes.

"Accompany Gennes and his rebel guard. The duozi can fight and advise Gennes' rebels when the Nala are near," Soris said.

Luriel considered his compromise. "I will agree to that, but I expect all duozi to have a say in whatever justice is meted out once Mudug is captured." She turned to Estos. "Our voices will not be suppressed, Estos. Not now, nor in the future."

"Why are you so worked up about the future?" Cal interrupted. Luriel turned an icy glare on her. "I'm not trying to be insensitive or anything, but what's the big deal? You're going to be cured, anyway, right?" Cal looked to Nat for confirmation.

"What is she talking about?" Luriel asked.

"Sister Natalie discovered something that may lead to a cure for the duozi." Soris spoke up, surprising Nat. "I should have told you before, Luriel." He looked straight at Nat. "It was a mistake not to." She met Soris' gaze and smiled forgivingly when she saw his apologetic look.

"Natalie's discovery is important," Estos acknowledged and glanced at Annin. "But the Healing Sisters may never have a chance to try any cure on the duozi unless we take out Mudug and wrest control of the southern part of Fourline from the Nala. Which brings us to you, Natalie."

CHAPTER
THIRTY-FIVE

"Me?" Nat pressed her back into her chair. Estos entwined his fingers and glanced at Gennes. The huge man lumbered past him and pulled a map free from a loose pile on the table. He strode toward Nat, who watched with interest as he placed the map in front of her.

"The Nala's attacking Mudug and his men is one advantage we don't want to waste," Gennes said as he smoothed the map. Nat caught herself staring at his eyes, thinking how similar they were in color to Soris' human eye. "Bolstering the Nalaide's belief that Mudug is holding you captive will help us maintain that advantage and weaken Mudug's position in Ballew."

"If the Nalaide discovers we've taken Rustbrook, she may send the Nala here to search for you," Estos spoke up. "We can't risk her turning her focus away from Mudug or attacking Rustbrook while the rebels are otherwise engaged in a fight with him. You understand that risk, don't you, Natalie?" He spoke to Nat as if she were the only one in the room.

"What do you want me to do, Estos? Try to trick her again?" Nat asked. She knew as exhausted as she was, she'd eventually fall asleep and have to face the Nalaide's attempts to invade her dream space.

"No." He kept his eyes focused on her. "The Nalaide will be more aggressive if you give her another opportunity to enter and occupy your dream space. Your remnant tie to her places you in a precarious situation, and we can't risk your exposing our plans if she takes hold of your mind," he added.

"She has the Nalaide's remnant?" Luriel gave Nat a horrified look. "Are you a fool?" she spat at Estos. "What is she even doing in this room? She'll give everything away."

"She's been carrying the Nalaide's remnant for almost two weeks and has given nothing away." Annin's voice almost sounded like a growl.

"How do you know?" Luriel countered. "The Nalaide could be in her head right now."

"She's not." Soris spoke up. "I watched her eject the creature from her dream space, and I don't believe she's slept since then." He cocked his eyebrow. "Am I right, Natalie?"

"Not a wink." Nat covered her mouth, stifling a yawn.

"What more proof could I want?" Luriel said sarcastically.

Nat ignored Luriel's continued grumblings and asked Estos, "If you don't want me to let her back into my head, what do you want me to do?"

"A small team, disguised as Mudug's personal guard, will take you close to his headquarters in the bluff above Ballew." Gennes pointed his thick finger at the map in front of Nat. "We know the Nalaide has active scouts in the area. If they see you, they'll report back to the Nalaide and she'll think Mudug still has you in his grasp."

Nat saw the logic in their plan. The Nalaide would be furious when she found out where Nat was, and she'd attack Mudug's headquarters to get to her.

"Natalie, the guard I've selected to accompany you is one I would take with me anywhere. But are you willing?" Estos asked.

I'll be that much closer to Mudug and the Nalaide, she thought, knowing how easily she could slip away from Estos' guard when the timing was right.

"Yes," Nat responded without hesitation. If it meant getting her closer to the Nalaide under her own terms, she was all in. She knew she had to confront the creature, and fighting her anywhere but the Nala den would be an advantage. "Yes, I am," she repeated.

She glanced at Soris, waiting for his usual outburst that she shouldn't go, that she was agreeing to this crazy idea only because Estos had asked. But he stood silently between Luriel and Annin with a look of resignation on his face. She tried to shrug off the sense that he'd expected her to agree.

"Good," Gennes said. "Your guard will leave with you late this afternoon. If you need to sleep, Annin can administer the drug to put you in a dreamless state for a few hours, but time is a precious commodity. The sooner the Nala catch a glimpse of you near Mudug's outpost, the better." He gave her an appraising look. "By the looks of you, it might be worth putting you under now while we finalize our plans."

"I'm fine, Gennes." Nat stifled another yawn.

"I'm not," Cal said in an agitated voice. "You're asking my sister to risk her life for you and for what?" She twisted around toward Estos. "So you can become king and your beyond-erratic sister resume being queen?"

"She's a Warrior Sister, Calpurnia," Rory said from across the room. "She's fulfilling her oath."

"She's *my* sister," Cal replied. "And you're using her like she's a piece of meat baiting a trap. Can't you figure out some other way to help yourself?" She splayed her fingers on the table as she challenged Estos.

"It's her decision, Calpurnia. It's always been her decision to help us," Estos replied, but his pale eyes flickered in Nat's direction.

"Would you excuse us," Nat said. She pushed her chair back and grabbed Cal's hand.

"What?" Cal stood swiftly and faced her sister. "You're willing to risk your life for them? What about me? What about Mom and Dad and MC? Don't we count for anything?"

From across the room, Nat heard Soris clear his throat. She kept her eyes on Cal. "Cal, don't do this, not here," she pleaded. "Come with me." She tightened her grasp on Cal's hand and pulled her into the empty hallway. She didn't let go until they were at the end of the hall next to one of the rolled-up carpets.

"I have to do this, and I can't go back home, not now," Nat said before Cal could start in on her.

"Why not?" Cal thrust her chin forward. "Why can't we leave now? I delivered your discovery to the Sisters. They've taken this city." She gestured to the air around them. "You and I can slip away from this place while they fight their own battle. This isn't your battle. Why are you agreeing to any of this?"

Nat settled onto one of the carpets and motioned for Cal to join her. "I have a story to tell you, Cal. Will you listen?" Cal didn't move. "After you've heard everything I have to say, tell me if you still think my decision's wrong."

Cal frowned but lowered herself onto the carpet next to Nat and pulled her knees to her chest. "I'm listening."

Nat took a deep breath and started from the beginning, from her first impression of Estos and Annin to her job interview with Barba. She told Cal about Andris and how much she'd hated him the night she'd stormed out of the costume shop only to be brought back by Estos. The story of discovering her dream space, agreeing to come to Fourline, meeting the Hermit, and encountering the Nala spilled from her lips. She remembered Neas' face and described his every detail to Cal. She faltered when she told her about first meeting Soris and how close she'd grown to him after she'd returned to Fourline to destroy the Chemist's tracking device.

Her voice caught when she told Cal about Soris and the Nala attack. She recounted the months of misery and guilt after returning home. She told her how she trained to become a real Warrior Sister, took the oath, and returned to Fourline to help Soris, only to discover the duozi children enslaved in the Nala den, turned over by Mudug to be used to regenerate the Nala. She shared how fiercely she'd wanted to protect the duozi children and Soris when she set off with Andris and the others to free Emilia. How her friendship with Soris had grown into something more, something she'd never felt before. Nat told her about finding Emilia and how she'd delayed telling Soris that the Nalaide was looking for her until the attacks put him and everyone else around her in danger.

"I've been through too much with them, know too much of their suffering, to ever leave them when I can help," she said, brushing away her last tear. "I swore an oath as a Warrior Sister, Cal, and when I was forced home, my sole focus was to find a way to end the hold the Nala have on the duozi."

"And you did," Cal said, still clutching her long legs to her chest. She had a confused look on her face.

"I hope I did." Nat sighed and looked into her sister's eyes, full of both gratitude and regret for her presence. "I should have waited for Annin to come back to our world, but I was impatient. I made mistakes, and you're here because of them." Exhausted from telling the story, she leaned her head against the wall, knowing she had to tell her sister the last part. "Cal, when we split up in the forest that night, I was captured and taken to the Nalaide. She put her remnant in me. And now you know that even if I turned my back on all of them, my life back home would be a slow slide into nothingness. You remember how bad I was last spring."

Cal touched Nat's bandaged arm. "You have to face this Nalaide thing and kill her?"

"I do. Even if I went home now, she'd keep after me in my mind. Do you understand now why I'm going? I have to do what I can to help them and then confront her. It's the only way I can really go home. And Cal, Fourline, all these people, are my family, and this place is my home now, too." Soris appeared in her mind, and she realized how true the memory she'd shown him was.

"If you have to face this thing, I'm coming with." Cal's lips formed a stubborn line.

"Cal, if something happened to you, I would never forgive myself. I promised I would make sure you got home safe, and I'll keep that promise, but you can't come with me. You can't come to Ballew. I'll come back and get you when the battle is over." *Or Soris and Annin will see you home.*

Cal opened her mouth to speak.

"You can't come. You are too precious to me to lose." Nat choked on her words. Tears welled in Cal's eyes, and Nat pulled her sister close. She looked up and caught sight of Estos lingering in a side doorway to the meeting room. "Everything's going to be okay, Cal. All of us will get through this," Nat whispered as she gazed at Estos. He didn't retreat, but stayed in the doorway watching her comfort Cal. She wondered if he'd said the same words to Emilia. Nat heard the buzz of voices coming from the open doorway and released her sister. Both of them wiped their eyes. "Head back in. I'll be there in a minute." She stood and gave Cal's hand a reassuring squeeze.

"You're not the only one who won't forgive herself if someone gets hurt, Nat," Cal said. A determined look flashed behind her blue eyes.

Estos approached the sisters. "Nothing will happen to Natalie, Calpurnia, you have my word."

"You better keep it," Cal said in a tone that bordered on threatening. She released Nat's hand and walked toward the doorway. She paused and turned around. "She's irreplaceable."

"I know," Estos said.

"At least we agree on something." Cal reluctantly stepped through the door.

Estos turned his attention to Nat. "Do you remember the day in the costume shop when I described my home to you?" he asked and set his hand on her shoulder. The question surprised her.

"Yes," Nat said, recalling the moment as if it were from a different life. "You told me about your sister. You told me about your home."

He gave her a tight smile that quickly vanished. "I had no idea then how much you would be willing to sacrifice for my home. But I promise to do my best to make it a place of peace for everyone. What you've given of yourself is too valuable to be wasted. I'll make Fourline a place worthy of what you've sacrificed." Another tear trickled down Nat's cheek, and she took a shaky breath. Estos folded her in his arms. "And I, too, promise to see you home safely."

CHAPTER
THIRTY-SIX

The two wagons rolled through the streets of Rustbrook, pushing through the crowds to the central square. Heads turned and people gaped at the occupants of the first transport. Estos and Emilia stood in the first wagon in full view. They held each other's hands and looked out over the throng of people. Annin, features hidden under a heavy robe, and Sisters Rory and Cassandra flanked the regents. The driver maneuvered the wagon down a corridor created by rebel guards waiting to accompany Estos south to join Gennes and the rest of the rebels outside Ballew as soon as he and Emilia publicly reclaimed the regency. The wagon halted at the base of the raised platform Mudug had used for public executions.

"This insanity is your doing," Andris accused Nat. He rose from a bench and alighted from the second wagon as it ground to a stop. "They are sitting ducks." His gaze lingered on Emilia as she and Estos climbed the wooden steps at a slow, deliberate pace. Cheers and shouts of their names accompanied each step they took.

"I didn't recommend a parade through town or an announcement in the central square." Nat glanced up at the gallows, shaking her head at the irony of Emilia's choice of location to reclaim the regency. "I had no idea Emilia would demand something like this when Estos shared my suggestion with her."

"No? Well, then, you don't know the queen at all." Andris' tone was blistering. "If anything happens to either of them—"

"If anything happens to them, it will be the result of Emilia's decision to do what she thinks is right," Soris interrupted his brother. "She's well aware of the risk. And besides, the public is cheering for her. Support her in her decision, brother."

Nat gripped Soris' arm, hidden under a concealing cloak, as she hopped from the wagon and wondered if he'd feel the same way when she broke off and tracked down the Nalaide on her own.

Soris' words didn't diminish the look of worry on Andris' face. He strode toward the stairs and took a defensive spot behind Emilia before Nat and Soris reached the base of the steps. Nat paused and released her orb, remembering her oath to protect the regents. As it rose, she heard a familiar voice shout from the crowd.

"Sister!" Fergus pushed into the line of rebels surrounding the platform. A hollow-eyed woman wearing a determined look stood next to him. Nat recognized the resemblance between them. She gave her old captor a brief nod, bewildered by the odd turn of events and the momentum of the change around her. The residents of Rustbrook were shouting cries of praise, and Nat could feel energy in the air, like a bright light suddenly shining in the darkest of rooms.

The steps to the gallows creaked under her boots. She scanned the square, realizing it was the location where she and Soris had first seen Sisters Rory, Pauler, and Camden on Camden's execution day. She came to a halt next to Soris at the rear of the gallows. His hand found hers under the folds of her cloak and pulled her close. He turned and she glimpsed his eyes under the hood. She caught her breath, thinking how much both of them had experienced together to get to this very point.

"Citizens of Rustbrook," Emilia's voice rang out, and the rumble from the crowd faded into utter silence. "I stand in front of you today after nearly seven years of imprisonment and torture at the hands of Lord Mudug and the Chemist." Cries of outrage erupted, and Emilia raised her hands in the air to silence the outburst. Nat's lingering misery over Benedict's death lessened as she marveled at Emilia's composure. *She endured and survived. I can't blame her for any of what happened this morning,* Nat thought as she watched her hold her head high and continue to address the throng of people in the square.

"Believing me dead, my young brother, powerless to overcome Mudug's growing control and lies, fled for his life." She paused and took a deep breath. Estos reached for her hand. "These are truths. And truths must be embraced by us all no matter how painful." She glanced at her brother. "One of the truths is that as your regent, I failed to protect Fourline from Lord Mudug. I failed to put a stop to the rumors and lies he spread about the Sisters. And I failed to protect all who have suffered at the hands of Mudug and the Nala. I say this to you now, because we are at a new dawn after the bleakest of nights. And with the new day, you need a new leader. I reclaim my right as regent, and in so doing abdicate and grant all my authority to my brother. My only wish is that you give him the loyalty you gave to me." Emilia bowed her head and stepped back. "Do you accept your rightful position as regent of Fourline?" she asked Estos.

"I do!" Estos' confident voice echoed through the square. Emilia bowed her head once more as a roar of cheering shook the square. Andris swept to Emilia's side, leading her away from the front of the gallows. Her strength faded with each step she took and she clung to Andris for support.

"Did you know she was going to do that?" Nat whispered to Soris, shocked by Emilia's declaration.

"I had no idea, but it seems as if Estos did." He gestured in his direction. The king now took center stage in front of the crowd as their shouts filled the air. "King Estos! King Estos!" they chanted over and over, shaking the very foundations of the platform with the vibration of their voices. Estos reached for Annin's hand. Nat could tell from Annin's agitated movements that she wasn't expecting to be beckoned, but she stepped forward and joined him. He lifted his hand in the air, and the crowd settled. Thousands of eyes, glittering from the cold, locked on the king and his robed companion.

"I am humbled by your solidarity, and I pledge to do all that is in my power to return Fourline to a time of peace. To a time when our lands weren't overrun by Nala. To a time when the controlling power didn't manipulate, abuse, and enslave its people for personal gain." The crowd erupted again. Estos waited for a moment before continuing. "But each of us must act individually to understand, rectify, and change so many of the wrongs and lies Mudug used to poison this land. My sister spoke of truths. As your new regent I implore all of you to open your eyes to the truth. The Sisters and the Houses were never in line with the Nala." Estos gestured to Rory and Cassandra, whose orbs hovered high above their heads. "The few that survived Mudug's purge deserve nothing but our support and respect as we rebuild this land."

A chorus of cheers rose from the crowd, and Nat's heart leapt when she looked at Cassandra's proud smile.

"Know that neither Emilia nor I would be standing here today without the support of the Sisters and"—he paused to lift Annin's hood from her face—"the duozi."

A ripple of shocked utterances replaced the cheers. Nat could see Annin's stunned expression even in profile. The muscles in Soris' arm tensed, and he squeezed Nat's fingers with a grip that bordered on pain.

"The truth is that this country and its people have for far too long treated the duozi with abject hate and suspicion when they have been nothing more than victims of the Nala. Lord Mudug exploited that prejudice. In the coming weeks and months, many of you will learn that children or siblings you thought lost were delivered to the Nala by Mudug to be turned into duozi. Mudug knowingly traded and exchanged your children and your loved ones for the Nala's services." A hush fell over the crowd as Estos' revelation hit them. "I speak nothing but the truth, painful as it is." He brought Annin closer to his side. "Now is the time for all of us to work together to overcome the nightmare and suffering Mudug and the Nala have brought upon this land. Will each of you join us in rebuilding Fourline into a country where we all have a voice? Where we all have the freedom to live lives free of fear and create futures full of hope and prosperity?"

Nat closed her eyes, fearing the crowd's response to his speech. But her fear dissolved instantly as individual voices in the crowd swelled to a roar of approval. The deafening shouts shook the gallows again.

Estos bowed and stepped back with Annin. They stood a few feet away from Nat and Soris as Cassandra, Rory, and the guards cleared the stairs and space around the wagons. Nat couldn't take her eyes off them.

"Why did you do that?" Nat overheard Annin ask. "There was so much to risk."

"I did it for you, Annin. You've been my friend and companion through all this, and I wouldn't be here but for you. Even if Natalie has found a cure, I want Fourline to know what it owes you and all the duozi. And the people need to get used to seeing your face."

"What do you mean?"

"I mean I want the person I love to be by my side as we rebuild this country. Are you willing?"

Annin swallowed, and Nat could see her struggling to hold back tears. "More willing than ever before in my life."

"Thank you, Annin Afferfly."

Rory ushered Estos down the stairs to join Emilia and Andris in the wagon. Annin stood on the platform as the crowd began to disperse and the wagon rolled away. She turned to Nat and Soris.

"Well, what are you doing just standing there?" Annin asked with her normal petulant look replacing her smile. "We have a Nalaide to trick."

CHAPTER
THIRTY-SEVEN

"Do I need to knock you out now?" Annin brought her chestnut-colored horse next to Nat's sorrel mare.

Nat sat up in her saddle, startled by Annin's voice. She blinked, taking in Annin's ill-fitting guard's uniform.

"Looks like you're about to fall off your saddle. Falling asleep now won't help the cause." Annin gave Nat a worried look and handed her a water flask.

Nat took the flask and glanced around. The band of Sisters disguised in Mudug's uniforms rode spread out along the Rust River toward Ballew. She took a deep breath, filling her lungs with the cold winter air. "No." She blinked again, irritated by Annin's doubtful expression. "I can stay awake." She took a drink from the flask and sputtered at the swampy taste. "What's in this?" She grimaced as she handed the flask back.

"Mild stimulant to keep you awake." Annin tucked it into a pocket of her coat.

"Will you tell me next time when it's something other than water?" Nat groused, remembering Malorin's trick.

"Why would I? I'd miss your delightful expression." Annin scrunched up her face, mimicking Nat's. "You get crabby when you're tired."

"I have a lot on my mind right now." Nat scanned the winter grass rolling down to the banks of the Rust River. A jittery feeling came over her and she clutched the reins tightly, wondering how she'd break from Annin and the Sisters after they'd deceived the Nala into believing she was still Mudug's captive. She had no intention of dragging anyone else with her when she confronted the Nalaide. *Hopefully the Nalaide's near the battle,* she thought. If she had to travel through the eastern woods back to the Nala den, the danger would be much greater, especially since she'd be traveling alone. She glanced around and saw the Sisters and two of Estos' guards riding in her direction. *At least Soris isn't here.* Breaking away would be easier without him around. The jittery feeling intensified.

"Thinking about Soris?" Annin asked, reading her mind.

"I'm thinking about a lot of things, Annin," she replied. "But now that you mention him, where is he? I thought he was coming with us. Is he traveling with Estos?" Nat asked, wondering where he'd disappeared to after Estos' startling proclamation to the citizens of Rustbrook.

"No, he's not with Estos. He's gathering information." Annin looked away toward the river. Something in her voice didn't ring true, and Nat brought her horse closer to get a look at Annin's face. Her horse snorted nervously and sidestepped away from Annin. She jerked the reins to the right, bringing the sorrel under control.

"There aren't any Nala near, are there?" Nat asked, wondering if her horse was jumpy because of Annin or something else.

"No, just me." Annin gave her a wry smile.

The two women rode a little farther together, following Sister Pauler. Nat's thoughts strayed to her sister.

"Annin," Nat said, breaking the silence. "I'm going to ask you again: if something happens to me, promise you'll wipe Cal's memory so she forgets all this and make sure she gets home."

"You sound like you're on the way to your own funeral. It would be a waste of my breath to say yes since nothing's going to happen to you. You're safer than a gunnel kit next to its mother." Annin gestured to the ring of Warrior Sisters.

"Just promise me." Nat leaned to the side in her saddle and clutched Annin's arm. "I've put her through too much, give her a memory that . . . that makes it easier for her."

Annin scanned Nat's face. A hint of understanding flashed in her eyes, then disappeared. "Fine, I promise. But I'm of the opinion that Cal deserves to remember everything."

"I don't disagree." Nat winced at the pain in her throbbing arm. "But memories can be a heavy burden, and I think she's earned the right to the peace that will come in forgetting about everything that's happened to her here," she argued and spurred her horse forward before Annin could answer.

Nat slowed her horse's gait when she noticed Pauler conferring with another Sister. The Sister disappeared up a hill, and Pauler turned her horse and rode through the dry grass toward Nat and Annin.

"Our scout's sighted a small band of Mudug's guards moving up the river. We'll ride east to avoid detection. There's a forest about half a mile from here where we can hole up until they pass. I sent a Sister on to scout it. Annin, do you sense any Nala around?" Pauler asked.

"No. Nothing," Annin replied, sitting straight in her saddle.

Pauler looked back down the river. "Then move out, ride toward the forest, and meet up with the Sister. We'll be right behind you."

Nat kicked her horse, urging her forward. The cold wind hit her cheeks as she rode next to Annin. The jostling of her arm made her grimace. Trees appeared along the crest of the next hill, and she caught a glimpse of a Sister disguised as one of Mudug's guards disappearing past the foliage. Annin glanced behind her and slowed her horse.

"Why are you slowing down?" Nat pulled on the reins of her sorrel.

"Pauler and the others should be behind us." Annin scanned the rolling hills beneath them. "Follow that Sister into the woods. I'll see if they've run into any problems, then I'll come straight your way."

"I'll come with you." Nat spun her horse around and pulled her orb from the folds of her cloak.

"Don't be foolish. You're too valuable to get caught up in a skirmish with Mudug's guard. Get to the woods and stay with the Sister. I'll be right back." Annin kicked her horse and rode quickly away. Nat watched Annin disappear over the hill with an uneasy feeling, but turned her horse to the forest and rode in the direction she'd last seen the Sister.

The rustling sound of dry grass under her horse's hooves vanished when she entered the woods. Her hands began to shake, and she tried to shrug off the now-constant jittery feeling. Whatever stimulant was in Annin's flask was making her jump at every snapping branch and crunch of pine needles. The sounds seemed amplified, as if they were occurring inside her head. Nat grasped the saddle horn, suddenly overcome by a wave of dizziness. A surge of pain shot up her arm. She cried out. Her horse bolted forward, startled by the sound, and plunged deeper into the woods.

"Whoa," Nat said, gasping for breath. The sorrel slowed. She slumped over the saddle and dropped the reins, completely exhausted. Her head spun and she tried to keep her eyes open. *Can't fall asleep,* she told herself. Sweat poured down her forehead despite the frigid temperature. *Where's the Sister?* Nat turned and caught a glimpse of a bright blur before something hard knocked her head, sending her falling from her saddle onto the forest floor.

When Nat came to, Lord Mudug was leaning back in a chair in front of her, stroking his long mustache.

"The troublesome Sister awakes." Mudug walked over to a chest-high table and shuffled through some papers. Nat tried to speak or cry out, but a cloth was tied tightly around her mouth, and her hands were bound behind her. Her eyes widened as she looked around. They were inside a large cave with a massive canvas cloth covering its entrance. Guards in blue coats paced in front of an open flap in the cloth. The light from the entrance flooded the area where Mudug stood while leaving Nat in shadow. She caught a flicker of light above the flap. Her orb hung in a cage, smashing against the metal bars.

"You're wasting your strength trying to free your orb, Sister," Mudug said over the clamor of her orb. He approached, holding a map in his hands. "Strength you'll likely need if I decide to let you live." He grasped the chair and pulled it closer to Nat. His shrewd black eyes searched hers. His hand shot out and he grasped her chin, squeezing it. "You have caused me more than a Sister's share of trouble," he growled and ripped the gag from her mouth. "Tell me, what were you doing wandering in the woods on your own?"

Nat hid her relief. Whoever had knocked her out hadn't seen her traveling companions. "I was traveling north, trying to reach the fringe," she lied.

"The fringe? Are you certain you weren't headed south from Rustbrook to meet up with your rebel filth?" A wicked look crossed his face, and he shoved the paper at Nat. She stared in horror at the map Gennes had set in front of her in the Representatives' Building. He tsk-tsked at her reaction and let the map fall to the floor. His thick-heeled boot ground the map into the dirt.

"You shouldn't look surprised, Sister. I knew the rebels were planning to take Rustbrook, just as I knew they'd follow me south right into the Nala fray. The timing of a fallout with my blue allies has been a sudden gift. I've sealed off all access to this outpost, leaving your rebels no choice but to engage the Nala. My location on the bluff above Ballew will provide me with quite the view while your rebels are forced to fight off the incoming Nala. When the battle is over, I'll send my guards to finish off the victor." He stuck his thick fingers in a tight pocket of his heavy coat, extracted a vial of clear liquid, and rolled it between his fingers. She watched him down the liquid, and his dark eyes settled on her.

"How did you know about the rebels' plan?" Nat asked. She struggled against the ropes binding her wrists, wondering what else Mudug knew and why he was sharing so much information with her.

"You have your spies, and I have mine, Sister. The better question is what to do with you?" He gave her a condescending look. "You're valuable to the Nalaide and possibly the rebels. I'll see who the victor of this battle is and then decide your fate." A hooded guard stepped into the cave and Nat cringed. "Knock her out so she doesn't try to escape."

Mudug pressed a vial of cloudy liquid into the guard's hand. The guard reached Nat in one quick step and pried her lips apart. The syrupy liquid slid down her throat. Nat gagged, to keep from swallowing, but he shoved her mouth closed, forcing her to swallow. Her head felt as if it were spinning. She blinked as Mudug's shadowy figure in the light of the entrance to the cave grew blurry, and her eyelids drooped.

A thick gray slime formed around her feet, and a low hiss rose from the ground. Nat began to sink into the liquid, first her ankles, then her calves. As she sank deeper and deeper, a large bubble protruded from the surface. The bubble grew in size as Nat's waist and arms were sucked under. Two black concave ovals emerged from the slime, and Nat found herself looking directly into the eyes of the Nalaide.

Nat thrust her arms up, forcing her head under the slime and away from the creature. She wriggled in the viscous liquid, trying to swim away. Her leg struck something solid and she blindly reached out, feeling the rough edge of her dream space. A sucking sound filled her ears when she pulled herself over the ledge and rolled onto the floor, her arm exploding in pain. *This is my dream space,* Nat said to herself. The pain began to ebb and she slowly opened her eyes. The Nalaide stood on top of the ledge directly above her.

"You weren't quick enough with your barrier this time, Sister. Let me in." The Nalaide's voice felt like a magnet, tugging at her brain and preventing her from creating the barrier. "You hold my remnant, Sister. You are part of me. You have no choice but to let me in."

Her voice reverberated through Nat's head. She doubled over, clutching her ears, unable to think of anything but the Nalaide's incessant demand. "Come in," she gasped.

The Nalaide landed on the ground. She stalked toward Nat and snaked her arm around Nat's neck, pressing into the back of her head and pulling her closer to her pale face.

"Does Mudug still have you, vessel?" The Nalaide yanked Nat's head back and stared straight into her eyes. A flash of white-hot pain burst through Nat's arm and radiated into her mind. Numbness overtook her body and brain. The images from Mudug's cave clicked through her head as if they were individual pictures, appearing slowly at first, then faster and faster. Mudug moved around the cave, picked up the map, and waved it in front of her. A low, angry hiss underscored Mudug's voice as he said, "I'll see who the victor of this battle is and then decide your fate."

"Throw her out of your mind, Natalie!"

Mudug's image splintered. Nat searched the memory, looking for the source of the faint voice. She felt herself jerked violently to the side and crashed into something hard. Her heart sounded like a drum drowning out all other noises. She opened her eyes. A blur of pointed white feet danced in front of her. *I'm in my dream space and the Nalaide's with me.* She sat up, and a wall of orbs shot up between the Nalaide and her. Nat struggled to her feet, holding the image of the orbs in place. The heat in her arm grew in intensity until it felt as if it were on fire. Losing her concentration, the orbs scattered over the floor. Nat lifted her head and watched as something jumped onto the Nalaide. *Soris?*

Soris clung to her back. She stabbed her daggerlike hands into his side, ripped him off, and sent him flying into the darkness of Nat's dream space.

"*No!*" Nat cried. A field of meldon flowers sprang up from the ground around her feet. They spread like water pouring from a broken glass and flowed over the ground. Soris landed in the soft field. Nat turned her attention to the Nalaide and spread the flowers in her direction. The creature jumped onto the barrier to avoid them.

Nat pressed her hands to her head and met the Nalaide's cold gaze. "Get out of—"

A deafening hiss interrupted Nat's command. The Nalaide thrust herself off her back legs and flew through the air. She angled her arm down and grasped Nat, yanking her out of the field. The creature crushed Nat against her slick skin, and the two of them rolled across a patch of empty floor.

"Such tricks will not work again on me, Sister," the Nalaide hissed into Nat's ear. Nat felt herself slipping into her memories. She writhed against the Nalaide's grasp, slowly forgetting she was in her dream space as memories flooded her mind and blurred at a sickening pace.

Soris' face flashed by and she clung to the image. The blur slowed, and she found herself in a memory of the Nala den. Soris knelt next to the dead Nala, cleaning its wound, while Annin stood screaming behind her. The memory shifted to the faces of the frightened duozi children fleeing the den. A sharp point seemed to stab at the memory, and it evaporated only to be replaced by the bright lights of her chemistry lab. Ethet's book lay open to the page containing the meldon formula, and Nat could feel the sensation of peering through the microscope and watching the Nala bacteria wither and die.

Pain exploded through Nat's body. The Nalaide released Nat and backed away. Her black eyes pulsed with a look of terror. The creature stumbled farther away from her as Nat's mind lingered on the memory of the dying bacteria. Streams of liquid erupted from the tips of the

Nalaide's hands. She convulsed in front of Nat's eyes and fell over the ledge of the dream space.

"Wake up, Natalie!"

Nat opened her eyes. Soris scanned her face, looking worried.

"Where am I?" she asked, completely confused.

"You're safe," he said. His hand tightened protectively around her shoulder, and she realized she was cradled in his arms. Annin sat on a bed of pine needles near her feet, breathing hard. She uncapped a water gourd, took a drink, and handed it to Soris. He accepted it and held it to Nat's lips as she sat up.

"It worked?" Annin asked Soris as Nat greedily gulped the water.

"Better than you can imagine. Natalie was unbelievable. The Nalaide saw the images you planted in Nat's mind, Annin. The cave, Mudug's disclosing his location, and his desire to keep Natalie for himself. The Nalaide saw all of it." Soris brushed the damp strands of hair away from Nat's forehead. His brow furrowed. "But the creature went farther into Natalie's memory this time." He pressed his lips together, and the lines across his forehead deepened. He studied Nat. "For a moment, I thought she had you. How did you eject her?" The bewilderment in Soris' voice equaled the confusion in his expression.

"The bacteria," Nat answered shakily. She wrung her hands, rubbing her skin. "The last memory she saw was of me in the lab looking at the meldon formula and the Nala bacteria . . ." Her voice trailed off. She sat up and leaned against the tree, wondering if the Nalaide's reaction to her discovery was a figment of her dream space or if the meldon compound really had weakened the creature's hold on her. "Mudug never had me?" she asked, unsure how to explain what had happened to either of them.

"No, he didn't." A satisfied smile spread over Annin's face. "I used fragments of your existing memories and built that one in your mind."

"You tricked me." Nat steadied herself against the base of the tree and rose to her feet. Her muscles trembled from the effort. The memory of the tight bonds around her wrists and the cave seemed so real.

"You're offended?" Annin brushed the pine needles off her cloak and stood. "Messing with your memories was a far sight safer than dragging you through Mudug's lines and dangling you in front of the Nala in hopes they'd scamper off and tell the Nalaide where you are. I can't believe you thought Estos, Soris, and I would actually put you in such a dangerous position." She crossed her arms over her chest. "I guess it's a good thing you're gullible and a willing martyr."

"I agreed to Estos' plan because there weren't any better options, Annin," Nat lied, knowing she'd wanted to travel to Ballew so she could confront the creature herself and not put anyone else in danger. She pulled her cloak tight across her chest and shivered. "And if you were so interested in protecting me, why'd you drag me out into this forest? You could have smashed me over the head as easily in Rustbrook." Nat rubbed the egg-sized lump at the base of her skull.

"I had to wait until Soris had rendezvoused with the Sisters to confirm where Mudug was on the bluff above Ballew," Annin explained. "He demanded that we know Mudug's exact location if we were going to subject you to the Nalaide again while you have her remnant."

Nat gave Soris a withering look. "You helped plan this?"

"Of course I did," he replied without a shred of remorse. "I had no intention of letting you slip away to go off and find the Nalaide on your own."

"What are you talking about?" A flush crept over Nat's face.

"Natalie," Soris chided, "I knew the moment I heard what happened to you that you'd want to battle the Nalaide. If I had any uncertainty, it disappeared after Sister Hanni revealed what she knew about the Predictions. Gennes told me you asked him to take you to the front. You've been planning to break away from us so you can fight the Nalaide by yourself. Did you seriously think Annin and I would let you do that?"

"It's not your or Annin's problem. It's my problem, and I have no interest in putting anyone at risk because of me." Nat's hands trembled, and she clutched them under her cloak.

"No. Unacceptable." Soris shook his head. He tilted her chin and gave her a fierce look. "You are not facing the Nalaide on your own."

"Why don't I leave you two alone?" Dried pine needles crunched under Annin's boots. "You know where to meet up," she added and glanced at Soris before jogging away.

"How is my going after the Nalaide unacceptable?" Nat clutched her hands to her chest. "What am I supposed to do, Soris? Stand back and let others fight my battle?"

"Natalie, when are you going to get it through your head that you're not alone in any of this?" Soris pressed one hand against the bark and kept his eyes locked on hers. Her chest grew tight as he stared down at her. "When people love each other, they stand up for each other, fight for each other. You've always done that for me, and it's my turn to do it for you. I love you too much to stand aside and let you fight this battle on your own." Nat sucked in a breath, and he gave her a surprised look. "You don't know that's how I feel about you?" He traced his fingers across her face.

The flush in her cheeks deepened. "You've never told me."

"Neither have you," he countered and leaned closer.

"I did. You heard me say it when you saw my memory." Her stubbornness evaporated as his expression softened. She felt as if he could read every emotion she'd ever had.

"Always arguing." He rolled his human eye. "You told Annin how you felt about me. Tell me now. To my face," he demanded, inches from her lips.

"I love—"

His kiss interrupted her. She melted against him, forgetting all her grief and pain. Walls crumbled inside her, and all her doubts washed away as she clung to him. His lips broke from hers, and a fierce light shined in his eyes.

"I love you, too, Natalie, and whatever the fight, I'll be by your side."

CHAPTER
THIRTY-EIGHT

A wide smile covered Nat's face as she and Soris ran hand in hand toward Annin and a trio of horses.

"Grinning like fools, both of you," Annin quipped, but her lips curved up. She tossed a set of reins to Soris. "Pauler and the other Sisters have already left, and we need to move out now if we're going to reach Ballew by daybreak."

Soris snatched the reins in the air. The sleek black mount jerked his head away from the sudden movement. He brought the animal under control and helped Nat into the saddle. His hand lingered on her thigh as he turned to Annin.

"Cheeky all of a sudden," Annin observed.

Soris dismissed her comment with a wave, but Nat caught his grin with one of her own. "Any news about the battle?" he asked as he mounted another horse.

"Before Pauler left she told me she'd received word that the Nala are attacking Ballew from the south and east."

"Why are the Nala attacking the city instead of Mudug and his outpost?" Nat asked.

"You've never been to Ballew, Natalie," Soris replied. "Mudug picked it for a reason. The city sits at the base of a bluff. The outpost on the bluff is only accessible through a series of ropes and ladders. Because the top half of the bluff is a sheer drop, the only way the Nala can get to Mudug is to go through the city and up the lower half. He's positioned most of his guard and archers in caves and crevices and can pick off any attackers. He's using the city as his buffer."

"That man is going to get half the city killed and the other half transformed into duozi." Nat scowled as she thought what a horde of Nala would do to the people who lived in Ballew.

Annin kicked her horse and he trotted forward. "The Warrior Sisters from the fringe will flank the Nala and do what they can to protect the city. Gennes and Estos will attack from the north and west, cutting Mudug off from any retreat. There are smugglers' entrances into those caves that the rebels and free travelers have used before. If Mudug thinks he's protected, he's dead wrong."

Nat spun her horse and spurred him toward Annin and Soris. "Can we use the smugglers' entrances to get to Mudug's cave?" she asked as their horses increased pace.

"Possibly," Annin responded. "But leave Mudug to Estos and Gennes."

"Not if the Nalaide has him pegged." Nat leaned over her saddle horn, trying to get a better look at both Soris and Annin as their horses' trot turned into a gallop.

Soris gave her a sideways glance. "That brings up the question of whether the Nalaide will search for Mudug and you herself or send her Nala army in to find you."

"If she's commanding her Nala but staying out of the fray, we have to figure out a way to lure her into the open." Nat gave Soris a quick glance as she spurred her horse closer to his, knowing he wasn't going to like her next suggestion. "She'll come out of whatever hole she's occupying if she sees me. We can attack all the creatures then," she said, thinking maybe there was something to the Predictions.

"A reminder: you are not going after her on your own." He gave her a threatening look. "The Nalaide will come after you mentally and physically if you give her the slightest opportunity, and you won't have the luxury of control that you had in your dream space."

"I know," Nat said, disliking the fact that Soris was right. "I need to think of a way to let her see me and get her out in the open where she's vulnerable." Soris opened his mouth as if to protest. "Without putting myself at risk," she added. He shook his head but held his tongue.

The day wore away. A thinly lit sky appeared as evening swallowed up the winter sun. They crested a hill near twilight, and Nat spotted movement along the Rust River. An open wagon packed with men and women, their faces and arms covered with bandages, rolled across a bridge spanning the river.

"Haruu!" Soris called out and waved his arm. A pair of rebel soldiers broke away from their position by the bridge and met the trio as they rode down the hill.

"What's going on?" Annin addressed a stout rebel soldier standing guard near the bridge.

Nat heard a dull thwacking sound. She dismounted and stared into the dim evening light. Two men swung broad-edged axes at the bridge supports as the dark water swirled around their calves.

"Moving the wounded to the other side of the river before we dismantle the bridge," the guard said. He gestured to a long tent leaning at a precarious angle as if someone had hastily set the center pole in the ground without securing it properly.

"Wounded are already being transported from Ballew?" Nat asked as she watched the cloaked wagon driver help a man whose arm was in a makeshift sling descend from the wagon bed.

"Not yet, no," the guard replied. "The wounded are from two merchant trains that got caught up in a battle between a band of Mudug's guard and the Nala just south of here." He gestured beyond the bridge.

Nat's heart skipped a beat at the mention of the Nala. She glanced at Soris and Annin.

"From what the survivors tell us, Mudug used the merchants as a shield while his archers attacked the Nala from the hills. We came across the merchants this afternoon. Luckily we had a handful of Healing Sisters with us."

"Are any duozi around?" Annin asked.

"Two," the guard answered. "They've been scouting with some of the rebels to help secure the area." Nat noted his respectful response to Annin and hoped it was a harbinger of the future.

"Good," Annin replied. "I don't sense any Nala near, but the duozi will warn you." She pressed her lips together. "You can trust them." The rebel guard nodded.

A bright light caught Nat's attention. An orb trailed behind a cloaked woman entering the tent. Nat recognized her bluish-black hair and the slight limp that punctuated her walk.

"That's Sister Tamara from Ethes' House." Nat handed her reins to the bewildered rebel and ran toward the tent.

"If you're heading to Ballew, best move on. Bridge won't wait for you, Sister!" the guard called out. "A smuggler's bridge is all we have after this one comes down."

"A smuggler's bridge will suffice," Soris responded and sprinted after Nat.

When Nat crossed over the threshold of the tent, the acrid smell of blood hit her. "Blessed Rim," Soris whispered as he entered the tent after her. She brought her hand up to cover her nose as she breathed through her mouth and moved deeper inside. A few orbs hovered in the air, illuminating rows of the wounded groaning on thin blankets on the ground. Five Sisters bustled around the tent, kneeling and examining them. Sister Tamara knelt in the far corner. Her stubby fingers flew over a woman's arm, suturing a deep cut by the light of her orb. The woman had hair the color of Cal's, and Nat shuddered, thinking of the dangers she'd put Cal through. Even though her sister was safe with a guard in Rustbrook, and Annin had promised to take her home if something happened to her, Nat desperately wanted to see her home herself.

Nat walked carefully down a row, taking in each of the injuries as she made her way toward Sister Tamara. Her gaze landed on the torn flesh hanging from the exposed leg of a young boy. Even in the faint light, she could see his skin turning a pale shade of blue. The boy's large brown eyes stared with a vacant look past Soris when he knelt next to the boy. Annin pushed Nat to the side and joined Soris. She quickly examined the boy's wound and unrolled the small apothecary she carried in her cloak.

"Orb," Annin snapped.

Nat released her orb, and it cast a beam of light over the boy. Annin pulled out a pinch of dennox from her apothecary and sprinkled it over the bite marks on his leg. "Apply that to the cut on his temple," she ordered and handed a small jar to Soris.

Nat pushed the boy's matted hair away from his forehead, and Soris slathered the thick balm across the gash. The three of them worked together, tending to the boy's wounds while he remained mute and motionless. Nat sat back on her heels after Annin secured a linen wrap around the boy's leg. *We can heal his body,* she thought. *But what about his mind?* Nothing would erase the trauma he'd been through from his memory. She glanced down the row of wounded. How many more people would end up like this, bleeding into the frozen winter ground?

"Annin?" Sister Tamara's voice broke into Nat's thoughts. "You are a wonderful sight to see. Extra hands, especially ones as skilled as yours, are always appreciated." A wide smile covered her face. Nat marveled at how anyone could smile when surrounded by such misery.

"I treated his leg wound with dennox and the linen wrap." Annin shuffled to the side to let Tamara inspect her work.

"Very nice, very nice indeed," Tamara complimented her. "The Nala wounds inflicted on these merchants were particularly violent. I have yet to find a clean bite. They make the arrow wounds from Mudug's archers look like porc-tree punctures." She shook her head and knelt next to the boy. Her cloak billowed out around her, and Nat stepped back to give her more room. The sinking feeling in her stomach grew as she again glanced from patient to patient. Was the Nalaide ordering the Nala to increase the severity of their attacks to show Mudug what she was capable of? She bit her lip and caught Soris watching her.

"How did you come to be here, Sister Tamara?" Annin asked as Tamara checked the boy over from head to toe.

"A few Sisters from the Healing House joined the band of rebels from the canyon, knowing our services would no doubt be needed. Ethet had some of us remain here while others traveled on with the band."

"Sister Ethet's here?" Nat asked, glancing around the tent.

"No." Tamara shook her head. "She should be near Ballew by now with Estos." Her eyes focused on Nat, and recognition flashed over her. "She has six other Sisters and some of the Healed with her. I believe more Sisters from the fringe are on their way."

Healed? Nat wondered what she meant.

"That's hardly enough to treat the wounded of Ballew if this is what the Nala are doing," Soris said grimly.

"All the Sisters from the Healing House wouldn't be enough," Tamara corrected him gently. "But we'll do the best we can. Help me with him, Annin." Tamara slid one arm under the boy, lifting his upper body off the ground, while with her other hand she slipped a small vial from the pocket of an apron tied tightly around her ample waist.

"That's darker than meldon juice," Annin observed as Tamara tipped the vial of dark-yellow liquid into the boy's mouth. The color looked familiar to Nat, and her heart beat faster. She watched the boy swallow even as his gaze remained unfocused.

A smile curled over Tamara's lips. "It's not meldon juice." She tapped the side of the vial. "It's the cure. We're administering it to everyone."

"The cure?" Soris grabbed the vial from Tamara's hand.

"Yes, blessed Rim. Sister Ethes had the first batch ready a few days after that crazy girl showed up in the Meldon Plain just outside our House. Little Neas volunteered to be the first to try once we'd created a batch. Brave little boy spent days in pure agony—mild convulsions within an hour of ingesting, delirium for at least a day. Oh, and fever. Very high fever, and then a solid two days of what we call the blues, or purging." She described the process cheerfully. "His body purged quite viscerally, from his nose, eyes, ears, mouth, and . . ." Tamara paused and frowned. "But he's now healed." The smile returned. "A little scarring, but not a sign of duozi in him."

"It worked," Nat whispered. Her hands trembled as she took the vial from Soris. Their fingers touching, Soris and Nat stared at the dark-yellow liquid clinging to the glass container. "It worked!" Nat whooped and threw her arms around Soris and Annin.

"You did it," Soris said with a look of astonishment.

"I did it." Nat smiled so wide that her cheeks started to ache. "You have to take this—now." She held the vial up in front of Soris and Annin, shaking with excitement.

"No," Annin said and stepped away, distancing herself from the vial.

Nat felt her exuberance fade as a stubborn expression formed on her friend's face. She thought of Annin's earlier comments. *It's her choice*, Nat reminded herself as Annin took a deep breath.

"If we take it now, we won't be able to do anything to help you. I wouldn't be able to sense the Nala, call in predators, or connect with Estos." Annin kept her eyes fixed on the vial as she spoke. "You heard Sister Tamara. If it took Neas days of spewing blue gunk to heal after he ingested the cure, how long would it take me? I've been a duozi since I was a child. I have no intention of convalescing for days while everyone else is fighting for control of Fourline."

Nat turned to Soris. He met her gaze with an equally indignant look. "I agree with Annin." He crossed his arms over his chest and stood next to her. "We can wait a few more days."

Nat clutched the vial tightly. She looked pleadingly at Soris. He'd never be able to pass into her world unless he was cured.

"Perhaps waiting would be best," Tamara interjected before Nat could say anything more. "I have a limited supply. Head Sister Ethes promised to send more once another batch is prepared, but I must ration what I have now for the wounded."

"Listen to Sister Tamara, Natalie," Annin said with a sharp edge in her voice. "The Sisters need the cure for the wounded. Visceral spewing can wait." She addressed Tamara. "Sister, we need to move on soon, but is there anything else we can assist you with before we go?"

Tamara bobbed her head. "The cure may prevent these poor souls from transforming into duozi, but it does nothing for their other wounds. I could use your skilled hands for suturing."

"Of course," Annin responded and removed her cloak.

"Sister, would you and Soris please administer a drop of the cure to those men by the entrance? They are the last who need a dose." Tamara gestured to the figures propped against the tent pole.

"Certainly," Soris responded and carefully wove around the wounded, leaving Nat with no choice but to follow. He knelt down next to the first man, and Nat gasped when she saw the man's head. Half his face was wrapped in a blood-soaked bandage, and a crimson stain seeped from a wide strip of linen covering his abdomen. Soris cupped his hand around the back of the man's head and touched his lips to get them to part. Nat carefully uncapped the vial, then froze as she was about to pour a drop into his mouth.

"Larkem?" Nat studied the uncovered portion of the man's features. His uninjured eye fluttered open. Clots of blood clung to his ginger beard.

"Sister," he whispered. "I must be dead if I'm seeing you." His voice sounded like gravel.

Nat brought her orb closer. "No." She glanced up at Soris. He gave her a questioning look. "Luck intervened." Larkem coughed and a trickle of blood trailed from the corner of his mouth. "But you weren't quite as lucky," she said, feeling a mixture of loathing and pity as she looked at the man who'd beaten her and turned her over to who he thought was the Chemist. She held the vial above his lips, knowing how many others deserved the cure more than he did.

He let out a laugh that sounded more like a gasping wheeze. "No, I wasn't as lucky."

"What happened to you?" Nat tried to keep her voice calm. She still felt the aching bruises from his blows.

"Paid a grain merchant to join his wagon and a merchant train. Planned on sneaking off after we got clear of the city, but the guard fell in behind us." He closed his bloodshot eye. "Half a dozen Nala attacked after we passed over the bridge. I've seen a Nala attack before, when my brother was taken, but that was nothing compared to this. They tore apart all the wagons and the contents like they were looking for something and tried to kill anyone in their way. And some of them were like the color of death." He took a deep, shuddering breath. "The guard did nothing to help us. Just used us as a shield as they picked the Nala off with their arrows. Left all of us for dead, even their own wounded after they managed to kill all the creatures." He opened his eye and stared up at Nat. "Maybe I deserved it, Sister. Retribution for my actions. But the merchants . . . They were innocent."

"I told you Mudug and his guards couldn't care less about the people, Larkem," Nat snapped, unable to control the well of anger building inside her.

"I know, Sister. But the Nala—"

She poured a drop of the yellow liquid into his mouth before he could say another word. He swept his tongue over his cracked lips. "Rest up, Larkem. Whether or not you deserve it, you're safe now." She stood swiftly and pocketed the vial before anyone noticed. She walked away toward the tent entrance. She wrapped her arms tightly around her sides and stared out at the starlit night. She felt Soris' presence next to her.

"The Nalaide sent her creatures up here looking for me," she said.

"She probably did," Soris agreed. He placed a hand on her shoulder and pulled her close. Nat let him enfold her in his arms. "But don't for a minute blame yourself."

"I don't, but she'll call off the Nala if she thinks she has me."

"How do you know that?" Soris turned her around so she was facing him.

"Because she's their queen. Attacking the merchants, Mudug's men, and Ballew put the Nala at extreme risk. I didn't see any duozi in the Nala den when Malorin turned me over. They can't regenerate without making and enslaving more duozi. She knows that."

"You're suggesting giving yourself up so she can regroup and create duozi?"

"I never said I'd give myself up." Nat fingered the vial in her pocket. Soris opened his mouth, but she held up her hand. "I need to think." Ideas raced through her mind.

Annin approached from the far end of the tent. "What did I miss?" she asked as she refastened her cloak. Nat stared at her orb, lost in thought.

"She's thinking." Soris leaned against the tent entrance and shook his head.

"Help us," Annin muttered under her breath. They followed Nat as she headed out into the night with her orb trailing behind her.

CHAPTER
THIRTY-NINE

Nat caught sight of the rebel camp just as dawn was breaking. She slowed her horse and patted his sweat-soaked neck with her cramped hand. Behind her, Annin and Soris descended a long open slope of trampled winter grass. They'd ridden over the flatlands all night without encountering either Nala or Mudug's guards. Taking a deep breath, she pulled her horse up short and stared at the lip of the crescent-shaped bluff above Ballew. Their quiet ride had come to an end.

Smoke from an enormous pyre rose into the sky and turned the dawn light a grimy shade of yellow. Wagons rolled to a stop near the fire. Two rebels removed bodies from the wagons and tossed them into the flames. Nat saw a woman's body in the rays of the sun before the flames engulfed it. She turned away, horrified.

Soris and Annin brought their horses to a halt next to hers, but neither looked at the pyre. They directed their gaze far past the lip of the bluff. Dark circles showed under Soris' eyes, and the blue skin around his neck looked pale in the soft glow of the morning light. Annin blanched.

"Hundreds," Soris whispered.

"What are you talking about?" Nat studied her companions and gripped her reins.

"Hundreds of Nala are down there." Annin gestured past the bluff's rim. "Down in Ballew." She paused and slowly turned her head so she was staring straight at Nat. "The Nalaide is here as well. I can sense her."

She's here. A nervous tremble shook Nat from head to toe. She urged her horse into a reluctant trot and headed toward a row of rebel tents sparkling with frost. Two guards met them at the entrance of the camp. Soris leaned over his saddle horn and spoke with the guards while Annin and Nat scanned the site. A row of long white tents similar to Sister Tamara's occupied the east end of the camp. Even though Nat was far away, she could see rebels and Sisters carrying bodies into the tents.

"Gennes and Estos are on the west side of camp." Soris interrupted her observation of the disturbing scene, and the three of them rode down the rows of small tents and morning fires. Only a few of the soldiers were cleaning their weapons and checking crossbows. The rest were huddled near the fires.

"Why aren't they preparing for battle?" Annin wondered out loud.

"I don't know," Soris replied with the same questioning look. The number of guards stationed along their path increased as they drew closer to a long tent set far back from the edge of the bluff.

Nat dismounted and followed Soris and Annin past another set of guards, pulling her weary horse behind her. She then turned her reins over to a teenage girl who disappeared with their horses. Two Warrior Sisters guarding the front of the tent stepped aside to let them enter. Estos, looking as if he'd aged ten years since Nat had last seen him, was leaning over a long table. Both he and Gennes looked up when the three companions entered. Relief washed over Estos' face.

"The morning brings a bit of good news," he said, embracing Annin. He placed a hand on Soris' shoulder in greeting, then turned toward Nat to give her a contrite look. "My apologies for keeping you in the dark about our subterfuge, Natalie."

"Don't apologize to her," Annin said as she warmed her hands by a small stove. "The memory manipulation worked. The Nalaide thinks Mudug has Natalie in the cave in the bluff." She regarded Nat and Soris. "And Soris convinced the Sister to give up her brainless plan to scurry off and face the Nalaide on her own."

Nat glared at Annin but swallowed her retort.

"We assumed you'd been successful, given the Nala's push against the city and the cliff last night." Estos returned to the table, looking more stressed than pleased. "But our plans may be working against us."

"How?" Nat joined him as he studied a worn map.

Gennes spoke up. "Mudug and his guards know we've blocked their escape routes. When the Nala approached the base of the bluff last night, Mudug's archers attacked the Nala, but they also deliberately sent flaming arrows into the houses and buildings of Ballew. They set part of the city on fire. The Nala retreated from the onslaught of arrows and attacked the residents trying to flee. A few townspeople escaped, but not many. Several were killed. Most are still holed up in the city." Gennes twisted his mustache and scowled.

"I've ordered Rory to hold off the Sisters' attack from the east for fear the wave would send Mudug's archers and the Nala into another frenzy and endanger the residents even more. Mudug's trapped, but so are the citizens." Estos lifted his head. His pale eyes were full of worry.

"And there's something else." Gennes glanced at his brother. "The number of Nala in Ballew is staggering. Our scouts have estimated at least two hundred, possibly more. They've infiltrated every quarter of the city." His green eyes settled on Nat. "We must get the residents out before we strike from any direction, otherwise they'll be caught between Mudug and the Nala."

Nat swallowed, feeling a heavy guilt settle over her. The Nalaide was pushing the Nala into Ballew because she wanted her and revenge on Mudug. She felt Soris' gaze fall on her and studied the map, hiding her emotions. Annin joined her while Gennes and Estos argued over options.

"Most of Mudug's troops are concentrated in the central section of the bluff, where the caves are deeper and offer more cover, correct?" Annin asked.

Gennes nodded. "The bluff face on the eastern and western ends is slick as ice with no decent trails up or down and little cover."

"What if the Sisters create corridors here and here, east and west of town?" Annin traced her finger over the map. "The curve in the bluff would keep Mudug's archers from reaching the Sisters with their arrows. If they can keep the Nala near the corridors at bay, we'd have a safe path for the residents to flee from the city. Once they're evacuated, you could attack Mudug through the smugglers' tunnels, and the Sisters could go after the Nala."

"That might work," Estos responded. "But how do we keep the Nala from attacking the townspeople before they reach the corridors?"

"Get the creatures to attack the bluff. That's where they want to go, anyway," Nat broke in. She looked up to find all eyes on her.

Estos sighed. "Mudug's archers will keep them back, Natalie. We've already been through this."

"We just need them there long enough for the residents to flee." She scratched her head. "We need something to draw them to the bluff and temporarily hold their attention. Some type of distraction."

"Anything come to mind?" Estos asked.

"Yes," she replied. "Me." Soris gave her an exasperated look. "Don't discount the idea," she said before he could argue with her. "The bluff is full of places to hide."

"It's full of places you could die, Natalie."

The tension flowing from Soris left her feeling torn. *This is about us, too*, Nat reminded herself. She pulled him away from the others and whispered, "I know how my impatience and mistakes have hurt you and other people I love. But I can't stand back and do nothing." He averted his eyes, but she brought her hand to his chin, forcing him to look at her. "What if I come up with a way to lure the Nala without risking much in the way of safety?"

A confluence of emotion crossed his face. Seconds that felt like hours ticked by before he finally spoke. "I need to be a part of your plan, Natalie. We are in this together to the end."

"We are." A feeling of calm settled inside her as she realized she truly wasn't alone in facing anything ever again.

"I hate to ask . . ." The tone of Soris' voice was light now, but he held her close to him. "But do you have any ideas? Because I'm not betting on some crazy Predictions to protect you against hundreds of Nala."

Nat let out a nervous laugh. "Trust me, neither am I." She felt the warmth of her orb hovering near her. She turned her head and watched it spin slowly in place, then inhaled sharply. "I think I do have an idea." She released Soris and stepped back to join the group. "Estos, is Rory here?"

"She's in the triage tents waiting for word from me," Estos replied.

Nat turned back to Soris. "I need to run something by Rory and see if it's possible." A tingle of excitement flowed through her as she backed away. "Wait here, okay?" She caught his nod of agreement, then bolted out of the tent.

The stable girl jumped back in surprise when Nat ripped the reins of a cream-colored horse from her hands and spurred the animal across the camp. She tied up the horse and ducked in and out of the triage tents until she found Rory in the back of the last tent not far from the pyre.

"Rory!" Nat skirted an aid station, nearly tripping over her own feet to reach the Sister.

"Sister Natalie?" Rory broke away from a clutch of Healing Sisters and approached her.

Nat took Rory by the hand and led her out of the tent. "Annin came up with an idea of how the Warrior Sisters can get the citizens out of Ballew, and Estos likes it."

"Excellent. We are getting a bit restless," Rory said. "What's the plan?"

Nat spoke quickly, explaining Annin's idea of creating corridors for the townspeople. When she finished, she asked, "Are any duozi with you?"

"Several, including Luriel. Why?"

"They can infiltrate the city. With so many Nala around, I doubt the Nalaide's army would detect a handful of duozi. They can spread the word to the residents and help them flee to the corridors once the Nala move toward the base of the bluff."

Rory's brow rose in question. "And what's to keep the Nala from attacking the people when they break for the corridors?"

"I'll let the Nala see me and lead them on a chase. We both know the entire pack will come after me." *And hopefully the Nalaide, too.* Nat bounced on the balls of her feet, too nervous to stand still while Rory considered her words.

Rory frowned. "It's too risky."

"What I have planned is safe." *If it works,* Nat thought. Rory looked unconvinced. "You and I took oaths, Rory. We both know Mudug and the Nala will continue killing people while we sit back and scratch our heads trying to figure out another plan. We need to do something now." She felt an anxious twist in her gut. If Rory didn't agree, she had no idea what she'd do.

"What do you need, Sister?" Rory asked.

"You'll help me?" she asked, hoping she hadn't misheard her.

"I did take an oath similar to yours, as you reminded me." Rory arched her brow.

Nat clasped her hands together to keep them from trembling with nervous excitement. "I need one of Mudug's guard's uniforms and use of all the Sisters' orbs." She thought of Soris. "Plus a rope and every archer you can round up."

CHAPTER FORTY

"Your plan is about as safe as sticking your face in front of a buler bug," Rory commented as they rode down the rocky eastern slope toward the outskirts of Ballew.

"I'll reach Soris and the rope before anything happens to me." Nat blew out a breath, thankful he had acquiesced to her plan. She was nervous enough as it was. Going into this knowing he had her back calmed her—a bit.

"You better, or you'll be dead," Rory remarked and slapped her horse when he balked from the smoke rising from the city.

The outlying farms came into view. Nat stood up in her stirrups to get a better look, and the stolen guard's uniform bunched up around her hips. Smoke poured from thatch-roofed houses and smoldering stacks of hay.

"I know what I'm doing," Nat responded, hoping there was some truth to her statement.

"I hope so. I was beginning to get used to your being around. It would be a shame if you got yourself killed."

Rory kicked her horse and Nat followed. They galloped down the hill toward the lines of Warrior Sisters assembled behind a stable. The sight of the confluence of Sisters and orbs made Nat catch her breath.

Dozens of orbs bobbed above the Sisters, creating a halo effect. The spheres shifted on their approach and linked together, forming a curve.

"You're certain all the Sisters are willing to let me use their orbs?" Nat asked as she scanned the bright spheres. Waves of heat emanated from them and caressed her face.

"Natalie, contrary to how you normally operate, Sisters rarely act on their own." Rory gestured to the spheres. "The Sisters' orbs will follow your orb's lead. No need for verbal commands." She dismounted in front of the band of Sisters. "But once you're safely hidden in the bluff, the orbs will snap back to their owners," Rory warned. "We'll need them in case the Nala decide you aren't worth the chase." She leveled a look at Nat. "It's up to you to make your way to the ridge where Soris will be waiting with the rope."

Nat nodded and ticked through the plan in her mind as she dismounted and tied her horse to a broken post. She secured her sword and tucked an extra dagger into the tunic she wore under her coat. The blade clanked against a hard object. Searching the folds of her garment, her fingers curled around the vial of the cure she'd taken from Sister Tamara's tent. She was about to give it to Rory when she realized there was a strong chance she might need it herself. She pushed the vial deeper into her tunic.

Nat turned and took in the ruined city. Her lungs burned from all the smoke, and her hands trembled slightly. *This will work,* she told herself. *Just pretend you're on a run from campus to town, Nat, that's all you have to do, run until the Nalaide finds you.*

Rory grasped Nat's shoulder. "You've certainly changed from that frightened whelp I saved in the woods a year ago. Good luck, Sister. I hope to see you soon." She motioned to the band of Sisters, and the linked orbs snaked through the air like a ribbon of white light. Nat grabbed her cloak from her saddle and released her orb. It rose in the air and joined the other spheres. She pulled the cloak over her shoulders, fastened the front to conceal the guard's uniform, and ran toward Ballew.

The orbs zipped around her on all sides at first, creating openings where Nat could see the burned-out houses and dead livestock scattered over the road. She glanced behind her. The Sisters spread out, moving swiftly to clear the area of any Nala. She thought of Cal and Soris and ran faster, sprinting down narrow lanes. People, their faces full of fear, peered out of broken windows as the ribbon of orbs flashed by. She gestured urgently for the townspeople to run the way she'd come, hoping the duozi that Luriel had secreted into Ballew had managed to get word to all the residents to flee once the Nala pressed toward the bluff.

A blue figure darted into the road and Nat skid to a halt. She locked eyes with the creature and drew her sword. A flicker of recognition crossed the Nala's features and a hissing cry burst from its mouth, sending an eerie echo down the nearby lanes. *They know I'm here now,* she thought and lowered her sword. The creature lunged and crashed into the wall of orbs. The orbs singed the creature's skin, and it rolled onto the charred remains of an outbuilding. Nat hurtled over the Nala's body and pressed on, sweating inside the protective dome of spheres. She turned onto a side road leading toward the bluff and looked for more Nala. The plan wouldn't work unless they and the Nalaide came after her. *Where are you?*

She glanced between the spheres. A Nala sprang from the eave of a house and landed in front of her. The orbs clacked together instantly and rammed into the creature, sending it into the side of a house. Burning thatch tumbled onto its bulbous head. A screaming hiss erupted from underneath the pile and Nat tensed, knowing the cry would bring more Nala her way.

The orbs opened up again. Nat quickened her pace. An arrow sliced through an opening in the orb wall, barely missing Nat's arm. *Mudug's archers.* She ducked into a narrow lane for cover. The orbs formed a single layer above her head, and she heard a pinging sound like raindrops.

Arrows ricocheted off the orbs and fell, broken, onto the ground behind her. She dodged an overturned cart and burst into a vacant square.

Three Nala jumped out from behind a cracked fountain in the center of the square and darted toward her. The orbs slammed into the creatures. Nat sidestepped the broken fountain and brought her sword across the neck of one of them. Its hissing ceased as its head spun in circles on the cobblestones.

Nat sprinted away, slowing briefly to ensure the Nala were following her. She ran down another lane and narrowly avoided two more Nala before again dashing toward the bluff. Hissing and the sound of the Nala's slapping footfalls filled the lane behind her. Nat dared turn her head and the orb wall parted, revealing a lane packed with dozens of Nala now scurrying after her. The spheres linked together. Nat raced toward the bluff. Her heart beat faster than ever.

Arrows whizzed above her, and the hissing behind her intensified to a deafening pitch. She drew near the bluff face and the orbs shifted. The cave opening she'd spied earlier in the day when she and Rory had viewed the bluff from the ridge above the city was tucked a good fifty feet up from the base. Under the cover of the orbs, she unhooked her cloak and reached for her crossbow. The orbs surged forward, creating a single set of glowing stairs leading toward the cave entrance. Nat glanced over her shoulder as she ran up the steps. Her eyes widened at the Nala pouring from the lanes of Ballew after her.

Her arrow flew from the crossbow, landing dead center in the slick abdomen of a Nala leaping through the air onto the stairs. It spun and hit the crowd of its kin behind it, trailing venom. The lower steps broke apart, and Nat was soon climbing higher and higher out of reach of the creatures. Arrows from Mudug's guards whizzed past her face and pinged off the orbs hovering near her head. Her foot hit the last step, and the spheres separated as she dove into the cave opening. She blinked quickly as her eyes adjusted to the dim light.

Crawling to the edge of the shallow cave, Nat looked out. The orbs flew east and west toward the Sisters and the stream of citizens. She was filled with relief. People emptied out of the city past the phalanx of Sisters. She rolled onto her side. *It worked,* she thought as her chest rose and fell in rapid succession. *Now for the next part.*

Nat glanced at the base of the cliff, searching for some sign of the Nalaide. Enraged Nala sprang from the smoldering ruins of houses and shops and skittered down the smoke-choked lanes. A mass of the creatures slammed against the bluff and clambered on top of each other, forming stairs with their angled bodies. The arrows from Mudug's archers picked out a few of the Nala, but the creatures kept swarming up the base of the bluff. A screaming hiss shook the air, and the Nalaide emerged from between two buildings. Her black eyes scanned the bluff.

Nat scrambled away from the edge into the shadow of the cave. She tossed her cloak against the rocks, slipped her orb into the folds of the uniform, and crawled on hands and knees to the wide eroded crevice leading to a narrow ridge. She needed to get closer to the spot where Soris was waiting before she exposed her location to the Nalaide. Nat squinted through the drifting smoke and looked above her. One of Mudug's archers knelt behind a rock in a cave about twenty feet up. He trained his bow on the Nala and didn't notice Nat creeping toward him. He released arrow after arrow into the sea of Nala forming the stairs.

Wasting no time, she crawled up the rest of the ridge. She stuck her foot in a toehold and released her orb before pulling herself into the cave where the archer knelt. The sphere knocked the bow from the archer's hand and smashed into his nose, sending him collapsing onto his back, unconscious. Nat grabbed his puffy blue guard's hat and pulled it over her head.

A blur of white and blue flashed beneath her. She glanced over the rocks and spotted Nala in the cave entrance where she had been moments before. The remnant rings in the white Nala bulged from their chests, and they had a fevered look in their dark eyes. Fear clutched Nat, and she froze in place as the creatures found her cloak and ripped it to shreds. *I need to get higher.*

A rope ladder connecting the cave where she stood with the one directly above her swayed near the unconscious archer. A warning cry burst from the upper cave, and the ladder began to ascend as guards pulled it away from the approaching Nala. She jumped up and grasped the end of the ladder with her good hand, praying the guards would think she was one of them when they saw her uniform. The ladder continued to rise.

"Give us your hand!" a guard hollered to her as the rope ladder scraped against the rocks. She reached for the soldier and scrambled over the ledge.

Two sets of dusty boots scuffed the ground in front of her. Nat pulled herself to her knees and pretended to be out of breath. She kept her head low and scanned the ground in front of her, looking for any more boots, then said in a raspy voice, "They're coming . . . the Nala are coming."

"Up to the next level!" one of the guards cried. Nat heard the springing sound of arrows releasing. She crawled to the far edge of the cave away from the soldiers and scanned the curve of the bluff for Soris.

Nothing but pitted rock met her eyes.

"Climb!" The frantic cry of the guards brought Nat to her feet. A blue spikelike hand slapped the ground not far from where she stood. The guards cried out again and scrambled up the next rope ladder.

A Nala's head popped up, and its silver eyes retracted when it saw Nat's sword tip in front of its face. She thrust her weapon into the Nala's open mouth, cutting off its hissing cry. The creature's hand dragged against the ledge, and it tumbled backward off the bluff. Nat spun around and jumped up to grab the ladder, but she crashed to the ground, landing on her back. The frayed ends where the soldiers had cut the rope lay next to her cheek.

Hissing erupted from beneath the cave. Nat scrambled to her feet and ran to a slab of rock opposite the cave entrance. She clambered up, then slid behind it. She found a tiny lip to balance on and pressed her body behind the slab just as a Nala crawled from below into the cave.

Her heart pounded so fast she was afraid the creature would hear it. She peered through a crack and watched it scurry around the cave. It let out a barking hiss, and three white Nala crawled up after it. Nat held her breath as they used the tips of their feet to balance on a ridge on the other side of the cave. More Nala climbed in and followed the path of the others as they scaled the face of the bluff. She heard cries above her, and a guard's body tumbled through the air. His arm hit the slab right next to her. She shut her eyes and heard his wailing, then a crashing sound.

Minutes passed. Nat slowed her breathing and watched from the protective shell of rock as more and more Nala climbed to invade the caves where Mudug's guards were positioned. Soon, hundreds of blue bodies covered the face of the bluff, making its surface come alive with movement. A surge of pain ripped up her arm, and fear gripped her. She scanned the creatures, looking for the Nalaide, but caught no sight of her in the mass swarming over the bluff.

Adjusting her hold on the rock, she glanced down and her heart soared. Dozens of Warrior Sisters poured from the city lanes and attacked the Nala scurrying around the base and climbing into the low caves. With the bulk of the creatures engaging Mudug's guards, the Sisters made quick work of the Nala in the city, then sent their orbs shooting into the sky. The spheres rained down on the mass of creatures swarming over the bluff. Nala fell from the cliff, and the air was filled with a horrid chorus of hissing.

Emboldened by the Sisters' storm of orbs, Nat climbed from her hiding spot and ran to the narrow ridge. She scanned the slope of the bluff again and spotted a long rope dangling from the top. Soris, standing on the rim in the middle of a row of rebel archers, caught sight of

Nat and waved to signal her. Nat waved back and watched him begin his descent down the rope.

Time to find the Nalaide and end this. Her orb hovered above her palm a moment, then shot out of the cave, blazing with light. She let the sphere linger in place and intensified its light. *Please let her recognize my orb . . .* She unsheathed her sword and waited.

A hissing cry broke through the clamor of fighting. A shiver ran down Nat's spine as she heard the call again and recognized the Nalaide's distinctive hissing. She edged a few steps up the ridge so the Nalaide would be in the archers' line of sight when the creature came after her. She glanced in Soris' direction, nervous about her escape route if the archers missed. Soris, clinging to the end of rope for balance, pivoted on the ledge. Their eyes met and his head jerked up.

"Natalie! Behind you!"

"Sissssster."

A fierce pain exploded in her arm. Blinded by the agony, she stumbled back, straight into the Nalaide's slick hands. Arrows struck the rock face but missed the Nalaide. The Nala queen crawled into the cave, pulling Nat with her. The creature flung her against the back wall. Nat crashed to the ground. Her sword fell from her hand and spun across the rocky floor behind the creature.

The Nalaide, backlit by the morning sun, crept deeper into the cave. Her spiked hands cut into the hard surface of the stone as if it were butter. Her black eyes were clouded with rage. Nat scrambled away, frantically searching the folds of her clothes for her dagger. Her fingers wrapped around the vial instead as the creature opened her fanged mouth and charged toward her. Nat brought her hand up to shield herself. The Nalaide crunched down, biting into her fingers. The creature's sharp teeth cracked the vial, and Nat's grasp flew open as a fiery sensation ripped through her hand, arm, and chest.

The Nalaide lurched back. Her fangs sliced into Nat's fingers, ripping the flesh from the bone as she pulled away. A scream erupted from Nat as she rolled to the side, clutching her mangled hand. Barely able to lift her head, she called her orb. The sphere wobbled in the air, then froze in place. Nat, her vision blurring, watched in confusion as the Nalaide staggered away from her. A deep gurgling sound slid from the queen's mouth, and she stumbled against the wall of the cave. She convulsed and clutched at her throat. A stream of white liquid poured from her nose. Nat struggled to keep her eyes open as excruciating pain and the Nalaide's venom coursed through her body.

Soris jumped from the ridge into the cave. The arrow from his crossbow pierced the Nalaide's skull, and she fell onto her back. He slashed at her neck with his sword, and her massive white head rolled across the cave and tumbled over the rim. Falling to his knees, he lifted Nat up and the light around them faded into darkness.

CHAPTER
FORTY-ONE

A low, calm murmur of voices filled the air, waking Nat. She opened her eyes. It was bright, and blurred figures moved in front of her. The air smelled of herbs. She blinked twice, clearing her vision. Healing Sisters wandered down rows of occupied cots.

"Natalie?" Soris' face appeared above her. His blond hair was unkempt, and dark circles hung beneath his Nala and human eyes.

"Soris." Her voice sounded like a croaking frog. She reached up and touched his cheek, needing to feel him to believe he was there next to her. "W-what . . ."

"The Nalaide's dead, Natalie. Finished." He gently caressed her face. Her pent-up fears and anxiety washed away, and tears trickled from the corners of her eyes. "It's over and you're—"

"Ethet, get over here! She's waking up!" Cal's face popped up next to Soris'. "Ethet!" she called out again anxiously, then stared at Nat as if it were the first time she'd seen her in years.

"Cal?" Nat struggled to sit up. Soris cradled her head. "You shouldn't be here, Cal," she protested. "There's a battle—"

"Not anymore, Natalie. It's over," Soris assured her and smoothed her wrinkled brow. "Mudug slipped away, but his army surrendered, and Gennes is on his tail. It's over," he repeated.

Cal knelt at the side of the cot. "Cassandra brought me after we heard what happened to you." She draped her arm protectively over Nat's legs.

"How long have I been out?"

Soris gave her a thin smile. "It's been four days since I pulled you from the cave."

"And he hasn't left your side since I arrived," Cal added, giving him an appreciative smile. She stared at her sister and her mood morphed. Deep lines formed in her smooth skin. "It's a good thing someone besides me is concerned about you, because—"

"Would you kindly keep your voice down, Calpurnia?" Ethet wore a pinched expression as she strode past a row of cots toward Nat. "You are louder than the bells in Rustbrook, and Sister Natalie is not the only patient in here."

"She's the most important. Estos even said so." Cal stood up, set her hands on her hips, and looked steadily at Ethet, whose height matched her own.

"I agree she's important," Ethet replied with a tone Nat imagined she'd used on many apprentices. "Now if you'd please move, I'd like to check my patient."

Cal let out a sigh that sounded more like a growl but stepped aside. "Fine. I'll go tell Cassandra and the others she's awake." Her gaze fell on Nat. "Don't relapse on me or anything, okay?"

"I won't, Cal. I promise." Nat gave her a shaky laugh.

"You made other promises, too," Cal responded and gave her sister a fleeting look before running out of the tent.

"Been under my feet ever since she arrived," Nat heard Ethet mutter as she settled onto a stool across from Soris. Nat and Soris exchanged glances, and he hid a smile behind his hand. "It is delightful to see you awake, Sister Natalie," Ethet said as she took Nat's pulse. The skin around her brown eyes wrinkled. "We weren't certain you were going to make it after Soris carried you up the bluff." She frowned. "You'd lost a lot of blood. And your hand . . . I'm sorry, Natalie." Ethet gestured to the bandage encasing her right hand. "You lost one finger and half your thumb. There was nothing I could do to save them. The bones were shattered."

Nat stared at the thick wrapping, and the memory of the violence suddenly resurfaced. Her breath quickened. "The Nalaide bit me."

"Yes, quite viciously, Natalie. But we gave you a dose of the cure. Thanks to your discovery, you, along with many who were fated to be duozi, will not be infected. Remarkable discovery, my dear. You've given hope to the lives of so many."

A knot formed in Nat's throat as she took in Ethet's warm smile. "It's really working, then, on everyone?" She was flooded with hope and fixed her gaze on Soris and his Nala eye.

"Yes, even Annin," Ethet replied and began unwrapping the bandage covering her forearm. "She's in recovery with other duozi who have chosen the cure."

"Annin?" Nat asked, surprised.

Soris cleared his throat. "She was . . . almost irrational when she saw your wounds. Estos had to carry her out of here." Nat caught a disapproving frown form on Ethet's face. "He told me later she decided to take the cure then and there. She said you'd met your fears head on and she needed to as well."

"She chose to change because of what happened to me?" Nat murmured. She glanced at Soris. *What about you?* she wondered.

He placed a firm hand on her shoulder as if to keep her from slipping away from him. "I had no intention of leaving your side to convalesce," he said, answering her unspoken question.

"Certainly could look worse." Ethet's strange comment pulled Nat's focus away from Soris. The Sister gently lifted Nat's forearm and examined it under the light of her orb. A thin jagged scar marred Nat's vine and spear markings, but the once putrid wound had healed, and her markings were vivid against her pale skin.

"My arm," she said in wonder and ran her finger down the scar.

"Yes, Natalie, the last remnant is gone from your body," Ethet replied.

"Sister Natalie!" Nat felt a breeze brush past her as Sister Rory, Estos, and Cal crowded around the foot of her cot.

"I'll need a separate tent for you soon if this keeps up." Ethet gave Cal a perturbed look as she stood. She adjusted her glasses and addressed Estos and Rory. "I know you have questions, but make them quick. Natalie needs her rest."

"Understood," Estos replied as he slipped onto the stool Ethet had just vacated. "You are a sight to see, Sister." His pale eyes shone and he scanned her face. "I can't thank you enough for what you did." He paused and a thousand unspoken words passed between them.

Rory knelt next to Estos. A deep gash marred the right side of her face.

"You're injured!" Nat gasped.

Rory laughed. "I'm better off than you, Sister. It's just a little scratch."

"Hardly little." Nat struggled to stay upright. Her muscles screamed with fatigue, but she refused to collapse back in the bed in front of Rory. "Were any of the other Sisters hurt in the fight?"

"Considering how long it had been since we'd taken on the Nala together, we fared well." She leaned closer to Nat and placed her hand on her forearm. "Your stunt worked, Sister Natalie. Most of the townspeople were able to flee before the real fighting began." The smile faded from her lips. "But there is more fighting ahead. The other Warrior Sisters and I will soon depart for the eastern forest to root out the remaining Nala. I have questions to ask before we leave if you're up to it." She glanced across Nat toward Ethet. The Healing Sister wore a pensive look.

"Of course," Nat replied.

Rory sat back on her heels. "You were unconscious when Soris pulled you from the cave, so you wouldn't have seen the dozens of white Nala converging in your direction." She touched the bottom of her scar and frowned. "Soris got you out just in time." Nat felt Soris tighten his hand around hers as Rory continued. "I led Pauler and a band of Warrior Sisters to the cave to finish the white Nala, but when we arrived all we found were their withered white corpses draped over the headless husk of the Nalaide. Do you have any idea what could have killed the white Nala?"

Nat tried to imagine the scene. "Why—" Her mind landed on a thought. *The white Nala were trying to regenerate their queen.* Moments passed as she considered the implication of what she was about to say. Finally, she met Rory's curious gaze and said, "I may have an idea. When the Nalaide attacked me, she ingested the cure. I was holding a vial of it in my hand." Nat stared at the bandage covering her wounded fingers, then glanced up at Ethet. The Healing Sister's eyes were wide with interest. "I think it's what prevented her from . . ." She thought about how close the Nalaide had been to implanting a remnant ring in her chest and shivered. "I think the cure poisoned her before Soris killed her," she said softly. "Ethet, if the white Nala were trying to regenerate their queen, could the cure have poisoned them as well?"

"It is very possible. The cure could be toxic to the Nala." Ethet brought her hand to her mouth, let out a small laugh, and gave Nat a wondrous look. "If only Barba were here . . ." Her voice trailed off, and her eyes danced with delight as she smiled at Nat. "It appears that your Head Sister's belief that you might be the Sister to live out the Predictions was not as far-fetched as I thought."

Now it was Nat's turn to gape. Ethet's smile grew wider as she took in Nat's startled expression. "Barba always had a keen eye for a Sister's potential." She touched Rory's shoulder. "You may have a new weapon against the creatures, Sister. Natalie's discovery could very well be the end of the Nala. Take our supply of the cure with you," she added hastily.

"I will." Rory stood and gave Nat a fleeting look. "I wish you were well enough to come with us."

"No, no, no." Cal's voice rang out and she brushed past Rory. "She's not going *anywhere* but home with me. Just like she promised." Nat could see the stubbornness in Cal's eyes as her gaze, full of challenge, swept over each person around them. "Does everyone understand that?"

Soris' steady hand pressed against Nat's shoulder. "We understand, and I'm certain Natalie will keep her promise to you," he said to Cal. The meaning behind his words pulled at Nat's emotions.

The challenge faded from Cal's face. "So we'll go home, soon?" Cal asked, her voice overflowing with anticipation.

"Just like I promised, Cal. I'll take you home." Nat felt Soris' grip on her shoulder ease, and she leaned back on her pillow, afraid she'd start crying if she looked at him. The thought of leaving him again made her feel as if her heart were ripping in two.

"Ethet, how long before Natalie is able to travel?" Estos asked. "I want my best guard accompanying both of them home."

"A day more of rest and she should be able to manage a horse," Ethet replied.

"I'll see that a guard is ready." He bent over Nat and whispered in her ear. "Know that you always have a home here and a place of honor among our people." He gently kissed her forehead. "Thank you, Natalie Barns, for giving me back what I lost."

The tears flowed freely from Nat's eyes as she watched Estos and Rory disappear from the tent. She wiped her damp cheeks with her uninjured hand and brought her attention back to Soris, who had a sad smile on his face.

"What about you, Soris?" Her voice broke and she felt as if she could cry forever.

"Don't worry, Natalie." He brushed away her tears. "You're not getting rid of me that easily." His hand clasped hers. "I'll find you when the time is right," he said and gestured to his Nala eye. He looked intently at Nat's injured hand. "But if you're leaving tomorrow, you'll need to come up with some explanation for your injury. I don't imagine your family will be thrilled when they see that."

"After all that's happened you're worried about what my family will think?" Nat couldn't help herself and let out a weak laugh.

"No, Soris is right." Cal's light eyebrows knit together. "You and I better think up some airtight lie to explain what happened to you. What happened to us," she added in a conspiratorial tone.

Nat pondered the quagmire that lay ahead. Barba would give her the tongue-lashing of a lifetime for disobeying her, but she knew for certain both Barba and Cairn managed to hide her absence. She doubted they knew Cal had passed through, though. She shifted up on her elbows so she could get a better look at Cal. "How often were you supposed to meet with your instructor during J-term?"

"Just the one time. I met with her the morning before I followed you into Fourline," Cal answered. "I was supposed to be researching and writing a paper all January. I guess one incomplete on my transcript won't kill me." She shrugged. "My roommate and most of my friends were taking J-term classes off campus. Hopefully no one's noticed we've been gone the last three weeks." She eyed Nat's hand. "Mom and Dad's freak-out over your injury is what I'm worried about."

"Barba is going to be a problem, too. I'm more concerned about what she's going to do to me than Mom and Dad. She may never let me come back to Fourline after she finds out I dragged you halfway across the country."

Ethet bustled around the cot and shooed Cal and Soris to the side. "You can figure out your string of lies tomorrow. Both of you go eat and rest. Sister Natalie needs her sleep."

Soris kissed Nat, leaving her lips warm and wanting more when he pulled away. "Ethet's right. Get some rest. I'll see you soon." He turned and joined Cal as she wove her way past the other Sisters. They exited through the thick canvas opening of the tent.

"Sleep now, Sister," Ethet said kindly. "And do not fear what your dreams will bring."

CHAPTER
FORTY-TWO

Soris held Nat's hand as she dismounted from her horse. The boulder marking the last leg of the trip to the membrane glowed in the winter-afternoon light.

"You are slower than sap," Andris remarked from where he stood next to Cal.

"Excuse me for holding you up." Nat still couldn't believe Estos had sent Andris as part of the guard accompanying them to the membrane. "I didn't ask for you as an escort."

"Don't mind Andris," Soris said. "He's just peeved he had to leave Emilia behind. They were about to make the trip to our family farm when Estos told him he had to come with me. Duty over love, eh, Andris?"

"Odd for you to remind me of that, brother," Andris shot back. "Sister, if you'd let go of my brother and limp your way over here, we might make it to the membrane before I turn gray."

Nat made a show of draping her arm over Soris and walked with mincing steps.

"You're horrible, Andris." Cal rolled her eyes and joined her sister and Soris. Andris strode ahead of them. Cal linked her hand through Nat's free arm. "It's a good thing Emilia's a little unbalanced. I don't know how anyone could put up with his—"

"I can hear you, Calpurnia," Andris barked from the path ahead of them.

"Good," she retorted.

Andris grumbled again, but kept his back to them as he checked the path.

"Thank you for seeing us off, Soris," Cal said. "It's nice to have at least one pleasant person around."

"There were others who wanted to come as well." Soris met Nat's gaze.

"Annin?" Nat guessed. He nodded. "I didn't even get a chance to say good-bye to her." She felt as though something precious were slipping away.

"It's for the best. She's still . . . purging." Soris' expression grew somber, and Nat took a deep breath as she imagined the cellular fight occurring in Annin's body.

Cal slipped her arm out of Nat's as if sensing they needed to be alone. "I'll catch up with Mr. Grumpy." She strode toward Andris, who peered into the crevice that hid the membrane. The moment Cal was out of earshot, Nat stopped walking.

"What about you, Soris? I know you didn't take the cure because you wanted to be by my side. But after I pass through the membrane . . ." She trailed off, knowing he couldn't follow her.

"I'll take it," he promised. "But . . ." Nat tensed as he continued. "With your agreement, I intend to wait. I told Rory I'd help the Warrior Sisters finish off the remaining Nala and find Mudug. I'm one of the few duozi rebels in the south who hasn't taken the cure. My ability to sense the Nala and call other predators will help the Sisters, Natalie. May even save a few more lives." Soris paused and pulled her close. "But without your consent, I won't go. I told you, you and I aren't alone in this anymore."

"You should help them. I trust you to keep safe," Nat said, her love and faith in him overpowering her hesitation and fear.

"Thank you, Natalie." He kissed her gently on the lips and took a step back. "I'm not sure I can watch you leave."

"I'm not sure I can leave," she answered honestly. "After everything I've—we've—been through . . ."

"Not that much," he teased gently. "You merely traveled into a world that shouldn't exist to you, became a Warrior Sister, battled a living nightmare, found a cure that will end the misery of thousands, and made someone fall deeply in love with you. Really wasn't that much you accomplished in a year if you think about it."

Nat couldn't help herself and burst out laughing. The laughter kept her from crying. She flung her arms around him. "I'll miss you, Soris."

"And I'll miss you." He held her close to his heart, then released her. "I'll find you soon," he said. "Trust me."

"You know I do."

He turned and left her with the memory of his smile as he walked slowly away.

Afraid she'd lose control and follow him, Nat turned swiftly and slipped past Andris, who was waiting with Cal.

"Neither of you should return until we've found Mudug and eliminated the Nala," Andris said as he followed Nat through the crevice in the cliff.

"Did you see me volunteer?" Cal lifted her long legs over a pile of rocks and shimmied through another crevice.

"No sneaking through—"

"We understand." Nat squeezed between another tight split in the rock and found herself in front of the membrane with Cal at her side. Her orb bobbed in the air next to her.

"No—"

She turned and gave him an exasperated look. "Really, Andris? I know you may miss lecturing me already, but would you lay off?"

"One more thing."

"What?" Nat clenched her fists.

"My brother could have picked worse." His expression softened. "Despite my misgivings, you turned into a decent Sister."

"Thank you." Her eyes misted over as her annoyance subsided. "Thank you very much."

"Now get your arse back where it belongs. Both of you," he gently chided and took a step away from the membrane.

"Ready to go home, Cal?" Nat asked as she took her sister's hand.

"Am I ever," she replied.

"Then let's do this—together," Nat said.

They set their hands on the vibrating membrane and pushed, and the two sisters—and one orb—disappeared into another world.

CHAPTER
FORTY-THREE
FOUR MONTHS LATER

"Solar panel for the well in the west pasture is out." Nat's father walked into the kitchen. Nat looked up from her plate of eggs and carefully set down her coffee cup. Her dad's eyes lingered on the stumps on Nat's hand where her finger and thumb had once been. She tucked her hand under the table, still feeling guilty about telling her parents that she'd smashed her hand and fingers while helping Cairn build a set for one of his plays. Her parents had never questioned the truth of either her or Cal's tightly coordinated statements, and Nat shuddered to think what their response would be if they had even an inkling of the truth.

"Did the storm knock it out, Dad?" Nat asked. She hadn't gotten much sleep last night after MC had climbed into bed with her during the thunderstorm.

"Looks like it. Gary Harris called and said the storm took out the power source to one of his pivots. With all the lightning we had last night, we'll be lucky if the solar panel is the only thing that's out." He walked over to the kitchen counter and poured a cup of coffee. "Where's your mom?"

"She left for town with MC already," Nat replied, using her left hand to drink from her mug. She managed just fine with her right hand, but she knew the sight of it still upset her dad. Cal strode into the kitchen looking bleary eyed but dressed. She retrieved a travel mug from the counter and filled it with coffee.

"See you," she mumbled and headed for the door.

"Whoa, hold up, Cal. I'm going to Gary's to help him with the pivot. One of you needs to fix that solar panel so the well keeps pumping." Their dad gave Cal an appraising look. "How about you? Your sister seems to be doing all your chores this summer." He tugged at his beard and missed the wry smile Cal gave her sister.

Cal adjusted her purse strap and leaned against the kitchen counter. "I told you I'm picking up a friend from campus who's coming here for the weekend. We're supposed to meet up in Albert Lea. Mom said I could use the truck."

"Your mom may have said you could, but I need the truck to get to Gary's."

"Cal can take you, Dad." Nat wiped her face with a napkin and rose from the table. "I'll fix the panel."

"When are you planning on driving home, Cal?" their dad asked.

"Early afternoon. Call me and I'll swing by and pick you up on the way back. There's plenty of room in the truck for all three of us."

He shook his head and turned to Nat. "You sure you can fix the panel on your own?"

"Dad, really? The theater set just took off some of my fingers, not my arm." She lifted the coffee mug with an exaggerated move. "See?"

"Yeah, don't get me started on that." His expression soured.

"It was an accident, Dad, and completely my fault. Barba and Cairn warned me not to mess with the set on my own," Nat replied.

The injury had truly upset her parents, but she'd been firm about taking the blame.

"I'm surprised they haven't fired you yet, Nat. From what I've seen every time I'm in the shop, you don't take instruction well. Barba must be keeping you on just because you got hurt." Cal winked at Nat behind their dad's back.

Nat cast an irritated look at her sister, but it faded. Cal had earned the right to verbally jab her every now and then.

"I know that shop's been good to you, Nat, but going through the rest of your life with a mangled hand hardly seems worth it." His displeased expression deepened.

"There are far worse things that could happen." Nat dumped her dishes in the sink and turned on the faucet. The sound of the water hitting the plate reminded her of the Nalaide's hiss, and her skin crawled at the memory. Cal gave her sister a thoughtful glance and turned back to their father.

"Hey, Dad, wasn't it a year ago you were sitting at this very table with your leg in a cast because you pulled a bag of grain from the loft by yourself instead of waiting for help?" Cal crossed her arms. "Must be some genetic weirdness you two share."

"Thank you, Calpurnia. Any more comments before I change my mind and decide you aren't taking the truck to Albert Lea?"

"Nope." Cal took a sip of coffee from the travel mug, hiding her smile.

"Good. I'll get the tools I need to help Gary. Pull the truck around in front of the barn, and I'll meet you in a few minutes." He walked out of the kitchen.

Nat rinsed her plate, careful to keep the tender skin of her injured hand away from the hot water. When she heard the mudroom door shut, she turned to Cal. "Thanks for deflecting—*again*." She wiped her hands on a dishcloth.

"Don't mention it," Cal said. She gently pushed Nat away from the sink. "Let me finish those. Your hand looks pretty pink. Not that I'm complaining, but you don't have to keep doing all the chores Dad asks me to do. You know I was kidding when I said you owed me when we were in Fourline. You don't owe me anything." She let the water out of the drain, turned to Nat, and gave her a smile.

"I don't mind, Cal. Keeps me busy." *And my mind off other things,* she thought to herself.

Cal's smile faded. "Such a selfless do-gooder." She shook her head and grabbed her mug. "Come on, walk with me to the truck. We haven't had much of a chance to talk on our own. MC's been glued to you since we got back from school."

Nat laughed, thinking of her little sister. Cal was right. MC had been her shadow since they'd returned home, and she loved every minute of it. "She's a pretty special kid," she said.

"She has some special sisters."

"Yes, she does," Nat replied. She shut the front door, and they stepped onto the small porch.

"I forgot to tell you, Barba called last night while you were out with Dad."

"What did she say?" Nat stopped in the middle of the driveway that looped around their house.

"She said to tell you Oberfisk came through last week. They finally found Mudug. He's set to be tried within the month."

"Who found him?" Nat asked.

"Cassandra." Cal smiled.

"I'm surprised she let him live."

"I guess now that the Nala are gone, Estos and Annin's reforms are starting to sink in. No more slash-and-gash justice. Cassandra's a little off balance, but she swore allegiance to the regency."

Just like me, Nat thought, remembering her oath. She glanced down the road to the barn and out toward the rain-soaked fields. She was happy and grateful to be home with her family, but Fourline pulled at her and she thought of Soris too often. Both Estos and Barba had forbidden her from returning to Fourline until all threats were gone. Since Barba's list of perceived threats grew by the day, Nat had no idea when she'd see him again. She didn't even know if he'd taken the cure yet.

"Earth to Nat." Cal waved her hand in front of her.

"Sorry," she said and opened the creaky door to the cab of the truck for Cal. "My mind's on other things."

"Hmm." Cal searched her sister's face and Nat forced a smile. After a moment Cal tossed her purse into the truck. "You sure you can handle the repairs by yourself? My friend and I can help after we get back."

"I'm fine on my own," Nat replied.

"No, you're not," Cal said. "It's just a good thing those who love you know it, because you still haven't figured it out." She wrapped her arms around her sister, giving her a tight hug. "See you this afternoon." She climbed into the truck.

Nat stepped away, disconcerted by her sister's words. She watched as Cal drove the truck down to the barn and helped her dad load up his tools. She trudged up the path toward their house with her sister's words lingering in her mind.

Nat's horse munched greedily on the blooming alfalfa growing near the fence line as she tied him up for the second time in the late afternoon sun. The heat was punishing and Nat regretted her late start. *At least I was smart enough to ride up here instead of walk.* She dropped her second load of tools and a special bolt. Her first go at fixing the solar panel had been a bust, causing her to return to the barn and root around for a wrench she could easily grasp with her left hand and a bolt she'd failed to bring with her.

She wrapped her hand around the wrench handle and torqued her wrist, trying to loosen the old bolt. Sweat trickled from her brow as she jerked on the wrench. The bolt gave suddenly and Nat fell back onto the grass.

"Do you need some help, Sister?" Soris swung his leg over the saddle on MC's horse and dismounted.

Her heart hammered in her chest as she took in his completely human form. His eyes were the same green as when she'd first met him. The tanned, exposed skin of his arms and neck showed no sign of blue tint, and his hand was perfectly normal.

"S-Soris." Nat stumbled over his name, not quite sure if he was real. "How'd you get here?"

"What kind of greeting is that?" He gave her a wry smile and tied MC's horse next to hers. Neither animal shied away from him.

"I . . . you . . ." Nat took a deep breath, knowing she was babbling. "You were the last person I expected to see riding my little sister's horse," she said, managing to complete a sentence. The air around her felt warmer as he approached.

"I asked Annin to bring me through the membrane so I could see you. Barba got ahold of Calpurnia. I'm still not sure how." He shook his head, looking confused. "Everything in your world is so . . . different. I almost threw up in that contraption your sister drove to get us here." He stood close to her now. His shadow shielded her from the hot sun.

"Cal drove you?" Nat stared at him and wondered if she was dreaming.

"I believe so. I had my eyes shut most of the time." He shuddered and Nat laughed. "I met your father. Had an interesting talk with him on the way here. Seems surprisingly normal for being your dad. I met your mother as well. Very gracious, although I think she was a bit surprised to see me. I think she expected Calpurnia's friend to be a woman. And your other little sister, MC, asks a lot of questions." Lines crinkled around his eyes when he smiled. *Not a dream*, Nat thought.

She laughed again and brought her hand to Soris' face. He flinched when he saw the stumps. Nat tensed at his response, remembering how she'd reacted when she'd seen his fused fingers for the first time in the Healing House. But Soris took his hand in hers, carefully examining the damage. He pressed his lips to the inside of her wrist, and heat radiated up her arm.

"I missed you, Natalie Barns," he said with an intensity that shook Nat.

"I missed you, too," she replied, feeling nothing but love as she kissed him. The sun beat down on them as they embraced. Nat dropped the wrench and twined her hand through Soris' hair, pulling him closer.

He broke off their kiss and brought her hands gently to his chest. "You owe me something." His smile was demanding.

"Do I?"

"Yes, I think it's about time the woman I love welcomed me to her world."

Nat's eyes misted over. Soris wiped a tear from her cheek and held her close.

"Welcome to my world, Soris," she said as she looked into his perfectly human eyes. "I've got so much to show you."

ACKNOWLEDGMENTS

This book is dedicated to my children, who tolerated my brain being in Fourline while I wrote this trilogy. Each of you is a blessing. Thank you for your patience, love, and cheerleading.

To my own siblings, my brothers Tom and Greg. I am awed by your strength, compassion, humor, and generosity. Thanks to both of you for giving me a source of sibling conflict and love to pull from while writing *The Last Remnant*. I love you both and am a very fortunate sister.

Thank you, Dad, for being my go-to science man, and Mom, for holding my hand through the early drafts.

Courtney and Tegan, I've accomplished things I didn't think I could do under your guiding hands. You are both wonderful editors, and I appreciate all you've taught me. Kamila, Janice Lee, Britt, and everyone else at Skyscape, thank you for all your efforts and hard work. It was a pleasure working with all of you.

Thanks to my agent, Valerie Noble, for her keen eye and reminding me what Natalie deserves.

To my readers, thank you for caring enough about Natalie's journey to see her through to the end.

Finally to my husband, thank you for the gift of time to write and pursue my dream and reminding me what's important in life.

ABOUT THE AUTHOR

Photo © 2015 Ally Klosterman

Pam Brondos grew up in Wyoming and watched her mom write novels on a manual typewriter. She graduated from St. Olaf College; worked in Shanghai, China; and received her juris doctor from the University of Wyoming College of Law. *Gateway to Fourline*, her debut novel, released in 2015. The Fourline Trilogy continued with book two, *On the Meldon Plain*, and concludes with *The Last Remnant*. For more information about Pam, visit her online at www.pamalabrondos.com.